THE BAD ONES

ALSO BY MELISSA ALBERT

THE HAZEL WOOD

The Hazel Wood
The Night Country
Tales from the Hinterland

Our Crooked Hearts

the
BAD ONES

MELISSA ALBERT

FLATIRON
BOOKS
NEW YORK

THE BAD ONES. Copyright © 2024 by Melissa Albert. All rights reserved. Printed in the United States of America. For information, address Flatiron Books, 120 Broadway, New York, NY 10271.

www.flatironbooks.com

Library of Congress Cataloging-in-Publication Data

Names: Albert, Melissa, author.
Title: The bad ones / Melissa Albert.
Description: First edition. | New York : Flatiron Books, 2024. | Audience: Ages 14–18.
Identifiers: LCCN 2023037589 | ISBN 9781250894892 (hardcover) | ISBN 9781250348241 | ISBN 9781250357694 (international, sold outside the U.S., subject to rights availability) | ISBN 9781250894908 (ebook)
Subjects: CYAC: Best friends—Fiction. | Friendship—Fiction. | Missing persons—Fiction. | Supernatural—Fiction. | Horror stories. | LCGFT: Paranormal fiction. | Horror fiction. | Novels.
Classification: LCC PZ7.1.A4295 Bad 2024 | DDC [Fic]—dc23
LC record available at https://lccn.loc.gov/2023037589

Our books may be purchased in bulk for promotional, educational, or business use. Please contact your local bookseller or the Macmillan Corporate and Premium Sales Department at 1-800-221-7945, extension 5442, or by email at MacmillanSpecialMarkets@macmillan.com.

First Edition: 2024

10 9 8 7 6 5 4 3 2 1

To Sarah Barley and Kamilla Benko,
the good kind of goddess.

And to my awesome dad (and unpaid publicist),
Steve Albert. Look what I made for your birthday!

the BAD ONES

"BE GOOD."

"Uh-huh." Chloe Park angled her head to look at the house's top-floor windows. Two were yellow-lit, edged in pale curtain. That would be Piper's bedroom. She could picture it already. Trophies and craft supplies, inspirational posters rendered in sugary neon.

"Chloe."

Her mother said it forcefully enough that Chloe looked. The older woman's hands gripped the wheel, manicured nails and a wedding band so delicate it looked like gold thread.

"Be good," she repeated. "Please."

"Okay, Mommy." Chloe shouldered her overnight bag and left the car.

Piper Sebranek had brown eyes, shiny brown horse hair that fell to the middle of her back, and a reputation for supreme niceness. Chloe got the sense Piper had been the queen of her junior high, but look at her now. Just another freshman nobody.

She and Chloe weren't friends, obviously, but their mothers worked together at a law firm in the city. Two days ago Piper dropped a birthday party invitation on Chloe's desk in American Lit, all the details written in swoopy calligraphy on lilac card stock.

Chloe had skimmed it, then said, "You couldn't have just *told* me this?"

Piper smiled with her glossy lips only, fingers fraying the end of her ponytail. "My mom made me invite you."

So. Maybe not that nice. Chloe smiled back. "Can't wait."

By 8 p.m. she was regretting her decision. She would've pretended to pass out early, but Piper's weird private school friend Diahann had announced she'd be drawing a mustache on the first person who fell asleep. A *mustache*. These dorks.

Diahann brought a Tarot deck, Anjali three cigarettes in a ziplock bag, two of them snapped and leaking. Ashley got really wild and pulled out a whole hard lemonade. Everyone but Chloe took turns sipping it, after which Diahann stripped to her bra and lay on the floor, whisper-screaming, "I can feel it!"

Diahann fell asleep first. Piper covered her with a fleece blanket and put on *Booksmart*, then dumped the contents of a fat cosmetics bag onto the green-and-blue rag rug. Good stuff, Chloe noted. Sephora brands.

"Makeup!" Ashley clapped her hands like the makeup had put on a little show. She approached Chloe with a brush in one outheld hand. "You have the *shiniest hair*," she began.

This happened a lot. People saw Chloe's size and prettiness and age, a year younger than anyone else in their grade, and thought, pet.

"Fuck off," she said.

After that, they left her alone.

When the movie was over the other girls hugged each other, then took turns going to the bathroom with their toiletry bags and their neat little piles of folded pajamas. The lamp went off and Chloe faced the wall. Bursts of giggly whispering broke out with decreasing frequency until finally the room was quiet. For a while after that she lay unmoving in the glow of Piper's night-light, tracking the shallow breath of the sleepers.

Chloe rolled over. She watched Piper's face, making sure she really was out. After a minute it started to feel like Piper knew she was being watched. Enjoyed it, even. Like any moment she'd open her eyes and wink. What a creep.

Chloe sat up. Hands braced on the floor, she slid both legs from her sleeping bag, then crab-walked to the rag rug. From the makeup still lying in a glitzy pile she selected a pot of blackberry gloss, a NARS eyeliner, and a ribbed tube of Charlotte Tilbury lipstick, pushing them into the bottom of her bag.

The other girls slept on. Their breathing was soft, their closed eyelids untroubled, their small dreams stocked, no doubt, with cute boyfriends. Chloe rose to her feet.

A unicorn mug full of pens sat on the desk between the windows. She selected a black permanent marker and crouched beside Diahann. In two thick lines she inked a mustache above the girl's upper lip, curling twice at its ends like a cartoon villain's.

The other three were squished together on the bed. Chloe considered their faces, but Diahann's mustache had scratched the itch. She moved on to their phones.

Piper's and Anjali's had passcodes. Ashley's had face recognition. Chloe leaned across the bed, held the phone over the girl's slack face, and nudged her shoulder. Then again, harder. Ashley's eyes shuttered open. She breathed in through her nose, blinked twice, and rolled onto her side, still asleep.

The phone unlocked. Chloe sat cross-legged on the floor, taking her time looking through Ashley's texts, DMs, photos, boring boring boring, then she stopped.

Two weeks ago Ashley stood in front of a bathroom mirror with one hand on her hip and the other at the level of her eyes, taking a photo of her reflection. Her expression was inward, absorbed. You could tell the photo had been taken for her reference alone. She was naked from the waist up.

Chloe considered it a moment, impassively. Then she texted it to herself, deleted the text from Ashley's phone, and replaced it where it had lain.

Restlessly she surveyed the room. The air that had felt so alive to her minutes ago, so shiny-dark with possibilities, was dead now. It lay like flat seltzer on her tongue.

But the rest of the house remained. A pocket world in which only she was awake.

If the feeling she had, easing into the hallway, were a sound, it'd be a tonic note. If it were a scent, it would be matches and cut lime. Sometimes she tried to imagine a future that would allow her an endless supply of it, but all she could think of was cat burglar. Or Manson girl. The closed double doors of the main bedroom pulsed invitingly at the end of the hall. But there was risky, and there was stupid. Down the stairs she went.

The ground floor was dark. Chloe turned left into the little den beside the stairs, a place of deep chairs, a cold fireplace, and a pretty cabinet full of bottles. Wine, port, gemstone liquors with Italian-sounding names. The only thing she recognized was a half-full bottle of Cuervo. It'd be funny, she thought, to stash the bottle in Piper's room, some place where her mom would find it before Piper did. The thought hardened into a plan. She tucked it under her arm, stepping noiselessly from the den.

A light had come on in the kitchen.

Chloe paused. Her heart was gently sparking, the way it always did when she got caught, or was about to, or almost did. She didn't notice it, but she was smiling. Tequila bottle hanging from her hand, she walked toward the light.

Then she stopped, thrown by the sight of a girl she didn't know.

The girl stood with her back to the doorway. Her head was bowed over the sink, hands braced against the imitation marble. Piper's older sister, she must be, but Chloe's brain supplied no name. Was she about to vomit? She'd probably just snuck in drunk.

"Hi," Chloe said brightly.

The girl whipped around. Chloe took an involuntary step back. The girl's breathing was audible, her pupils massive. Chloe revised her guess: not drunk. High.

"Chloe," she said. Her voice was odd, her face a little bit familiar.

"Yep." Chloe gave a derisive sniff. There was a smell in the kitchen, plasticky and unnatural. It was coming from the girl. "No offense, but you reek."

Piper's sister nodded without speaking. Eyes fixed on hers, nod, nod, until her bobbing head seemed toylike. Chloe felt a rare stab of unease and crossed her arms over her chest, hugging the bottle of Cuervo. The other girl hadn't even mentioned it. "You're staring at me."

"I'm sorry," the girl said softly.

She *sounded* sorry. Like, genuinely. It creeped Chloe right out.

"Thirteen."

"What?" Chloe snapped. She was still standing on the threshold, and forced herself to take a step into the kitchen.

"You're thirteen," Piper's sister repeated. Her eyes ran over Chloe's face. As if, just by looking at her, she could smell the matches, hear the tonic note. "That's a bad age for a girl."

A prickle ran over Chloe's neck. She rolled her eyes to hide it. "Whatever. I'm going upstairs. Maybe you can go find a shower."

"Stop," the girl said.

Chloe did. Why, though? There was something in the way the girl said it. The word a wick of sharp command, her voice burning around it like a flame.

So. Chloe did stop. She did turn and look and feel all her superpowers—cruelty and nerve, a cast-iron stomach—dissolve like cotton candy at the sight of the blackness that massed around and behind the girl's head, not shadows nor hair nor anything else she could put a word to.

"I'm sorry," the stranger said one more time.

And Chloe remembered. Piper was an only child.

Away, away. Over a mile of winter-cracked blacktop and freeze-dried lawn to a car parked crookedly on a pastoral suburban road. Benjamin Tate sat in the driver's seat.

He was crying. Not crying as a grown-up cries, though he was past forty, but like a child, loud and snotty and unchecked. Faint heat spilled from the vents and the car's windows were covered with a censoring steam. Its interior smelled like clear liquor and stomach acid and a cologne so popular, once upon a time, that just one whiff of it could induce instant flashbacks in an entire generation. The song he'd put on repeat ended and began again.

Benjamin pressed his forehead into the wheel's slick hide. "What am I supposed to *do*?" he asked the air.

The car was a green Kia Soul, its paint job rendered inoffensive by moonlight. To its right, a row of sleeping two-stories. To its left, a gray expanse of fields, pocked here and there by soccer nets. Benjamin had grown up in this place. Everywhere he looked he could see ghosts of his younger, better self. Here came one now, sloping across the field in baggy Umbros like a slacker godling.

"Oh, Jesus," he said. "Help me."

He was speaking, again, to no one. But this time, someone answered.

"Stop."

The word was heavy with disgust. The man sucked in a gasp that lodged in his chest like a swallowed cough drop. With it came an odor that overwhelmed even the Drakkar slathered over his wrists. It was the house-fire scent of things that should not have been burned.

There was a girl in his backseat. Her face was in shadow but he could see right away that she wasn't *his* girl.

"What are you doing in my car?" With every tick of his shitty old heart embarrassment was replacing fear. Embarrassment and fury and a different kind of anxiety: What did she see? What did she know? He was drunk enough that he didn't stop to wonder how she'd gotten past a locked car door.

As fucked as he was, things could easily get worse. So he breathed in deeply and made his voice low. His *voice*, that gritty golden thing he used to believe would carry him free, up and out of this mediocre town. At least he could still use it to convince.

"I hope I didn't scare you," he said, though he'd been the one near to screaming. "Are—are you supposed to tell me something? Did she send you out here to give me a message?"

The word *she* cracked in the middle. It added another layer to his shame, and shame kindled anger. "Well? *Talk.*"

The girl leaned forward until just her mouth was caught in a beam of streetlight. The smile it illuminated filled him with an instant, atavistic terror. The kind that hid in your backbrain, only showing itself when you were on the brink of something irreversible.

Get out of the car.

The thought was electrifying and immobilizing in equal measure. He got as far as moving his hand toward the door.

"Stop."

And he did, mesmerized by the horrible something happening to the girl in the backseat. The darkness thickening around her, the sense of barely concealed *wrong* just behind. Like she might tilt to the side and reveal a black hole where the seat should be.

"I'm sorry."

She didn't sound it, though.

Up now. North over gridded roads, half a mile as the crow flies. To a cemetery.

Alastair and Hecate walked among the stones, tending to their ghosts. Since junior high they'd come here to lay wildflowers and cigarette ash on the graves of their favorites. Every week, it used to be, but not so often lately. Alastair greeted his old, cold friends silently in his mind. Leonora Van Cope. Lucas Tree. Mary Penney: Sweet Violet, Gone Too Soon.

Hecate wore a ground-sweeping coat of embroidered black, Alastair the collared shirt required to sell phone plans at the mall. Hecate rolled her eyes when she saw him in his work clothes. Must be nice, he thought, to have all your shit taken care of by Daddy.

Alastair had been in love with her for so long, so unreservedly and without expectation of return, that it was disorienting now to find that love was gone. Not fading from overuse, not cracking under pressure, but *gone*. Like someone punched a drain hole in the place where love had lived and let it run out.

Everything was dimmer on the other side of love.

"I talked to my new roommate yesterday," Hecate was saying. "Her friends all sound amazing. We're gonna be, like, this total artists' house."

It used to be that Alastair would plot to be alone with her. Logging every minute, every glance, every accidental-or-not brush of skin on skin. Now he dreaded it. Every time they met it grew clearer: that she was shallow. That she thought of him very little. That she was *just like everyone else*.

And where did that leave him? Alone. Even more utterly than he'd thought.

On top of everything else, Hecate was *boring*. Since her early acceptance to RISD, it was all she talked about. Each fresh revelation punched another little wound into his skin.

"Hey. Hello?"

He looked up. Hecate was pouting against a time-eaten headstone. "You're not *listening* to me." She pushed her lips into a lazy kiss, no sound.

She'd noticed, lately, the loss of his unrequited love. It bothered her just enough that she'd started to flirt a little, crumbs of attention he once would've fallen on like a starving man. Now he looked at her kissy face with cold fascination.

"You have to come visit me in Providence," she said unconvincingly. "Just wait till, like, October, so I know all the good places to take you."

"I'll need my money for rent," he said stonily. "Here. Remember?"

She fidgeted her handmade dress into place, checking the pretty swell of her breasts above it. She really was talented. The road at her feet was paved in sunny brick.

"Well. If you pay for your flight, I'll pay for half your food." She laughed. "It's so funny, my roommate actually gave herself a fake name, too, back in junior high. She thought it was so cute we used to call ourselves Alastair and Hecate."

She spoke the names in a mocking upper-crust accent. Horror clamped around his spine like a calloused hand. "You told her our True Names?"

"Oh—come on." She was still smiling, but she knew enough to look ashamed. "We haven't called them our *true names* since . . . Kurt, that was a kid thing. We're almost eighteen."

Alastair stood abruptly, wishing he was wearing something more dramatic than work clothes beneath his open coat.

"Fuck you, *Madison*," he hissed, and stalked off into the dark.

She called after him, but only once. Even dazzled with rage, he wove among the stones without stumbling. He knew the graveyard like he knew the piece of shit house where he'd grown up, in all its nicotine-stained, decorative-chicken-bedecked glory. Fuck his mom and her chintzy chicken collection. Fuck Hecate—Madison—and her perfect new life in Providence. Fuck—

He tripped. He banged his knee on a stone that shouldn't have been there and went ass over teakettle in the dark. When he stood, eyes damp and knee throbbing, he wasn't sure where he was.

Not that he was *lost*. The stars were out in force, the moon a bobbing silver boat, but every familiar thing they illuminated seemed strange. Not Alastair's haven but the realm of an indifferent dead.

He spun in place, anger souring into fear. Madison was back there somewhere, unseeable in the dark. Lost to me, he thought grimly, dramatically. She's lost to me. Then he looked ahead, orienting himself by the Eyeless Angel. It was perched atop the old Petranek mausoleum, stone wings extended.

Alastair squared his shoulders and struck out toward it. He would rest in the Angel's shadow, see if Madison even bothered to follow. Maybe he would play the old game, reaching up to grip the Angel's stone fingers with his own. But he stopped before he reached it, shoes sliding a little on a damp stone marker.

Someone was already sitting on the mausoleum steps. A girl, hair around her face, bare palms flat against the stone. Her posture told him she was very cold. Alastair's skin lit up with a pleasurable anxiety. She looked like an urban legend.

"Hi," he said.

The girl turned just a little, face hidden behind her hair.

He thought she might have been crying. He'd been crying some, too. Softly he approached. A sour chemical scent flavored the air around her; distantly he pictured closet backs and bug spray. "Are you okay?"

There was a catch in her throat. Sadness. Or laughter. "I've had a long night."

"Me, too." Alastair hesitated, then slipped his long coat off his shoulders and held it out. "You look cold."

The girl made a tight sound. "That's nice. Thank you." But she didn't reach for the coat.

It wasn't until he saw the quick white gems on her hair that he realized it was snowing. Fat flakes from a clear sky. And maybe it was that ordinary miracle, or just the unfamiliar act of chivalry, offering his coat to a stranger in the middle of the night, but something shifted in him.

As the frozen stars touched down and melted to nothing he saw, with swift and perfect comprehension, that he would have a life after Madison. After high school, after his mother counting down the days until he was no longer hers to deal with. The fog would clear, the black hallway end. Somewhere, a place of light lay in wait. He was suddenly sure of it, and so full of relief he could've lain down over the stones and wept.

But. Something was happening. A dark mass, gathering behind the girl. The stone of the mausoleum dissolved in it, curling in on itself like paper eaten black by flame. He squinted and shifted a step to one side, trying to see it more clearly.

It was coming from the girl.

He stepped back. And again. Thinking, Madison, stay. Stay far away.

The girl said, "Stop."

Just the word made him feel heavy. "What . . . what is this?"

She tipped her head to see him, clearing the hair from her face. "I'm sorry."

The bright future he held in his mind slipped free like a tumbling coin, gone. "Wait." His hand out, warding this new destiny away. "*Wait.* I know you. I know who you are."

Now, on her face, a smile. "No. You don't."

CHAPTER ONE

HER TEXT CAME JUST BEFORE midnight.

I love you

Only that. I'd read it and my eyes went wide in the dark. I replied in an anxious flurry.

Hi

I love you too

Okay I just tried to call. Lmk youre ok

Becca??

I'm coming over

I'd had to go on foot. In January, at night. As I walked my mood flipped from fear to fury and back again. The text was weird, but on the other hand it was classic Becca: dropping a line in the water. Waiting to see if I'd bite.

Now I stood, a little dizzy, at the bottom of her snow-dusted driveway, watching her unlit house. How long had I been standing here? Time felt slippery, the night endless. My body ached with cold and the lateness of the hour.

I shook it off and headed up the drive. Around the side of the house, over the screechy gate. The last time my best friend and I had spoken was three months ago. Now I moved to her bedroom window and tapped our particular tap. The one that said, *Wake up, come outside. It's not a serial killer, it's me.*

The light stayed off. The curtain didn't twitch. Becca slept like a frigate bird, half her brain awake at all times. If she was in there she was ignoring me on purpose.

I slapped my palm against the glass and stalked over the lawn, shoes crisping through a rind of new snow. I climbed the steps to the little deck Becca's dad built around the aboveground swimming pool and sat in the less grimy lawn chair. The pool beside it was dank as a cauldron. Last year Becca and her stepmom didn't cover it until Thanksgiving. This year they hadn't bothered at all.

There was a smell coming from somewhere. It was noxious, scraping my throat. I looked askance at the surface of the water, then typed out a text.

I'm on the deck. Get out here it's freezing

A light blinked on below me. I looked, then reached through the chair's gaping slats to pluck Becca's phone from the boards. Its screen was lit with the text I'd just sent. Behind it, a stack of my other texts, unread.

I looked up at the silent house, neck prickling. Then down again, at the deck. There was a stained green mug beside the place the phone had lain, half-full. Something made me pick it up and sniff its contents.

Then I laughed a little, rolling my eyes. Coffee, spiked heavily with citric vodka. Now the text out of nowhere made sense: Becca had always been a sentimental drunk. Also a drunk with a tiny bladder. Probably she'd swayed inside to use the bathroom.

I watched the dark glass of the back door, waiting for her to walk out of it. I was nervous but I was ready. On the boards near my feet was a smear of ashy black. I smudged it to nothing with my heel. I ran my fingertips over my palm—raw and stinging, scratched on my dash through the night. After a while I lay back to look at the stars.

I was lying in the quiet rift between the two halves of my life: before and after. Fear was lapping at my edges, dark as ink. But now that I was still I could feel how tired I was. Exhaustion swooped over me like a long-winged animal.

And the stars were so clear tonight, so coldly burning.

I fell asleep.

CHAPTER TWO

I WAS HAVING THIS DREAM. The kind that evaporates as you wake, leaving just the taste of itself behind. The thing about it was, it was really a memory. I'd dreamed it before.

In the dream I couldn't breathe. Water pressed in on me like the walls of a pine-box coffin. Usually in the dream the water was green and warm as spit, but this time it was icy black. I felt my heart slowing, my vision shrinking to a keyhole, a pinhole, gone. Then, her voice. Becca's.

Nora, she whispered. *I'm sorry, Nora.*

I wanted to reply but I was just so cold. My jaw locked tight and my lungs were dead flowers and I thought, *Don't go away, not again, don't leave me, Becca, don't—*

Something jabbed my side. I woke into a world of white sky, dry air, the plastic slats of the old lawn chaise bending beneath my weight.

Becca's stepmom stood over me, blocking the sun. She'd poked me with two fingers.

"Nora. *Nora*, wake *up.*"

My elbow slipped through the slats as I struggled to rise. "Sorr—sorry." A thin layer of fallen leaves stuck like cling wrap to my coat. I'd never been so cold in my life.

"My god." Miranda was swaddled in a thick pink robe that looked like the fluffy stuff you find inside walls. Her face was scared. "How long have you been out here?"

My mouth tasted like a penny jar and my brain felt scrubbed. Like someone had lifted it from its pan and run it over with steel wool. "I was waiting. For Becca."

"You could've frozen to death," she said bluntly. "Come on, come in the house."

"Is Becca awake?"

"Not that I know of. You're waiting inside while I heat up the car."

"Oh." I balled my fists. "No, thank you. I'll walk."

For a second Miranda looked helpless, her pale lashes standing out in the cold sun. "Are you serious?"

"Um." A shiver ran through me. I was regretting the instinct that made me refuse the ride. But Becca and I were still in a fight, probably. I wasn't sure I could afford to be caught making nice with her stepmom.

Before I could decide Miranda gave a small, humorless laugh. "Have it your way. Enjoy the walk."

"Wait." I held up the phone I'd found under the chaise. "Becca left this out here."

She was already picking her way down to the grass. "Leave it."

I watched her disappear into the house. When she was gone I levered myself stiffly upright, all my joints crackling like tinfoil. It was so early the birds were still calling to each other one by one. In the dawn light the pool looked even grosser than it had last night. And there was something under the water.

My heart gave an acid pulse. I leaned over, peering through the scrim of dead leaves. Whatever it was lay in a hump over the pool's concrete bottom. Blackish, the size of a small animal. Maybe it *was* an animal, a squirrel or an outdoor cat. Miranda and Becca would probably leave it down there to disintegrate.

I dropped hard from the deck onto the frosted grass, trying to wake up my feet. The old trees that circled the yard gave a long rushing sigh. A second later the breeze that ran through them washed over me. It shook loose that weird bad smell from last night. It had soaked into my hair while I slept.

Becca's bedroom curtains were closed. She'd better be asleep in there, not peeking through a crack while I talked to her stepmom, thinking, Better her than me. I stomped around the side of the house and down the drive. Everything ached as it came back to life. How the hell had I fallen asleep last night? How had I *stayed* asleep in this cold? I pulled my phone from my pocket to check the time.

Then I cursed, suddenly ten times more awake. It was half past seven on a Sunday morning, and my screen was filled with missed calls from my mother.

I hit play on her first voicemail, left at 6:34 a.m.

"Nora, where are you?" Her voice was just south of frantic. "Call me back as soon as—"

I stabbed the message off and called. She picked up after half a ring and right away I started talking.

"Mom, hey, I'm so sorr—"

"Where are you?" It was my dad. His voice sounded hard and flat. It sounded *afraid*.

"I'm just leaving Becca's. I'm sorry I didn't tell you I was going, I just . . ."

"Come home," he said tersely. "Now."

"Wait." I curled a hand around my throat. "Did something happen? Dad? *Dad.*"

He'd hung up.

CHAPTER THREE

IF YOU KEPT TO THE bike path that ran through the forest preserve, you could run flat out between Becca's house and mine in twelve minutes. We knew, we'd timed it.

I made it in ten. My body coursed with electricity as I ran, wind-chapped and sweating in my coat. I cut down the path that bisected our cul-de-sac, emerging half a block from my own driveway. Then my stomach dropped out.

Two police cars were parked across from the house. Mom, I thought. A prescription pill mix-up, a stroke, a fall. No, wait, I'd heard her on my voicemail. My little sister, then. Cat used to have seizures. And she was fearless, the kind of scarred-up show-off who never said no to a dare.

All these thoughts overlapped each other, flooding my head in the half second it took me to notice the third car. Dark and featureless in a way that screamed *unmarked vehicle*, it was parked in the driveway next door.

Not our house. Not us.

My dad was already opening the front door as I passed our mailbox. One hand on the frame, the other gesturing at me to hurry, like he wanted me to cross the driveway unseen. He was the kind of man who would find it unseemly for us to be seen going about our usual business, at our usual pace, when something so ugly was unfolding next door.

"What—" I began, and he gestured sharply, cutting me off. When I was inside he closed the door and crushed me into a hug. "You *tell us* when you're going somewhere. You *answer* when you're not where you're supposed to be."

"I know." I spoke into his chest, arms wrapped around his back. "I'm sorry. What's going on?"

He sighed heavily, holding me. Then, "Your coat," he said. Showing me his fingers, smeared in black ash. I stared, remembering the ash smudge on the deck. There must've been some on the deck chair, too. My stomach turned. What had Becca been burning?

"Nora?" My mom called from their bedroom. "Get up here."

She was lying on the bedroom floor, knees up and hair half lost beneath the dust ruffle. Bad back night. The sight made my stomach hurt worse.

"Hey." I crouched beside her, my dad hovering behind. "Are you okay?"

She gripped my hand, eyes roaming over me like she was making sure I was all there. "A girl went missing from the Sebraneks' last night. The police came by about an hour ago to see if we'd seen or heard anything."

It took me a second to make sense of her words. "Oh, my god. What girl? Piper?"

"One of her friends. A girl named Chloe Park, she's a freshman at PHS. Do you know her?"

I shook my head. "What did they say happened?"

Mom blinked up at the ceiling, face tugged back by gravity. "Piper had some friends staying over. In the middle of the night something woke her up, some noise from downstairs. Chloe wasn't in the room, Piper figured it was her. But all she found was a liquor bottle smashed on the kitchen floor." Her breath hitched. "There was blood. In the glass. Like someone had stepped on the pieces."

I winced. "But probably the girl was just trying to steal the bottle, right? And panicked when she broke it? Maybe she went home, or to someone else's house."

"Rachel called her parents first. She's not at home. And all her things are still at the Sebraneks'. Her phone, her coat, her clothes. Her *shoes*. Wherever she is, she's barefoot in pajamas. With bloody feet. In January."

"Shit," I said hoarsely. "They don't think someone broke in and *took* her?"

"There's no sign of forced entry." Mom ran her free hand restlessly over her eyes. "I keep thinking she must've let them in. Whoever they are. Some internet predator? She's thirteen."

Tears slid over her temples, into her ears. I squeezed her fingers, still warm from the heating pad laid over her middle. "What else did they tell you?"

My dad shifted heavily on the mattress. "Not much. They think she went missing between midnight and one."

"Does Cat know?" My little sister was a freshman. I didn't know the missing girl, but she might.

"She's still asleep." Mom pressed a hand to the floor like she might sit up. "Sweetie, could you pull some food together to send over there? Cupcakes, or . . . oh, lord, what am I saying. Not cupcakes. Something savory."

"Yeah, of course." But food was for illness or grief. For bereavement. It wasn't even seven in the morning yet, and slumber parties were always a shit show. The girl could've stolen a pair of Piper's shoes and gone for a very long walk.

But I didn't really think so. There was a hum in the atmosphere, a back-of-the-neck kind of dread. It wasn't just the early hour, the sharp shock of empty beds and cop cars. Whatever happened last night, it left a stain on the air.

Or maybe that was just in my head.

Mom checked me over beadily. "So you spent the night at Becca's."

"We had a sleepover." I tried for a smile, felt it falter and slide.

"A sleepover," she said flatly. "Really. Did you get any sleep?"

"Not good sleep."

My mom used to be so protective of my best friend. She'd known Becca since we were in the first grade, had watched her lose both her parents in the space of three years. But at some point she'd decided I was the one who needed protecting.

"Nora." She sounded half-apologetic, half-pissed. I knew what was coming. "Are you sure that's what you were doing last night?"

The pressure in my temples was instant, familiar. The feeling of a lie folding in on me, even though this one was half-true. I looked away. "*God*, Mom. I'm sure."

Her voice went spiny. "Don't you *god, Mom* me, you scared the crap out of us. And I think I have good reason to—"

"Laura." Dad spoke sharply, for my dad. Sharp as a tarnished butter knife. Then he changed the subject. "How are Becca and Miranda handling each other these days?"

I grimaced a little. "About the same. I'm gonna shower, okay?"

Mom gave me a last hard look before beckoning me in to kiss my forehead. "Go. Get cleaned up." Dad ruffled my hair.

When I was alone I started to text Becca, then changed my mind and called. My anger had dried up and blown away, now I just wanted to know she was okay. The call went straight to voicemail, like she'd let her phone sit up on the deck and die.

"Becca, where *are* you?" I paused like she might actually answer, then went on. "You can't text me like that, then nothing. You can't just . . ." When I took a breath I could hear it shaking. "You know what, never mind. Just— goodbye."

I dropped the phone from my ear, then replaced it. "And now I'm worried about you. Something weird happened next door and it's messing with my head and you have to call me, okay? You have to call me as soon as you get this."

SIX MONTHS AGO

BECCA BURST FREE OF THE woods.

She wore a green sundress. Her phone was in her bra, her camera around her neck. Blood ran from a gash below her left knee and pooled in the canvas of her high-top.

Two hours ago she'd walked into the forest preserve to take photographs. She hadn't thought twice about going out alone with her camera in the middle of the night, half a mile from home. She didn't rate her personal safety too highly these days. And what could hurt her in her own woods?

If she had the breath she might laugh at that now. She stood on the grass strip between trees and parking lot, head pulsing with what she'd just seen. It was terrifying and grotesque. It was awesome and impossible.

When she took a step toward the lot, she cried out. The adrenaline was waning, and now she could feel the pain in her knee, ripped to shit when she fell running away. The pain was whatever, the pain she could handle. But how loud had she been when she fell? Had she been heard?

Probably. Definitely. Okay, but had she been *seen*?

The thought set a match head to her back. She jerked

around to face the trees, hobbling away, keeping watch on the shadows. There was a sickening buzz in her brain, like bees crawling around in there, asking her, *What did you see what'll you do who will you tell?*

Not *who*. Nora was the only person she ever told anything. The real question wasn't who she would tell. It was whether she would tell her.

Of course she would. Becca dropped to her butt in the gravel, eyes pinned to the trees, and called Nora.

The sound of her voice after five rings was a cool palm to the cheek.

"*Becks.* I was sleeping. Shoot, I spilled my water everywhere. What time is it? Becca. Hello?"

Becca gripped the phone. Drinking up her best friend's voice, shaking her head like Nora was right in front of her. She hadn't known her throat would lock up.

Nora snapped from groggy to very clear. "Becca."

"Hey." Finally words came. "Hey. Um. Could you come get me?"

"Yep. I'll be there in fifteen minutes. Twelve."

The way Nora's tone went businesslike filled Becca with a mix of shame and loving irritation. Nora still didn't know what the hell to do with her bereaved best friend. Nothing soothed her like a direct order.

Becca dared a glance at her knee, then looked straight back at the woods. "I'm not at home. Can you pick me up in the Fox Road lot?"

She heard Nora hesitate. Then, "Why are you in the . . ."

"Get me. Please?"

Now she was waiting. Gravel dug in from ankle to thigh, every twitch of the trees hit her like a static shock. The night was summer soft, quiet, but even without a head full of bees Becca would've been bombarded by all the information in it. When she was upset she couldn't keep it *out*.

When she closed her eyes it rolled over her in a nauseating rush. Wet dirt and resin, the yellow-green perfume of chlorophyll and dandelion clocks. The tinny scratch of a bat call, the high chirruping of a toad. In her mouth, the sweet penny flavor of bit tongue and raspberry Tootsie Pop.

She spat on the gravel. She opened her eyes but it didn't help. Her vision was as restless as it always was, framing and reframing, finding the places where the light did something that could masquerade as magic.

Magic. Automatically she pressed the palm of her hand, gritty with gravel bits, hard into her ripped-up knee. The pain made her gasp, pulled her back from the brink.

Nora's car turned in a half minute later, headlights bathing Becca in white. The car swerved to a stop, tires spitting gravel, and she knew Nora had spotted her bloody leg.

Becca saw herself from the outside, like a photograph. Not a girl escaping the woods' grasping dark, but a creature that belonged to it. Slow and secretive, basted in its own blood.

That was how she knew. Even as Nora threw the car door open and clattered over the gravel in flip-flops. Even as her arms opened and her mouth formed Becca's name, she *knew*. The thing she'd just seen in the trees was hers. For now. For a little bit longer. She needed time, and the dark of her mind, to consider what it might mean.

Nora crouched in front of her, gnawed lips and split ends and a face that showed everything, every emotion, that had once made her the world's most hopeless liar.

Becca lied less, but she lied better. What you did was

you kept it simple. So. She'd keep it simple. Say nothing until she was ready.

Becca let her best friend hug her, and didn't breathe a word of what she'd seen in the woods.

CHAPTER FOUR

THE DAY BRIGHTENED BRIEFLY, THEN drained away. I showered and dressed and made a hot dish for the Sebraneks. I ate pancakes because my dad put them in front of me and watched cars come and go from the house next door. I kept my phone beside me at all times, sound turned up for when she called. It was starting to feel like a cursed object, like a stone, speechless and obsolete. I turned it off, then on again.

I told myself it was the stuff going down next door that perfumed the air with paranoia, giving my worry a shrill edge. But I couldn't shake the feeling I'd had when I got her text, the certainty that I had to hurry to her, had to *run*. It felt good, finding the spiked coffee and convincing myself I was about to receive a drunken apology. But had it felt *right*?

It was five in the afternoon when I finally cracked. I found my dad in the garage, tinkering with something he'd broken down to pieces on a paint-stained tarp. He'd never fix it, whatever it was. He just liked the busywork.

"Dad."

I said it quietly. But something in my voice made him look up quick, wiping his hands on a grease cloth. "What's up?"

"Last night, with Becca. It wasn't exactly a sleepover."

"Nobody thought there was a sleepover, Nor." He spoke evenly, flooding me with guilt. I didn't lie the way I used to, and I'd told my parents so. But why would they believe me now?

"Oh. Sorry." I cracked my knuckles as I spoke. "Becca texted me last night out of nowhere, telling me . . ." I swallowed. "Saying she loved me. Which made me, you know. Worried. I called her and texted her back a bunch of times but she never replied. That's why I went over there. I spent the whole night on the deck but she never showed. And now I can't reach her."

Dad was wearing sweatpants and battered 574s and a T-shirt with a sea turtle on it, picked up on a vacation so many years ago I could only recall it as a long bright smear of salted sun. I felt such gratitude as he rose to his feet. Believing me.

He ticked his head toward the car. "Let's go."

When we pulled into Becca's drive I got the feeling she wasn't there. Maybe it was the vacant way the house looked back at me. It was a ranch with funny eyebrow shutters and a dented garage, sinking quietly into disrepair. Its demise had come on faster over the year and a half since her father died.

Dad came around to open my door, squeezing my shoulder as I stepped out. On the way to the porch I went on tiptoe, peeking through one of the garage windows. "Her car is here." It should've been comforting. It wasn't.

Miranda answered the door wearing jeans and a sweater, expression closed off and her hair in a wet twist. She addressed my dad through the screen.

"Paul. What can I do for you?"

"Miranda. We're checking in on Becca."

A crease drew itself between her brows. "Why's that?"

"Nora's been trying to reach her all day, but no joy. We'll feel better if she can come out and say a quick hello."

Miranda finally looked at me. I met her eye, feeling guilty after the morning. "She's not locked up in here, Nora. When she wants to talk to you, she'll call."

I thought of the way Becca used to widen her eyes and hold up a single finger when Miranda was pissing her off, shorthand for *one more year*. One year until Becca could walk away. Her dad left her enough money to do it, but it wouldn't come through until she was eighteen. Just over a month away now.

"But you've seen her today, right?" I said. "I don't need to talk to her, I just want to make sure you know where she is."

Miranda flapped a dismissive hand. "You know more than I do. I should be asking you."

My dad looked between her and me. I hadn't told my parents just how badly things had deteriorated between my best friend and her stepmom since Becca's dad died.

"A little girl went missing from our neighbor's place last night." His voice dropped into the low, slow register that meant he was furious. "Thirteen years old, up and disappeared from a slumber party. It's got us pretty upset. So I want to be clear on what you're saying. You do know where she is, or you don't?"

Miranda's fingers crawled up to her neck. She looked

left, toward the hall that led to Becca's room. "I haven't seen her yet."

But my heart knew. My skin knew, and ran with a feverish goosebump trail. I grabbed the screen door handle, pulling it open before I could think.

"Can I come in? Just to check. Please."

She pressed her lips together. "Shoes off."

My dad stayed on the mat as I toed off my shoes and ran down the oatmeal carpet. The hall was dim, with a haunted-house smell that might've been dry rot. I threw Becca's door back, letting it bang against the wall.

The room was empty, the bed neatly made. Only the walls, lined with dried flora and her own black-and-white photographs, gave the space an eerie sense of motion.

"She's not here." I said it quietly, to myself. Then louder. "Dad! Becca's not here!"

Miranda had followed me. Now she pushed past, edging me back into the hall. I hovered there as she charged to the closet, wrenching it open, then to the window, pushing the curtain aside. It was closed tight, the glass frosted over.

"Again with this shit." She glared at me. "You're telling me she's not at yours?"

"Obviously not!"

"Not that obvious," she snapped.

She wasn't wrong. Becca used to slip off to our house without asking almost every day, until my mom imposed a "tell Miranda first" rule. I don't think Becca ever fully forgave her.

"This isn't that," I insisted. "She's not with me. I haven't heard from her all day."

Miranda gave me the smallest, grimmest smile. "I should take you at your word on that?"

I stepped back, stung by the subtle emphasis on *you*. My dad had joined us and in a gentle voice said, "Can you think of anyone we should call? Anywhere we should go looking?"

Miranda sighed. "Come on, Paul. It's barely dinnertime. And she's run away a thousand times."

My neck flushed hot. "No, she hasn't! Not *once*. She was always at our house."

But doubt was seeping in. Being back in this house after three months away, I could really feel how cold it was without Becca's dad inside it. Maybe, without me to escape to, Becca had gotten to the end of what she could handle.

Dad put a hand on my arm. "Her car's in the garage. Nora said she left her phone behind? You know that's not normal for a teenager." That bit he said in a stab at lightness.

"She's willful as a cat." Miranda wasn't looking at us, or even talking to us, really. "I don't know how to do this. I don't know how to do this alone."

I dug my nails into my palms, almost shivering. I'd known how it was between Becca and Miranda, but until right then I didn't really *know*.

"You're probably right," my dad said. "She's probably off in a sulk somewhere."

I shot him an incredulous expression.

"But if she's not back by tonight, I think you should call the police," he went on. "In case it *isn't* nothing. At least you'll have started a paper trail."

"She's seventeen. Eighteen in a month." She was still blocking Becca's doorway, keeping my dad and me in the hall. "She's smart enough to know you can't hide when you're carrying a phone. And she hates it here. Hates me."

The emotion in her voice surprised me. "She doesn't—hate you."

"Think about it," my dad said quietly. "No phone, no car . . ."

Miranda clapped her hands firmly together. The gesture was so decisive, her face so impassive, he fell silent.

"Rebecca has made it very clear she has no interest in being my responsibility," she said. "She'll come back when she decides to come back. And wherever she is, I'm sure it's exactly where she wants to be."

CHAPTER FIVE

WHEN WE GOT HOME THE Sebraneks' house was dark. The driveway was empty, the garage door closed. I considered texting Piper, but we weren't really friends. She'd think I was pumping her for information.

My little sister was waiting on the stairs when we walked through the front door.

"They still haven't found Chloe Park," she announced. "And now Becca's missing, too?"

Her eyes were big and shiny with gossip. It was the first time I'd seen her all day.

"What?" I said irritably. "No, she's not. She's just . . ." I didn't know how to finish the sentence. "She's fine."

Cat considered me, bright as a bird. "Okay, but does she know Chloe Park? Because people are saying—"

I cut her off. "People. *What* people?"

She hesitated, folding her lips together.

"Cat, what the hell. Who'd you tell about this?"

"Just Beatrice," she mumbled.

"Bullshit. You put it on your dive team thread, didn't you?"

She said nothing, but her eyes flicked to her phone. I

snatched it from her fingers and whipped it into the family room. "Grow. *Up*."

"Eleanor Grace!" my dad said, as Cat snapped, "Guess who's buying me a new phone."

"It landed on the carpet." I stomped up the stairs to my room.

Mom came in a few minutes later. My eyes were closed but I knew her tread, her weight on the foot of my bed. She put a hand on my knee, a mild tremor running through it from the amitriptyline. When I didn't open my eyes she lay carefully down beside me.

"Sweetheart." I could smell her cough drop breath.

"I'm not apologizing to Cat," I said.

"I'm not asking you to."

I kept my eyes closed. "How's your back?"

"Better." But she always said that. Dad had called her on the drive home with an update, his voice drenched dark with anger. All the while I looked out the car window, thinking, I did this. This is my fault.

"Becca ran away because of me."

She sighed. "Oh, honey. Because you've been fighting? All friends fight."

I rolled my face into my pillow, but no tears came. I rolled it out again. "It was bad, Mom. *Bad*. It was—not just her. It was both of us."

"Most fights are. That's why it's a fight."

She didn't see Becca that night. Didn't hear her. Didn't walk away. "I guess. But I cut her off after. I just needed . . . but I never thought it would go on this long."

"This is not your fault. Whatever it is. *Becca* decides what Becca does. Not you."

I didn't think she believed herself, either. I'd never told my mom exactly what the fight was about, because she'd have lost her mind. But she knew enough to know I was right.

"It's more than that. She's been so *weird*, Mom. Before we stopped talking, even. Ever since . . ."

Ever since that night over the summer, when she'd called me to pick her up from the forest preserve. But I'd never told my mom about that. Because the whole thing was unsettling, and because I'd had to sneak her car keys from her purse at one in the morning.

Mom was nodding. "Ever since her dad. I know."

"Yeah," I said dully. "So they still haven't found Chloe Park?"

"Not yet."

Tears clotted my lashes together. This I could let myself cry about. "God. Her parents."

"I know." A quiet minute went by. I could see her arranging her words, had some idea what was coming. Finally she tucked my hair behind my ear and said, "I understand you're worried about Becca. I know you want to find your way back to each other. But honey, please don't let this derail you. Don't let her do her—Becca thing."

"Her *Becca* thing?"

"Yes," she said firmly. "I know what she's been through. And I know she will always be a part of you. But I've been watching you these past few months. You have to see a little space has been good. You're doing new things. You're making new friends. By god," she added dryly, "you've even joined something."

I rolled my eyes. She'd been almost too proud when I joined the school literary magazine.

"Baby, you're blooming." She cupped my chin. "You're letting your light out from under that bushel."

I looked at her beautiful face. Big mouth in strawberry ChapStick, tired screen-siren eyes. Becca used to say she looked like Sally Bowles. How could she not understand me wanting to treat my best friend gently? I had my mother right *here*, close enough to touch. Becca had no one. No one but me.

"I'm all she has, Mom." I'd thought it a million times. Actually saying it gave me the stinging satisfaction of ripping off a scab.

"Nora, no," Mom said softly. "She has Miranda. She has me, and your dad, and Cat. Well," she tipped her head ruefully. "She doesn't have that much of Cat."

I responded as gently as I could. Because she was trying to make this better, but what good did lying do? I knew better than most that the truth didn't just give way.

"No, Mom. There's just me."

I couldn't have known, a year and a half ago, what it would mean to become someone's only person.

Becca's mom died when we were twelve, in a hit-and-run. The aftermath was a nightmare in the literal sense: surreal, endless. But at least I understood my role. I grieved with Becca, held her hand, hugged her when she cried.

What I didn't really get was that her dad absorbed the worst of it. The bulk of it. I only ever saw Becca's grief and anger with their edges sanded down by his steady presence, his constant love. And when he got sick three years later, speedy stage-four lightning-strike *sick*, it felt so cosmically unfair I couldn't believe he might actually die. Right up until he did, a few months before the start of our sophomore year.

Becca was the only child of only children. Her grandparents were long gone. She was left with a wrecked step-mom, a house full of ghosts, and me.

I wasn't prepared for the grinding dailiness of her grief. I didn't know how to help her as she shrunk her life, shrunk her*self*, retreating at times so deeply her pupils would contract, as if the spectacle of her own sorrow were a scorching light. Someone else might've known what to do, how to bring her back. But not me. I was failing her, failing myself. I was insufficient and terrified, watching my best friend travel through a shadow country I couldn't reach.

After that first terrible year was behind her, she started to come back. But it seemed to me she came only partway. I thought of girls out of fairy tales who walked Death's halls without precisely dying. Who breathed its black air and were changed by it. Their steps lighter, underworld shadows pressed like bruises into their skin.

Sometimes I thought I was being dramatic, thinking this way. My best friend still laughed, still made art and housed pizza and fixed her eyeliner when it smudged. She talked hungrily about the future, more than she ever had. But she could also be so *vacant*. As if loss had turned her into a passenger. She could be reckless, too, gathering cuts and bruises like they were wildflowers. I had the terrible sense she needed to take her life in both hands just to feel it.

Whatever happened on that night when she called me from the lot by the woods, I feared it was rooted in this recklessness. On its heels came a long sticky summer of eerie yellow skies and sudden pressure drops. Like the weather, we were constantly out of sorts, the air between us staticky with things left unsaid.

Then came autumn, and our fight. When both of us said too much.

CHAPTER SIX

I WAS SURE I'D NEVER fall asleep. But it seemed to me I blinked just once and was dreaming. It was one of those blurred dread-dreams, more texture than content. I got a sense of shadow, of stone, of absolute quiet.

When I opened my eyes it took me a long time to understand I was awake. It had snowed while I was sleeping, snowlight painted the walls white. It gave my room the strange luminosity of the dream. Then I woke up a little more and thought, Becca.

I squinted at my phone. Only the time obscured the lock screen photo of our faces: 5:55. I made a wish by reflex.

My parents were asleep, my sister already on her way to dive practice. And Becca. At not quite six on a Monday morning, in a suburb gone silent with snow, where was she?

Back in her bed, I hoped. But, no. If she'd come home— maybe even if she hadn't—she'd be headed to the school darkroom by now.

I sat up.

Downstairs I pulled on my coat, still smudgy from my attempts to get the ashes off. At least it was navy.

It was 6:20 when I left a note for my parents and

stepped into the black-and-white world. Still no sign of daylight, barely a graying over the tops of the houses. It was early for me, but not for Becca. She was a night owl and a dawn riser, one of those people who make sleep look like a choice.

The plows hadn't come through yet. My mom's car lumbered and squeaked over snowdrifts all the way to school. Wind leaked uneasily through the driver's side window, chilling the cup of my ear. I put music on, then turned it off again. The sound just made everything seem more desolate. The unfamiliarity of the snowbound world gave me the unsettling sense that I was still inside my dream. Or it was inside me.

The thought made me tilt my head unthinkingly, like I might tip it out.

The lot, at least, was cleared. I took the closest spot and walked to the side door, the only one unlocked before seven a.m. The security guard waved me through with a Dunkin' cup.

Palmetto High School was a weird place. Not the people, who I assumed were no worse than people anywhere, but the building itself. It started as an eight-room school back in the 1910s. Rather than being torn down and rebuilt as the population grew, it was expanded piece by piece. The original build was still lodged inside, the creaky core of PHS. Ancient lockers, water-stained wood, the atmosphere itchy with the buzz of aging fluorescents. The first eight rooms—now down to five, walls knocked out to combine them—were where the arts classes were taught.

It wasn't lost on me that it was the art kids who were exiled to the part of the building most likely to be haunted. But I liked the old section. Its proportions were subtly wrong, traveling through it gave you this off-kilter Wonderland vibe. Even the sunlight that filtered into the classrooms seemed vaguely antique.

But now the dark morning lay like curtains over the windows, and I was moving as fast as I could without breaking into a full-on run. I hurried down the half stair to the art department.

And then I *did* start running, because the door to the photo lab was open. Its lights were on. I rushed into the room, chest bubbling with relief. No one in sight but the bulb by the darkroom shone red, letting me know Becca was in there. Knock? Wait? Throw the door back, negatives be damned? It would serve her right.

The bulb blinked out. The door swung open. My heart kicked hard against my ribs as I moved forward to meet her.

But the person who came trudging out, eyes on the prints he held, was someone I'd never spoken to. Black sweatshirt, black hair to his shoulders, Levi's tattered to strings at the knees. He looked up just before running into me. Reflexively he raised both hands, dropping his photos and catching my shoulders in a startled grip.

His hair was tangled. His touch was warm even through the sleeves of my shirt. There were violet shadows around his startled eyes. I registered all this in the half second it took for him to let go and step back.

"*Je*sus," he said. "I thought I was alone."

He crouched to pick up the prints. I went with him, our heads bumping in the middle.

"Ouch," I muttered, rocking back on my heels. "Sorry."

"It's fine." He gathered his prints into a pile. They'd fallen facedown.

"I didn't mean to rush at you, I'm just looking for Becca Cross. Have you seen her?"

When I said her name he looked up. Hands still, eyes wary. "Why? Is she . . ."

I leaned in. "What?"

"I don't know." He shook his head. "I haven't seen her."

"But you do know her?"

He looked back at his pile, tidying its edges. "Yeah."

That was when his name came to me: James Saito. He was the new kid last year. I knew *of* him, because everyone did. But I didn't *know* him, because nobody did.

"Hey. James."

His mouth quirked, like he was surprised I knew who he was.

"I really need to find Becca. Do you know where she is?"

He hesitated just long enough to make my curiosity spike into suspicion. Then he said, "Hey. Nora. I really don't."

He stood and walked back into the darkroom. The door closed, the red light clicked on. And I stayed a little longer on the floor, wondering why Becca had told him my name. And what else she'd said about me.

Here's what I knew about James Saito.

He moved to town late last year, when we were sophomores. I remember the day exactly, because it was the Monday after spring break. We rolled back in after a typical March holiday of drizzly Midwestern blegh and there was this new guy moving through the halls. Startling face, black hair, the grainless skin of an influencer. The unmistakable aura of someplace bigger and better rolled off him like heat off a bonfire. Everyone who bought a new shirt or whatever over break and thought that counted as reinvention felt the futility of it when they saw James.

Just a tiny bit of effort and he could've upended our entire social order. But he didn't bother. He had the untouchable air of a man doing his time, counting down the clock until he could go back to his *real* life, in Manhattan or Milan or Middle-earth. If you told me he was an ancient vampire being forced to go to high school for the twentieth time, I'd have been like, *Yeah. That makes perfect sense.*

James seemed kind of unreal, honestly. He didn't act arrogant or shy, he just wasn't really *there*. In a matter of days he went from mystery man to . . . I don't know what. Background noise. It was kind of inspiring, actually. He genuinely did not give a shit whether and what we thought about him.

But he was a photographer, too, apparently. One who, like Becca, used the darkroom in the early hours. And his face, when I said her name—it wasn't neutral.

As the halls filled slowly with people, I did the thing I liked to do. I reimagined reality, turning it into something better. A tale I could run like a movie.

In my movie James and Becca met printing photos. They talked every morning in the dark. And when she decided to leave, he was the one she confided in. Maybe he even helped her go.

CHAPTER SEVEN

I WAS SO FOCUSED ON Becca I'd nearly forgotten about Chloe Park, the actual missing girl. It didn't take long to remember. As the halls filled, you could literally see the story of her disappearance spread.

Students gathered in gossipy clots, heads dipped like lions over a carcass. Here and there girls drifted through with damp eyes and holy expressions, books clutched tightly to their chests, already trying to attach themselves to the possible tragedy.

There was one now, beneath the caged hall clock, a beautiful senior in a long black dress. She was flanked by friends on either side, reaching to comfort her like she was a war widow. Except her face was swollen with *actual* tears, the skin between her nose and mouth rubbed raw. I must've stared too long because one of the friends gave me a look, moving to block the girl from my sight.

I wondered how many of these people really knew Chloe. Not many, I'd guess, but hey. Any excuse for drama. Especially the kind that was happening to other people.

Pieces of conversations washed over me as I walked to class.

"My sister was supposed to be there, but my mom found vodka in her overnight bag. Thank *god*."

"Under the Angel, apparently. That thing is cursed."

"Two people gone in one night? That's some serial killer shit."

I stopped. Retraced my steps to the girl who'd said the thing about a serial killer. She was a senior with a mop of hennaed curls and a sweatshirt that read *BOWIE* in an athletic font.

"Two people gone?" My voice sounded cracked. I would *kill* my little sister if her mouth had dragged Becca into this, pairing her name with Chloe Park's. "Did you say two?"

Bowie's friends—a guy in big glasses and locs to his shoulders, and this girl Jordan, who played Miss Trunchbull in the fall musical—gave me the eye. Bowie *tsk*ed and said, "You haven't heard about this?"

"No, I did. I heard about Chloe Park, and . . . I just want to know what *you* heard."

Bowie's expression cleared, sharpened. "About Kurt Huffman, you mean."

There was a jolt in my spine. "Kurt Huffman," I repeated. "What about him?"

"He's the other missing person?" She turned it into a question, asked of someone very dim.

"Oh. I guess I didn't know about that."

I spoke faintly. But the memory that pinned and held me was icicle-bright. I shook it off, still facing a trio of seniors whose patience with me was waning. "What happened to Kurt Huffman?"

Bowie looked at Jordan like, *Do we bother with this awkward child?* Jordan shrugged and took pity. "I got this from

Kurt's friend, Madison Velez. She was with him when he disappeared. Have you seen her? She's a total mess right now."

"She's a mess in general," the guy in glasses murmured, barely moving his lips.

Madison. *That* was her name, the girl I'd seen crying in the black dress.

Jordan went on. "Saturday night they're at the cemetery, right? The old one up the hill, where the Eyeless Angel is. They had some kind of fight, and Kurt took off running toward the Angel. Like two minutes later Madison followed him. She found his coat lying on the bench in front of the mausoleum, in the Angel's shadow. But Kurt? Was gone."

"Spooky," whispered glasses guy.

I thought of little Chloe Park, disappearing into the winter night. She'd left her coat behind, too.

Jordan was relishing this. All she needed was a flashlight under her chin. "Madison says the way it happened was impossible. The Angel's near the back of the cemetery, the gates are way up front. The fence is basically unclimbable. If Kurt left she'd have seen him. Plus his car is still where he left it." She checked herself, studying my face. "Uh. You look kinda . . . are you okay?"

"I'm fine," I told her. "I just—I've gotta go."

I spun around and took off. Tried to. The first bell had rung but the crowd was moving sluggishly, still passing gossip hand to hand. I didn't want to hear anything they were saying. I needed to think, needed five minutes alone in the quiet so I could *think*.

Becca and Chloe Park didn't know each other. I doubted they'd ever exchanged one word. Chloe disappearing, my best friend running away, these were two distinct happenings of differing badness that had nothing to do with each other.

But Kurt Huffman. If he was really missing, could I say the same thing about Becca and Kurt?

Because it wasn't entirely true that Becca and I hadn't spoken to each other since autumn. We had, just once. Week before last, she found me at my locker. I was digging something out when she came to rest beside me, left hand on the locker next to mine.

I stopped what I was doing, but I didn't turn. I just looked at her fingers. They were banded in blue agate and tipped with opalescent polish, picking at the locker grate. I'd never seen those rings, that polish. This was a stranger's hand.

I looked at Becca's hand and knew with a rush that I *should* have called her on Christmas, on New Year's, something I'd agonized over and ultimately chickened out on. I was bracing for her to tell me off about it when she said:

"You see that kid?"

It was so abrupt I finally looked at her. After weeks apart it was a shock to see her face so close to mine. There was a hard gloss on her, an aura of such careless impenetrability I felt a stab of real grief.

"Which kid?"

Becca kept her eyes on mine just long enough that I thought she'd been hoping for more. Then she glanced away, and I figured I was wrong. She tipped her chin toward a guy down the hall, crouching to rummage in his backpack. A lanky senior with blond hair and a *Bob's Burgers* T-shirt, who managed to be both imposingly tall and nearly invisible. One of those kids. Kurt Huffman.

"What about him," I muttered.

Becca's voice stayed cool and distant, even as she leaned in so close I could smell the licorice on her breath. She was the only living person under seventy who liked Good & Plenty. "I need you to stay the fuck away from that kid."

Very quietly I said, "Is this about . . . what you said? That night?"

The night we fought, in October. She knew what I meant, and her indifference flipped to ferocity. "I don't," she spoke in a hiss, "want to talk about that night."

When she turned to walk away, I let her.

As the news about Chloe and Kurt spread, it mutated. It sprouted unproven details and wholly invented asides, until everyone was working off slightly different versions of the tale. At least nobody was talking about Becca. By the time I got to fourth-period comp I'd settled into a state of relative calm.

Miss Caine didn't even try to hold our attention. She put on *Dead Poets Society* and pulled out her phone. Everyone else either did the same or commenced whispering. I slumped over my desk and listened.

"I can't stop thinking about it," Athena Paulsen said tearfully. "I was home alone Saturday night. I could so easily have been the one who was taken!" The girl beside her rolled her eyes and patted Athena's back.

The kid next to me turned in his chair. "Do you think Kurt did something to Chloe Park? Like, *something*?"

"So obviously Huffman abducted the hot freshman," said a boy with a Chalamet quiff. "But what about the other girl?"

My breath caught. I waited, head cradled in the crook of my elbow. Tracey Borcia was sitting on the desk above him, feet planted between his outspread legs. "What other girl?"

"Whatshername, with the camera. That Tinker Bell–looking saddo."

Tracey laughed. "No *way*. Little orphan girl's missing, too? I guess she finally offed herself."

I stood so fast my chair scraped and fell.

Even Miss Caine looked up. Chalamet and Tracey watched me with bored irritation, just a momentary interruption to their mating ritual. And what was I going to say? Something super original and scathing like *fuck you*?

"Ohhhh, shit, girl." Tracey's eyes lit with malice. "You're friends with her, aren't you?"

Before I could reply, the strangest thing happened.

Don't bother, my brain told me. *They don't matter. Their lives will be so small.*

My vision shimmered and I could see it. Tracey at twenty, thirty, fifty, the smirk on her face settling into permanent creases. And Chalamet. Just pretty enough and lazy enough to be ruined by it, an early bloom eaten by early rot.

I caught myself on my desk before I could stumble. Quietly I righted the fallen chair and grabbed my bag, mumbling "Bathroom" to Miss Caine as I hurried to the door.

. It was *my* thoughts that stopped me from saying anything. My own easy assumption that my mediocre classmates were already living their best years.

But I had the unshakable sense of having heard them in Becca's voice.

CHAPTER EIGHT

I KEPT MY EYES DOWN as I washed my hands. I pushed the darkest thoughts away. My face in the bathroom mirror was creeping me out. Anxiety darkened my gaze, drew the blood from my lips. And Becca's voice still burrowed into my ear, so crisp it made me shiver. *Their lives will be so small.*

It wasn't like it was hard to put those words in her mouth. She'd always been disdainful of people who weren't us.

We met in the first grade. Becca was a rare midyear new kid, not new to town but transferring in from some local nature school.

I was, at the time, an absolute outcast. Since preschool I'd had a reputation as a liar, and early in first grade a particularly dark untruth had led to my social ruination. When Becca showed up I recognized the opportunity for what it was: a chance to make a friend who didn't know about me.

The trouble was everyone else wanted her, too. Rebecca Cross was heather-eyed and autumn-haired and wee as Thumbelina. She looked like a creature you'd see peeking out from behind a leaf in a Brian Froud book.

And she was canny for a six-year-old. For a month she

had all the little girls gunning for her favor. She floated among them like Scarlett O'Hara, accepting tributes as small and adorable as she was: fruit-shaped erasers, thumb-sized pots of glitter gloss. I burned with envy. I would've traded places with any of them, including the cute rubber strawberry she used to correct her worksheets.

Long after I'd given up, she found me at recess. I was playing HORSE against myself when she came walking up in one of the eccentric handmade dresses her mom used to put her in, that would've deep-sixed the popularity of a less self-possessed child. She looked like a flower floating toward me on a breeze. I tugged at the waistband of my Carter's jeans and focused on sinking the ball into the basket. Kept my expression stoic as it went sailing past the backboard completely.

Becca watched it go, then turned her attention to me. "I heard you told Chrissie P. she's gonna die in a car crash on her sixteenth birthday."

My heart gave a defeated squeeze. That was the lie that undid me.

Just before Halloween, I made a desperate popularity grab by pretending I could see the future. I had a few kids halfway convinced when Chrissie P. stomped over at recess. *Nobody believes you*, she said, *and nobody likes you, either.*

The truth of it hit me deep in my belly. And from that same deep dark well I hadn't even known was there, the lie poured out. It was made of fairy tales and hurt and I didn't really think she'd *believe* me. My stomach still ached remembering the way her sneering face had crumpled into tears. Parents were called, a conference was had. I was toast.

Of course the other kids told Becca. I was sure that if

I turned around I'd see them watching us, whispering. I pretended I didn't hear her, trudging after the ball.

"But," she went on, pausing for effect, "I also heard you're a liar."

"So what," I snapped, turning. "Chrissie and her stupid friends lie all the time. They're just jealous because my lies are *interesting*."

Becca grinned, and I realized I'd never seen her do that before. I would've remembered. Her teeth had the pearl-string sameness of a china doll's.

"Tell me the future," she said. "Tell me what's going to happen to everyone."

I narrowed my eyes. Then I turned in a slow 360, looking for Chrissie and her henchmen. They were all the way across the yard, playing double Dutch. I could hear them chanting to the beat of the turning rope. . . . *count to three. If I'm good, will you pick me?*

"Okay," I said, chest swelling with cautious hope. "You see that boy over there?"

She let me talk for the rest of recess, and through every recess that week. I'd never had an audience like Rebecca Cross. Her shining eyes and respectful silence spurred me to ever greater heights of invention, ever deeper trenches of imagined horrors. By Friday I'd pegged half our class as speeding toward some kind of astonishing doom. And Becca was mine. We'd been written off as weirdos together.

Together! Some girls treated their friends like athletes in competitive trials, constantly moving them up and down the ranks. But for us best friendship was deadly serious, more permanent than a tattoo. We invented code words and handshakes, we made repeated blood pacts. We scratched each other's arms with pine needles and sipped unholy potions we invented in our parents' gardens, out of some nebulous but passionate desire to prove our devotion. We snuck clothes into each other's drawers so we could swear to anyone who asked—no one ever asked—that we lived together.

Our moms conducted hushed phone calls, worried we'd burn bright, then break each other's hearts. They set up playdates with other children, who never asked to come back. Our parents didn't get it, that was all. They didn't believe you could find your soul mate at six.

As I stood in the school bathroom, avoiding my own reflection, I felt a surge of painful longing. Not for Becca as she was now, but for that bold little girl with the firework hair, whose love I won with lies.

I'd already checked my locker, hoping she'd slipped a note through its slats. Now I trekked across the building to hers. Maybe she'd left something for me, maybe I would just rest my eyes awhile on her familiar mess. I spun the dial lock until the door came open with a crisp snap.

For a disoriented moment I thought I had the wrong locker. Gone was the riot of taped-up prints and balled thrift-store sweaters and the textbooks she barely cracked. Gone were the mason jar full of film canisters and the Francesca Woodman postcards and the Tenth Doctor Funko that had belonged to her dad. The door, the hooks, the locker's dented metal sides, all were bare.

But the locker wasn't entirely empty. One black-and-white photo remained, stuck to the locker's back.

In the photo a girl lay supine in open water. Her white dress was wet, heavy, it shaded to drowned grays and threatened to drag her under. Her limbs were loosened and submerged. Only the oval of her features remained above the surface.

Everything about the photo spoke of surrender except that face. The eyes wet-lashed and open, watching the camera with an expression of absolute challenge. The contrast it made with the rest of the image prickled my skin. On the photo's rim, marked in soft lead: *The Goddess of Impossible Chance.*

The girl was Becca. The photo was the last in a series we made: our Goddess series. It was a collaboration that began when we were ten, inspired by a strange interlude in the woods. I wrote little stories about goddesses we thought should exist, and she set up the photos to go with them. We took turns playing the goddess.

This photo, taken the summer before our sophomore year, was our last one. She was born just after Becca's dad got sick, when he needed the intervention of an impossible power. On the day he died in hospice, we fed our whole pantheon to Becca's backyard firepit. All those glossy, powerful deities who wore our faces, gone in a cloud of chemical smoke.

Becca must've kept the negatives, then, and reprinted this one. Another secret. How many had she been keeping from me?

There was one more thing in the locker, set perfectly squared on the shelf: a silver butterfly knife, closed up tight. It had been placed there with precision by someone who knew exactly who would find it, and how I would feel when I did. I'd seen the knife just once before, years ago, on a late-summer evening.

It came over me in a sensory wave. Thick heat, purple

twilight, the odors of honeysuckle and rust. A sunburnt Becca gripping the knife in her fist, blood lying blackish on its blade.

Down the hall a classroom door swung open and a teacher walked out. It wasn't until I slapped the locker shut that I realized I was smiling. Because it wasn't a *bad* memory, the one with the knife. It was one of my best.

When the teacher was gone I opened the locker just long enough to slide the knife and photograph into my bag. Here was my first hard proof that Becca's departure Saturday night wasn't an impulsive act or a temporary flight or, god forbid, an abduction. She'd known since last week at least that she wasn't coming back Monday morning.

CHAPTER NINE

THE BELL RANG AND THE halls filled and I couldn't even remember what class I was supposed to go to. Everything that wasn't Becca had a glassy texture to it. Only she felt alive in my mind.

Then I saw Madison Velez. Her eyes were down, her black dress dragging. She radiated meaning now, too. If Kurt really was missing and Becca did know something about him, something bad, Madison might know it, too. I followed her.

She moved with a sodden grace, telegraphing her sorrow. The halls thinned out but she was too busy being sad to see me. Even when we were the only ones in the echoing stairwell, she didn't turn. I didn't call out, either. I followed her all the way to the threshold of the bathroom, where I hesitated before going in.

Madison was already in a stall. I couldn't hear her peeing or anything, but I could see the shadow of her skirt on the floor. I planted myself in front of the mirror to wait. My reflection looked even more discordant than before. Hollow-eyed, imprecise at the edges. Like there was a flaw in the glass, reflecting me twice.

"Good god," Madison said through the stall door. "I came in here to get away from you. Was that somehow unclear?"

I flushed red, mumbled an apology, and fled.

After that I kept my head down. I went to class, ate lunch in my car to avoid making conversation. As the day played out around me, I kept running through the same questions. Where was Becca keeping herself? How far was she willing to let this go? What did she know about Kurt Huffman?

I should've left the knife in the car, but its weight in my bag centered me. Made me sharp and humming, ready to do *something*. Problem was I didn't know what. After last bell I walked through the parking lot, considering my options. Go back to Becca's house? Check her favorite coffee place, technically a used bookstore with a burnt pot of dollar drip in the back?

Or the forest preserve. I could look for her there, her camera in hand. But I didn't really think I'd find Becca among the frozen trees. I would find only endless echoes of her, my best friend at every age, with a thousand versions of me in tow. I felt haunted enough, I didn't want to go to the woods.

Book coffee, I decided. I could use it.

Then I saw Ruth. She was leaning against the passenger door of my mom's car, studying me as I approached. She was good at it: the fearless editor of the school lit magazine, Ruth had a perfect poker face. She was intense, unflappable, wearing big Gloria Steinem glasses and tweed pants that came up to her ribs under an open men's car coat. Her hair was swept off her pale forehead and pinned to one side because she was letting her bangs grow out. It was her one sign of weakness.

"You weren't at lunch," she said. "Then I heard some possibly bullshit rumor about your friend Rebecca Cross?"

I guess my face gave me away. When I got close enough Ruth stepped forward and folded me into a firm hug. "So it's true. I'm sorry, I hoped it wasn't." She patted my back once, twice. "It'll be okay."

The platitude almost helped. Everything that came out of Ruth's mouth had the ring of fact-checked truth. Then she leaned back, mouth pursing, shifting into journalist mode. In another era Ruth would've been the sharp-dressed shark at the edge of the party, telephoning her editor with a scandalous tip. The only reason she ran the magazine instead of the school newspaper was because the paper had died of budget cuts.

"Rebecca and the other missing students. Do they share any—"

"Becca ran away," I cut in. "Alone."

Ruth's brow went up. "Okay. Well, I'm here to personally drag you to Ekstrom's. You skipped lunch, I figured you'd try to skip lit mag, too."

Meeting day. Right. I considered my other option: bailing in favor of lurking at the back of the bookstore, waiting for someone I knew in my heart wouldn't show. Drinking coffee until my stomach burned, browsing secondhand paperbacks.

I followed Ruth. I wasn't super pumped to parse the bird symbolism in some sophomore's breakup poem today, but anything was preferable to being alone.

CHAPTER TEN

I DID FEEL BETTER JUST walking into Miss Ekstrom's classroom. Leafy plants lined the tops of the windows and clustered along the sill, tinting and dimming the daylight. The air smelled of bergamot and crumbling paper, and a collection of vintage library posters covered the walls, all featuring random celebrities holding up books. Half of them looked like they'd never seen a book before.

Ekstrom was our faculty advisor, her staff four people strong: Ruth and Amanda, seniors who'd joined up their freshman year, and me and Chris, both juniors. I could've pretended we were small because we were elite, but I think Ruth just scared people off with her commitment.

Now she was watching Chris with crossed arms and a look of waning forbearance. He leaned back against the windows, wedged between a monstera plant and a mother-in-law's tongue, holding a submission in his hands.

"'I ran back to my room,'" he read aloud. "'It was definitely the day of doom!'"

"You're going to hell," Amanda told him, standing up and grabbing at the paper.

He twisted out of her reach. "Just let me get to the part

where he rhymes *they canceled lacrosse* with *my after-school job boss*."

Chris had a rosy apple-pie face he did everything he could to neutralize: growing his hair to his chin and dying it black, black polish on his nails, an endless wardrobe of vintage band T-shirts—black—emblazoned with names like Nightwish and Mastodon. All it did was make him look like an evil schoolchild in a horror film.

He was also the only one of us who lacked the karmic terror of making fun of someone else's writing. Miss Ekstrom manned the submissions inbox and gave us printouts with their authors' names excised. Today she'd made the mistake of leaving the stack of printouts unattended on her desk, and he'd slipped one off the top.

Clearing his throat, he continued in a sing-song. "'My mom made my favorite meal, in the hopes that my sadness I'd no longer feel.'"

"*Ahem*," Ruth said in cold imitation, then took on a pretentious tone. "'Like zipper teeth they come together, separate. Crooked boys in a cut-clean row.'"

Chris's face reddened but his voice stayed level. "Yeah. I wrote that. What's your point, Ruthless?"

"My point is everyone's shit sounds embarrassing when you read it in a shitty voice. People are *trusting* us. All these submissions are from writers who had to be brave enough to put themselves out there. Don't mock them."

"*Writers*." He curled his fingers into the okay symbol. "Sure."

"News flash, Christopher," Ruth snapped. "You're not the arbiter of what's good."

He looked around exaggeratedly. "I actually am, though? That's literally what we're here to do?"

"The vibe in here sucks today," Amanda commented mildly. Her pale brown eyes looked faintly electric against her darker brown skin, and were ringed around with stress circles. She was waiting for news on college admissions with a grim fanaticism at odds with sleep.

I raised a hand. "It's me. I'm weirding everyone out."

"No, it's definitely Chris," Ruth said, while Amanda gave a little grimace that proved my point.

"It's fine," I said. "You can talk about what's going on. I know you want to."

Chris sharpened up. "Okay. I wasn't gonna ask, but since you told me I could. What the hell is happening here? Did your friend tell you where she was going? Did she and Kurt and that freshman go somewhere *together*? Is it teen cult activity? Ooh." He tilted his head thoughtfully. "Teen Cult Activity." Chris was always looking for a name for the band he didn't have.

I shrugged. "No idea."

He smirked at me. "Great. Glad you let me ask."

"Are you worried about her?" Amanda asked, then winced. "Of course you are."

I avoided the question. "What's grossing me out is how *into* it everyone is. They're acting like it's a TV show."

"This is the most exciting thing half these people will ever experience," Ruth said flatly. "And it's not even happening to them."

Chris scoffed at her. "Why do you get to make fun of people and I don't?"

"You make fun of their *art*. I just make fun of their bad ideas and the stupid things they say and the general way that they are."

I laughed, one hard bark. Everyone looked at me.

"I'm feeling the misanthropy today." I gave a double thumbs-up. "Thanks, guys."

Miss Ekstrom swept in then, hair a static cloud and her long coat carrying the smell of cigarettes and snow. "Hey, kiddos. Sorry I'm late. Got called into a last-minute meeting."

She glanced at me when she said it, a quick look that made my skin tighten. I figured the meeting was about the missing students, and wondered what exactly was discussed.

Ekstrom had been a PHS fixture since the 1970s. She was a Palmetto lifer who loved to travel, and always came back bearing edible gifts: wasabi Kit Kats, rose macarons, crumbling blocks of halvah.

Right now the big bowl on her desk was full of lychee taffy. Ekstrom sat beside it, hair spilling over her shoulders in a fuzzy silver sheet. I assumed she'd make us talk about what was happening, but all she said was, "Small stack today." Discreetly Chris slid the submission he'd lifted under the monstera. "Ruth, you want to hand these out?"

Ruth circled the room, divvying printouts among us facedown. When she was done Ekstrom slipped her glasses on and said what she always did. "Somebody read me something good."

Ruth read first. That, too, was enshrined. It was a winter poem that compared icicles to monster teeth and had nicely itchy slant rhymes. We all voted to advance it to the next round.

Amanda went next, with an overheated "The Raven" pastiche about—could it be?—a breakup. Breakups and unrequited love were the fuel on which our submissions box ran. We looked at each other in the silence that followed. "Special filing cabinet?" Chris said.

Amanda balled up the page and chucked it into the trash. Ekstrom pursed her lips but said nothing. She was a mostly silent partner, keeping things civil while rarely telling us what she thought. Even when we broke the "discuss it before you shitcan it" rule.

Over the course of four bad submissions and two good ones, and a poem I would've known was Chris's even if he hadn't spent the entirety of its reading with his ears glowing neon red, my spirits settled. The routine of it lulled me, and the warmth of the room. When there was nothing left to read, Ruth brought up the lockbox that lived at the back of the room, below a sign reading SUBMIT YOUR LIT! in purple Magic Marker. It was meant to entice spontaneous submissions from shy geniuses. Mainly it inspired our classmates to submit drawings of dicks, but Ruth lived in hope.

She unlocked it with her usual sense of ceremony, and smiled in triumph. "We've got one. Nora, I think it's your turn." It was folded into a football, and she flicked it at me.

As I unfolded it Amanda made jazz hands and said, "Penis time!" Still laughing, I began to read.

"'Goddess, goddess, count to one. Who will you . . .'"

I stopped, scalp prickling.

"What is it?" Ruth asked instantly.

The paper was in my hands but I didn't see it. I saw midday sun turning the hair of my schoolmates into strands of bright tinsel, lit clouds. I smelled playground rubber, heard a chorus of girls' voices.

"It's not a real submission."

"What do you mean?" Ruth's expression went scalpel-sharp. "It's plagiarized, isn't it."

"Wait." Amanda ran a hand over her shaved head. "Read it again?"

I didn't want to. It wasn't meant for them. It was another message to me, from Becca, delivered sideways. First the knife and the photo in her locker, now this. What was she playing at?

But everyone was watching me, waiting. Ekstrom, too. Steadying my voice, I read the poem through.

> *Goddess, goddess, count to one*
> *Who will you pick when the day is done?*
>
> *Goddess, goddess, count to two*
> *Which one will the goddess choose?*
>
> *Goddess, goddess, count to three*
> *If I'm good, will you pick me?*
>
> *Goddess, goddess, count to four*
> *Is that you knocking at my door?*
>
> *Goddess, goddess, count to five*
> *In the morning, who's alive?*
>
> *Goddess, goddess, count to six*
> *Who will you pick for your bag of tricks?*
>
> *Goddess, goddess, count to seven*
> *Whose hand will you take when you go to heaven?*

The room stayed quiet when I was done. No sound but the abacus click of Ekstrom messing with her necklaces. Chris scooted forward on the window ledge to see us better. "Hello? Anyone?"

"I forgot—" Amanda began, but Ruth cut in. "Why bother submitting *that*? Did they think we wouldn't recognize it?"

Chris looked annoyed. "*I* don't recognize it."

She gave him a scathing look. "It was a recess thing. You were probably too busy lighting things on fire to notice."

In third-grade recess Chris got caught running the flame of a Zippo over Palmetto Elementary's brick corner. Eight years ago now, but people still called him Pyro Pete.

"It's a jump rope rhyme. Here, listen." Amanda took the page and read the first line aloud. "'God-dess, god-dess, count to one.' Hear it?"

I did. The militant slap of sneakers on asphalt, keeping time with the rhyme's bratty cadence. Two jumpers, two ropes. The rhyme was for double Dutch.

Ruth made a face. "I'm not good at jumping. But I played the bad kid version once."

"You're not good at *jumping*? Bad kid version of what?"

"Of the goddess game," she told him impatiently. "You know, the urban legend."

"Suburban legend," Amanda corrected. "For real, Chris, you haven't heard the goddess story? It's all murder and vengeance. You'd love it."

Ruth chewed her cheek. "No, it's more supernatural than murdery."

Amanda turned quizzical eyes on me. "Nor? You ever play the goddess game?"

"Nah," I lied. "I'm not a bad kid like Ruth."

"How about you?"

Amanda addressed Ekstrom with a little smile on her lips, like she couldn't imagine our teacher ever being young enough to play anything. But Ekstrom nodded.

"I have." The slant of the light turned the lenses of her glasses into two gray moonstones. Then her voice went dry as she tapped her hip. "Back in the Stone Age, when my body had all its original parts."

Chris's ears went red again, maybe at the thought of a body existing under Ekstrom's layer cake of cardigans. "Is anyone planning to tell me the story, or is my ignorance too amusing?"

Ekstrom shook her head. "Save it for next week. Our time's up."

"Carry my bag," Amanda offered brightly, "and I'll tell you on the way."

It was a true trade-off. Chris bent beneath the weight of her traveling library like King Koopa. "What is *in* this thing," he said, trailing her out the door.

I wondered which version of the story Amanda would tell. Before I could follow them, Ekstrom touched my wrist gently.

"Nora. Stay a minute?"

"What?" Then, trying to hide my reluctance, "Okay."

I knew it would be about Becca. At some point Miss Ekstrom must've gleaned we were friends. It was always funny to be reminded our teachers could see us, too. That they were probably fully aware of all our crushes and friendships and breakups and fights, all our griefs and alliances right there in plain sight.

Ruth lingered a bit, maybe hoping to overhear. But

Ekstrom waited until she was gone to turn toward me and kindly say, "Rebecca Cross."

After an awkward pause I said, "Yeah."

"How are you doing? Can I do anything for you?"

"I'm good. No, I don't think so. Thank you, though."

She nodded. "Let me know if you need to talk, okay? Or if you just need to take a breath. My room's usually free."

I tightened my fist around the goddess rhyme, which I'd folded into a little square when nobody was looking. What would she think if I told her Becca had submitted it? Would she be annoyed, intrigued? Would she think me paranoid?

But Ekstrom spoke before I could. "Do you know where Becca is?" The words were quick, and tempered with an apologetic smile. "People are saying some outlandish things."

How disappointing, I thought, to watch my favorite teacher dig for gossip under the guise of sympathy. I answered curtly. "Whatever they're saying, it's got nothing to do with Becca. She ran away from home."

Ekstrom blinked at me. "Ran away. Really?"

"I'm her best friend," I said bitterly. "I'd know, right?"

"You would," she said, then made a rueful face. "Good ol' Palmetto, huh? It's an easy place to want to run from."

I wrinkled my nose. Adults rarely acknowledged the limitations of the suburbs. "You stayed here, though."

It didn't seem rude until I'd said it. She didn't take offense, just laughed. "Ran away from it plenty of times, too. My best friend and I would take it in turns, coupla drama queens."

Her eyes crinkled and softened when she said it. I bet she wasn't seeing me. I bet she was seeing two teen hellions in bellbottoms or whatever, racing around town on roller skates. And I felt suddenly, unaccountably jealous. Ekstrom's runaway years were long behind her. She'd built a life right here.

When Becca and I dreamed our overlapping futures, they were always set elsewhere. New York, Los Angeles, London, places whose names conjured up a sensory rush and a taste on the tongue: coffee, sunshine, smoke. For the first time I imagined us growing old where we were raised. Passing paperbacks and cut herbs and bottles of beer over property lines, partners and maybe-kids a blur in the background. Right then the idea of staying in Palmetto didn't feel so claustrophobic.

I was going to say something self-pitying. The words were forming on my tongue. But I looked at Ekstrom and something in her face made me stop. There was a hard curiosity in it that made me wonder if I'd really seen any softness there.

And it made me think she didn't believe me when I told her Becca ran away.

Maybe no one did. Maybe everyone but me was already in the process of writing her off: a mystery or an abduction or something even worse.

So I gave my teacher a big fake smile and walked out the door. She and everyone else could think what they wanted. I was the one Becca was talking to. I just had to figure out how to listen.

CHAPTER ELEVEN

I CALLED MY MOM FROM the car.

"Hey, sweetie." She sounded distracted. I could hear her typing as she spoke. "I'm sorry, I let the day get away from me. How are you holding up? You want me to check in with Miranda?"

"Oh. Later, yeah. But hey, Mom? Did you ever play the goddess game?"

The sound of typing stopped. "The goddess game. The old slumber party game?"

"Right. Or—yeah."

"You know what, I did." Her voice was thoughtful. "Once or twice. What made you think of that?"

"Just thinking about Becca. Stuff we used to do."

"Ah," she said softly. "You heading home?"

"Pretty soon." I hesitated. "Do you remember where you learned it? The game?"

Mom made a *hm* sound, not quite a laugh. "Where does anyone learn these things? They're just in the air."

But I knew exactly where I learned the goddess game. The bad kid version, the one that mattered.

Becca and I used to tell our parents we were going to the playground. Then we'd walk right past it and into the woods. There we played one long lovely game of make-believe, interrupted by dinner and sleep and our lives outside the trees but at the same time never-ending.

Now I could see Palmetto's forest preserve for what it was: a cultivated wilderness. A green playground for bikers and power walkers and parents with jogging strollers. But our woods had been wild once. When we were children, they were as wild as we could make them.

Here's something that happened to us. Once upon a time, in the course of one of those endless summer days.

We were playing in the clearing by our tree, a gorgeously gnarled oak with a hollow in its trunk. We liked to hide things inside it, small stuff, candy and woven jewelry and folded notes. The game that day was what it always was: the Kingdom. In the Kingdom the clearing was a throne room, and we were enchanter-knights to a demanding Queen, forever sending us off on some mission or other: finding magical objects, working spells, waking ensorcelled sleepers. We were just young enough that the game closed over our heads, sealing us off from the real world completely. Playing didn't work that way forever.

Back then I didn't think of my own face and body as foes or friends, I just moved through the world and kept my eyes on Becca. I looked at her more than I ever looked at myself. But I can picture us both if I try.

Becca in summertime, age ten: bright as a spark in a pair of dirty overall shorts and a revolving assortment of tank tops, shoulders freckling beneath her tangled hair. Grown-up women used to clutch their hearts when they looked at her.

And me. I never made a stranger's heart spill over, as far as I could tell. I had the same hair then that I have now: a sloppy shag that hits somewhere between chin and shoulder, brown dark enough to call it black. I wore slip-on Vans and T-shirts so big they swallowed my shorts completely. Becca was tiny and I was tall and I'm sure we made a cute picture. A girl witch and her faithful protector.

That day we were looking over a scroll from our Queen, talking in pretend Old English. One minute we were in the clearing alone, and the next it was filled with girls.

They probably weren't even that old. Eighth graders, maybe. But they were old enough, all tangled metal necklaces and bikini tops, T-shirts scissored away into irreplicably cooler shapes. There were five of them, I think, but the way they moved made them hard to count. They managed to look both entirely distinct and as identical as birds of the same species. They spoke in a musical round, each voice overlapping the next.

"Oh, my god. Look at these literal cuties."

"You guys are lil' witch babies, aren't you?"

"I love it. All potions and shit." Picking up and inspecting the mortar and pestle I took from my parents' kitchen, lined with crushed alder leaves. "You're so much cooler than we were. Can you do a spell for me?"

"Do her a love spell."

"Shut your mouth, I want a *money* spell."

I'd risen to my feet, like I really was Becca's protector, and one of them bumped her shoulder into mine. "Look how big she is. How old even are you?"

Another touched Becca's hair, first lightly, then really getting her hand up in it. "Ugh, so pretty. Can I, like, carry you in my pocket?"

Their attention was glittery and dizzying and a little bit nauseating, like a carnival ride. They smelled like a carnival, too, their skin cheap-sugar sweet and their breath warm and sour. There was something mesmerizing about their certainty that what they had to say was worth saying.

One of them squatted beside Becca. I moved to hide the paper we'd been reading, dipped in tea to make it look like parchment, but the girl was too quick and snatched it.

"Ooh, what's this?" Her mouth curled and my whole body burned with slow-moving shame as I realized what she was about to do.

She cleared her throat.

"'By proclamation of the Forest Queen these my faithful knights may move freely through the Kingdom and its six surrounding lands, in tireless search of . . .'"

The girl read the entire thing. Her friends giggled inanely throughout, and Becca hunched beside me, each of us alone in our embarrassment. As this stranger recited the words I'd been so proud of when I wrote them, I felt the Kingdom fall. Its forests toppled, its oceans dried to glimmering salt, its meadows curled black beneath scouring fire.

A great age had ended by the time she was through.

"So cool." Lightly she dropped the page. "We would *totally* be best friends if I was your age."

Just because I was younger she thought I wouldn't catch the way she smirked at her friends above my head.

"Hey, you know what we should do?" The other girls turned toward her, smoothly automatic, in a way that told me she was their leader. "We should teach them the goddess game."

"We know the goddess game," I muttered.

"You know the recess rhyme," she said dismissively. "I mean the *real* goddess game. The fucked-up one."

The f-word hit me like a drop of sizzling oil. The girls were arrayed immovably around our clearing now, stretched out in the grass or on a fallen log, ripping up handfuls of clover.

"Oh, my god, we totally should."

"Do they know the story yet?"

"Everyone knows."

"Little kids don't know."

"Chelsea, you tell them."

The ringleader—Chelsea—settled back on the grass. "Yeah, okay," she said lazily. From the pocket of her cut-offs she produced a flat silver bottle and wagged it. "Want some?"

"You're corrupting the babies!"

"There's hardly enough for *us*."

Chelsea shrugged. "Benny's obsessed with me. He'll get me more."

The bottle made its way around the wobbly circle, each girl taking a drink. I watched its approach with mounting anxiety. When I glanced at Becca, I could see in her face that her soul had gone to ground. This happened sometimes when she got overwhelmed. Her hands were folded, her expression as smooth as a bead of plastic. But when the bottle reached her she surprised me by tipping it to her mouth without hesitation before handing it over.

The summer light was honey thick, insects floating in it like flecks of black tea. I slapped at one, then took a sip, determined not to cough. Whatever they'd put in the flask was sweet beyond recognition. It made me think of old-fashioned medicine.

"Good job, sweetie," the next girl said softly, as I passed her the bottle.

"Okay, so, the story of the goddess," Chelsea drawled. "Way back, like, eighty years ago, a girl died at the high school."

One of her friends, sitting with her back to our tree, shook her head. "It was fifty or sixty."

"Shut up, Tegan." Chelsea spoke with the regal certainty of a cat bringing its paw down on a mouse. "Anyway, it was a long time ago. Right after her funeral, her friends broke into the school in the middle of the night. They wanted to do a ritual in the place where she died." She leaned in. "A ritual that would bring her back to life. So they made a fire right in the middle of the hall and they burned all this stuff. Like, the dead girl's diary, and all these special herbs, and her pearl ring and the key to her house and one of her teeth and literally the dress she wore to prom and—"

"How'd they get her tooth?" I interrupted.

"Stole it from the casket," she said, unblinking. I nodded, one liar respecting another. "And they all threw in a lock of their own hair and prayed for her resurrection."

"No way," Tegan said stubbornly. "My grandma actually went to PHS when it happened, and once she got super drunk on vodka tonics and told me—"

"Tegan, shut *up*, I swear to God. I'm the one telling it."

Fiercely Tegan yanked a chunk of bark off the tree's crumbling base and was silent.

"As I was saying." Chelsea rolled her eyes. "Something happened when they were doing their spell. Right in the middle of all the praying and stuff, they stopped praying to God." She paused, small blue eyes intensifying. "And they found themselves praying to the *girl*. It was like *they* were the ones under a spell. And then? The girl appeared to them."

The bottle had made its way back to me. Sickening, but it lit a small warm ember in my throat.

"What'd she say, Chels?" one of the girls asked when it became clear a prompt was required.

"She was floating over the fire. Sixteen years old, looking just like she did when she was alive. Her ghost wore the very prom dress they were burning, and the pearl ring. And, um, these satin dancing shoes."

I glanced at Tegan. Her arms were crossed over her chest, ends of her mouth turned down.

Now Chelsea's eyes looked almost sad. "She told them she didn't *want* to be resurrected, because it was too much fun being dead. She told them that when they burned all her favorite things they'd freed her from her last bit of sadness, missing her life.

"And then she told them how good it felt when they prayed to her. It felt like, she said it felt like being in a video game, where your body just eats up golden coins."

Nobody asked how a ghost could've made this analogy eighty or sixty years ago. We were listening too hard.

"She said that if they prayed long enough it would fill her whole body up with gold, and transform her into a goddess. Because she might get bored one day of being a ghost, but she'd never get bored of being a goddess. And if they kept on praying to her, and giving her burnt offerings and stuff, she would grant them each a wish. So they did. And she did."

"What were their wishes?" Becca said suddenly. She'd sat still as salt through the telling, only moving to take the flask. She seemed fully present again, soul tugged back into place by the ghost story.

Dramatically Chelsea smoothed the air. "Nooobody knows." I bet she didn't feel like thinking up a bunch of wishes on the spot. "And nobody knows whether the goddess died when the girls did, or if she just stopped existing the day they stopped praying and forgot about her, or whether she's still hanging around, waiting for someone to believe in her again, and grant their wish."

"If she *had* come back to life," I asked on a burst of courage, "do you think she would've been mad they took her tooth?"

"What?" Chelsea squinted at me. "Why are you so obsessed with the tooth thing?"

I wasn't sure, either. The story kaleidoscoped around me, too many interesting pieces to look at all at once. Also my head felt . . . fuzzy. Imbalanced. Exactly what our anti–substance abuse assemblies had told me would happen if I drank. My heart seized and I reached for Becca's hand, but she didn't notice me.

"So what's the game?" she asked. "You said there's a, a messed-up version."

Chelsea grinned. She made her eyebrows go up and down twice, the most confident girl I'd ever seen. It filled me with a grudging awe that she'd figured out how to do the thing that eluded me: draw people in with her lies.

"The goddess's friends tried to steal her back from death," she said. "From the *ground*. They turned her immortal with their faith. Summoning the goddess takes two people who can prove their bond is as strong as *that*. It's like a trust game. But not the summer camp bullshit kind."

Becca's brow furrowed. "What about the rhyme? How does that fit into the story?"

Goddess, goddess, count to one. Who will you pick when the day is done? I sang it through, silent in my mind.

Chelsea shrugged. "It's asking the goddess who she'll choose. To give her favor to. So. Do you think your bond is powerful enough to bring her back?"

Becca was already standing.

"Let's play."

Chelsea gave her a spotlight smile, hot and bright and exclusive. "Somebody gimme a blindfold."

One of the girls stripped off her tank top and tossed it over.

Chelsea kneeled in front of me, so close I could see the stained glass bits of her irises. She twirled the tank top into a thin rope and tied it over my eyes. The fabric was rough-grained and brightened the light. It still held the warmth of the other girl's skin.

Close to my ear Chelsea said, "Stand up. Wait here."

"What's the game, though?" No one answered, and after a moment I stood. As soon as I was on my feet the two swallows of alcohol in my system felt like ten.

For a while it was quiet. A quiet that hissed with voices. Then I got confused and thought the hissing was leaves, the breeze. But there, a thread of laughter. The pinprick of a whispered word.

Becca spoke from right beside me.

"Turn," she said hoarsely. "A little to the left. Okay, stop. Now take six steps forward."

I put my hands out, disoriented before we'd even begun. "What are we doing? What's the game?"

"Trust me. That's the game."

I did. Trust her. So I followed her voice where it led me.

Sometimes she was farther away, sometimes right beside me. I tripped once and came down hard on my knee, and once a branch whipped so sharp and wet over my cheek I couldn't tell whether I was bleeding. I knew Chelsea was somewhere close, directing us, but I couldn't sense her. After an indefinable stretch of time, Becca told me to stop.

"Put your hand out," she said.

My fingertips met the furrowed hide of a tree. Maple? Its familiar feel was a candle flame in the dark.

"There's a branch just above you. Grab it."

I did, loosely. I heard a whisper, then Becca letting a breath out slowly through rounded mouth.

"Both hands. *Tight*. Now—climb."

Eyes wide behind white cotton, I climbed. Every branch seemed fatally thin, every reach through empty space another small act of faith. Of devotion. Maybe Becca could feel them all, like golden coins melting into her skin.

"Okay." Her voice was breathless. "Stop."

At her direction I'd crept, belly down, onto a long thick branch. The way the breeze moved around my body made it feel insubstantial. "Now what?"

"Take off the blindfold." Her voice was just over a whisper. "I changed my mind, I don't want to play."

The branch beneath me bowed with a creaking sound. "But. How are we supposed to win?"

"You're supposed to fall. Jump, whatever, out of the tree. But it doesn't *matter*," she added fiercely. "We're already better than the girls in that stupid story. I wouldn't have let you die in the first place."

"I know," I said, and let myself fall.

Did I know I was over the water? Or did I really believe Becca's love would catch me, no matter where I fell? I wondered about this later, and never settled on an answer.

Everything happened at once. Rushing air, the grainy suck of tepid water, warm mud under my feet. Then my whole body was under, stretched long over the creek's plush bottom, and a sharp wrong pain filled my head.

I really did black out for a second or two. That was real. The blindfold dipped down, clinging to my nose and mouth, and I opened my eyes onto a dusty green world. Then a submerged explosion went off beside me: Becca, jumping into the water.

I would marvel, later, at how quickly I thought.

I closed my eyes. Kept them closed as she put her arms around me and pulled me up, as my face broke the surface, as she touched the raw place at the back of my head and made an anguished sound.

I let my fingers tighten on her where they wouldn't be seen, tugging at her to come closer. She did, dipping in like she was checking my breathing. I whispered without moving my mouth.

"Play along."

Becca took a small sharp breath and straightened. Lacing her arms around my chest she dragged me through the water and up the rocky bank. An exposed shale point drew a sizzling line up the back of my thigh and still I was silent. Gently she settled my head onto a softish place. I let it loll.

One of the girls spoke, sounding strangled. "Is she okay?"

"Of course she is." But Chelsea's perfect confidence was gone. "She's fine, she's faking it."

"Does this look fake to you?" Becca, believably terrified. Holding her fingers up, she'd tell me later, smeared with blood from my scalp.

"Oh, my god, oh, my god."

"Should we do a—what's that called. A tourniquet!"

"On her *head*?"

"We're fucked, *fuck*, what is wrong with you, Chels!"

"Go to the path, go get help. Someone call 911."

That was when I sat up. *Fast*. Eyes wide, hair plastered to my cheeks and neck in black strings. My arm straight out and pointing to the place where I'd heard Chelsea's voice.

Two of the girls screamed. Chelsea rocked back like I'd pushed her.

My whole skull throbbed. I thought of the way she'd torn our Kingdom down in the space of a minute. She and her friends were nothing but a band of raiders and charlatans, unwelcome in our woods. They wanted to play with us? I would play.

"I've just returned from the land of the dead," I intoned in my somberest magical knight voice. "And I spoke to the goddess there."

"Um," said a girl to my left. I ignored her.

"My heart is pure," I went on. "And I have won her favor. But *you*. The goddess is angry with you."

Chelsea's mouth was working. "But. What did I . . ."

"You turned her death into a joke with your lies. Sleep well," I finished darkly. "The goddess will find you in your dreams."

For a radiant half second I think she really believed me. Then she rolled her eyes and said, "You absolute *freaks*. Have a nice head injury!" and stormed off toward the bike path.

The other girls followed. One of them said, "Are you really okay?" The girl named Tegan hung around until last. "I'm sorry," she said before joining her friends. "Also that was awesome."

When they were gone I looked triumphantly at Becca.

She wasn't smiling. She was *shaking*. Big-eyed and sopping with her legs curled under her, palms flat on the tops of her thighs.

"What?" I said nervously.

"Was any of that true?"

I touched the back of my scalp. The extent of the wound was hidden by my hair. Before the sun went down I would be at the ER getting stitches. "Any of what?"

"What you told them. About talking to the goddess."

"The goddess?" I smeared bloody fingers over the grass. "There is no goddess, it's a game. I was playing pretend. Like in the Kingdom."

"The Kingdom is gone," she said softly.

I nodded. I knew already, but it hurt to hear her say it.

Becca yanked her hair. She looked like an agitated mermaid. "Why did you jump, Nor? You could've *died*."

My head rang with a sound like bells. If I'd fallen a little harder, if the thing that cut my scalp had dug a little deeper.

I said, "You would never let me die."

I watched the words hit her bloodstream, making her eyes shine. "I didn't like her story anyway," she said. "You could tell a better one."

I nodded. "Definitely. Why would the girls put a *tooth* in the fire? Everyone knows teeth don't burn."

"You should, though. *We* should."

"Should what?"

Her agitation was gone now, she sat up straight. "We should make our *own* goddess."

"Okay," I said cautiously. "I guess we could."

But pain was biting away at my victory. I was woozy and tearful by the time I got home, Becca pale at my side.

My parents kept me close for a while after that. They knew there was more than I admitted to the story of how I hit my head, and anyway you rested after a concussion. Days would pass before we returned to the forest preserve.

When we did come back, I knew it was right that we'd waited. The woods were so good that day, so green and deep. There was a void left by the Kingdom, but it didn't make us sad. It felt like a listening ear.

We filled it. Together we invented a goddess who would protect us, ensuring our safety in the land of play. I posed for the photo in my favorite dress-up outfit, and Becca used a long exposure to turn my face into a blurred library of expressions. I wrote an origin story to accompany the photo, inspired by the illustrated book of world mythology I'd gotten for my birthday. We named her the goddess of make-believe.

We made an altar to our first goddess, out in the woods. On it we burned the Queen's final tea-stained scroll, and the blindfold I'd been wearing when I followed Becca's voice through the woods and into the water.

Sometimes in dreams I'm wearing it again. Muddy water dragging it over my nose, over my mouth, as I drown.

CHAPTER TWELVE

IT WAS PAST FOUR WHEN I got home, the sky the dead white of printer paper. Against it the bare trees looked like pieces of an unconvincing stage set. When I turned onto my street there was an unfamiliar car parked next to our driveway, a boxy mustard-colored station wagon. James Saito sat on its hood.

I laughed. I did that sometimes when I was nervous.

Despite the flat light he was wearing intensely black sunglasses and one of those brown jackets with the sheepskin collars that smell like rain. His posture was loose and with the glasses on he looked utterly indifferent. But he couldn't have been, could he? He was here.

James said nothing as I walked toward him. I guess he was watching me but I couldn't make it out through his lenses. I stopped a few yards away.

"Hey."

"Hey." His voice was deep, with a quiet quality to it. The kind of voice that would sound peaceful even at a yell. He sat very still except for the fingers of his left hand, picking at the frayed cuff of his jeans. "Have you heard from Becca yet?"

I eyed him. "So now you want to talk about her."

"Have you?"

"No."

"Do you have any idea where she is?" He didn't move, his voice didn't get any louder, but I could feel his intensity climbing.

"No. Do *you*?"

He gave his head a little jerk, like the question wasn't important. "When did you see her last?"

His urgency was infecting me. My neck and temples pricked with sudden heat. "Why are you asking me this?"

"You should've told me she was gone, when I saw you this morning," he said abruptly. "I hadn't heard. I'd have tried to be helpful, if I knew."

"Okay. So can you be helpful now?"

He pulled something from his pocket. It fit neatly on his open palm: a package the size and roughly the shape of a Ping-Pong ball, wrapped in rubber-banded paper. "I found this with my stuff in the photo lab. Becca left it for me."

"For you," I repeated. I hadn't actually believed myself that morning, when I'd imagined him knowing where she'd gone. Now I wasn't sure. Who *was* this boy to her?

James had good hands. Artist's hands. Blunt and practical in this indefinable way, made for work. He unsnapped the rubber band and peeled off the paper, revealing a roll of undeveloped film. Then he handed the paper to me. It was a note in Becca's handwriting, all pointed peaks and exaggerated serifs.

tell nora I'm off to play the goddess game

I'm sure he saw the way my shoulders jumped, the way I curled in around the paper, blocking it from his sight.

Though of course he'd already read it. When I looked up he was turned partly away, like he was trying to give me some privacy.

"Why . . ." I began. But there were too many whys. I picked an easier question. "When did she leave it for you?"

"Could've been anytime since sixth period on Friday. That's the last time I checked my stuff."

"What's on the film?"

He made a faint grimace, a polite way of saying, *It's undeveloped, dumbass.* "I don't know yet. What does the note mean?"

I shook my head. The goddess again, three times now, surfacing like stitches in a seam. I was seized with a frustration bordering on fury: yes, Becca, I can hear you. But what are you trying to *say*?

We'd only ever played the game twice: once in the woods, when we were children. And again three months ago, the night we fought. I was hit with an intrusive flash of Becca's face as it looked that night, right before I walked away from her. I shuddered.

Then I stepped forward and gripped his arm. To hold him there, to steady myself. The curling edge of his license plate dug into my knee.

"You know her. You *know* Becca. Don't you?"

With the arm I wasn't holding, he pushed his sunglasses into his hair. Like he knew I'd need to see his eyes to trust him. They were a clear clear brown, fierce and focused. "She's hard to know. But yeah, I think I do."

"Even getting that much about her, that she's hard to be close to, it's more than she gives anyone. And I don't know what to do. I don't know what to think. She's leaving me all these—clues, I guess, and it's all so *Becca* I could just . . ." I swallowed, throat aching. "So. Are you only here to give me this note? Or are you here because you give a shit, and you're willing to *help* me?"

The whole time I spoke I hung on to his arm like he was a life raft. When I realized what I was doing, I let go. James leaned forward, putting his elbows on his knees.

"I want to help," he said in his peaceable rumble. "This morning, when you were looking for her—I kinda knew something had happened. I think I've been waiting for it."

"For what?"

He didn't answer that. "She's been different. Or, the same, maybe, but *more*. All highs and lows, like she's lost her middle. Not that she had much of a middle."

I nodded, drinking it in. I'd never heard anyone else put into words the way Becca could be. For me she just *was*, like the weather.

He went on. "Usually we talk about what we're working on. That's how we became friends, being the only people in the darkroom every morning. But lately the only thing she'd talk about . . ."

I leaned hungrily into his pause. But he only sighed and said, "Lately the only thing she wanted to talk about was you."

There was a bitter rush in my throat. "Me."

"It was nice." He pushed a fall of black hair away from his face. "I'm not complaining. She told me all this stuff about the two of you being kids together. But it was the *way* she talked about it."

James had been looking at me all the time. Now the

nature of it changed. He really *looked*, his attention on me in a way that made my skin hum subtly to life, electric.

"Until today I didn't really think about it. But the way she's been talking . . . it was like someone much older. Someone looking back across their life." He spoke with supreme gentleness. "At the end of their life."

It took me a beat to understand what he was getting at. When I did my blood rushed up, making my temples pound.

"Oh. No. That's not—god, that's not what's happening. That's not what this is. Are you . . ." I held up the note. "You can't actually think this piece of shit sentence is a *goodbye* note."

Now even his hand was still. A red flush stained his cheeks. "I don't know."

"No, you don't. You said you know her. You know what she can do, how talented she is. How *much* she is. Her life is gonna be," I gestured at the air. "More. More than this."

But: her recklessness. The joyless daring that had possessed her ever since her dad died. And that late-night text. *I love you*. I wasn't angry because James had put this fear in me. He'd only opened the door it hid behind.

He gave a single nod. "Okay."

My skull felt buzzing, toxified. In that moment I think I hated him. "*Okay?*"

"Yes," he said softly. "Okay."

I glared at him. Trying to hold on to my anger even as I could feel it break and dissipate like a whitecap. It wasn't really him I was angry at. Or frightened for.

He held up the film canister. "I wanted to talk to you

before I did anything with this. Should I take it some-where, get it printed now? Or should I wait and print it myself?"

My stomach churned at the idea of turning it over to a stranger. The photos could be anything. They could be nudes.

"You should do the printing," I said grudgingly. "Just in case."

"Okay. You want to meet me in the darkroom tomor-row? Like, 6:30?"

I nodded, mollified by the fact that he knew I'd want to be there. As he slid off the hood of the car I thought, Vampire. Hot vampire. Then, paranoid he might somehow have heard me, I said, "How do you know where I live?"

"Becca showed me. We drive around sometimes."

That made an ache in my heart, tangible as a bruise. I was glad she'd had someone these past few months. It eased a portion of my rising guilt.

"Thank you," I said as he opened his car door. "For talking to me."

James seemed nonplussed. "No problem?"

"Like, because you don't talk to anyone." I flushed. "I mean, you don't *bother* with anyone. Not that you have to! Just, you don't." I ended there, pressing my lips firmly together.

He gave me a funny look. "Yeah, I'm not good at . . . high school. All the high school stuff. I'm not used to it."

I figured by *high school* he meant big, underfunded sub-urban public high school. My new theory, invented on the fly: James had transferred in from one of those thriller-novel prep schools, full of rich kids and scandal. He'd probably gotten kicked out after his secret society murdered the dean.

As I wasted time polishing my hypothesis, he was climbing into his car. His eyes met mine in the rearview mirror, a flick of cool brown, then he was gone.

SIX MONTHS AGO

BECCA SAW A MOVIE ONCE about a woman who discovers she has a doppelganger.

What that meant, in the film at least, was that somewhere in the world there was a person who looked like her, had a brain and a soul like hers, was her exact double, in fact. Yet they were leading two entirely separate lives.

After that night in the woods Becca split in two. She became her own doppelganger.

There was the self she knew. The one who wanted to tell Nora everything, work through the fallout, stick to the path she was on. This self tried to forget what she saw in the trees. She turned her face to the sun.

And there was the doppelganger. The Becca who crept to the forefront late at night, when she was alone. This girl was obsessive and unreasonable. She had seen something that couldn't be explained, and it moved like grit beneath her skin. Her life was one of late-night research and persistent fear. She needed to dig beyond that fear, needed to *know*.

These two selves clashed uneasily, overlapping like a blurred photograph. Nora knew something was amiss but said nothing, waiting it out as she always did. Becca fought the battle alone.

Then, about a week after the night *it* happened, she woke with a feeling of certainty. As she slept, the conflict between her two selves had been resolved. She'd made her choice. But before advancing into an altered future, she was determined to have one good summer day.

It was early morning when she picked up Nora. They got iced coffees and almond croissants and drove to the beach. It was one of those rare days when Lake Michigan was Mediterranean clear, flashing with minnows and polished stones. When they were sated on sun they drove back to Palmetto and moved lazily through their summer paces: trying on rings and patchouli rollers at the old-hippie jewelry shop, browsing paperbacks at I'm Booked. They sedated themselves with Sno-Caps and arctic air conditioning at a late matinee.

When they got out the light was soft and blue and the theater parking lot was full of parents. Corralling, hugging, scolding, tucking snacks into capacious purses, one two three *swing*-ing little bodies between their clasped hands. Nora saw it, too. It was a sliver of ice melting slowly between them in the summer air.

Taco Bell drive-through. Creamsicle shakes at the Dairy Dream, fireflies blinking in the weeds. Becca's hands were sticky on the wheel. Coasting on waves of sugar, filled with a sense of vivid daring, she drove to the parking lot at the edge of the woods.

They hadn't been near the forest preserve since the night she fell. Lightly she touched the scabbing wound on her knee, destined to settle into a messy scar. She and Nora sat on the hood of the car, backs to the windshield. Music drifted from the dashboard speakers like songs from another planet and the whole lot was a dreamy block of purplish streetlight. If you cupped your hands to block it you could almost see the stars.

Becca thought, Ask me, Nora. If you ask, I'll tell.

She saw them in black and white. Two girls on the hood of an old sedan, shoes kicked to the ground. Their hair thick with lake water, their skin plump and shiny with youth and processed foods. Americana as anything, a small-town summer dream.

But if you looked close you could see a darkness between them, shaped like a question mark. A complicit edge to the way they looked not at each other but straight ahead. That was what made it an interesting photograph.

Nora made a joke. Becca snapped back to herself. It had been a good day, that was all. A day very nearly free of shadows. Her best friend just wanted to keep it that way.

They stayed in the lot until the sky was black, and a police car with a bored officer inside it slow-crackled over the gravel. *Park is closed, girls.*

Still they stretched out the night. Or Becca did, driving around until Nora's phone buzzed on the dash. She sighed and said, "Curfew."

The car smelled of lake and patchouli and fast-food tacos and it all seemed so suddenly, unutterably sweet. Becca pulled all the way up Nora's drive, like she never did, making Nora waggle her brows and say, "Well, *well*." Then she was out of the car, head down in search of her keys. Almost without meaning to Becca said, "Nora."

Her best friend looked at her, startled by her tone.

"I love you."

"I know," Nora said, cool like Han Solo. Then she seemed

to think better of it, dashing in three big steps to the car window and hugging Becca through it, quick and tight. Then she was gone into the dark of the house, into the warmth of a life where your mother sends you a text reminding you of your midnight curfew at 11:45 on the nose.

That's why, the doppelganger told her darkly. There were things that weren't *for* Becca anymore. But guess what? There were things that weren't for Nora.

Still her chest felt like it was made of crushed candy. If she cried now she'd cry beads of strawberry sugar. Instead she drank the gross warm hours-old iced coffee Nora never could finish, imagining the caffeinated drops lining up in her veins like a string of little soldiers. It was after midnight. Becca's daylit self was a spell that ended when the clock struck twelve. Now the doppelganger took her turn.

She drove through sleeping streets to a house she'd never been to. Before this moment it was just an address she'd found and memorized. It was a cottage, really, small and tidily kept, robin's egg with black shutters. And it was the only place on the block where a light was burning. Two lights: one over the porch and one inside.

What Becca was doing was so stupid, so dangerous, she was actually laughing as she walked up the drive. Now she got why it took her a week to get here, to psych herself up into taking that first step toward shedding her old self completely. She'd had to reach the place where *not knowing* felt worse than anything else she could imagine.

And wouldn't you know it. The door swung open before she could knock.

CHAPTER THIRTEEN

I HUSTLED INSIDE WITH BECCA'S note in my fist.

The house was murky, all the lights off. "Hello?" My voice sounded thin. "Anyone home?"

"In here."

I stuffed the note in my pocket and followed my mom's voice to the kitchen. She was sitting at the table in her tricked-out work chair, face drawn in the lunar glow of her laptop.

"Hey, Nor," she said when she saw me. "You doing okay?"

I *had* been okay, ish, until I saw her. "Oh, honey," she said as my face crumpled, and held out her arms. I crossed the room to nestle gingerly against her, careful not to tweak her back. She smelled like Vicks and coffee and the French bath oil Cat and I gave her every Christmas.

"Should I not have sent you to school today?" she said into my shoulder. "Did I get it wrong?"

I could've let go right then and had a really big cry. The kind that leaves you with a headache and an appetite. But I had the superstitious feeling I shouldn't. Like crying over Becca might make it so there was really something to cry about. I just breathed steadily until I could speak with minimal wobble.

"Mom. Do you think Becca would hurt herself?" I squeezed my eyes shut. Listening to her sharp intake of breath, feeling the press of her lips against my temple.

"No."

Her voice was so definite I sagged with relief. "Why not?"

"Because . . ." She paused, smoothing a hand over my hair. "Because Becca has been hurt enough already. Has had enough taken from her already. That girl is not going to give up one more thing. Not without a fight." A small, wry smile. "And Becca fights dirty."

I bit the side of my tongue, focusing on the dull pain instead of the question that sprang immediately to mind: Why hadn't Becca fought harder to hold on to me? Or had she? *Was* she? Maybe that was what this was all about.

I said, "I don't know what to do."

"Is it your job to do something?"

"Who else will?"

And god, I was hoping she'd have a good answer. But she only sighed and said, "The police will, Nor. If Becca's not home soon they'll have to get involved." Her voice dropped ten degrees. "Not that I have much faith in Palmetto's finest."

I slumped lower. "Because of what happened with Becca's mom."

"Well, yes. That, and—do you remember me telling you about Logan Kilkenny?"

I thought about it. "Maybe?"

"He was that classmate of mine who went missing our senior year. Good guy, really well-liked. Good grades, played baseball, did the musicals. Not the kind of kid you'd think would just disappear." She pursed her mouth. "Not to say there is that kind of kid."

"No, I know what you mean." Kurt Huffman was that kind of kid.

Then it hit me that my classmates would probably say the same thing about Becca.

"Anyway," she said, "the cops decided he was a runaway, and they wouldn't budge. It took them ages to treat it as a missing persons case, to actually *look*. The thing I most remember about my senior year is this feeling of heaviness. Paranoia. Everybody uneasy, everyone with their theories. Fights breaking out in the halls. It was different then, we didn't live on the internet. All we had to think about was what was in front of us."

I rolled my eyes internally at the internet comment. "They never found him, did they?"

"No."

She spoke shortly, looking sorry she'd brought it up. When she didn't say more, I crossed the room to stare into the fridge. "So why are you sitting in the dark?"

"Rubberneckers," Mom said succinctly.

I slid out a pan of leftover bread pudding. "Rubber what?"

She made a discontented sound, closing her laptop. "Turn them on. Come sit with me."

I flicked the lights and sat down with my pudding. Mom looked at me squarely.

"There've been nosy people nosing around out there. Different cars in the cul-de-sac. A couple hours ago I saw a girl pass the window with her phone in the air, taking a video. She was going for the Sebraneks' back gate. That was when I turned off the lights."

"Ew. Did you call Mrs. Sebranek?"

"They're staying out of town for a bit. But I promised Rachel I'd keep an eye on the house, so I called the police. They said they'd send a patrol car around."

I looked at the space between houses, lined on either side by narrow garden beds. "What do people think they're gonna find? A big clue dropped on the ground?"

"I think we have to be realistic." Her voice was strained. "In terms of how interested people might get in what's happening here."

The bread pudding tasted like nothing. I kept shoveling it in anyway, each sugary bite filling, briefly, that empty spot in the nexus of my ribs. "Right. I know."

"I don't just mean local idiots. I still—I'm very hopeful Becca will be home soon. That she's just cooling off somewhere, mad at Miranda. But combined with the other missing students . . . this is the kind of story that gets out there. And I do not want your name to be a part of it."

My fork scraped the bottom of the dish. I'd eaten every bite. "My name? Why would my name be part of it?"

She gave me an exasperated look. "You've been Becca's best friend since the first grade. You were there, at her house, the night she—the night she left. How many people know that?"

I put my fork down, suddenly queasy. "Just Miranda. But Cat's probably screaming it all over town."

"No, she's not," Mom said tartly. "I've talked to your sister. She knows I will be good goddamned if some shit-raking journalist tries to write you into their story."

"*Mom.*"

"Oh, you puritan." She mimed throwing a dollar into a swear jar.

I looked down. Unwilling even now to break Becca's trust by telling my mom about the breadcrumbs she'd left for me, but needing her to know some part of the truth. "I just feel like she's trying to tell me something," I said carefully. "Like . . . okay, fine, she's doing her Becca thing, but she wants me to figure out what's going on. And I'm just *stuck*. I don't know where she, when she'll . . ." My throat closed up around the words.

"Nora." Mom put a hand on mine. "I hear you. I do. You've got enough to worry about already. But I want you to brace yourself. This isn't the nineties. And it's not one boy. Three students, all from one school? This thing could turn into a wildfire."

CHAPTER FOURTEEN

SHE WAS RIGHT, OF COURSE. I looked online and there was nothing about the disappearances yet, but it was only a matter of time. The story wouldn't be just ours for much longer.

I needed to think, needed to start figuring stuff out *now*, before other people's ideas crowded out my own. But all Becca had given me to work with were pieces of our past. The photograph, the jump rope rhyme, the knife. *i'm off to play the goddess game.* If there was an explanation there, I couldn't see it.

My laptop was open. I thought for a second, then typed in *logan kilkenny palmetto*. I was curious about this "good kid" my mom went to school with who never was found. Luckily the *Palmetto Review* had a scanned backlog of old editions, because he didn't show up anywhere else. I leaned in to read the smudgy PDF'd article about his disappearance.

In October 1994, Kilkenny drove himself, his girlfriend, and another couple to the homecoming dance held in the PHS gym. According to friends, he went to use the bathroom and never returned. None of the chaperones posted at the exits saw him leaving. That didn't mean much—chaperones weren't exactly trained guards—but it was still creepy that the last confirmed sighting of Kilkenny was in the school itself. I read through the article twice, then studied the class photo that accompanied it.

Even in grainy black and white, Logan Kilkenny was extremely cute. He was dark of brow and high of cheek-bone. His smile was close-mouthed but not insincere. And just looking at him made my stomach turn with absolute aversion.

I wasn't sure why. Yes, he had a horrible '90s butt cut—parted dead center, falling just past his ears—and his hemp necklace looked grimy. But I could cut the guy a break, couldn't I? His ending would not have been a happy one.

Still, I didn't like looking at him. And I wondered if he was as good a guy as my mom recalled.

I searched a little longer, but nothing else interesting came up. Then my dad came home with pizza and I set my laptop aside.

CHAPTER FIFTEEN

HOURS LATER, DINNER DONE AND homework glanced at, I was still thinking about that photo of Logan Kilkenny: thirty years gone, looking doomed only in retrospect. How would Becca's school photos look to me in a few years' time? And Chloe's, and Kurt's?

I thought of the photo I'd found in her locker, and slid it from my bag to look again. Maybe she'd written something on its back that could knock an idea loose in my head.

When I picked it up, I realized something: it wasn't one photo, but two. Stuck lightly together, like she'd stacked them before they were fully dry. Even as I carefully peeled the top one away, my heart was sinking. I knew what would be hidden behind it.

The only one of our goddesses I wished we'd never made.

The day I jumped into the water only tightened my and Becca's bond. And the goddess project we began soon after sent us tunneling ever further into our private world.

We read everything we could find on the subject of creation myths, invocations, pagan worship. We loved that there were gods of things as specific as silence and as grand as the sea. A goddess could wrap her arms around the cosmos, or conceal herself in human form.

But nobody had made deities for the things we were living through, the things we were feeling right now. And we thought, if there can be a goddess of fevers and of door hinges, a goddess for every hour of the day, a god literally of *poop*, no kidding, then why not a goddess of crushes, of white lies, of the middle of the night?

Becca's talent grew with the book we kept our goddesses in. And my compulsion to lie was funneled into mythmaking. Two years passed this way, happily. Then, in the spring of our seventh-grade year, at a little past nine on a weeknight, Becca's mother was struck and killed while biking home from Target.

Becca's dad erected a ghost bike in the place where she was hit, about a quarter mile from their house. A three-speed cruiser sprayed white, chained to a yield sign.

My memories of the days after her death were similarly colorless, blown over with drifts of bad sleep and grief and confusion. The way my mom cried out when she got the call, the sight of my stoic dad with tears running down his face. Those are the memories I could bear to handle. There are others, with Becca in them, that I still couldn't touch.

Through some combination of negligence and the driver's awful good luck, there was no video of the car that hit Mrs. Cross. There would be a lawsuit down the road, leading to a cash settlement Mr. Cross poured straight into a trust fund for his daughter. But Becca didn't care about that. Money wasn't what she was looking for.

Two months after her mom died, Becca told me we were

adding a new goddess to our pantheon. One who could step in where the police had failed.

We were twelve, remember. Too old for such pure belief in magic. Past the point when we truly believed the world could bend to please us. She wouldn't say a thing like that lightly, but she couldn't exactly mean it, either. Could she?

I knew the idea was a bad one. That it would endanger that thing our parents kept referring to quietly as her *healing*. Becca's internal borders between real and not had always been porous—that was part of what made her a good photographer, a tireless playmate. But even I found the notion of enlisting an invented deity to help bring a very real murderer to justice an unhealthy one. The goddesses were protectors of *our* world, not the real one. They were an art project that allowed us to dress up and play pretend, act like kids a little while longer.

But. I'd have done anything for her. Anything she asked of me.

This new goddess was depicted, of course, by Becca. She had a vision and I helped her fulfill it. I painted her features entirely away, blotted them white as a ghost bike. On her two closed lids she directed me to ink staring black dots, like twin centers of the evil eye. Where her mouth was painted out I drew in a sharp vertical wedge of absolute red, resembling the curve of a dagger. Even on black-and-white film you could sense how red it was. I spent ages arranging her hair into the fiery corona she required.

We named her the goddess of revenge.

After we got the shot she wanted, Becca set out a trio of candles at the base of our tree. She lit them with her left hand, and with her right set a photo ablaze on each snapping flame: her mom as a teen, then pregnant at thirty, then leaning against Mr. Cross with baby Becca between them.

I wanted to ask if they were the only copies. If she would one day regret burning them for no good reason. But I never got the chance.

Three days later Mr. Cross got a call. The driver who killed his wife had been found. Her name was Christine Weaver, she was a fifty-four-year-old resident of nearby suburb Belle Pointe. Fifteen minutes before she struck Mrs. Cross's bicycle, she was closing out her tab at one of Palmetto's downtown bars. The police determined it was her based not on this but on the confession of her husband, who broke down while talking to them about a different matter.

A different accident. The one they'd come knocking on his door to discuss. Not seventy-two hours after we consecrated the goddess of revenge, the car that killed Becca's mother stalled out on a train crossing. Or maybe her killer just parked it there. Because she was mortally guilty or blackout drunk or or or. The cargo train that hit her did not derail or catch fire. It sheared her car neatly apart and stopped half a mile away. Christine Weaver was the only casualty.

We didn't tell anyone about the goddess we'd made. My parents only knew that I cried and cried. That I crawled into bed between them each night. Cocooned by my mom's soft snoring, the whirring of my dad's CPAP machine, my thoughts rising above us in a vast mushroom cloud of wondering. Of fear, at my own imagined power.

I overheard them talking about it once. My mom said, "I don't feel sorry for that woman, and I don't feel bad about that, either. It feels like poetic justice."

"I wouldn't call it poetic," my dad replied.

"You know what I mean." She sounded irritated. Then: "Nora's taking it so hard."

"She's too young," he replied. "First the hit-and-run, now this? Such random brutality, twice. How's she ever gonna believe us when we tell her we can keep her safe?"

Random brutality, I repeated to myself. Random. Brutality.

And I knew it was—random, I mean. But there's believing with your head, in the daylight hours, and there's believing with your belly, with your nervous system, when you're lying awake at one in the morning.

Of course my best friend was changed in countless ways by the death of her mother. The fact of it, the conditions of it, the way people treated her once they knew.

But it wasn't just loss that changed her. I was the only person who knew the other piece of it. How some part of Becca truly believed what I couldn't. What I refused to: that the vengeful deity we'd made might truly have acted on our behalf, putting her holy thumb down to pin a woman in the path of Death.

CHAPTER SIXTEEN

I HID BOTH PHOTOGRAPHS IN the pages of one of my old picture books and lay back on my bed.

The images bookended the horrible landscape of Becca's losses. One created to save a parent, the other to avenge one. But in leaving them for me, what was she trying to *say*? In her maddening way, she was telling me something, leading me somewhere. I just had to think.

My room vibrated around me with half-done things that mattered last week. Two bookmarked novels on my bedside table, a composition notebook full of the beginnings of stories I might finish one day. A string of open tabs on my laptop, college websites and lists of creative writing programs and a FAFSA info page.

Closing my eyes, I pushed it all away. My own fears and my mother's. My dad's gentle good night through the door and the sound of my sister coming home late, tromping up the stairs to hover on the landing outside my room. What could she have to say to me? It didn't matter, she never knocked. I pushed that away, too.

Across my emptied mind I unrolled a flat black map. On that map I picked out all of Becca's crucial places.

Point by glowing point, they came into view, a crooked constellation.

Our houses. The darkroom. The playground and the woods where we'd played, the places she liked to take photographs. Tentatively I added to my map the sites where Chloe and Kurt went missing: the house next door. The cemetery.

That was where my attention caught. The sleeping city of the dead, overseen by the Eyeless Angel. Its marble glowed against the dark of my mind, brighter, brighter, obscuring the rest of the map, until it flared and shattered like an old-fashioned flashbulb.

I sat up gasping. When I checked my phone more than an hour had passed since I closed my eyes. I'd drifted off. I must've dipped into a dream, because I found myself blinking away a phantom afterimage: Kurt Huffman, slipping his coat from his shoulders beneath the Angel's lofted wings. There was a surreal HD fineness to the dream vision. I could see the thumbprint shadows under his eyes, the disaffected curl of his mouth.

I had the strangest, strongest feeling that if I got up and went to the cemetery now—right now—I would find Kurt there waiting for me.

It was a ridiculous notion. So I didn't stop to think, I just moved. Out of my bed, into my clothes. Out the back door, over the grass. My bike had a flat, so it was Cat's cobwebbed Huffy I wheeled from the warm-smelling dark of the garden shed.

The night was milder than the day had been. Snow made parapets along the curbs and the road was a wet black stripe. The wind smelled big and wild, whipping my hair back as I sped down the street beneath a storybook moon.

I pedaled faster and faster, like I was outrunning some-thing, like I could leave a piece of myself behind. I felt closer to Becca than I had all day. She was right beside me, smiling up at that Mellowcreme moon.

The fat front tire of my sister's mountain bike ate up the glossy asphalt all the way to the base of Liberty Hill. There I paused, and felt whatever I was running from catch up with me.

The cemetery was waiting at the top of the hill, its bor-ders obscured by snow-crusted thickets of rye grass. I took a breath and pedaled hard up the rise. When I reached the top, its gates were open. Not much, just enough that I could slip between them. I propped my bike on wrought iron and walked through.

Becca and I hung out here sometimes. Most Palmetto kids did. Past its gates were a hundred places you could tuck yourself away in, to do all the things you couldn't do inside your house. And at the cemetery's center was the cool white point around which everything turned: the Eye-less Angel. Wings spread, palms open, head downturned, with sinuous stone curls framing a Roman face. Beneath its pale brows were two unnerving empty sockets. It was said they were once embedded with two crazed orbs of sap-phire, in honor of the blue eyes of the long-gone woman it grieved for. The stones were stolen immediately, of course.

The Angel was mother to a host of scary stories, and the crux of countless dares. Everyone who came here would, at some point, reach up with a racing heart to grip the Angel's stone fingers. If its empty sockets ran with tears, the person holding its hand was destined to die young.

The Angel was a little ways ahead of me now. I could just make out its wing tips. Then the base of the mausoleum came into sight. I'd come here half expecting to find Kurt waiting. Still the sight of a figure in a dark coat, crouched in front of the mausoleum's ironbound doors, made shock pop in my chest, sending a glittering burst of floaters over my sight.

The figure straightened. Not Kurt. Madison Velez.

She wore another black dress. This one was overlaid in lace that dripped over her hands and scratched at the tops of her boots. Her mouth was a brisk impeccable red, flanked with the kind of dimples that stick around even when you're not smiling. Madison wasn't smiling. She watched my approach, her posture so stiff and wary I thought she might bolt. By the time I reached her, there was steel in her stare.

"So you're stalking me."

I responded before I could think. "I thought Kurt would be here."

She recoiled. "What? Why?"

I shook my head a little. "I'm sorry. I had a weird dream. I'm friends with—"

"I know who you're friends with." She looked at me appraisingly. "It's true, then, about Rebecca Cross. Do you know what happened? Were you there?"

My mom would want me to say no. But there was a pained edge to Madison's questions that I couldn't ignore. "I got there right after. I think she'd just left."

"So you didn't see it. You didn't have anything to do with it."

I laughed bitterly. "I didn't say that."

Her posture softened. She gestured to the thing that lay in front of the mausoleum doors, nearly invisible in the moonlight. A Ouija board made of wafer-thin wood, its white plastic planchette perched over the BYE in GOOD BYE.

"I tried to talk to him," she said. "But no luck."

"Oh," I said, involuntary. "God. So you think . . . he might be . . ."

"*No*," she snapped. Then her furious face crumpled. "I don't know."

I winced. Feeling like Tracey Borcia, like Miss Ekstrom, all the curious people digging for information that didn't belong to them. "So . . . why the Ouija board?"

"I don't *know*," she repeated, looking miserable. "All I know is, what happened wasn't possible. Because what happened is he *vanished* while I was standing fifteen yards away."

I looked at the rickety clutter of old stones and forgotten mausoleums that surrounded us, all glazed with melting snow. It seemed to me there were lots of places a person could disappear here. "But. Couldn't he have—"

She talked over me. Suddenly animated, up on the balls of her feet. "I was mad when he ran off, because he *does* this, you know? I wasn't even planning to follow him. But then . . ." Her chin tipped up. "It started to snow. And it was weird, because the sky was cloudless. When I looked straight up it was like being inside a snow globe. The sky was perfectly black and all these individual snowflakes were coming straight down out of the dark. Did you notice that?"

I flashed on myself standing frozen at the edge of Becca's snowy driveway, seized by a kind of anticipatory trance. "I'm not sure. I don't think so."

"There's a name for that, for snow that falls from a clear sky. It's called diamond dust." Madison sounded wistful.

"Pretty, right? Kurt told me that. He's a meteorology geek. So it felt like a sign, you know? That things would be okay with us.

"But I couldn't find him. At first I assumed he was messing with me, but when I reached the Angel I knew something bad had happened. The air tasted wrong and it smelled wrong and he'd left his coat behind. Do you know how many hours Kurt worked at the Verizon store to buy that stupid coat?"

"No," I said softly.

"I was standing right *here*. Kurt was gone. I looked up at the Eyeless Angel and thought about poor old Alexander Petranek."

Petranek was one of the two bodies interred beneath the Angel. As the story went, his bride died at nineteen. He commissioned the Angel to honor her, and crept in each night to keep a vigil over her corpse. Until one morning the doors stuck, and he perished by her side.

"I remembered what happened to him and I guess I kind of lost it. I started shouting and banging on the mausoleum doors, like Kurt might actually be in there." Madison balled her hands into loose fists and showed them to me. They were bruised a faint blue-black.

"But he's not there," she said with finality. "He's not anywhere. And who's gonna believe that? Even *you* don't believe that." Her lip curled. "Nora Powell, the compulsive liar of Palmetto Elementary."

I made a face. "What the hell?"

"Sorry." She flipped a hand, like that could erase what she'd said. "Look, I'm used to covering for Kurt. Trying to convince people he's not just the way he acts. So now everyone's tired of hearing it from me. Nobody wants to listen when I say that what happened *could not* have happened. Even my parents won't listen. Kurt's mother, don't get me started." She spat on the ground, actually spat. "So, no. I *don't* think Kurt is dead, and I don't know what I'm doing, but I'm trying to do *some*thing. Aren't you?"

"Of course I am!" I said too loudly. "But it's different with Becca. She didn't disappear, she ran away. She left *because* of me. Because things were so messed up between us."

"You think things weren't complicated with me and Kurt? He was my best friend in the world until he decided he was in love with me. He's spent the past two years *punishing* me for not loving him back. You know he never even bothered asking me out? He hates himself so much he skipped straight to being miserable." She stared down, flexing her bruised hands. "But Kurt's barely got a family. All our friends are actually mine. If I dropped him, he'd have no one."

Her expression was a mix of weary and defiant, a look so familiar it knocked the breath right out of me. It was hard, sometimes, to remember I wasn't the only one who felt messy inside, who carried around a tangled yarn ball of weirdness and sadness and unplaceable thirsts.

"Yeah," I said. "I get it."

There was a little mourner's bench in front of the mausoleum. I took a few unsteady steps toward it and sat. "Becca told me something before she went. Two weeks ago. Like I said, we haven't been talking, but she found me in the hall. She pointed Kurt out, and she told me—she said to stay away from him."

Madison stiffened. "Do you think I haven't been hearing that stuff all day? Kurt's a guy. Rebecca and Chloe are girls. She's not the only person at school who doesn't like him. He's *quiet*. People who don't know him don't get him."

I shifted uncomfortably. Kurt *was* kind of creepy, with his watchful, washed-out eyes and his Mr. Cellophane vibe. It hit me, suddenly, that I hadn't thought at all about the possibility of Kurt having hurt Becca. That was weird, wasn't it? Even knowing she might have something on him, some troubling intel, the thought hadn't struck me at all. In a confused way, I'd only wondered whether she might have done something to *him*.

"I'm not saying he did anything," I told her. "But it's the timing, right? Is there anything she might know about him that—"

"Your friend ran away." Madison cut me off sharply again. "That's what you said, right? And if you listened to anything *I* just said, you'd know Kurt was here. He disappeared *here*. He has nothing to *do* with her."

"Right, I didn't say he did. Honestly, all I'm trying to—"

"*Stop it.*" She jammed her fingers in her ears like a little kid. "I came out here to be alone. I came out here to think about my friend, not about what other people think of him. I need you to stop following me, you got that? I need you to leave me alone."

I nodded. "Understood."

Madison blinked like she'd expected more of a fight. Then she sighed, long and slow, her mouth blurring behind the smoke of her breath.

"Look, I'm just sad. And so tired." Her eyes were closed. "My stupid plan didn't work. I'm going home to think up more stupid plans."

"Good luck. I mean, really."

She gave me a pinched smile. "You, too. But seriously, never follow me again."

As she walked away it struck me how foolish we were being. Both walking alone at night in the place where Kurt—according to Madison—had disappeared into the air. But I didn't dare call her back.

When she was all the way gone I stood, taking a final look at the mausoleum.

I walked closer, reaching toward the Angel's lightly splayed fingers. When I tipped back to see her, moonlight was caught in the sunken cup of her eye. It looked as if it were filled with tears already.

I dropped my arm without making contact. Then I ran fast to my bike.

CHAPTER SEVENTEEN

AFTER MY MIDNIGHT RIDE I was sure I would dream more bleak cemetery dreams.

Instead I fell out of consciousness and into a high-ceilinged room full of cheap decorations and bobbing bodies. The PHS gymnasium, stiff with sweat and laughter and freesia body spray, and music so loud it blurred.

I was there in the crush of the dancers. Looking past them at a boy jumping around in a white waiter shirt. His tie was undone, his skater boy hair pasted to his cheeks. In the photograph I'd seen he was black and white and I didn't like him. In my dream Logan Kilkenny's hair was sun-bleached brown and there was something wrong with his face.

Not his features. Not his expression. The wrongness hung over him like a stamped shadow, warping what lay below.

I watched as he put his two first fingers together and tapped them to his mouth in a cigarette gesture, looking questioningly at the pretty girl beside him. She shook her bright blonde head, kept dancing.

Now Logan was moving toward me, slipping kinglike

through the heaving crowd—a nod here, some manly hand-shake stuff there. He didn't see me watching him, even as he moved right by. I trailed him through the double doors.

Outside the gym it was cool and relatively quiet. A cry-ing girl, a kissing couple, a boy still wearing his coat, sitting on the ground. I could've been a ghost for all the attention any of them paid me. Maybe I *was* a ghost. The doors to the parking lot were blocked by a teacher tipped back in a folding chair, eyes closed and arms crossed.

But the hall leading to the old part of school was un-monitored. That was where Logan had gone.

I was behind him now. Walking, floating, dreaming, but it felt so real. I watched him pull a pack of cigarettes from one pants pocket, a lighter from the other. He was head-ing toward the steps to the art hall, he was starting the descent, he was—

My alarm went off, yanking me like a tick from the dream.

I gaped at the ceiling, breathing hard. The dream wasn't fading. All of it was as bright as if I'd just watched it on a screen. My door swung open and I shrieked.

Dad stood on the threshold, big and bleary as a spring-time bear. "It's not even six, kid. Turn off your alarm."

"Oh, shit. I mean, shoot." I grabbed the phone, poked at its face until it was silent. "Sorry."

He rubbed a hand over his stubble. "You doing okay, sweetheart?"

"Good. Yeah."

I smiled at him until he stepped back and closed the door.

I had to get up now if I was going to meet James. But I stared into space, trying to think what I'd been mashing up with the newspaper image of Logan Kilkenny to create such a vivid dream. Some low budget '90s romcom, or the video for "Smells Like Teen Spirit."

I took a shower. The dream stuck to me, filming my skin like oil. When I got out the mirror was misted over. I reached out to swipe it clear.

And stopped. My face in the mist was a featureless patchwork of dark and light. I lowered my hand and leaned closer and the shadows that were my eyes spread disconcertingly. My mouth—the place where it would be, barely a darkening in the glass—smiled.

I jerked back. Touched my lips.

Stupid. I could barely *see* my reflection. Taking my towel from its hook, I went to dry off in my room.

No time to eat. I drove to school with wet hair and my stomach already growling. At 6:35 I was pulling in next to James' mustard-colored car.

I thought we'd meet in the lab, but I found him leaning against the wall just past the security desk, waiting for me. He looked extremely good in that looks-like-shit way almost no one can pull off. Like he'd rolled out of a ditch twenty minutes ago and put on shoes. But he smelled clean and incongruously sweet. Like lily of the valley. He had a to-go cup in each hand, from the good place on the downtown strip. He lifted them one at a time.

"I've got black. I've got cream and sugar. I don't know what you like. I'm at the shop every morning anyway," he added hurriedly, like he was worried I'd mistake a cup of coffee for a proposal.

I took cream and sugar. "Thanks. I didn't know they opened this early."

"They don't. They're just used to me 'cause I live right there."

"Ah," I said diplomatically. Imagining the fluttery-hearted barista who opened a whole shop early just to give beautiful James Saito his morning coffee. "So you live downtown?"

"Yeah. Palm Towers."

I took a sip of coffee, wished it had more sugar. "Palm Towers? I thought that was a . . ."

"Senior residential community, right. I'm almost fifty years too young to legally reside there. My grandma's into it, though. It's her first time living outside the law."

"That's cool," I said, trying to hide my surprise.

"It is. Check this out." He lifted his hand, turning it so the yellow-metal bracelet he wore caught the light. "I won it last Friday at bingo. It was this or a plastic cast of a giant penny. Which, honestly, I couldn't see the point of. My grandma was pissed, though. She wanted that penny."

"A difficult choice," I murmured. It was coming home to me that James was nervous, and his nerves were making him *chatty*. I'd assumed he was too cool to be capable of either.

Then again, I'd also assumed he wasn't spending his Friday nights hanging with a crew of elderly bingo ladies in green gambling visors. My perception of him kept re-arranging itself.

"Should we . . . ?" He tipped his head in the direction of the art wing.

The empty hall echoed with every strike of our feet. I spoke over it, because I was a nervous talker, too. "So. Do you come in early every day?"

He nodded. "That's how Becca and I started to hang out. It's always just us."

That made sense. In his own way James seemed as guarded as she was. It didn't surprise me that it took silent hours alone in the lab to make their friendship happen. Or—I snuck a glance at his profile—whatever it was between them.

We passed the locked doors of the gym. Seen through gridded windows, lit only by safety lights, it looked like a deep orange sea. Briefly I saw it as it was in my dream, throbbing with music and Mylar balloons, and looked away.

"It's creepy here this early," I said.

"I know. Even more so since Becca told me about the bad shit that's happened here."

The fluorescents made insect sounds over our heads. "Bad shit?"

"With the boy who went missing. And the girl who died here back in the day."

"The girl who died," I repeated. "In the *school*?"

"Yeah. Sixties, I think."

I stopped walking altogether. "Becca told you this?"

James stopped, too. "Yes. Is that—weird?"

I frowned at him. Remembering the ghost story we were told seven years ago, about a girl who died here decades ago and was turned into a goddess. I never considered the possibility that it was based on anything real. "What was the girl's name?"

"Becca didn't say."

"Did she say how she died?"

"She was found in the bathroom, with—I don't know, quaaludes? Whatever drugs were around in the sixties. It was written off as an overdose. But Becca said it was an open secret that the story was a lie. There were . . . it got around that there were marks around the girl's mouth. The kind you'd get if somebody taped your mouth shut." He winced. "Then ripped off the tape."

Pain spread across the back of my skull, cradling it like a hot palm. "That can't be true. The police would notice something like that."

"I'm sure they did."

He said it evenly, and I stared at him for a beat. "That's . . . very messed up. Where'd she even get this story?"

"She didn't say. I think it's weird people *don't* know the story. The sixties weren't that long ago."

"I guess." I took a slug of coffee. The story might be unrelated to the goddess game tale. It might not even be true. But Becca believed it. She wouldn't have told anyone if she hadn't. When we reached the half stair to the art hall, I felt a pulse of foreboding. If a girl died here way back when, it would've happened down there, in the school's original rooms.

A burst of sound cracked the quiet. It came from the direction of the photo lab, just out of sight: static and a woman's voice, so balled up you couldn't understand it. James and I traded a startled look, then clattered down the steps. At the bottom we stopped short.

The photography teacher, Miss Khakpour, sat on the floor with her knees drawn up, back against the lab's closed door. When she saw us she cursed under her breath. I'd never heard a teacher do that before.

"James, I'm sorry." Her dark hair, cut Cleopatra-style and usually impeccable, was in a wavy halo. "You *cannot* be here right now."

The lab was closed and dark, but light spilled from the

open painting studio next door. James nodded toward it. "What's going on? Is Mr. Tate in there?"

Tate was the painting teacher, the studio was his domain. But Khakpour startled at the sound of his name. "No," she said tersely.

That staticky yawp came again from inside the studio, filling my joints with Pop Rocks. I knew that sound. It was a police radio. I paced toward it, but before I could go in Miss Corbel met me in the doorway.

Corbel was the main office manager, head of PHS in everything but name. Her graying twists were pulled back in a bun and she wore one of her usual bright pantsuits, but her eyes looked tired. She narrowed them when she saw me and James, pulling our information up out of her frightening computer brain.

"Miss . . . Powell. Mr. Saito. I need you to clear the hall."

I stepped closer, angling to see what was behind her: a male police officer crouched behind Mr. Tate's desk, going through a drawer.

"Miss Powell," Corbel repeated icily. "Back *up*."

I retreated a step. "What's going on? Is this about Rebecca Cross? She's here, usually, in the morning. In the darkroom."

The officer glanced at me, maybe in response to Becca's name. Corbel sighed.

"You need to be somewhere else. Both of you. Go." She turned back into the studio and shut the door.

"Miss Khakpour—" James began.

She didn't look up. "Not now."

"James," I murmured, and gestured toward the other end of the hall.

Glancing back to make sure Khakpour wasn't watching,

I led him past the stairs. Past the defunct newspaper office with its faint inky odor, to the place where the art hall petered out into a dead end. It was dark down here, the frosted panel in the ceiling spotted with dead-bulb gaps. To our right was a door. I hipped it open and beckoned James to follow me through.

CHAPTER EIGHTEEN

A FULL SECOND ELAPSED BETWEEN my flipping the switch beside the door and the fluorescents coming on, filling the space with staticky light.

It was an old girls' room, barely used. The ceiling was coffee-colored with rain damage, the walls the wan green of a dinner mint. The frame of its one frosted window was so warped it didn't fully close, letting weather in through a gap the width of an index finger. If you pressed your cheek to the wood and closed one eye you could make out a sliver of parking lot.

Becca and I used to hang out in here sometimes, to avoid the cafeteria or look over her prints or just pee in privacy. We'd claimed it because no one else seemed to remember it was there.

James was wide-eyed, skin greenish under the lights. "Shit. What do you think they're looking for?"

I resisted the urge to wrap my arms around myself. "I don't know. If it is about Becca, why the studio and not the darkroom?"

"Maybe they'll go there next. And that's why Miss Khak-pour is here."

I didn't respond. I'd caught sight of myself in the mirror and for a weightless instant didn't know what I was looking at. Even when I lifted my hand to see it move I felt a sense of disconnect.

I hurried past the mirror's eye.

James looked around like he'd just noticed where we were. "This is . . . why are we in here?"

"I wanted to show you because I'm pretty sure this is the bathroom."

He looked at me strangely. "It's definitely the bathroom."

"No, *the* bathroom. Where the girl died."

I watched him absorb the shift in topic. "Okay," he said slowly. "How do you figure?"

"This part of school used to be the whole school. Back in the sixties, I think this was the only girls' room in the building."

"Does that feel . . ." He thought. "Important?"

I chewed my lip, trying to order my thoughts. "Becca and I heard a story once. About a girl who died at PHS a long time ago, whose friends tried to resurrect her." I laughed a little. "A mean older girl told us that was the origin of the goddess game. We didn't believe her, obviously, except now I'm wondering if it was based on something real. On *someone* real, and Becca found her."

It was grating on me that Becca hadn't given James the dead girl's name. The story was just the kind of injustice she would've carried around like a rock in her shoe, until she broke open and bled. It wouldn't be like her to minimize the person at its center.

Unless she'd omitted the name on purpose.

I considered the possibility as I hoisted myself onto the

windowsill. It was covered in carved graffiti and burn scars from when the bathroom must've been a smokers' hide-out. James joined me, pulling himself up with such athletic grace I stared, then pretended to adjust my contact lens.

"So," he said. "The goddess game. What is it?"

"It's just this thing people play."

He gave me a dry look. "That much I got."

"Right." I breathed out, not quite a laugh. "So, there's this jump rope rhyme kids use around here. Double Dutch. It goes like, 'God-dess, god-dess, count to . . .' whatever, it's a counting rhyme. And it's all about asking the goddess to *pick* you."

"Like an invocation."

I looked at him sharply. "Yeah. Exactly. Then you get older, and at some point somebody teaches you the *real* goddess game. The rhyme is, like, goddess junior league. The actual game is one of those slumber party things. Like truth or dare, or light as a feather, stiff as a board. Except it's only played here in Palmetto. At least, I assume so. People like to say it's based on something that happened here a long time ago, which I assumed wasn't real, but— now I'm wondering.

"People tell the story different ways. It's always about a girl who died and the way her friends avenged her. By res-urrecting her as a goddess, or summoning one, or *becoming* one, however you want to tell it. And the point of playing is you have to impress the goddess enough that she'll—you know, *pick* you, like in the rhyme, and appear. And grant your wishes or whatever."

"Goddesses grant wishes?"

I shrugged. "According to drunk people at sleepovers, yes."

"How do you impress a goddess?"

"Acts of devotion."

"Okay." He took a breath, palms up on his knees like a yoga person. "Show me how to play."

I reddened and said, "Right, so, you have to really know the person you're playing it with. Because the way you play it is, you put your life in their hands."

He did this frown-smile. "You—*how* do you do that?"

So Becca *hadn't* told him what happened the night we fought. I could speak more steadily knowing that. "All sorts of ways. It's just a name people give to whatever risky trust game shit they're getting up to. Like theater kids doing falls into the pit before a show. Or stupider stuff, like playing the blackout game. The happy nice take is the goddess rewards the power of friendship and trust." I candied my voice, traced a rainbow in the air. "The hardcore version says the goddess will only appear to you if she believes you're willing to die for it."

The way his eyes snapped to mine, I could feel it. And I knew we were both thinking of Becca's note. *i'm off to play the goddess game.*

After a beat, he said, "And this is just a Palmetto thing."

I swallowed. "Pretty sure. It's been around for a while, though. My mom said she's played it."

"Oh, *shit*." Suddenly James stiffened up. "I think my mom has, too."

"Your mom's from Palmetto? Wait. You *have* heard of the game?"

"Yeah, no, I thought I hadn't. But now I'm remembering something she told me. About this thing she used to do back in high school." His eyes dark, he plucked at his bracelet. "In the middle of the night she and her best friend would go out in someone's car. One of them would drive, and the other would cover the driver's eyes and direct her. They'd see how far they could get before running up on a curb or hitting a mailbox. Or, you know, committing manslaughter. She definitely referred to it as a *game*."

"Yeah," I said flatly. "That's the goddess game."

"Hey." His voice was so low it sent a shiver over my shoulders, hit my stomach like a swig of something hot. "We'll print the film. Whatever's on it could be all we need to find her."

I tried to think what that might look like. Becca holding a map with an arrow drawn on it. I AM HERE. "Maybe."

We were both quiet then, wrapped in thoughts that may or may not have looked alike. He was running his fingers idly over the graffiti gouged into the fat paint of the sill. After a minute he started to read it aloud. "Annie plus Miriam. R.E. hearts P.D. Sublime *rox*. Wow, okay. Mind the Gap? Oh, I get it." Below the phrase was a touchingly skillful drawing of a butt. It was the art hall, after all.

I pointed to a phone number half-hidden by a slick parabola of spilled nail polish, scratched beneath the timeless words FOR A GOOD TIME CALL. "We called that once."

His brows went up. "Did you have a good time?"

"A woman answered. She asked if we wanted to hear a story." My skin prickled. "She was already talking when she picked up. It was like walking into the middle of a conversation. Then Becca said hello and she stopped. That's when she asked us, 'Do you want to hear a story?'"

"Tell me you said yes."

I gave him a look. "Of course we did. Don't ask me what it was about, though. I can't remember."

It was true. Her story hit our brains like rain on dry dirt, cool and sweet, then gone. I wanted to write stories like that. Tales that filled people up like a meal or a song they loved. The *good* kind of lie.

The woman on the phone had inspired an entry in our goddess series: me lying on a white-sheeted bed, surrounded by old phones we picked up at donation shops and thrift stores. My body wound around with their cords, a book of fairy tales open in my arms. The goddess of open endings.

James made a face. "Palmetto is a strange town. More than you'd think for a place that has two Chili's."

"The Chili's on Oak is the old location," I said automatically. "They just haven't taken the sign down yet."

He smiled.

I smiled back. I couldn't help it. It was hard being this close to him. He was actually *better* up close, because he looked realer. Chapped lips, scrub patch of stubble that he'd missed on his cheek. He had two freckles bracketing the corner of his mouth, and another on his jawline and on his neck, one two three four. I leaned in, noticing for the first time a pie wedge of gold in the brown of his left iris. He saw me looking and touched a self-conscious fingertip to the eye's outside corner.

"Fairy-kissed."

I straightened up, flustered. "What?"

"The discoloration thing. It's something my mom used to say." He looked a little flustered, too. Like he hadn't meant to bring it up, but now he had to see it through. "She told me . . . ugh. She told me I was stolen from the hospital the day I was born, and when she got me back I had this yellow stripe. Because a fairy took me, and kissed my eye before giving me back." He shook his head. "It's classic my mom. Doing her whimsical artist act, while I'm sitting there terrified."

"Your mom's an artist? What, um. Medium?"

"Bullshit," he said with zero hesitation. "It's lucrative, if you're good."

"Is she good?" I spoke lightly, trying to figure out how much he meant it.

"She's the best."

There was no teasing in his words, just a kind of flat resignation.

"I used to be a bullshit artist myself." I smiled at him thinly. "Becca tell you that?"

He tipped his head like he was trying to see me better. His eyes were so brown they made me hungry. And that stripe like clover honey. "Becca's told me a lot about you."

I couldn't tell if he was doing that thing with his voice that made everything sound like it had six possible meanings on purpose. It could just be how he talked. I looked down. "The kiss isn't yellow," I told him, gesturing toward my own irises. "It's more of a gold color."

There wasn't much room on the ledge. We were holding our bodies carefully apart. I think I would've been less self-conscious if we'd just allowed our knees to bump, our feet to tangle. As it was I couldn't stop feeling all the places we almost touched, glowing like a heat map. James took a swallow of black coffee, head falling back and throat working.

I dropped my gaze, curling my fingers under the window. Outside air seeped in and chilled my thighs. When he spoke again his voice was consciously blank.

"Why would Becca say what she did in her note?"

I puffed my cheeks up, blew out. "She told you we had a fight, right?"

"Just that you did. No details."

"That's what we fought about."

I was radically simplifying the issue, to the point that it was almost a lie. I thought he'd try to pin me down about it, but he only said, "I thought the note might have to do with your goddess series."

I felt a rush of—what? Not betrayal, exactly, but surprise. Besides us, only our parents knew about the series. Just my parents, now. "She told you about that?"

"A little bit. When we were talking about our favorite things we'd ever made. She said it got lost, though."

"Lost," I repeated softly. Thinking of the flames that took our brimming goddess book, the way it felt like they were burning away a piece of me. "She's made way better stuff since then. We stopped making goddesses when—"

He spoke softly. "Her dad. I know."

He knew a lot. I pulled my knees in tighter, away from him. Wondering again if friends was all they were.

"The game gave us the idea, but the goddesses were ours." I made my voice light. "Just a way to keep playing make-believe when we got too old for it."

Then I looked down, reset, and tried again. Tried to say it more honestly.

"We just *wanted* so much, you know? Inventing our own religion was our one big idea. The only way we could think of to *get* what we wanted. Or to pretend we might."

Something flickered in his eyes. A bright depth charge of an emotion I couldn't name. "What did you want?"

I wasn't sure what made me talk so straight with him.

Maybe it was his steady X-ray eyes, that made me feel like he could already see my secrets. Or maybe it was that he was the closest I could get to Becca right now.

"What does everyone want?" I said. "Talent. Power. Love. Then, you know. Becca's life changed. And it didn't feel . . . it stopped being just fun."

I wondered if she'd told him about her mother's death, and what happened after. I watched him, wondering, and he watched me back. When it became too much, I looked down. "What was yours, though?"

"My what?"

"Your favorite thing. That you've ever made."

"I could show you," he said. "Sometime."

The first bell rang, distant but distinct. Neither of us moved.

"Think the cops are still out there?"

I stirred, feeling a ripple of nerves in my chest. Somehow I'd almost forgotten about the police. "God, I hope not. Everyone'll be so excited."

I wondered how long we'd have lingered if the bell hadn't brought the outside world in. James sighed, shouldering his bag, and I spoke before he could rise.

"What else did Becca tell you about me?"

His jaw shifted. I gave myself half a second to slide my eyes down that line of freckles, lip to jaw to neck, then sideways to the hollow of his throat. He was deciding what to give me, shuffling through possible answers. Finally he said, "She told me you were obsessed with the TV show *The Outer Limits*."

I stared at him. "What?"

"*The Outer Limits*. You know, the . . ."

"The ridiculous sixties sci-fi show," I interrupted. "I

know. Because *Becca* was obsessed, not me. She liked it because her dad made us watch it with him on the weekend when it rained. She liked the terrible props and the weird acting and the way people always think of it as, like, this *Twilight Zone* runner-up, but in some ways it's actually *better*."

James cocked his head. "Okay. But it kind of sounds like you also like *The Outer Limits*."

"Yeah," I said quietly. "I kind of do."

He didn't smile, exactly, but I was learning to read him a little. The smile was there.

"Here's something else Becca told me about you." His voice was low and tinged with heat. "She said you saved her life. After her dad died, she said you kept her alive."

My stomach filled with ice water. "She told you that?"

His brows went up, like he knew he'd said the wrong thing. "Yeah. Sorry if . . . I'm sorry."

"Why?" I slid off the sill, boots hitting the floor with a hollow thunk. "It's a nice thing to say."

"Right, but . . ." He let the silence finish his sentence. I hated when people did that. I probably did it all the time.

I gave him a tight smile. "I should get to class. Let me know when you can try the darkroom again, okay? I'll meet you whenever."

For a second he looked confused, almost hurt. But the next he was sliding out of reach. Back to his usual self, the one who moved through the halls like a permanent tourist. "Sure," he said coolly.

I'd have felt guilty if I had any room for it. But all I could think about was that horrible phrase. *She said you kept her alive.*

CHAPTER NINETEEN

LET'S SAY YOU'RE THE GIRL who saved your best friend's life. The person who, apparently, *kept her alive*. With your love and your constancy. With your steadfast disregard for the worser parts of her nature. Like the way she had of acting like she and you were the only real people left on Earth.

Then let's say she changed overnight. Became elusive, unpredictable, treated your love like it was a cage. Until you hit your limit and canceled your constancy. Held your love in reserve. Saw her for what she was and let her *know* it, too.

What happens then? What becomes of her life when you're sick of saving it?

Becca's voice in my ear, dragging me backward out of sleep.

"Wake up. Let's play the goddess game."

This was it. Three months ago, the night we fought and broke. I think I'd been waiting for it to happen. Something had to give.

I wanted to pretend I didn't hear her. Snap my fingers and watch the sun come up in triple time, washing the night away. But her fingers pressed cold into my arm and her hair grazed my bare shoulder like an irritant, and any- way she'd keep shaking me until I opened my eyes.

Oh, god. Let's go back further. It wasn't always that way.

You'd think we would have talked about it: the brutal death of Christine Weaver, three days after we made the goddess of revenge. Instead we both pretended it hadn't happened. Me because I wished it hadn't. Becca because she could see how much the coincidence had terrified me. The way it made me—lightly—pull away.

I didn't love her less. I was just chafing against the bor- ders of our time-stuck world. Sometimes I craved the greasy normalcy of my junior-high peers, as I imagined it: sports practice, McDonald's, convoluted telephone chains of gos- sip involving the finer points of second base and who got there. The stupid dances they taught themselves, a ritual Becca mocked with unsettling ferocity. *I* thought it looked kind of fun. The thing was, we were coming up on thirteen, and our shared obsessions had barely shifted since we were six. They'd only deepened.

I didn't know how to say it, and when did I ever get the chance? A year after her mother's death, Becca's dad reconnected with his college girlfriend, a freckly paralegal named Miranda. A year later he had the audacity to marry her. Not much more than a year after that, he was gone.

Through it all Becca's grip on our status quo tight- ened. I loved her still, always. I loved our weird little world. But there were times I could hardly breathe think- ing about how much it would hurt her if I tried to stretch or change.

And then *she* changed, lightning fast. It started after she hurt her knee in the woods. It wasn't just the injury that made her call me. Becca was *afraid*, I was sure of it.

For a week or so after that night she was thoughtful, a little pensive, but herself. Then all of a sudden she flipped. Became distant, bordering on cold. She missed my calls, left my texts unread for hours. She treated me with impatient irritation, while insisting nothing was wrong. Like I could be convinced to believe *I* was the one being weird. After all those months—years—of bending myself into the shape she needed me to be, her defection seemed like the cruelest possible thing. I felt gaslit and heartsore.

Summer passed, junior year began. We limped along, not talking about the thing we weren't talking about. Then, that autumn night.

"Wake up. Let's play the goddess game."

I tensed before I could stop myself. Then there was no use pretending to be asleep.

We were sprawled on blankets in the family room. Earlier that evening my dad had made us a fire in the fireplace, first of the season. We'd listened to the *Nightmare Before Christmas* soundtrack and toasted marshmallows on sticks, a longstanding annual tradition. But all the time I was alert to her darkening mood, like a sailor tracking the black line at the horizon.

Now the room was a low orange, painted with the light of dying embers. Beneath their crackle I heard the homey *whoosh* of the heater and rain hitting the sliding glass door in scattered fistfuls. The sky behind it was greeny black.

I put an arm over my eyes. "Go back to sleep."

"I can't go back to sleep, I haven't slept. I never sleep." She gave an odd little gasp. "I have to tell you something."

I pulled a flap of blanket over my face. A premonitory

dread was creeping up my body in a blue-black tide. But when she spoke again the raw note in her voice had gone.

"Come on, Nora," she wheedled. "Nora. Eleanor Grace Powell, you beautiful bitch, get up." A pause. "If you get up now I'll buy you an Icee."

"It's too cold for an Icee," I said plaintively, but I was already sitting up.

By the time we pulled coats over our pajamas and stepped outside the rain had passed, leaving the air soft and rich with autumn rot. Clouds swaddled a gold-bellied moon. We'd made it to the bike path when Becca unwound her scarf and held it up to me in silence.

I pretended not to understand. "What?"

"We're playing the goddess game. Like we did, that time."

I ducked away. "The time I got a concussion? Becs, no."

"Playing is the whole reason we're *out* here."

Her mood was balanced on a knifepoint. Edgy high, threatening a plunge into brooding low. When I didn't immediately comply, her jaw shifted into an underbite. "You're being weird. You're mad at me."

This Becca I recognized. The tarnished flipside of our joyful mindmeld was that whatever she did or felt, she accused me of doing or feeling. She had trouble thinking of me as a separate person. We were plaited together too tightly in her head.

"Now why," I said slowly, "do you think I would be mad at you?"

She swallowed hard. Her eyes were wet. "I know. I do. Just, please."

It was her first acknowledgment that I wasn't making it up. That she had been different. I guess that was why I let her tie the scarf around my eyes, winnowing the world into steaming cold air and a path that seemed to buck beneath me once I could no longer see it.

"Walk straight ahead." She spoke in a self-serious intonation I hadn't heard since the first time we played. And I obeyed.

I used to close my eyes in the car and try to track its path turn by turn, betting myself I could open them again right as we reached our driveway. But I always got it wrong. As Becca led me over pavement and grass and pavement again, the ground canting gently up or down, I didn't even try to keep track.

A couple of times I stumbled. But I didn't fall.

"I won't let you fall."

I didn't reply. When I spoke, the scarf she'd tied over my eyes tickled my lips.

"Nora. Did you hear me?"

"I heard you."

Somewhere far above us, hidden in a skein of white cloud, the moon was making her solitary rotation. What would that sound like, if you could hear it? A scrape of stone over stone. The closing of an ancient door. You'd have to get right up close to hear it over the stars' silver chatter.

I stumbled again, and it yanked my thoughts back to Earth. My heart was beating very fast for no good reason. No good reason yet.

When Becca spoke again her voice sounded like it used to. When we were very young and she hadn't lost a single thing that mattered.

"I want to tell you something. Are you listening?"

Her scarf smelled like jasmine shampoo and crackly October and I was so tired. Trudging over the suburban badlands with a blindfold on, envying the moon her solitude. But love can look like this. It can look like anything. You make sacrifices for the people you love.

"I'm listening."

"Lie down."

I broadened my stance, flexing my toes to plant myself on the pavement. I guessed we were in the parking lot by the pickleball courts. They were locked at night, the whole lot chained off. "Here? Why?"

"Trust me."

That was the game, after all. She kept hold of my hand as we lowered ourselves together. Grit crunched under my hair, the knot of the scarf tilting my head off-center. It was raining again but I imagined above us a scoop of endless stars, glittering like salt on a black tablecloth. Her hand in mine felt exactly as it had when we were six, ten, fourteen. Despite everything the quiet between us was a place of comfort, where I could rest and tell myself, *It was so good between us for so long. It will be again.* But I knew we were lying on a trapdoor. One tick away from a free fall into places I didn't want to go.

"Okay," she said. "Okay." Then:

"You know that night, when you picked me up from the woods?"

I squeezed her hand without meaning to, then loosened my grip just as quick. "Yes."

Her breath was rattly. She was steeling herself. She said, "Nora."

I was no longer listening, because I'd just registered a sound that made my whole body ping with alarm. I'd heard it a thousand times before, but lying on my back was so odd an orientation I couldn't place it right away.

The long sizzle of tires over wet road. First the sound,

then the vibration. Up through my chest, through my hand placed palm down on the ground. I started to sit up.

"Wait." Holding my hand tighter, anchoring me. Trapping me. *"Wait."* Then, "Now! *Go!"*

I didn't know which way to go. Even through fabric I could see the glow of headlights. Then she was crushing me, body thrown over mine with a wordless cry, rolling us out of the way. I heard the long haunted wail of a car's horn warping as it blew past us, felt the dragon's lick of its exhaust. It hadn't even tried to brake. The driver must not have seen us until the very last.

Becca was making a sound I took for gasping, but when I ripped the scarf from my face she was *laughing*. Her color was high, her eyes were shining. Beautiful. She looked like a fucking demon.

We weren't lying safely on a locked-up lot. We were in the gutter of the two-way road that ran between Walmart and the woods. Trusting her, I'd lain blindfolded on my back in the middle of the northbound lane.

I tried to spring to my feet, but my legs were boneless and I crumpled. My pajama pants rode up to my knees and my skin was sparking in all the places I'd been dragged. Later I'd find long stippled patches of road burn along my hips and back and down one leg.

"It's okay, we're good." Becca beamed at me, tremulous. "Nora, we're amazing."

She reached for me and I pushed her away with as much ferocity as I could muster, sending her back onto her palms. "Don't *touch* me!"

"Hey." She sounded surprised. It just made me angrier.

"What are you . . . what were you . . ." I could hardly get the words out. "Are you trying to get us *killed*?"

"What?" Again she reached for me. "No, that's not—"

I swatted her hand away. "I said, *don't touch me*."

Her eyes darkened. "That's the game, Eleanor. That's how it works."

Another car went by. Nowhere close to hitting us but I crab-scuttled onto the grass. "Seeing if we die or not, that's a game?"

"No! Do *not* put words in my mouth. I told you, I've got something to—"

"*Shut up*." I shook my head convulsively. "What do you want from me, Becca? After lying to me for months, treating me like I'm *nothing*, what do you want from me now? Because it's always on your terms, isn't it? When you need me, I come running. When you want me gone, off I go. It's embarrassing is what it is. It's pathetic. I'm *pathetic*."

"I'm trying to tell you something!" she half shouted. "Do you think none of this has a point?"

All the fear in me, the adrenaline and the fury, had boiled down into something purer. One of the base metals I was made from: the will to survive. "I know it has a point. Do stupid shit, see if we die. Well, I don't want any of this." I gestured to encompass the night, the road, the place we'd almost become roadkill. "I love you, Becca, but I'm not gonna *die* with you."

Rain glazed her face and pearled her lashes. It hissed off the ends of her hair. "I would *never* let you die."

She spoke each word like she was scorching it onto the air. It was an echo of what I'd said to her the first time we played the goddess game. But I wasn't a kid anymore. My skin still felt scalded where the headlights lit me up.

"That sounds really great and it means fuck all. You're not God, Becca. You don't pick who dies."

"Not God," she hissed. "*Goddess.*"

I gaped at her, feeling some measure of the prickling fear I felt when I learned about the death of the hit-and-run driver. "What the hell does that mean?"

"Don't play stupid, Nor." Her head was down, bullish. "You're asking, but do you really want to know?"

I felt—dissociative. I didn't want to be here, didn't want to think or talk about this. Whatever it was.

Because what if she was *right*?

For a beat I considered the possibility that she'd been protecting me from something all along. Understanding I simply couldn't go as deep as she could into the dark. Knowing I was tethered firmly to life as I knew it, when her own tethers had snapped.

The thought made me hate myself too much. So I buried it.

"Whatever you're trying to tell me," I said, "almost killing us is not the way to do it. I don't understand what's going on with you, Becs. I can't read you like I used to. Sometimes I feel like I don't even *know* you anymore."

"You are," she said numbly, "the *only* person who knows me. The only person alive."

There was a time when these horrible words might've flattered me. Or at least pulled me back from the edge, reminding me how much was at stake. Now they just made me feel ill.

"Do you think that's a *good* thing? Do you have any idea how it feels to be your only, to be your *one*, to be your . . ."

The look on her face then. It boiled my words to nothing. "No. Wait." I put a hand up. "That was—shit. I didn't mean it like . . ."

"No, I don't think it's a good thing." She spoke through

whitening lips. "Yes, I do have some idea how awful it must be for you, how hard. How much it must cost you to have to keep dealing with me when you could be finding *new* friends, who'd make it all so easy."

"I don't want easy! My only friend is *you*. You think that'd be my life if I wanted *easy*?"

"Hell yes, I do. Otherwise you'd have said all this to me ages ago." Her lip curled back. For a second I thought she might spit at me. "If you pity me so much, why've you stuck around all this time? Where's your spine, Eleanor? I swear you used to have one. You say you don't know me, well, what about you? When did you become such a goddamned *people pleaser*?"

Shock made my ears ring. Pain exploded like red powder behind my eyes. "I learned it from *you*! I learned it from spending half my life folding myself into a sad little pretzel to please *you*!"

We stared at each other, the air between us hissing with poison. Both appalled, I think, at how far we'd gone. Becca gave her head a dull shake. When she spoke again she sounded surprised.

"I don't know why I said that. Any of it. I don't mean it, honestly I don't. I would never hurt you. I *love* you. It's everyone else who's the problem. There are so many people walking around looking harmless but under all that they're wicked. They're *wicked*, Nora."

Her mouth hung open like a black cavity. I could hear her grabbing for each breath. She sounded like an undone stranger.

The rain came into my mouth and it tasted so dirty. "What are you talking about?"

"You ask me, but you still don't want to hear it." She

squeezed her eyes shut like it hurt to look at me. "Nora, I swear. If you knew what I know, you wouldn't look at me like that. I'm trying to be okay, Nor. I am. But there are just so many . . ." She struggled to find the words. "So many *bad people*."

My heart beat fast and high, just under my skin. Slippery lights skimmed over my vision. "Becca," I said tentatively. "Did someone do something to you?"

Her jaw went hard. "To me? You don't have to worry about me."

I glared at her, needled by the hairpin swerve. "I . . . *what*? Of course I worry about you! I'm worried about you right now. But you can't just expect me to read your mind!"

The hurt on her face was so pure. As if she were the victim, not the one who'd almost gotten us pancaked by a passing car. "You've always been able to read my mind."

Then another swerve, and now her voice was trembling. "But I swear I wouldn't have let you get hurt. I swear there really is a reason. I wanted to tell you but I think I fucked it all up. Did I, Nor? Did I fuck it up?"

I knew my line. *Of course you didn't, of course you never could!* But I was sick with adrenaline. And beneath it, a rising suspicion that all the things I didn't know were more than I could handle. I forgot all the very good reasons I protected my bereaved best friend and rose on trembling legs.

"You know what, Becca? You did."

And I left her there, alone by the road.

Over the days that followed my anger shifted into something more complicated. Becca was struggling, but she loved me. She couldn't really have wanted to *hurt* me.

But when I closed my eyes that car's headlights were waiting. They burned me from the inside out. They summoned up the vision that used to keep me awake at night: the fast approaching lights of the cargo train that killed Christine Weaver.

For *once* I needed to be the holdout. The one who accepted the apology. Some acknowledgment that she understood how badly she'd messed up. A *text*.

I got nothing. When I passed her in the halls, my breath thickened in my chest. She looked like the Becca I knew from that very first day, back in elementary school. Composed and catlike. So far from me I wondered if I was misremembering the things she'd said that night. How could that Becca and this one be the same?

I wondered what it was she'd wanted to tell me, what point she'd tried to make by risking our lives. But the question was overshadowed by this weird bifurcation happening in my brain: half of me longed for her, feared for her. The other half tingled like a dead limb coming back to life.

Me, without Becca: that was a person I barely remembered. I thought she might be worth knowing. She was the one I'd been focused on, right up until my best friend disappeared.

CHAPTER TWENTY

IT FELT LIKE COMING BACK to Earth, leaving James behind and walking unsteadily through the bathroom door. I didn't get far. The art hall was nearly empty, just Miss Corbel locking up the painting studio, but when she saw me she made a brisk *come here* gesture. I trudged toward her as slowly as I could get away with.

"You should be in class," she said, "but you're saving me a trip. The police would like to speak with you."

My mouth dried. "So they are here about Becca Cross."

Corbel marched briskly on without answering. I trailed her up the stairs. "You'll be in Mr. Pike's office," she said over her shoulder. "He'll be present for the interview."

Mr. Pike, the school social worker, was waiting in his office doorway. The room was a windowless walk-in closet with which he'd done his best. On one wall hung a trio of insipid sunset paintings rumored to be Mr. Pike originals. A mini garden of succulents died in a quiet row atop the bookshelf, its contents a candy-toned mix of self-help, memoir, and young adult. I spied an acoustic guitar case in the corner and glanced quickly away, as if its earnestness might be catching. The circular table was topped with a

Kleenex box and a pink daisy in a glass, and behind it sat two uniformed officers.

On the left, a fiftyish Black woman with freckled cheekbones and close-cropped hair. On the right, the cop I'd seen in the photo lab. A white man whose age was hard to place, his baby face offset by a gray crewcut and flint-pale eyes.

The notion of a police interview hadn't felt concrete until I saw them. The awful machinery of the vanishings was changing gears, thunking over into another magnitude of real. Ugly, industrial, police-tape *real*.

The woman spoke first. "I'm Officer Sharpe. This is Officer Kohn. Thank you for agreeing to speak with us."

Agreeing? I thought I'd been frog-marched here. "Sure."

"We want to ask you a few questions about Rebecca Cross. I understand she's your good friend."

The months of our estrangement crumpled to nothing under the weight of the years that came before. "Best friend," I said firmly.

"Okay." The way she said it told me she didn't really respect the distinction. I was still standing, and Mr. Pike took a stutter step forward, gesturing at the table's third chair.

"Go ahead and sit, Eleanor." He had this slow-moving voice that made him sound like he was on muscle relaxants, but he looked nervous. "I'll just be over here. Don't pay any attention to me."

When I'd perched on the edge of the chair Officer Sharpe addressed me with a crispness that made it clear preliminaries were done. "Eleanor, thank you again for speaking with us. We'll try not to keep you too long."

"It's fine," I said swiftly. It had occurred to me this talk could work both ways. There were things *I* wanted to know. "I doubt anyone's paying attention in class anyway."

"I can imagine. I'm sure this hasn't been an easy few days for you." She paused like I might jump in, then continued.

"Rebecca was last seen Saturday afternoon by her stepmother. We're looking into her case on a more aggressive timeline than we usually might because of the . . ." She stopped to think, eyes tracking over the air above my shoulder. "Unusual circumstances."

"Three people disappearing in one night?"

She made this funny gesture—tipping her head, lips pursed, like she might correct me. But all she said was, "It's unusual."

I leaned forward a little. "Have you found any connections between them?"

Officer Kohn *hm*ed. His hands—older than his face, no wedding ring—lay flat on the tabletop.

Sharpe ignored him. "I bet you've been asking yourself that question. Has anything come to mind?"

"No." It was a small lie. "Becca doesn't know Chloe Park *or* Kurt Huffman."

"Doesn't know them at all, or isn't close with them?"

"Neither. She isn't close with anyone. Except me."

Officer Sharpe cocked her head like I'd said something interesting. Suddenly my neck felt hot. "Why's that?"

"No reason. She's just one of those people."

"Which people?"

"The ones who don't need a lot of friends," I said tightly. "She's a photographer. So she's pretty busy with that."

"Mm-hm." Sharpe's eyes were on me, her thoughts elsewhere. "Was she dating anyone? In person, online?"

My pulse flickered faster, in my temples and neck and the hollow of my throat. I was almost fully sure she wasn't dating James. "No."

"Mental state." Sharpe said it like she was laying it down on the table between us. "Any reason to believe—"

"No," I repeated.

"How's her relationship with her stepmother?"

"Bad," I said baldly. "But not—*Miranda* isn't bad. They just aren't close."

"I got that sense. Did Rebecca ever talk about having problems socially? Any bullies, any incidents, even if she didn't name names?"

"Not having a million friends doesn't mean you have problems socially." We both heard how defensive I sounded.

"No, of course not," Sharpe allowed. "I'm just trying to get a picture of her situation. Anything you can tell us could be useful. Odd behavior, a stray remark. Times she couldn't meet you and wouldn't tell you why. Any attempts she's made to contact you since Saturday."

Odd behavior and stray remarks were Becca trademarks. And what about the note she gave James, and the undeveloped film? Did that count as trying to reach me?

"She hasn't contacted me."

"How about before Saturday? Did she ever talk about running away?"

"Not really." I fisted my hands beneath the table.

Officer Kohn cleared his throat. "You were there the night she went missing." It was the first time he'd spoken. His voice had the unsettling characterlessness of an unmarked car. "Miranda Cross said she found you there in the morning, holding Rebecca's cell phone."

"Yeah." That threw me off balance, but it shouldn't

have. Of course Miranda told them that. "I went there to talk to her late Saturday night. Her phone was outside, and a cup of coffee, like she'd just been out there. It was after midnight. You can look at the texts I sent if you need the exact time."

"We already did," Kohn said.

I stared at him, wondering what they'd made of Becca's last message. My mind bounded back across years' worth of our texts. How far had they read? "Is that legal?"

He hooked a thumb toward Sharpe. "This is the kind of information she was talking about, when she asked if you could think of anything useful."

My face was burning. "Well, you already had it."

Sharpe leaned over the table, as if to pull my attention from her partner. "Walk me through it from your perspective. Everything that happened before and after you arrived at Becca's."

Through numb lips, I recounted the night in Becca's yard, the frozen morning, returning hours later to find her empty room. "Also she cleaned out her locker. All her books and everything are gone."

"We did check her locker."

I allowed myself a heartbeat's length of relief that I got to the photo and the knife first. "What about the painting studio this morning? What were you looking for?"

Officer Sharpe smoothed her hand over the tabletop. "I understand Becca spends a lot of time in the art department, including off hours. Is that right?"

"Yeah. Like I said, she's a photographer."

Sharpe's voice was bland, her face gave nothing away. But I understood at a level below thought that her next question was the one she'd been working up to all this time.

"Did Becca ever say anything to you about Benjamin Tate?"

It took me a second to place the name, to realize she meant *Mr.* Tate. I frowned. "The painting teacher? No."

"Even in passing."

"Nothing. Never. I mean, she probably had Intro to Art with him at some point—anyone who wants to take lab or studio classes has to—but since then she's only done photography. That's Miss Khakpour."

"Did she ever attend art club meetings?"

Tate ran the art club, I was pretty sure. I couldn't resist making a dismissive sound. "She's not a club person."

Sharpe looked down, like she was checking invisible notes. "What about Sierra Blake? Did Becca ever talk about her?"

Now I was completely lost. Sierra was a wildly intimidating senior who strode around in Dickies and men's work shirts, hair twined around a paintbrush. From what I'd seen of her work at the annual art show, she was the only person in school at Becca's level.

"No," I said. "She's never mentioned either of them. What do they have to do with any of this?"

Sharpe glanced at Officer Kohn. He gave a very small nod, and she trained her gaze back on me.

"Benjamin Tate also went missing Saturday night."

The air thinned, went vaguely astringent. "What?"

"He seems to have gone within the same timeframe as the three students." She tented her fingers on the table. "So I need you to *really think* about whether Becca has any kind of connection to this man. Even if she told you to keep it a secret. Even if you're not supposed to know. I can't overstate how crucial it is that you share with us any information you've got."

The room felt smaller, suddenly. Too small. I could see Mr. Pike in my peripherals, ready to dart in and offer me a Kleenex or a song on his guitar. I wouldn't cry. I wouldn't. "What are you saying? What do you think he did?"

"Some things have come to light," Sharpe said. "About Benjamin Tate."

"What things?"

"Mr. Tate is not a nice man."

The childlike simplicity of the phrase sent goosebumps sliding over my skin. It didn't seem like the kind of thing a police officer was allowed to say. But this woman was fully in control. She reminded me a little bit of Ruth. Whatever she told me, it was exactly what she meant for me to hear.

"What did he do?" I asked hoarsely.

"Nothing I'm at liberty to talk about."

"Are you serious?" My whole face was burning. "You can't just imply my best friend has been, what, *taken* by a teacher, then drop the subject. That's unacceptable. That's *sick*."

Then I did start to cry. Was this what Becca was getting at, the night we fell apart? Could Mr. Tate have been one of the *bad people* she'd talked about?

Everyone at PHS loved Mr. Tate. He was loud and funny and passionate. He'd even been in a band that was famous for like two minutes, twenty years ago. You still heard their big single on soundtracks sometimes. He wore checkered Vans and tight T-shirts and shabby cardigans pushed up to his elbows to show off his tattoos. Some of my classmates even had crushes on him.

But not Becca. Never Becca. Even as the tears were falling I could feel it wasn't right. No, I decided. Officer Sharpe was chasing a dead end. And if *this* was their big angle, all they had on Becca, I'd been right from the start. I really was the one who would have to figure out where she'd gone.

"There's no way." I gave in and took a Kleenex. "No *way* she's got anything to do with him."

Sharpe held her peace for a beat, then said, "Okay. Thank you for your time."

The room was windowless but I sat there blasted and blinking, like I'd just looked right at the sun. "That's it? You're done with me?"

"Unless you've got something else to tell us."

I shook my head. Then, "Wait."

They waited. Feeling faintly ludicrous, I said, "What about Logan Kilkenny?"

Officer Sharpe's face didn't change but for a slight narrowing of the eyes. I couldn't tell if that meant she'd already been thinking about him, or if she was trying to remember who he was.

"Logan Kilkenny went missing in the mid '90s." She spoke patiently. "It's a separate case."

I couldn't think of anything else to say, other than, *But I had this weird dream about him.* I nodded. They stood. Officer Kohn checked his phone, Officer Sharpe thanked me again and dismissed me just as quickly. "We'll need the room again in ten," she told Mr. Pike. "That work for you?"

Pike nodded. When the cops were gone, he smiled at me with mealy sympathy.

"Can we set up a time to talk, Eleanor? I think it would be a good idea."

I replied as politely as I could manage. "I've had enough talking."

I hustled to the nearest bathroom to splash my face.

Then I retraced my steps, parking myself as far from Mr. Pike's door as I could get while still keeping it in sight. I was rewarded after a few minutes of lurking by the sight of the cops returning with their next interview: Madison Velez. Her head was down but I could see her swollen eyes.

As soon as the door closed behind her, I went for the exit.

CHAPTER TWENTY—ONE

LATER I'D HEAR HOW MR. Tate's vanishing was discovered.

It was a woman walking her dogs who first sounded the alarm. Out early on a Sunday morning, a bouquet of leashes in her fist, walking along the soccer fields on Gorse. That whole block was one long no parking zone, but a car was parked there anyway, bumped up against the curb. A green Kia Soul. No one was inside it but its engine was on. She could hear music playing through its sealed windows.

The woman noted that, but didn't think too much about it until she passed the car again an hour later. Still running, still empty. Still playing the same song.

Suburb-dwellers are nosy. They take note when things are out of place, when someone isn't abiding by the rules, written or not. Whatever else was going on with that empty car, its owner was not being a good neighbor. So she called it in.

It was Mr. Tate's car. Locked. Keys in the ignition, his phone on the seat. Speakers playing a single midtempo indie rock song on endless repeat.

That was the detail that really stuck, making you laugh

or wince with sympathetic embarrassment. Before whatever happened to him happened, Mr. Tate had been listening to his own song. Or, his band's, I guess. Their one famous song.

CHAPTER TWENTY-TWO

I GOT IN MY MOM'S car and drove aimlessly for a while, past the rambling properties behind school and through the residential blocks clustered around Palmetto's downtown. The houses there were the colors of Jordan almonds, ship-shape and repetitive. I went up the hill and around the cemetery, glancing in the direction of the Angel.

And all the time my brain was hitching around what I'd learned, attempting to remap the contours of what the hell was going on here. Not three people missing. Four.

My thoughts felt like splatter paint and I was *hungry*. All I'd had today was coffee and bad news. When I saw the pink-and-green lights of the Palm Diner sign coming up on my right I was swept with breakfasty visions so intense they bordered on delirium. Waffles covered in powdered sugar crepes with chocolate chips melting in little puddles pancakes drowning in syrup sugar grit swirling in the dregs of a coffee cup—

Then I was lurching into the lot without losing speed. The car whumped hard over the divot between road and parking lot.

There was a blank space in my head. A small white cavity,

like something—time, thought—had been hole-punched cleanly away. I hadn't slowed because I hadn't *turned*. Not consciously. I had no recollection of deciding to go to the diner.

I slid sloppily into an open space, turned off the car, and sat there breathing hard. My blood beat loudly in every part of my body. I was hungry, that was all. I was *regressing*, is what I was, to the days when Becca and I were gross little sugar Hoovers. I got out of the car.

The Palm was a local landmark. The kind of place where you could still pay $7.95 for eggs and toast and a cup of bottomless coffee. It had an eternally sticky enamel counter and a dead jukebox stacked with midcentury hits and it smelled like mop water and maple syrup. Outside the world was starched and gray, but in the diner all was the sun-dusted colors of a place that never changed: burgundy stools, green booth backs, green-and-burgundy tile. The only nod to passing time was a fake Christmas tree still hanging on weeks past the new year, glinting with dollar-store tinsel. I paused beside it, taking great swallows of the burnt-coffee air.

"Seat yourself, hon," said the hostess. She'd been working here as long as I could recall.

I scanned the room. Moms with bored children, old men with folded newspapers, a middle-aged couple tucking wordlessly into their food. There was a six-top of construction workers sitting in the circle booth. I thought of Becca and me at age seven, seated with our four parents in that very booth, coming down off the high of our holiday dance recital. They'd let us leave on our Baby Jane stage makeup, our peppermint-stick dance outfits beneath unzipped parkas. We ate club sandwiches and drank root beer floats and felt famous.

I took the booth backing up to the broken jukebox. A very pregnant waitress came by to take my order. When she was gone I tipped a raw sugar packet into a spoon and ate it in pinches. After I'd crunched the last grain I turned the spoon over and looked at my warped reflection.

I turned my mouth up into a smile, thinking of my face that morning in the steamed-up glass. And that feeling I had in the old green bathroom, when I looked in the mirror and didn't know myself. I couldn't quite shake it. That lack of recognition, as if the girl in the glass had an agenda that ran counter to my own.

I'd felt off since I opened my eyes. Really, though, I hadn't felt right since I woke in Becca's yard Sunday morning, chilled to the bone and ignorant of the ways the world had changed. I slapped my palms against the tabletop, then again, harder. I stamped my feet firmly on the floor. Just to *feel* myself in my body. I needed sleep, that was all. Or maybe I needed to wake up.

The food came then and I was grateful. My waffle glistened with strawberry syrup, uncanny pink and so sweet I felt it in my spine. For a few blissful minutes I stopped thinking. When I came back to myself my plate was an empty red slick.

I blinked at it and saw something else. White tile, red blood. Broken glass and liquor on the Sebraneks' kitchen floor. I pushed the plate away, stomach turning, even though part of me wanted to lick it. When the waitress came around, I ordered a short stack.

Food hadn't helped as much as I wanted it to. I still felt so flyaway, I needed something to *ground* me. I shook out my hands, rolled my neck, thinking. Then I dug in my bag for something I should not have been carrying around.

The butterfly knife I'd found in Becca's locker sat heavy in my palm, solid and satisfying as a ripe plum.

I looked around. No one looked back. The waitress with her big aproned belly was across the room, delivering a tray of omelets. Carefully I opened the knife. Its blade had a wicked curve. It looked more like a prop than a thing you'd actually find a use for. I pressed its point lightly to the pad of my index finger.

I couldn't feel it. Because it was that sharp, or because I was that disconnected? I pressed a little harder.

Nothing. I looked around again, as if someone might look back to commiserate. This was weird, right? It was weird. A slow hum started under my sternum. A need to focus myself, *feel* myself, shed this persistent sense of detachment. I pressed harder, testing the matrix of my skin.

Right as it broke I did feel *something*. In my belly, in my ribs and along the T-bar of my shoulders. It was a kind of internal recoil, separate from the bright surprise of the pain—finally—in my finger.

"Ugh!"

I jerked my head up and the waitress was standing beside me, coffee pot slack at her side. I looked down to see what she saw.

A knife in my hand. The other running red from its highest point, palm turned up. The blood dripped onto the table when I turned my hand to hide it.

"No," I said. "I didn't . . ."

"This is a *restaurant*," she said, disgusted. "Save your little blood magic for your house."

"Sorry. I'm sorry." I dropped the blade into my bag, smearing blood on the handle. Squeezing a napkin in my cut hand to stanch the blood, I used the other to extract a twenty for the waitress.

Grabbing my coat, not quite myself, I charged into the open air. I sprinted to the corner and kept going, crossing against the light at a run. Cars honked and I felt it again: that tiny pulling back in my rib cage. Across the street was an Amoco and I pushed through its smeary door, because they sold candy and I never would get that short stack. I'd probably never get anything at the Palm Diner again.

One-handed I scooped up peanut butter M&Ms and a Milky Way, then doubled back for a clattering box of Good & Plenty.

The cashier was bent over a chessboard set up in the lottery-ticket window. Their opponent was a girl in paint-stained jeans and a hoodie. "Just a second," they said, turning a rook in their fingers.

I recognized them. Aster something, they'd been a PHS senior when I was a sophomore. Their graphic novel-in-progress had been excerpted last year in the lit magazine.

"Oh, hey," I blurted, wobbly on my feet. "I loved your thing in the . . . thing. The school magazine."

Aster looked up, their face lighting. Then it fell. "Dude, fuck. You're bleeding."

I looked down. The napkin I clutched was reduced to red strings.

Aster was backing up, face turned away. "Oh, yuck. Icky. It's blood. You have to stay away from me."

"Get it together, Az."

The girl in the hoodie tipped her chin up and peered critically at my hand. She had blonde hair, arching dark gull brows, a scatter of freckles the color of cassia cinnamon. I breathed in tightly: she was Sierra Blake, the girl the cops asked about. Skipping school, like me.

"That is a lot of blood, though," she said. "Come on, let's see if you need stitches."

"Once a candy striper, always a candy striper," Aster said, smirking. They seemed happier once I was moving away.

I followed Sierra into the bathroom, closet-sized and stinking of mildew. She turned the water on cold and gestured at me to stick my hand in it.

"Clean cut," she said, leaning close. "It's deep but it's short."

"You're Sierra Blake."

She threw me a wary glance, turning the water off with a hard twist. "Keep your hand up, like this. Here, dry it really really well. Where'd they get this first-aid kit, Goodwill? It looks like it's from 1972. Whatever, the gauze seems clean. Hand, please."

"I'm Rebecca Cross's best friend," I told the crown of her head. "Do you know who that—"

"Yes." She wrapped my finger, tight and neat. "There, that'll hold. Keep pressure on it for ten minutes to start. I'd set a timer, it's longer than you think."

I pinched my cut fingertip firmly. "Okay, it's clear you don't want to do this, but . . . the police talked to me today. They asked me about Mr. Tate." I grimaced apologetically. "Then they asked me about you."

Sierra sighed, running her hands over her face. They were winter-rough like mine, nails clipped short. "Well, that's disappointing. I hope you're not the kind of asshole who went around repeating that to a bunch of people."

I shook my head. "I promise I'm a different kind of asshole."

A smile, very faint. "Sorry about your friend."

"Look, I don't want to bother you," I said. "But. Please."

She made a noncommittal sound, eyes switching to the door.

I pointed with a thumb. "You want to talk out there?"

"Nah, just thinking Aster'll rip you up if they think you're pushing me about this. I mean, not physically, obviously, they can't stand blood. Psychologically. So let's make this quick. What's your name?"

"Nora."

"Okay, Nora. I'll tell you what actually happened. And when people come at you with some bizarro version, I want you to correct them. Okay?"

"Yes. I promise."

"Good. So, yeah. Tate is a straight up predator."

My heart sank. I'd figured, but it sank for her anyway.

"I'm smart," she said. "I'm not a shit-taking type of person. But guys like him . . . he's wily. I've been in art club since freshman year, and I always thought he was pretty okay. Harmless." She rolled her eyes. "A little pathetic, always bringing up his sad band, wanting us to think he's cool. It's funny how I can see it now, like, thinking back on the way he's been with other girls. And the way he's kind of . . . *favored* me, all year. Bringing me monographs to borrow, telling me about painters he's allegedly met, gallery shows I should go to. Doing the casual kind of," she gestured like she was touching my elbow, my back, then gave a little shudder. "But anyway. Hindsight.

"So Tate went to Pratt. Then last month *I* got into Pratt, early decision. He said we had to have a toast to celebrate. He invited me to his house Sunday before last, middle of the afternoon. I thought, fine. His wife and daughter'll be there, I'll drink an inch of cheap rosé.

"But when I get there, his family's nowhere in sight. He's got this Shins album on, and he's making us drinks in a *cocktail shaker*." Her laugh was disbelieving. "Still trying to decide why I didn't leave right then."

"He's a teacher," I said softly. "We're trained, right? To do what they tell us."

Sierra considered that. It was when she stopped talking that you noticed the shadows under her eyes, the unhappy cant of her neck. "Yeah. Maybe. Well, for whatever reason I stayed. Tate poured the drinks and we sat at his kitchen table. And he told me—"

Her voice cut out. She shook her head, as if that were a personal failing.

"He told me I have a big talent. He told me I'm gonna go off and live this big life, full of art and travel and *lovers*." She ejected the word with disgust. "And he said he'd be honored to be my first. He told me his first was an older woman, another musician. He said artists should always learn from other artists." Her eyes flicked briefly to mine. "He said I could learn a lot from him."

The whirr of the bathroom fan grated over my skin. Tate was a *grown-up*. Arm hair and crow's feet and a wedding ring. "That prick," I spat.

"My *first*," she said, laughing a little. "What a perv.

"Anyway, I got the hell out of there. And I just . . . I don't want to hear your opinion on this, but I didn't report it right away. I was kinda stunned, I think. Then all last week he acted like nothing had happened. Just, polite. Distant, kind of. And I started to think, it did happen, right? And when I *do* tell, is he gonna try to pretend it didn't?

"Then last Friday in class I was telling someone how my mom and stepdad were staying in the city for the weekend. And I guess Tate must've heard me. Because Saturday night I'm sitting around in my empty house, in my pajamas, and there's a knock at the door."

My stomach lurched.

"My front door has a window. I look and he's out there wearing a leather jacket and a band T-shirt, for *his own band*, waving a six-pack of Busch around. If I'm still drinking Busch when *I'm* ancient, please put me out of my misery.

"I dialed 911 and held my phone up so he could see it, with my finger over the call button. He yelled some incredibly sad shit through the door, and then he went home. Or, I assumed he did." She lifted one brow, cold and precise. "I guess something happened on the way."

"What'd the police say when you called them?"

"I didn't call them. Yesterday they showed up at my house."

I frowned. "But. How'd they know to come talk to you?"

For the first time, Sierra looked more sad than angry. "His wife. I guess a little while back she got this anonymous email. Tate lost his phone, and whoever found it dug up all sorts of incriminating stuff and sent it to her—old text conversations, photos he'd saved of art club girls. Including, like, *photos*. And there were some of me that he took when I wasn't looking, at school. My feeds are all set to private, but he'd screen-grabbed some shots of me from other people's accounts, too." She sighed, long and exhausted. "His wife took their kid and moved out, but she hadn't told the school anything yet. I get that she wouldn't want him to lose his job, but . . . yeah, she screwed up. She feels so bad about it now that she called my mom to apologize. That's how I know all this."

My hand was throbbing, along with my head. "Someone found his phone. Or someone *took* his phone?"

She ticked her tongue. "Right?"

I could hear my breath in my ears. "It just seems like a big coincidence. That someone would find a phone and randomly decide to break into it. Are the police trying to figure out who it was?"

"I think the police are trying to figure out a lot of things. And *all* of this seems like a big coincidence."

"Do you think he had anything to do with the rest of it? Becca and them?"

Sierra considered it, leaning against the dirty bathroom door with her arms crossed. Even when she was still she had an animating restlessness that made me think Mr. Tate was right about one thing: she did seem destined for a big life. He'd tried to stain it.

"None of it is mine to tell," she said, "so all I'm gonna say is this: I've checked in with some girls since the Tate thing began, people who've graduated. And Nora, the guy should be in prison. When he shows his coward fucking face in Palmetto again, we're going to make sure that happens. So practically speaking, he could be smart enough to be hiding out somewhere.

"But I have this vision," she went on. "Or maybe it's a daydream. In my daydream one of the girls he hurt came back to town Saturday night. Grown. She found Mr. Tate. And he learned a lot from *her*."

CHAPTER TWENTY—THREE

WHEN BECCA AND I WERE eight years old, one of the girls in our ballet class kept creeping away during barre time to steal little things from other kids' dance bags. Candy, lip gloss, my glass owl keychain. It stopped after Becca snuck away during class herself, to write THIEF in Wite-Out pen all over the girl's dance bag, her coat, the toes of her suede boots.

Once we were at the movie theater and a trio of drunk teenagers sat in front of us. They spent the whole movie yelling *Penis!* and pelting people with Mike and Ikes. Somewhere in the second half Becca went to concessions to buy the largest cup of syrupy fountain pop they had, and dumped it over their heads.

I've watched her key the absolute shit out of cars—multiple cars—belonging to people who left their dogs inside them on summer days. She didn't do it with anger, but a cool sense of cause and effect.

I liked this about her. It taught me you don't have to take the world as it's presented to you. You can be the dissenting vote. *You* can be judge, jury, and hangman, so long as you're ready to run from sticky teens and irate car owners like the devil is after you.

Then her mother was killed. And that thing in Becca, that bright crystal spike of moral certitude, changed its color.

There was a boy we used to see at the playground, a couple of years older than us. He was one of those mystery kids who's always there, no parents in sight, sunburnt in summer and underdressed in winter, always conscripting other kids into wild and occasionally violent games. He had a thin feral face and shining hair that fell nearly to his waist, resulting in a general consensus that he was the child of hippies or zealots or no one at all, spit like a cuckoo from the trees. But there was a live-wire spark in him that spilled over too easily into shoving, split lips, blood on the wood chips. Nobody ever made fun of him twice, not for the hair or anything else.

We avoided him when we could. Joined his games when we couldn't. And by the time we were twelve, his bad-kid energy had clarified into a different kind of poison. Puberty molded his face into something lean and sly. He wore his hair pulled back in a low gold tail, like a soldier in a history book. He started meeting girls at the playground, pretty and slouching and barely older than us. They'd follow him over the path and into the forest preserve on the other side. Sometimes a second boy would join them. The way they'd flank the girl, the prowling knowledge in it, made my stomach turn like I'd drunk spoiled milk.

Five months after Mrs. Cross died, just before the start of eighth grade, Becca and I lay on the merry-go-round beneath the lowering sun, turning it in lazy circles with our feet. We heard the shush of approaching shoes and suddenly the merry-go-round was speeding up. The boy and two of his hangers-on heaved at it in turns, spinning us faster, laughing as we pulled our feet up and hung on.

"Stop," Becca yelled. "Stop it!"

Bile rose in my throat and I knew I was about to throw up. Then the boy said, "Yeah, stop it," and jerked us to a halt.

I was too woozy to stand. He blocked my way before I could try, looking down on me with the sun draped over his shoulders.

"Price of getting off is a titty twister."

He wasn't smiling. There was a sharklike flatness in his eyes and picked zits around his mouth. One of the boys trailing behind him said, "Oh, shit!" into his fist while the other doubled over laughing. I glared at him, face heating with humiliation. I felt ashamed of being such an easy target. Ashamed that I had no idea what to say. Ashamed to have tits, to be a girl at all.

"Come on," Becca said, linking an arm into mine and pulling me bodily off the merry-go-round. As she dragged me past him he snaked a hand out, grabbed a fistful of my thirteen-year-old breast, and twisted.

The pain was dull but the shame was sharp and I didn't make a sound. "Screw you!" Becca screamed over her shoulder. Even that was agonizing, the fact that she used a baby swear.

I should have known she wasn't done.

It was the very end of summer, the last heat wave. The air was thick as tar, sticky on the teeth and slow in the lungs. We spent all the next day in Becca's pool, breathing just enough to make our bodies float. By six the brutal disc of the sun had slipped behind the treetops, splintering gold among their branches. I closed my eyes and waited for the heat to break. My breast still hurt where the boy had twisted it.

I was half propped on a pool float, legs dangling like weeds in the water. My hand was palm up on the float, fingers curled in. I had an image in my mind of holding something bright and burning, something fierce. When I unfolded my fingers it bounded away from me, true as an arrow. The pain in my chest receded.

I opened my eyes and the sun was lower. Becca was gone. I looked to the end of the yard and saw one bike where there had been two.

I was out of the pool and onto my bike in a dizzying instant. Flip-flops slipping on the pedals and wearing a soggy red one-piece, my hair wind-drying as I rode. The playground was full of the slow shapes of families finally venturing out in the twilight. I rode past them to where Becca's bike lay in the brush at the edge of the woods. I dropped my own bike beside it and went straight to our clearing.

He was with her. In all the years since she never told me how she got the boy to follow her into the woods.

Neither saw me. They stood facing each other on opposite sides of the tumbled grass circle. In Becca's hand was her dad's butterfly knife. Her voice scratched like she'd screamed it raw, though I'd spent the whole day with her and neither of us had been talking.

"Get down," she said. "Get on your knees."

The boy laughed, a little breathless. "You've got to be kidding me." His tongue pushed lewdly at his cheek. "You get on *your* knees."

"Do it."

He could've flipped her off and turned around. Jogged back to one of the paths and been done with it. But he was too arrogant. He lunged at her.

The boy had seemed so cunning to me, so dangerous and quick. That was when I realized his was the limited cunning of an animal. No thought to it, just base desire: he wanted to hurt her, to get that knife. But she was ready for him, and held it out, and in trying to grab her he wrapped his fingers briefly around its blade.

He snatched his hand back, folding his arm to his chest like a broken wing. "*Fuck*. You *bitch*."

"On your knees. On your knees, now." Her voice was quelling. Like she was gentling a horse before the branding.

"I'll kill you." He spoke with deadly calm. "You're dead, I promise you. You're *done*." But when she darted at him, feinting toward his belly with the blade, he cried out and fell into a crouch.

Head low, the boy cradled his bleeding hand and kept talking, making more and viler promises. She ignored them all, circling at a distance until she stood behind him. He stiffened, visibly afraid once she was out of his sight.

"Nora," she said.

She hadn't looked my way once, but she'd known I was there all along. I moved forward, kneeling to grab a muddy rock as I went. It nestled sweetly in my palm. The boy glared at me with uncut hate as I waved at him with the hand not holding the rock. My shame was burning off me like alcohol.

"Watch him," Becca said, and I'd never loved her more. In that moment I loved her with all the commitment of a subject revering her queen. Or an acolyte. Worshipping her goddess.

She stood behind him and raised the knife. Then she brought it down and began to saw. He closed his eyes and made no sound as she ground it back and forth, until all that wealth of hair came away in her hand. She'd cut it off right up against the scalp.

My best friend inspected the ponytail a moment, clotted with the blood his fingers had left on the knife. Then she lifted it high.

"For the goddess." She dropped the gory gold to the dirt, to the place where we'd made our altar to the goddess of revenge.

Inside me, something released. Because the goddesses had always been us, just us. Making them wasn't magic, it was a way to remind ourselves: together, we were enough. I could let go, at last, of my lingering guilt over the death of Christine Weaver. I could try.

Finally Becca looked at me. In her eyes I could see she'd do anything for me, always. Whether I asked for it or not.

"Good?"

I lifted my chin. I was six years old again, younger, all the way back in a place before shame. "Good."

We didn't run. We walked away together, elbow to scabbed elbow, the knife summer-warm in her hand.

So. Officer Sharpe's apparent theory—Becca as victim, Mr. Tate as predator—made sense. It was a story that played out again and again and everywhere.

But it wasn't *right*.

What if I flipped it. Mr. Tate as victim. Becca as—not predator, but avenging angel. Working again, always, to redress wrongs where she could. Stealing his phone, finding her evidence. Going from there.

I couldn't imagine how it would work. But the way it clicked into focus, more instinct than thought, made the hair rise on my neck. When she left the knife for me in her locker, maybe she wasn't just reminding me she'd once been my champion. The message could be something more direct.

More than once I'd wondered what my best friend—imperious, intense, wildly gifted—was capable of. Now, for the first time, I wondered what she'd *done*.

CHAPTER TWENTY—FOUR

MY FINGER WASN'T BLEEDING ANYMORE. No stitches needed. But my mom would ask about the gauze, so I stopped at Target for a box of Band-Aids.

I spent a while roaming the aisles. Filing my fingers through shirts I didn't want, picking up face wash bottles to stare at the words on their backs without reading them. A long-haired girl stood in the makeup aisle, stealthily sampling the nail polish. For half a second she was Becca.

It was disorienting, I thought, to be questioned by the police. To feel so manipulated, flipping on a dime between worry and anger, nails grasping at normalcy as you're dragged sideways into an altered version of your life. Who *wouldn't* look into the mirror and feel like a stranger to themselves? Who *wouldn't* feel numb all the way to their fingertips?

The knife burned through the canvas of my bag, through the denim covering my hip. What was it I'd felt when its point broke my skin? It was unlike anything. It was . . .

"Ex*cuse* me."

I startled out of my reverie and found myself in the cereal aisle. A man side-eyed me as he pushed past, two little kids tangled up like puppies in the bottom of his cart. When they were gone I looked at the Lucky Charms I'd been squeezing. Shook it a little, licking my teeth. I'd stress eaten half the box just standing there.

I paid for the cereal and a bottle of water I chugged on my way to the car. While it warmed up I checked my phone and saw two texts from Ruth.

Stop skipping lunch, we miss you
You hear about Tate?

I let my thumbs hover over my screen. *I heard.*

She replied within seconds. *They interviewed you right?*

Of course it had gotten around. Everything did.

Yeah but they already knew everything I told them

You need to talk? she replied.

Ruth. Flinty, heat-seeking Ruth. I ate a marshmallow horseshoe and a pot of gold and a tiny marshmallow rainbow, thinking. Even if she was trying to be a friend, which I believed she was, Ruth was too interested.

Thanks, I said. *I'll let you know*

The person I wanted to text was James, but I didn't have his number. I kept thinking about the way his walls went up when I hurt his feelings in the green bathroom. And I *had* hurt him, as much as I'd like to deny it. If I could text him I would say this:

I'm sorry

I wanted one thing to be simple.

I didn't mention my talk with the police to my mother. She'd be pissed when she inevitably found out, but that was a problem for future me.

Instead I went straight to my room. First I checked for news, looking up the names of the missing—nothing yet.

Then I spent a grueling half hour trying to track down the girl who might or might not have died at PHS, sixty to eighty years ago, possibly of an overdose but probably not. The one whose story could—but who knew?—be the origin of the goddess game.

I was immediately angry at myself for being so naive, for thinking I might actually find something. There were too many more recent deaths to get through. Ones I'd heard about and ones I hadn't, students as well as graduates. Athletes and artists and members of Model UN, accidents and actual overdoses and medical conditions. Eyes hot, brain waterlogged with other people's heartbreak, I slapped the computer shut.

I was just distracting myself, really. Despite the possible link between this long-ago death and the goddess game, despite my strangely lucid dream about Logan Kilkenny, I still didn't think the cold cases really mattered.

Becca mattered. Her rage, her warnings, her perception of herself as a righter of wrongs.

How could it have gone? I lay on my bed and stared into space, a mental movie coming into focus as delicately as frost flowers on glass. It opened on the summer night I picked Becca up from the forest preserve lot. What happened before I got there? She caught Kurt Huffman doing something awful, let's say, and hurt herself getting away. Then school restarted, and she learned something ugly about Mr. Tate. Together they'd shaken what was left of her faith in the world. Driving her back toward the mythology of our childhood play, where we possessed great and terrible power.

This was where the story cut out. Because no matter what Becca might have believed, goddesses *weren't* real, neither the one jump ropers chanted to nor the ones we made. And there was nothing Becca on her own could actually, physically have done to either Kurt or Mr. Tate. Not without leaving a trail. Not in one night.

There was, too, the fact of Chloe Park, whose vanishing could not be squared with any of my terrible hypothesizing. Thirteen years old, slight as a music-box ballerina. Friends with *Piper*, who I once saw cry with sympathetic distress over the hatching of a butterfly. Who offered free pet-sitting services to all the neighbors out of a sheer surfeit of love. What could possibly be wrong with a friend of Piper's?

I pulled her up in my contacts. We weren't exactly friends, but I'd hung with her a few times back in the day. And there was a summer or two when we'd run for the ice cream truck together, then eat our Choco Tacos in the shade of the willow at the corner. I considered texting a soft open, then skipped it and just called.

"Nora?"

She sounded stuffy, sad. Had I *really* caught her crying or was she playing it up? The thought was uncharitable and made me speak with an awkward compensatory heartiness. "Piper, hi! I've been meaning to see how you're doing."

"You have?"

Her tone was two degrees off nice, the equivalent of someone else saying, *Bullshit*. I recalibrated, straight to emotional manipulation.

"I'm sorry I didn't call earlier, but I've been a wreck. Because of Becca."

I could hear her remembering, almost see her putting a hand to her cheek. "Oh. Geez, of course. *I'm* sorry, I should've called. How are you doing? Have you heard anything?"

"Not yet. I'm doing okay."

"I'm so glad," she said fervently. Our shared connection to the tragedy seemed to have opened the doors. "I'm doing okay, too. I guess. We're staying in the city, in an Airbnb. My parents watch me all day, waiting to see if I'm traumatized. My mom took two weeks off so she can watch me during business hours. I'm literally hiding in the bathroom right now. I don't even know when they'll let me go back to school."

"That sucks," I said sympathetically. "Plus you must be so worried about your friend Chloe."

Her silence was my first confirmation. Then her voice, shot through quartzlike with veins of disgust. "Chloe Park is not my friend."

I was gripped by a dread so intense I sat up and swung my feet to the floor, pressing my toes into the carpet.

There are just so many bad people.

It was Becca's voice, again. Her *voice*, so thickly present in my ear I could feel the nerves humming. I curled in on myself, trying to slow my breath.

Piper kept talking. "Do you know what the police found on Chloe's phone? The last text she got? It was a photo sent from my friend Ashley after midnight. Except *Chloe* must've sent it to herself." Her voice pressed a little closer to the phone. "In the photo Ashley's topless."

My stomach twisted as I played it out. In this reality, Chloe Park went missing. In another she left Piper's house Sunday morning with a stolen nude on her phone. It wasn't hard to imagine the ways she might've used it.

"How well do you know Chloe?"

"I don't know her at all. My mom works with her mom, she made me invite her. That's why she's acting so guilty. If

I am traumatized, it's her fault." She gave a very un-Piper-like laugh.

"Do you know anyone who *is* friends with her?"

"Nope," she said flatly. "Chloe Park has no friends, and it's not because she's shy. Did you know she lives all the way in Woodgate? She transferred to Palmetto at the beginning of the year. Her parents drive half an hour every day just to drop her off. She takes a car home. So why doesn't she just go to school in Woodgate? What the heck happened there?"

Woodgate was a notoriously overfunded Ivy feeder school north of Palmetto. Word was they had actual stables on the grounds, probably a lie but the point was they *would*. PHS kids despised Woodgate's student body on principle. Even me, who on the record couldn't care less about school rivalries. Fuck those guys. "Do you know?"

Her pause was even longer this time. I could hear water running in the background, like she'd turned on the tap so she wouldn't be overheard. "I'm *really* not supposed to tell anyone."

I didn't try to convince her. I waited for her to convince herself.

"But I know I can trust you," she added after a minute. I winced, because eh.

"My dad is convinced Chloe's parents will try to sue us, even though my mom keeps telling him there's no case. And they had this whole big fight because he said something rude about her being *just* an intellectual property lawyer, and then *she* said—blah, never mind. Sorry. What I wanted to say is that finally my mom called one of her friends who does practice the right kind of law, and the friend said . . ."

The faucet turned up higher, thundering through the

phone like a waterfall. What did her parents think she was up to in there?

Her voice came through, low. "I'm not sure it was legal for him to have told my mom this, so you *really* can't repeat it. But something happened at Chloe's old school. I don't want to say too much, but there are *police reports*. Chloe was a bully, but the kind they make, like, Netflix shows about. And you know what? I'm not even surprised. She's so pretty and she has really good clothes but I got this feeling, being around her? Like, I can't really explain it, but . . . okay. I was the one who woke up in the middle of the night on Saturday and saw that she was gone. I heard this noise in the kitchen. But before going down there, the *first* thing I did was go to my parents' room. And it wasn't to tell them, you know? It was because I needed to see that they were both okay."

"Wow," I said quietly. "I'm really sorry."

"Thank you. Don't tell anyone any of that."

"I won't. And—I really hope your parents let you come home soon. We have your spare key somewhere, if you want me to mail any of your stuff? Or I could drive it to you."

"That's so nice of you, Nora," she said sincerely. "But I'm okay. My parents keep buying me clothes and books and everything, because they didn't give me enough time to pack. And because they feel guilty. It's starting to seem kind of weird, to be honest, the way they keep saying yes? Hopefully we'll be home soon. But I guess it's been pretty good just reading and doing nothing for a few days."

It was comforting hearing her natural positivity rebound in real time. I made a note to invite her out for coffee or something when she got back. Not that Piper drank coffee.

"Well. I'm glad you're mostly okay. And that your parents are mostly okay. You can call me, if you ever want to talk."

"I can?" She sounded so pleased I felt guilty. "I will, then. Definitely. Bye, Nora."

"Bye, Piper."

I ended the call and leaned back, rubbing my temple with a fingertip.

"Was that Piper Sebranek?"

My sister stood in the crack between door and frame. It was too dark to see her face.

"*God*, Cat!" I switched on the lamp clipped to my headboard. "How long have you been standing there?"

Then I shut up, because, impossibly, her eyes were welling with tears.

"Hey, so. I think Beatrice might've told some people about Becca." Her voice wobbled. "Like, about her being missing. I think that's how it got around."

I sighed heavily. "No shit."

She came a step closer, wiping tears out of her lashes. "I'm really sorry. I wasn't lying when I said I only told Bea. *She* put it on the dive team thread."

I wasn't sure what to do. My little sister never cried, never panicked, never got too upset. She was like one of those baby toys that won't stay down no matter how much you push it. Cat ran with a crew of perpetually chlorinated girls who woke at four each morning by choice and liked to do superhuman feats like flip upside-down and rattle off ten handstand push-ups. She left for practice at five in the morning and didn't come home until dinner and half the time she'd already eaten Little Caesars in somebody's car.

All that was to say we *knew* each other, right down to childhood terrors and first words and how best to drive each other up the wall during long car rides, while also not really knowing each other at all. I felt that distance now, unsure whether to double down or to comfort her. And how to comfort her if I tried.

I shrugged. "It was gonna get out anyway. Now that the police are involved."

"So Becca's *missing* missing?" she said miserably.

"No one knows where she is, so—yeah."

Cat cursed, looking down. "I swear I thought she'd be back in like a day. I assumed she was just trying to scare you, so you'd be her friend again."

I hadn't even been sure she'd noticed Becca and I were fighting. "Hey," I said. "Can you keep a secret? For real this time."

Her face brightened. "Yes. I promise. I really can."

Still I hesitated. Our mom was a dreadful gossip, and Cat had more of that than she could admit. I looked at her ready expression and thought of whatever I said next finding its way onto her group text, then into the world.

And I didn't say the dangerous thing I was dying to put into words. I didn't ask her: What if Becca isn't just a part of this? What if Becca is the *heart* of this?

"Becca left stuff for me," I said instead. "Like, clues. A note and a photograph and a roll of film."

She crossed the room to sit gingerly on my bed. "Damn. The police are looking for her, and she's playing scavenger hunt."

"Cat."

She exhaled. "I guess it's a good thing. At least you know

she wasn't kidnapped or something. It's just hard to believe she'd choose to leave you, like, unattended."

My stomach turned over. "That's a weird way to put it. She's basically left me *unattended* for the past three months."

"Uh, no, she hasn't. She drives by the house all the time. Or bikes. Or walks by on the path. You didn't know that?"

"No," I said faintly. "Does she really? Someone should've told me."

Cat picked at her thumbnail, red creeping up her neck. "You can't be that surprised. You know Becca thinks you belong to her. If she didn't creep around checking on you all the time, we might actually become friends."

"We?" I looked at her, startled. "Like, you and me?"

"Well, yeah." She wouldn't look back.

"That's—Cat, that's ridiculous. You're my sister."

"Exactly. I'm her biggest competition."

I opened my mouth, reaching for a denial that wouldn't come. Cat was still, waiting for me to absorb what she'd said.

"Becca is difficult," I said at last.

"That's an understatement."

"She's had it *rough*. That's an understatement, too."

"I know," she said softly.

I was leaning against the headboard, facing her profile. She sat at the edge of the bed, feet on the floor. "I'm sorry," I said.

"Okay."

There was more to say, so much that I fell silent in the face of it. But she didn't leave. So I said something I *did* have the courage for.

"Have you ever played the goddess game?"

Her face did a weird thing, this electric pulse of surprise. "Where'd that come from?"

"I know, it's random."

"No, I mean, I was just talking about that today. A bunch of us were, at practice."

"Really? What were you saying?"

She turned her eyes to the ceiling, thinking. "I don't remember how it came up. Naomi—she's a junior—was telling us about two girls playing it in the hotel pool during a meet last year. It ended in this big fight, one of the girls accusing the other of trying to kill her. We were all saying how it's kind of shocking no one's ever died playing the goddess game."

A sound came out of me, involuntary.

She narrowed her eyes. "What?"

"I don't know," I said hoarsely. "I'm just . . . I'm messed up, Cat." When I lifted a hand to push my hair back, it was trembling. "Can you look at me a sec?"

I squared my shoulders. "Do I look weird to you?"

Her pupils jittered, taking me in. Our faces were similar, only she got my dad's blue eyes, his squared-off jaw. And she was infused with a kind of core comfort with herself that even my spiraling couldn't shake.

She blinked a few times and said, "You look tired." Then she leaned way over and hugged me. The angle was awkward, the hug was all elbows. We didn't have a lot of practice.

"Hey." My sister spoke in my ear. "You know I don't love Becca. But I don't think this is just her being manipulative. Making you run around worrying about her. There's something else going on."

My heart felt shimmery in my chest, unstuck. "Like what?"

"I don't know." She was almost whispering. Not a gossipy whisper. The sound of someone genuinely afraid of the words they're saying. "But I think it's something nobody's thought of yet. Something nobody's saying."

I nodded, chin wedged into her shoulder. "I think so, too."

We stayed quiet awhile, each of us imagining our own version of a thing too big and strange to be spoken. Something that could explain four near-strangers dropping off the earth at once.

CHAPTER TWENTY—FIVE

I DIDN'T TALK MUCH DURING dinner. Usually my mom was chatty and pleased when she had both her daughters at the table, but tonight she was quiet, too. At one point my dad said, "Any word from Becca?" and my mom said, "I think she'd have let us know, Paul." And that was the end of that.

"How's the pain flare?" I asked as my mom stood to help clear the table.

"Better," she said, not quite looking at me. And it was, I could see by the way she moved. Then she nodded at my plate and said, "Hunger strike?"

I looked, too. Chicken in cream sauce over yellow rice and bright boiled carrots. I'd moved it all around, cut the chicken into little pieces. The few bites I'd taken had sickened me.

"Sorry," I said.

When the kitchen was clean, everyone headed off to their corners, I lingered. A strange sensation rolled through me, glittering everywhere, then compacting in my gut. It was so intense it took me a minute to identify it as hunger.

I stood at the counter dipping a spoon in peanut butter, then in honey, and licking it clean on unhygienic repeat.

When the honey was gone I ate half a pack of stale chocolate wafers. It wasn't enough.

You look tired, my sister said. But had there been something in her eyes? A certain widening? And my mother. Had she looked at me at all?

My stomach made a sound it had never made before. I went to stand in front of the pantry. On its bottom shelf were baking supplies: white sugar, brown sugar, a can of sweetened condensed milk. I surveyed them with a sense of doom.

Then I shut the pantry firmly, went to the sink, and filled a glass. I drained and refilled it. I drank water until my stomach hurt, until I could hear it sloshing, until I didn't have space for anything more.

When I got back to my room I had another text from Ruth. A link to an article from the *Chicago Tribune*, posted an hour ago.

Four vanish in northwest suburb

The article was short. It gave their names, their ages, the general timeframe of their disappearances. It stated that three were students at Palmetto High School and one was a teacher. My breath came in hard bursts as I skimmed it, her name catching my eye like a fishhook. *Rebecca Horner Cross, 17.*

The whole thing was matter-of-fact, empty of prurience or speculation. But it was undeniable. In black and white it laid out the terms. One town, one night. Four people gone.

CHAPTER TWENTY-SIX

I SHOWERED AGAIN BEFORE BED. The Band-Aid peeled off my finger and the cut beneath it opened like a rippled white mouth. Disgusting. Hotter, I thought. Hotter. Turning the water up and closing my eyes, breathing in the steam. When I looked down my skin was the boiled red of a sunburn and I could just barely see a bruise on my chest.

I turtled back to really see it, the way you do when you're trying to do up a necklace clasp. Then I realized it wasn't one bruise, it was four, starting above my left breast and going down. Little black smudges like I'd run hard into some obstruction. But what?

Hotter.

The word rattled in my skull. The water was hot enough, I could hardly breathe. The longer I stood there the more the thought seemed like a cockroach that had crawled into my ear, in me but not *of* me.

Fast, I turned the water all the way to cold. It rained down on my skin and I swear I didn't even shiver. I could barely feel it. But inside me, that funny little rubber-band recoil.

I turned the water off and climbed out, and didn't look at the mirror.

I crawled into bed knowing I would have a bad dream. About Becca or Kurt or Logan Kilkenny, a dream with the texture of life.

I was half-right. My dream was about no one I knew or had ever seen. But it felt as real as walking through my own room.

In the dream I stood in a bar lit by shaded bulbs and a red-and-blue Strongbow sign. Fewer than a dozen drinkers were scattered around the booths, the bar, the beat green pool table. All of them looked as if they'd just climbed off some grueling night bus.

I moved among them, peering into their faces. Some looked back, irritated or wary. Others turned from me. I didn't know what I was looking for until I found it in the face of the seventh man.

A shadow, just like I'd seen in Logan Kilkenny. Not exactly visible but there, like a star that only shows in your peripheral vision. In the hardness of his eyes I saw challenge, in the curl of his mouth invitation. But I couldn't take his features in all at once.

The dream folded and now the man was outside. Dim mosquito light, two dumpsters pushed against a brick wall and his wiry body between them. The shadow in his face stood out more in the dark.

Until then I couldn't feel my body in the dream. But I found I had feet to plant myself before him. I had hands to grab at the front of his sweat-stained T-shirt. A mouth I could feel turning up in a smile.

Something about the feel of smiling, so small inside the landscape of sleep, made me know I was dreaming. I twisted in the yoke of it, struggling to shrug it off. And with a physical wrench, I woke.

I was sitting upright. My feet were pressed to the floor, my hand curled around something hard and thin. It was dark still and I wasn't in bed. All was quiet, but my ears echoed with sound.

For a few seconds I shivered and blinked, hunched against fear like an animal. Then I started to take in the waking world.

I was at the kitchen table. Thin moonlight came through uncovered windows. The thing in my hand was a pen, and our old ceramic napkin holder lay on the tile in pieces. I'd knocked it off the table. The crash must have helped wake me.

I whimpered. The sound snapped me back to reason.

I wasn't hurt. I was fine, I was safe in my house. I'd never walked in my sleep before, but it was a thing, right? A thing people did? There was, I realized, a piece of paper in front of me, scrawled with a line of black scratches.

Words. It was too dark to read them. They were scarier to me than a knife would've been, waiting between my hands. I understood I'd been writing them before I woke, and flung the pen away. It rolled and settled on the floor.

With two fingers I lifted the paper, a sheet peeled from a Marriott scratchpad. I tipped it toward the window until I could read the words.

play g gm rembr

The letters were all lowercase, and it wasn't my handwriting. It wasn't anyone's. It was too erratic. My heart was pounding so hard I could hear it, a slick, sick whumping. I was right-handed, but I'd been holding the pen in my left. Like *she* did. I peered through the dark.

"Becca?" I whispered.

I was alone.

AS FAR BACK AS SHE could remember, Becca had been aware of a grand and secret world overlaying the one everyone else saw. It spoke in a language of shadow and light, of pooling energies she could almost trace with a finger.

But she didn't have the gift to explain it in words. When she looked for the first time through a camera lens, she felt like an alien finally receiving a translator.

Then she and Nora created the goddess of revenge. And Becca discovered a *third* layer to the world. One that, she suspected, almost no one got to see.

They'd done something magnificent, built a vengeful force out of little but film and fury. The goddess who ended the life of her mother's murderer. But Nora was so terrified by what they'd made that, in order to protect her, Becca had to let her believe it was a *coincidence*.

Maybe that was the ultimate unbridgeable thing. Together they'd done something that should have changed the nature of their souls. But in closing her eyes to the truth, Nora kept her soul unchanged.

Becca, possessing an altered soul, was able to accept that what she witnessed in the woods wasn't evil. It wasn't profane. It was, simply, *too much at once*. Now understanding was coming to her at the proper pace.

Each night she visited the blue cottage at the edge of the trees. Each night she heard another chapter in a story that kept changing genres: love to horror to revenge and back again.

This impossible tale, and all the discoveries that came with it, snapped in her mind's eye like the pennant of a new country, as yet unmapped. But it weighed heavily on her, too. Some days it seemed a slinking thing with a hidden face, and paws that tracked damp dark prints across her life.

Because the thing about the story was, it needed a new protagonist. Someone with a transformed soul and an eye for dark and light, and enough bruises that she had learned to make herself numb.

CHAPTER TWENTY — SEVEN

IN THE MORNING THE PAPER was on my desk where I'd left it. Like a black eye, it looked worse in daylight.

play g gm rembr

Play goddess game remember.

A response of sorts to the note Becca gave me, via James. But what did it mean?

Better question: What was happening to me? Why was I writing myself notes in the night, and why, when I woke in the kitchen, had I felt Becca's presence so powerfully? Even now I could almost smell the jasmine scent of her shampoo.

My altered appetite, my face unfamiliar in the mirror. These haunted dreams, so utterly real they made my waking hours seem dimmer. I didn't know how to talk about any of it out loud.

And who would believe me, anyway? Not my parents. They'd get that pained look on their face, that *Nora's lying again* look.

No. That wasn't true. They would soothe me, fear for me. But they wouldn't be able to *help* me. I had to see

James, we had to develop the film. I didn't have his number, which meant going to find him in person.

I got dressed. I was halfway to school when I realized I hadn't done much more than that. My face was unwashed, my teeth unbrushed. In the parking lot I pillaged my mom's glove box and did my best with a wet wipe and the nub of a dusty rose lipstick. There was half a bag of Hershey mini bars in there and I ate them, businesslike and fast.

I moved toward class in a fog of my own thoughts, not seeing what was actually in front of me, until someone stepped into my path and said, "You're friends with Rebecca Cross, right?"

She was younger than me, with a sly smile and straight black hair. Behind her, more girls stood in a little knot, watching us. I stared at her without speaking, until her boldness shifted into uncertainty and her eyes dropped. "I hope she's okay," she muttered, and moved away.

After that I didn't stop for anyone.

Mrs. Sharra wasn't in the room when I got to first-period chemistry. A trio of boys clustered around the whiteboard. I ignored their sniggering until the one holding a dry-erase marker said, "Aliens, sex ring, serial killer . . . what else?"

"The Blip!" called Opal Shaun.

The boy laughed and turned back to the board. His name was Kiefer and his arm ran with all these thin colored bracelets. Supposedly they had to do with the people he'd hooked up with and the things they'd done, but I was vague on the details. He'd probably made them up.

Opal pulled out her phone. "Nah, put me down for sex ring. I'm paying you right now."

That was when the words on the board came into focus.

Serial Killer. Mr. Tate Sex Ring. The Upside Down. Alien Abduction. The Blip. Next to each was a name or two. Sex ring had five.

It was a betting pool. They were putting money on what had happened, or was still happening, to the missing people.

I lost time. Just a little bit. I was at my desk, then I was standing next to Kiefer. He wore a knit cap over dirty blond hair and I yanked it off with enough force that he yelled, "Ow, what the *hell?*" and I knew some hair had come with it. I smeared the hat across the board, wiping away the betting pool. Then I threw it in his face.

"You know nothing," I snarled.

The room had been bubbling with *ooooohs* and laughter. Now it fell silent. Kiefer blinked at me with what looked like honest concern.

I blinked back, because something was happening to my sight.

I saw Kiefer's narrow jaw and his hazel stoner's eyes. I saw his messed-up hair and the dent in the middle of his bottom lip that made lots of people want to kiss him. But there was something else in his face. Something more.

I grabbed his wrist. To steady myself, I thought. But that wasn't true. In the moment, it was instinct: I knew that touching him would help me understand that unnamable *more*.

It wasn't like the shadow I saw in my dreams, veiling the faces of Logan and the wiry stranger. It was fluid, unsettled, a mist with truths glittering in it. Kiefer's weakness was there, and his vanity, which together made him easily led. I saw his fear, and his pride in the wrong things. I saw the pettiness he might grow out of, and selfishness born of having less than he pretended to.

And I saw shame. Shame in the proper measure, balanced neatly against his sins. I understood that it worked like a scouring fire, burning away that sin.

I wasn't looking for shame. I was looking for the shameless.

The thought jabbed me like a needle. It made an actual pain in my head. I dropped Kiefer's wrist and put a hand to the place where the pain had come and gone. He was gaping at me, and by their silence I knew everyone else was, too.

Very quietly he said, "What just happened?"

My vision was throbbing like I'd stared into a very bright light. When I pressed my palms to my eyes everything color-reversed in the dark. Someone put an arm around me and I thought it was Kiefer until she spoke.

"Why are you all just sitting there?" Mrs. Sharra snapped as she led me to the door. "Opal, get her things."

Out in the hall she stopped, letting me breathe and blink until the throbbing receded. Opal stood beside us, my bag hanging from her fingers.

"Good. Better." Mrs. Sharra set a hand, featherweight, between my shoulder blades. Once she was satisfied she turned to Opal. "Take her to the nurse's office, then come right back."

When Sharra was gone Opal held my bag out wordlessly. I took it. As we walked she kept sneaking glances at me, until I said, "*What?*"

Opal had the weirdest look on her face. We'd been going to the same school since we were five, but right then it was like she'd never seen me before. She said, "What was that? When you grabbed him, what did you . . ."

"What did I what?"

I must've sounded too eager. "Never mind," she muttered. "Come on."

"No, tell me."

"I said never *mind*."

"Opal, just . . ."

I reached for her arm, trying to make her face me. She jumped back so fast she tripped on nothing and fell hard to the floor.

For a second she just sat there, looking stunned. "You okay?" I put out a hand. "You need help?"

"Not from you." She scrambled to her feet and took off. I watched until she hit the corner and veered out of sight.

Opal Shaun was unpredictable. One of those people who'll do anything to be popular. She'd drive a bus over last week's best friend if that was the quickest route to a better lunch table. Anyone ill-informed or foolish enough to get close to her lived in fear. But when I reached for her *she* was scared. I liked it.

The nurse gave me a cup of paper-tasting water and two white tablets and disappeared. I swallowed the pills, then lay flat on my back.

I felt my pulse moving with a slow liquid repetition, like juice glugging out of a bottle. I smelled the burnt-dust smell of the overworked radiator. The nurse was reading behind her crispy folding curtain and I could hear the hiss and flap of turning pages. But none of it seemed real. What was real was the dark unfolding I'd seen in Kiefer's face that made everything else look so flat. Opal's fear, as juicy and tangible as a section of orange, that was real.

And my own fear. Of the way what happened with

Kiefer echoed what happened in last night's dream. Of thoughts threaded into my mind that didn't feel like my own. That was real, too.

I planned to lie there for a few minutes, then slip away, but I'd barely slept since three a.m. I fell asleep.

When I woke James Saito was lying on the other cot. His feet were crossed at the ankles, his hands behind his head. He was watching the ceiling with such absorbed dreaminess I looked, too, half expecting to see clouds sliding across it.

After a minute he turned to look at me. When he saw I was awake he stood, refilled my paper cup, and handed it over. I drank it down.

"I heard you were in here," he said.

What had he heard? *You know that missing girl? No, the other one. Her weird best friend just went full* Exorcist *in chem class.*

My tongue felt thick. The aspirin I swallowed had made a small clear place in the center of the pain, but I could feel that it would crash in again soon. "I don't know," I began carefully, "what's happening to me."

It was too much to explain. James didn't make me. He just nodded and said, "Let's find out what's on the film."

CHAPTER TWENTY—EIGHT

WE TOOK THE FILM IN for one-hour printing. Miss Khakpour was out, the photo lab locked. I couldn't wait another day.

James' station wagon smelled of soft things, petals and powder. There was a green-and-pink embroidered tissue holder behind the gearshift, and in the backseat a folded walker. Nudging at my heels, stuck halfway under the passenger seat, was a pair of tiny women's Keds patterned with daisies. It was an easy guess that it was his grandma's car.

At Walmart we dropped the film with the surly twenty-something at the photo counter. I pivoted, walked a few paces, and dropped to the linoleum. James stood above me, uncertain.

"So just . . . here?"

I leaned forward so I could see around him. The surly guy was doing something behind the counter, out of sight. "I don't want to leave the film."

James sat beside me as a Beatles song came on through the overhead speakers. I closed my eyes and Mr. Cross was setting the needle of his record player down. Becca was singing to herself about the King of Marigold as she walked ahead of me down the hall.

I brought my knees up and rested my cheek across them. No one but James was close enough to hear, but I whispered anyway.

"It's her, James. It all comes back to her. She knew things about Kurt, and Mr. Tate, and I think even Chloe. Bad things. And I have this awful feeling. Like maybe she *did* something about it."

I opened my eyes to see him watching a square of worn-out floor. He looked troubled, absorbed. Not surprised, though. "Like what?"

"I don't know. But . . ." I hesitated. "I walked in my sleep last night. I've never done that before. I made it all the way to the kitchen, where I sat down and wrote myself a note. When I woke up—for a second I was sure Becca was there."

His fingers were doing this nervous thing on his knee, counting out a rhythmic tattoo. "What'd the note say?"

"It was like the note she gave you. It said, 'Play goddess game remember.'"

"Huh," he said softly. "Had you been dreaming about the game?"

I twitched. Seeing the dingy bar with its pool table and Strongbow sign, the stranger with the bad face. "I don't think so."

"Did you try going back to sleep, see if you'd write anything else?"

"I couldn't sleep after that."

"Tonight put a pen and paper next to your bed. That way, if it happens again, you won't have to get up."

His calm instructions were a rope thrown into dark water. "That's . . . a good idea. Thank you."

Two old women power walked past us, arms pumping.

Even that reminded me of Becca. I was tense, waiting for James to ask me what happened in class, trying to think how I'd even put it into words. But he didn't ask, and I relaxed by increments, until finally I felt calm enough to say, "Would you mind if I check something?"

He looked at me, expectant.

"Can I touch your wrist for a second?"

Without hesitation he held up his left hand, palm to the ceiling. I hadn't deliberately touched him since grabbing him by the arm on Monday and practically begging him to help me. Now I reached out tentatively, watching his face as I wrapped my fingers around his wrist.

My hand was cold, his wrist was warm. His curled fingers grazed my skin and I felt it all the way to my shoulder. But there was no psychic mist, no shadows. No rush of information that was impossible but felt so real. When I looked into his face, all I saw was him. Posture soft, mouth turned up a little at one corner. His eyes doing that focus thing, intensifying invisibly like water just off the boil.

"Thanks," I murmured, sliding my hand away.

He gave a half smile. "Get what you needed?"

"I don't know what I need." Then I laughed a little, hearing how pitiful I sounded. "Sorry, I'm—what I need is to talk about something else. At least until the photos are ready." I glanced at Surly, leaning against the counter now, staring blankly in our direction. I turned quickly back to James.

"You said—yesterday you told me you'd show me your favorite thing you've ever made. Sometime." I raised my brows at him. "How's now?"

"Oh." His hand moved to his pocket, cheeks reddening. "Yeah, I could show you." But he didn't take out the phone.

"You want to tell me about it first?"

James nodded. "Sure. So, uh. I'm a photographer."

I bit my lip. "I know."

"Right, of course. So I've always preferred taking photos of people. I want to work as a photojournalist one day. But then, a couple years back, I moved to Reykjavík." He paused. "Have you ever been?"

To *Reykjavík*? I couldn't think of a place that sounded farther flung. I tried to picture it and saw Björk standing on an iceberg. Or, wait, wasn't it Greenland that was so cold?

"Not yet," I said.

"I spent about a year there, right before Palmetto. The city, it's . . ."

He looked up, focus turning inward. And I thought, I like watching him think. I like watching him find the right words. Most people spend words like they're dirty pennies, myself included. Not James, though. His sentences were seaworthy.

"It feels," he said, "like a colony built on the moon. Wherever you are, you can feel this big empty wind blowing straight through it, like the city isn't even there." He showed me with his hand, moving in a push broom motion. "Like it's an illusion. I've never felt so lonesome as I did in Reykjavík. Not even here."

He was lonesome? But why would that surprise me? I'd already figured out he wasn't what I'd imagined him to be. "Why'd your family move there?"

"It's just me and my mom. We went to live with her girlfriend. Wife, now. My mom was a working artist in New York. In Iceland she's a spouse. Which—that's fine if it's what you want, but . . ." He shrugged. "It's fine. And my stepmom is fine. Warped utterly by inherited wealth, but. Fine."

"Sounds fine," I murmured. New York, he said. I *knew* he was from someplace big.

He smiled faintly. And now he did take out his phone. "I lived inside my head the whole year I was in Iceland. I read, I took long drives, just seeing, like, random waterfalls. And I took a *lot* of photos. I couldn't look at them for months after I left, but when I finally did, I felt proud. Not—I'm not saying they're good, but they're *right*. They feel exactly the way I felt when I lived there. So, here," he finished nervously.

We were both nervous as he pulled up a photo grid and handed it over. I wanted so badly to like what he was about to show me. I looked at the first image and breathed out with relief.

He was a real photographer. Like Becca. But where her shots were rich with information, James' were simple compositions taken from perfect angles. Each was framed like the first paragraph of a story. A block of pure blue window, hanging like a painting on the wall of a dim room. A stripe of sun over stone, sharply defined at one end and melting into prisms on the other. The corner of a bed, a book lying open on its smooth white sheets.

The images breathed petrichor, salt, that hot non-smell of fabric dried in the sun. Not one gave a concrete hint as to their location—no skylines or street signs or specific landmarks. Each was suffused with solitude.

He watched me sideways as I scrolled slowly through, with the look of someone who'd peeled their rib cage back to reveal their beating heart. I could've cried, but I wouldn't know who I'd be crying for. Becca or myself, James right now or the person he'd been when he framed the world into these lonesome photographs.

"They're so good," I said quietly.

His hair managed to be both silken and tangled, in this way that made me want to put my fingers through it. He pushed it out of his eyes. "Thank you."

I slipped past a picture of black sand, a solid square of it, rippled with tide marks. At the very bottom of the frame was a slight impression in the black, hinting that a person's feet were just out of sight.

The next image was of an old woman. She wore a jaunty blue hat thing over very short silver-white hair. Her smile was bright, her chin up in a way that said she enjoyed having her picture taken. When I looked at James, his eyes had softened. Even the line of his shoulders seemed tender.

"My grandma," he said. "I'd been in Iceland almost a year when she showed up at my stepmom's house. I felt like I was hallucinating. She and my mom had this big falling out, I hadn't seen her in three years. She hadn't been on a plane in forty. She's got mobility issues, she's scared of cities, Iceland might as well *be* the actual moon. But she was worried about me. I think she knew I wasn't actually going to school. So she came for me and she scraped me off the ground and she brought me home to Palmetto."

There was so much glittering in the gaps between his words, big swathes of story sifted like sand among floorboards. I put what he'd told me against what I'd thought of him before this week: that he seemed like a person moving between two better places, gliding through PHS like it wasn't a place he wanted to belong.

I felt a genuine ache, understanding it wasn't snobbery.

That maybe he didn't feel like he *could* belong. And I was the snob, who almost missed out on knowing him at all.

Before I could reply, I heard something that made my head snap toward the photo counter. A mechanical screech, then a hot *whoosh* that sent me to my feet.

Behind the counter, the photo printer was in flames.

FOUR MONTHS AGO

BECCA SAT IN THE KITCHEN of the egg-blue cottage. The windows were open and the breeze came in, edged with smoke and the vinegar tang of windfall apples.

It was late September now and time was moving very quickly. Becca fell like a plumb bob through her days. Mornings passed in a blink, evening bruised the edges of the afternoons. It was half past ten at night now, and there were two fresh cups of coffee on the table. The person sitting across from Becca waited for her to put her cup down before saying:

"Have you thought about who you'll choose?"

Becca's stomach tightened. She'd been anticipating the question, but it was different hearing it out loud.

Her companion went on. "When it's your choice to make, whose harm will you cut out of this world? Don't think about politicians, or someone you've seen on the news. This isn't a thought experiment. Think seriously, and just this first time, think close to home."

And Becca realized she *did* have an answer. Or a place, at least, to begin. A maybe-monster, very close to home.

A memory crept into the light.

Becca told her dad and Nora that she didn't join the PHS
art club because she wasn't a *club person*. And while it was
true she wasn't a joiner, that wasn't the real reason.

At fourteen Becca was a good photographer. Some days
she thought *really* good. And freshmen weren't allowed
free access to the darkroom unless they joined art club,
so. On a Wednesday, on a whim, she lingered at her locker
after ninth. Then, why not, she walked down to the art hall.
It was meeting day.

Voices came from the painting studio, and the sound
of the Talking Heads. When she got to the doorway she
stopped there. The room was full of intimidating older
kids, cross-legged on the tables, sprawled on the floor,
leaning over canted drawing desks. The room was warm,
David Byrne singing from a paint-stained cassette deck.

"You need something?" a girl called from the corner.
Becca looked at her and flushed.

The girl wore a boxy black T-shirt and denim shorts unraveling up the sides of her thighs. She was straddling a
boy with shaggy ash blond hair, giving him a back massage.
Her bare legs tensed on either side of his body, smooth and
shiny as two hot dogs. The boy lay flat across a drafting
table, but when the girl spoke he lifted his head, turning it
to see who she was talking to.

His face gave Becca a shock. It was the feeling of picking
up a piece of fruit to find its underside caved in with mold.
Because he wasn't a boy, he was a man. He was Mr. Tate.

"Hey, chica," he said casually. "You here to join the club?"

Becca never went back. Nor did she tell anyone what she'd
seen, not even Nora. All the cool art kids seemed fine with

it. She must've misunderstood—what teacher would do something that wrong in plain sight?

But she thought sometimes about the expression on Mr. Tate's face when he saw her. It was the alert look of someone caught doing something he shouldn't, followed by pure relief. Because it was just some freshman standing there, witnessing an underage student perched atop his adult ass, and what was *she* going to do about it?

For a long time the answer was nothing. But two years later Becca sat at a kitchen table drinking coffee and was asked a different question. *Who?*

It was easy to steal Tate's phone, after watching him unlock it enough times to catch the code. Its background photo was a *Spin* cover from twenty-plus years ago, of him and his band. She could almost feel sorry for Benjamin Tate.

Until she saw what was inside his phone.

CHAPTER TWENTY—NINE

I STARED FOR A FEW seconds at the photo machine, too stunned to speak. The surly counter guy leapt back, hollering, "Holy—fire!"

He catapulted himself over the counter with surprising ease. The equipment behind him was fully ablaze.

"Fire!" he yelled again, darting past kids' shoes.

"Ffff," James said. I think he was too surprised to finish swearing. We were on our feet now, watching flames issue in pale tongues from the mouth of the machine. Up, up, almost threatening the ceiling. Then abruptly they spent themselves, snapped out. Gone.

James found his tongue. "Fire does not act like that!" he yelled, the most rattled I'd ever heard him.

An older woman in Walmart kit was barreling toward us on sensible shoes, holding a red fire extinguisher. When she reached the counter she slowed, looking around then down at the machine. "What in the world," she said.

It wasn't even smoking. There was no odor of seared plastic or mechanical malfunction. The thing looked untouched.

"Are my photos okay?" I asked desperately.

"Your photos lit the machine on fire." That was Surly talking. He'd crept up behind me. A crowd was gathering, mostly old men and moms with little kids.

The woman gave Surly an exasperated look. "I'm so sorry," she told me. "You won't be charged."

"No. No, you don't understand." My voice cracked. "Those photos were important. I *need* them. Please, can you check? Are the negatives okay, can anything still be printed?"

A woman behind me said, "What are they, prom pictures?"

"It's not prom season," said another, then dropped her voice to a loud whisper. "Pictures for her boyfriend."

The first woman made a negative sound. "They do *that* with their phones."

The older employee hovered a hand over the machine like it was a cooling stove. Then she said, "Huh." She leaned over. A grunt and a tug and she stood victorious, a photo in each hand.

"Two printed before the, uh." She thought, then firmly said, "They're free of charge."

I grabbed them rudely and took off.

"Nora." James hustled along behind me. "*Nora.* Stop. I want to see them, too."

I was so upset I could barely look at him. "There's hardly anything to *see*."

"I know. I'm sorry."

I turned in a circle, then nodded toward the dressing rooms, empty and unmanned in the middle of the day. "Fine. Let's sit."

We picked the first stall. The bench was too small to fit us both so we sat on the floor, shoulders pressed together.

James was so close I could see him only in pieces. His good hands, that soft stretch of skin between his jaw and ear.

I held the measly two photos pressed tightly to my chest. They felt hot, almost, packed with potential. As I pulled them away I was bracing myself for her face, her light, that specific density of mood she packed into her photographs. But the first photo had none of that.

It looked like a movie still. Horror, low-budget.

You saw the trees first. Summer-dressed, looming out of the dark in a nightmare diorama. Deeper in, not fully in focus, were two figures. One had their back to the camera. A hooded jacket covered them up completely, dark bleeding into dark. The second figure was clearer, turned toward the place Becca must've been hiding: a thirtyish white man in a T-shirt and ball cap. Though his face was out of focus, you could see it was angry, mouth caught in the middle of snarling speech.

"Do you . . ." James began.

"No idea. You?"

He shook his head. My body coursed with frustration, confusion. I tried to glean *some*thing from the sight of these two strangers arguing in the woods. What had made Becca stop to spy on them?

I flipped to the second photo and sucked in a breath.

She'd moved closer. Her framing had changed, both figures now caught in profile. The first person's hood was pulled too far forward to catch any part of their face. But the man I could see perfectly.

His mouth was open, head thrown back. His arms drifted in a way that evoked a body caught in water. You could almost hear the scream.

His twisted face was chilling, but it wasn't the strangest

thing about the photograph. Moving from left to right you could see: the woods behind the man's bent back, fuzzing in and out of focus. The man himself. A stretch of about five feet, then the hooded person. And behind them, stretching all the way to the photo's right edge—nothing. A thick vertical strip of it, faintly warped, lined up exactly with the hooded person's back.

"Light exposure?" James murmured.

"No." I traced a finger along the black, showing him how it followed the shape of the person's body. And there were textures in it. A glistening, a strange undulation. It didn't look like a printing error, it looked like something *physical*, inside the shot. It looked like . . .

I tipped my head back, frowning. It almost looked as if it were coming from the hooded figure. Like a rippling cape, or a sweep of tall black wings. It wasn't in the first photo, just the second. What might a third have looked like? With a ravenous regret I longed to see the rest of the sequence.

I held the two photos up side by side. Taken in summer, judging by the lushness of the trees and the man's T-shirt sleeves. I pictured Becca on the other side of the camera, wearing her summertime uniform of cotton sundress and filthy Cons.

Then it clicked: I was imagining her as she looked that night last July, when I picked her up from the Fox Road lot. The nocturnal shine of her eyes when I caught her in my headlights. Camera around her neck, leg running red to the ankle.

She'd been running from something that night. Through the woods, busted knee but she kept on going. I'd bet she was running from *this*. Whatever these photos had captured. A screaming stranger, a covered face, and this stripe of rippling black. As if the hooded person stood on the lip of another world.

But why didn't she tell me then? Why wait half a year, then talk to me *this* way? She could've told me everything that night.

And I could've asked. There were so *many* things I didn't ask about. What really happened that night. What exactly she had against Kurt Huffman. And the *big* question, the one that went back to the very root of my avoidance: whether she truly believed our goddesses existed apart from us. Whether she thought they could exert real power on the world. Cause real damage.

Before the goddess of revenge we believed in magic together. *Made* it together. But afterward I shut the door. Locked and barred it, refused to hear any calls that came from behind it. Because if magic were real, wouldn't that mean I was an accomplice to Christine Weaver's violent death?

Don't play stupid, Becca said to me last October. *You're asking, but do you really want to know?*

I was ready, finally, to know. And once I stopped pushing away the impossible, the clues she'd left for me lined up with almost audible clicks. The rhyme to petition a shadowy local legend, the true mother of our goddess project. The knife that brought a bully down, cutting his Samson hair off his head. Prints of the two goddesses we made for her parents, when we believed ourselves capable of everything.

And this roll of film that captured something so vast and unearthly it set a fire rather than let its face be seen.

I got it now. Not the *answer* to the question of four people gone without a trace, but its nature. An impossible problem could only have an impossible solution.

"What do we think this is?" James was still bent over the pictures, oblivious to my revelations. "Not to sound like a mob movie, but what if she *witnessed* something?" He poked at the hooded figure. "What if they knew she saw?"

"Or." I pointed to that strip of dark. The most delicate black damask, unseeable things embroidered inside it. "What if whatever *that* is didn't want to be photographed."

He looked at me narrowly. "Didn't want."

"Like you said, that was not an ordinary fire."

"Okay." He was shaking his head. "It did seem weird. But . . . maybe that's what it looks like when photos burn."

"I can tell you it's not," I said hotly.

"Or photo *equipment*, I mean. I'm just saying, there's some kind of explanation."

"Or *not*." I had to make him see what I was seeing. "Just think about it—is anything going on here explainable?"

"Probably. Right?" He gave me a pleading look. "I want to help you. I want to find out what *could* be going on here. I mean, what it really *could* be."

"I know what you mean!" I stood too fast, got dizzy, and had to lean against the mirror. That just made me madder. At who, though? I didn't stop to think about it.

"You say you want to help me, but you're not even listening to what I'm telling you. The fire was not normal. Whatever is happening in this photo isn't normal. Nothing that's going on has a rational explanation. *God*." I rapped a fist against the glass. "Why would Becca bother getting you involved in this if you're not willing to see what she's trying to show us?"

He got a look on his face I couldn't quite read. "Do you really think solving this is why she threw us together? That's the *whole* reason?"

"What." I squinted at him. "Why else would she?"

James was still on the floor. He looked hyperreal against the buzzing dimness of the dressing room. "She didn't just give me a roll of film, she gave me a note, basically ordering me to talk to you."

"Ordering you." I knew my voice would tremble if I let it, so I made it hard. "Well, shit. I'm sorry. I didn't realize it was such an imposition."

"Are you serious?" He was looking at me like he'd never seen me before. "You're . . ."

"What?"

"Going through a lot," he finished flatly, and stood. "Any more errands you need me to run? Or can we go back?"

I had a slow sinking feeling I refused to look at or recognize. "I don't have any errands."

"Good. Let's go."

CHAPTER THIRTY

AFTER THE DARK TERRAIN OF the photographs, the parking lot was so sunlit it felt like a dream. Dirty snowdrifts and abandoned shopping carts, the desolate brightness of the Party City sign.

We didn't talk, not in the lot and not in the car. I stuck the photographs in my bag as he pulled into traffic. I didn't need to look at them again, they were etched into my mind. When we got back to PHS James parked, turned off the car, and said, "Hey."

I half-turned.

He watched the lot as he spoke. "I wasn't implying I won't keep helping you. I said I would. I *want* to."

I nodded without speaking. The whole ride I'd been re-running our conversation. *Do you really think solving this is why she threw us together? That's the* whole *reason?* What had he meant by that? Trying to figure it out filled me with a shimmering anxiety.

"What did you—" I began, but he cut me off.

"I need to think. Please."

Still he wouldn't look at me. "Got it," I said shortly, and let myself out.

*   *   *

It was halfway through my lunch period when I walked back through the school's side doors. I felt like I'd been away for days. Nothing had been decided by the two photos we'd managed to get developed, nothing fixed. When I thought of James sitting in his car, *thinking*, I had this intense feeling of preemptive loss. For a thing I didn't even have.

And when I thought about Becca I just felt helpless. That moment of clarity in the Walmart had collapsed into nothing. All I'd really figured out was that everything was even bigger and stranger than I feared.

But I couldn't do anything about it right now. I walked to the cafeteria.

When I dropped my tray onto their table—cherry yogurt cup, sweetened iced tea, bag of Famous Amos, one of those packaged crumble-top muffins that's always mysteriously damp—Ruth and Amanda looked up with identically cagey expressions. Amanda smiled, close-mouthed.

"Nora. How are you?"

Scared. Sad. Facing the rapid disintegration of reality as I understood it. "Good." I popped a cookie in my mouth and spoke around it. "Hey, Ruth. Hey, Sloane."

Ruth raised a brow. Her hot monosyllabic girlfriend, Sloane, up-nodded imperceptibly. Sloane was six feet tall. She played the standing bass and looked like Joey Ramone and based on the handful of times I'd heard her speak at any length her brain was as vast and wild as a nebula. But good luck getting her talking.

"We heard what happened in class," Ruth said.

I swallowed. "What'd you hear?"

"That you told Kiefer Shitforbrains to go fuck himself, then had a breakdown."

"Huh. Pretty close, actually." I peeled back the wrapper on the gross addictive muffin.

They were still staring at me. Amanda shook her head, laughing a little. "Yeah?" she said to Ruth, who nodded.

"Yeah."

Ruth squared up, focusing on me in her unnerving way. She was wearing a white oxford buttoned to the neck, its collar so crisp you could file your nails on it. She'd styled her overgrown bangs into a pompadour. "May I say something?"

I *tch*ed. "Could I stop you?"

Ruth pursed her lips, then chose the high road. "You're *part* of this, Nora. This whole story. But you seem to think no one can see you. Everyone knows you got questioned by the police about Becca. Everyone knows you had a . . ." She thought. "Weird incident, in class. Everyone's talking about Becca and them, but they're talking about you, too. And Sierra and Madison and everyone at that sleepover Chloe Park was at. This is *out* there. Like, nationally. There's a . . ." She looked apologetic. "There's a hashtag."

"There is?"

"Ew," Sloane muttered.

Ruth went on unrelentingly. "It'll get worse before it gets better. You can't keep trying to push through this alone. You need to start asking for help from your friends. Let us *help* you. Let us stand by you." She leaned in. "Let us share information."

"You're gonna write something about this, aren't you."

Ruth shrugged, unembarrassed. "Eventually. Aren't you? I was wrong when I mocked our silly classmates for getting weird about this. It's worth getting weird about. What is going *on*?" Her face was all sparky, she was practically rubbing her hands together. "Just practically speaking, all the theories so far are unworkable. Does anyone really think *Mr. Tate* could've lured three people from three different places and taken them out of town? Do they actually believe he has the personal charisma to pull off a sex cult?"

Sloane said, "Ruthie."

Ruth glanced at her and reset, some of the hungry shine going out of her eyes. "The answer isn't obvious, but it's there. And I don't think the police or some newspaper's going to figure it out. But I bet we could. We go to school here, we *know* these people."

"We do?" I said. "I know one of them, out of four."

"I took Intro to Art with Tate," she said defensively.

"All right, Ruthless." Amanda was watching us coolly, scooping hummus into her mouth with popcorn chips. Now she smiled at me, kind but firm. "Whatever else is true, you're walking around looking like someone just set off a firework in your face. You're ditching class and yelling at Kiefer Fucknuts and skulking around like Hamlet."

"I'm *skulking*?"

"Yes. You're not invisible. I know we're not Becca, let us help you anyway." She elbowed Ruth. "Even if you don't want to share notes with J. J. Hunsecker over here. Even if it's just walking with you between classes, in case people start getting in your face. Okay?"

I chugged half a can of iced tea. Its dull sweetness made my molars pulse, and I still felt like crying when I was through. They let me eat lunch with them, but until right then I hadn't been sure Ruth and Amanda were my actual friends. "Okay. Thank you."

Ruth's eyes went beady. "Good. So, I've been doing

some digging. Did you know a student disappeared from PHS in the nineties?"

"Logan Kilkenny," I said.

She was only briefly stalled. "Right. Well, what about the teacher, back in the sixties?"

"What, went missing? Just a teacher?"

"*Just* a teacher?"

I lifted a shoulder. "I mean, they could've . . . moved to California or something. Left their wife. Husband. I bet it was super easy to disappear back then."

Ruth considered that. "True. But people tend to wash up eventually, if they're alive."

If they're alive. I tapped a nail against my lunch tray. Maybe I had it wrong, going about this in such a personal way. What if the key to unraveling all of it *wasn't* in the clues Becca left me? What if Ruth was on the right track, looking at it from the outside, like a journalist?

I said, "What about the girl who died here?"

Amanda made a face. "Here as in the *school*?"

"Brutal," Sloane said, and Ruth lit up with unhealthy curiosity. "Tell me."

I told her what I'd heard from James. "I don't know her name, though. Or whether it's true."

"So we find her name. We figure out if it's true."

"There's a possibility," I said, "that this girl might have to do with the goddess game."

Ruth's brow went straight up, like it was on a jack. "Have to do with. As in, she might *be* the story? That the game is based on?"

Amanda put her elbows on the table, face avid. "There's an actual girl in that story?"

"I don't know for sure."

She nodded at Ruth. "Look at her. She wants to run to the nearest library, start digging through the basement files."

Amanda was right, Ruth did look itchy. "Hey." Sloane put a hand on her knee. "Eat."

Ruth patted Sloane's hand absently. "No, but think of it. People die. Sometimes badly, sometimes young. There are tragedies every day, everywhere. But there's a death in our town's history that for some reason became legendary. In a literal sense. Maybe it started with this girl you heard about, maybe not. But she's worth finding, if she's real. God, why didn't I ever think to look into it?" Then her head snapped up. "Yearbooks."

"Yearbooks?" Amanda echoed.

"In the school library. They go back to the fifties, I think. Remember when we were freshmen, that girl who overdosed on Oxy? There was a memorial page in the year-book. We might find other memorials from way back, at least get some names to look into."

She cadged a jalapeño slice off the dregs of her girl-friend's nacho boat and stood. "Now I literally am off to the nearest library. Hope you're happy, Manda. Nora, you coming?"

Sloane shook her head fondly. "Bloodhound."

I stood, feeling a little bulldozed. Like I had a type, friendwise. I followed Ruth out the cafeteria doors.

CHAPTER THIRTY—ONE

"THEORETICALLY," RUTH SAID. "WHAT DO *you* think happened Saturday night?"

I'd just tipped half a bag of mini cookies into my mouth, and swallowed painfully before answering. "I'm trying to figure that out. Skulking all the way."

We were walking to the library the long way, to avoid going past the monitor at the front security desk. "'Goddess, goddess,'" she said under her breath. "It keeps coming up, doesn't it? That stupid game. You lied, by the way, you poker-faced faker. You've totally played."

I put my hands up like, *You got me.* "What do you expect? I'm Nora Powell, the compulsive liar of Palmetto Elementary."

"Well, *I'm* not in your grade," she said starchily. "You can't fool me. What happened, did someone get hurt when you played?"

I laughed. "I've played twice. First time I needed stitches in my head. Second time, I think I almost died."

"You *think*. Maybe don't play a third time." She bumped my elbow with hers.

"How about you? You said you played once."

"I did say that, didn't I."

There were ten minutes left before the end of class, the halls were empty. But she lowered her voice enough that I had to lean in. "Before Sloane I dated this girl. One of those *prove you love me* types—big scenes, high drama. *Gorgeous.* Obviously.

"Her parents were divorced and her dad had this terrible divorced-man houseboat. And a mullet and a gambling problem, but that's not part of the story. He let us stay on the boat one night, just the two of us, and my ex manufactured this big fight. It ended with her locking herself in the tiny bathroom. I'd have left, but it was after the last train, so I stayed. I fell asleep on this weird built-in couch thing, with like a life jacket for a pillow. We'd gotten pretty drunk, so I was *out*. Until my ex woke me up in the night. It was dark except for these strip lights, and she was holding a handgun. And she says something like, 'I don't think you love me the way I love you, but I'm gonna let you prove me wrong. We're playing the goddess game.'"

My nerve endings shrilled.

"She pointed the gun at my head. Before I could move she said, 'I love you,' and pulled the trigger. It made that empty click sound, just like in the movies. Then she handed it to me like I was about to do the same thing to her. And I *barreled* past her, up onto the deck, and threw the gun into Lake Michigan. I would've gotten off the boat but she'd taken it way out over the water while I was sleeping. The city looked amazing. The stars were out of control. Once the gun was gone I could notice all that.

"By then she was crying and telling me she was sorry,

the gun was empty all along, her dad's gonna kill her for losing it, on and on. I felt like a salt pillar just staring at the stars, I could not care less what she had to say. Finally she sobered up and took us back to shore, and I got off and walked straight to Union Station."

By then we were standing outside the library, leaning against the wall so she could talk without looking at me. It seemed like that kind of story.

"The thing that broke my heart was this girl was my friend back in grade school, before either of us had come out. I used to, like, turn the rope for her when she jumped. We did Brownies together. But, I don't know. Her parents suck and she got messed up about love.

"Anyway," Ruth finished. "Life is hard enough. We all get hurt without trying. And that was the first and *last* time I played the goddess game." She gave me a wry look. "Now. Let's go depress ourselves further digging through yearbooks for dead people."

The PHS yearbooks were shelved in the very back row, facing the window. They were sun-bleached and ugly as hell, bound in synthetic maroon pretending to be leather. They'd been exactly that tacky all the way back to 1951.

"I'll take the fifties to start," Ruth said briskly. "You take the sixties. We'll go from there."

It started out fun. The hairstyles, the clothes, the curious way midcentury girls looked like smooth-skinned old women, while the boys all looked like nine-year-olds dressed up as salesmen. Things started to loosen up around 1963. The hair got longer, the smiles less tight. I'd found two memorial pages by then, one for a boy wearing heavy computer programmer glasses, the other for a teacher with an astounding bouffant.

My hands were dusty, my throat dry. By the end of 1964 I needed a break. I rolled my shoulders, doing a little math, then pulled down the books from my mom's student years.

I found her first in 1992, a big-eyed adorable freshman. A year later she was a sullen sophomore wearing a turtleneck under an open flannel. Junior year she tied her hair into two knots high on her head and wore overalls and dark lipstick. Senior year my grandma must've stepped in, because she was wearing tortoiseshell hoops and a dress with a sweetheart neckline. She was Laura Mason back then. I centered my phone over her picture-day smile, then remembered: her senior year had been haunted by the vanishing of Logan Kilkenny.

I put my phone aside and scanned the Ks, but of course he was gone by the time photo season rolled around. The picture I'd seen in the paper would've been from his junior year. I flipped to the front of the book, and there it was. A two-page spread.

I wasn't sure how it worked with disappearances, whether and when you pronounced someone legally dead. But it wasn't quite a memorial. Logan's name was written in a vaguely churchy font across the middle of the spread, some of its letters lost in the binding. Below it were the words, *Whoever lives by believing in me will never die.—John 11:26.*

Circling the text was a photo collage showing Logan at all ages. He was a baby lying on a blue blanket, a toddler grinning in a Cubs hat. A lanky boy standing with, presumably, his family: two tall, tan parents and two equally handsome younger brothers. Twins, I thought. He was a teenager jumping to catch a Frisbee, lounging on a ski lift, leaping off a dock with a girl in a red bikini, her blonde hair a cloud around her face and their hands linked. I wondered if the girl, all exposed skin and flying yellow hair, had given her permission for the photo to be printed.

I checked the index to see if he showed up anywhere else. A whole string of page numbers appeared next to his name; the yearbook staff must've used everything they had. Some photos, according to the captions, were from previous years. I flipped around looking at Logan swinging a baseball bat; wearing an ill-fitting suit and shooting craps as Sky Masterson; sitting on the grass in a Phish T-shirt with his arm around a blonde girl, beaming at the camera.

Recognition hit me so hard and squarely I looked fast at Ruth, as if she might've felt it, too. She was turning pages methodically, head down, still working her way through the beehives and bowties of fifties Palmetto.

I looked back at the girl in the picture. Logan was smiling but her expression was pensive. I knew her face. She was in the dream I'd had about Logan, dancing beside him, shaking her head *No* when he gestured at her to come smoke. I'd never seen her before then, I *knew* I hadn't, not ever. Only in my dream. If I'd thought about it at all, I'd have assumed I made her up.

Below the photo, in tiny print: *Logan Kilkenny and Emily O'Brien have some fun in the sun.*

Emily O'Brien. According to the index she appeared in two other photos, though I'd bet she was also the jumping girl in the red bikini.

I looked at her senior photo first. At some point between having some fun in the sun and getting the photo taken, she'd cut off her blonde hair. The cut was striking, severe, her expression somber.

It made sense. If she'd been Logan's girlfriend, she would've spent the rest of the year being treated like a celebrity widow. Some people would like the attention. I bet Emily wasn't one of them. I looked at the photo a while, then turned to the final place she appeared in the book.

My heart gave a hot little rush. I was looking at a photo of the lit mag staff. The crew was slightly bigger back then, six people. And off to the side, looking both amazingly young and exactly the same, was Miss Ekstrom.

Thirty years ago her folksinger hair was brown. She wore wide-legged trousers with a vest top, and glasses even bigger and squarer than the ones she had now. The look was probably dorky at the time, but in retrospect seemed kind of cool. She was looking not at the camera but at the kids, her features vivid with pride.

I studied each face. These could've been my friends if I were born at a different time. A spooky-looking girl with circle specs and a boy doing a Cobain thing, long blond hair and a flower-print dress. A grinning kid with a skinny teen 'stache and a girl with relaxed hair and her hands up like a boxer, so you could see the straight-edge X inked on the back of each. A lounging boy in a white T-shirt working a super self-conscious James Dean thing, one hundred dollars down on his being a poet. And Emily O'Brien, so different here she was almost unrecognizable.

In this picture, Emily *glowed*. She was mugging for the camera: open-mouth smile, freeze-frame high-fiving mustache boy. Her other arm was slung around the shoulders of the straight-edge girl.

With fresh eyes I flipped back to the shot of her and Logan. Her face was turned toward him, but the rest of her pointed away: knees bent and tipped onto the grass, one arm wrapped protectively across her body, hands laced tightly together.

You could look at them and think, happy boy with an arm around his shy and pretty girlfriend. Or you could see what I did. A boy radiating entitlement and ease, using one muscled arm to anchor in place a girl whose entire body was straining to be away.

Back to the lit mag photo. Ekstrom proud as a mother hen surveying her brood. Emily surrounded by people who made her beam with confidence.

In my dream I'd watched Logan dance with Emily, then walk through the crowd and away, toward some uncertain fate. A darkness in his face, like the aftereffect of a photo flash.

It was the same darkness I'd seen when I dreamed of a stranger in a nameless bar. That hovering rottenness I searched for in Kiefer's face and couldn't find. The mark of shamelessness. The mark, I thought with an icy dread, of *bad people*.

What *were* these dreams I'd been having, of such needle-fine clarity? What did they signify, and what the hell else would I have seen if I hadn't woken up?

Their shadowy faces mixed and blurred, smearing like fresh paint. There was a thread I was reaching for, some greater idea yanking itself fishlike from my grip. I felt a numbness crawling up my arms, down my legs, until my whole body felt heavy. My hands tingled, and when I slapped them hard on the table I couldn't feel them at all. I closed my eyes, just for a second. I drifted.

"Hey. *Hey*."

Ruth kneeled in front of me, gripping my hands. The yearbook was sprawled on the floor and I was sitting beside it. I'd dropped into the dark again.

"What happened?" she said tensely. "Low blood sugar?"

I could answer honestly. Tell her everything. Before I could decide, she dropped my hands and answered her own question.

"Low blood sugar. I'll get you something."

When she was gone I stood slowly. Feeling the borders of my body, tracing them with a kind of possessive tenderness. My body, *mine*. I wouldn't let it float away from me again.

I tried, too, to recapture the thread I was tugging, and drifted over to the shelf of yearbooks. I wasn't sure of the timing, so I started with 1960. This time I skimmed only the class photos.

I found her in 1965. Rita Ekstrom. Even as a freshman Miss Ekstrom had that thick, center-parted hair, but back then it flipped up at the ends and just grazed her shoulders. Her wide mouth was unsmiling, her narrow blue eyes challenging, impatient. As if the photographer had annoyed her.

Ruth came back with a vending machine haul and dumped it on the table.

"Thank you," I said gratefully. I stopped a spinning Coke can with a finger, cracked it open, and drank it down. Then I went for the Hershey bar. When I looked at Ruth she was watching me with her mouth slightly open. She blinked a couple of times and leaned over the open book.

"What'd you find? Oh!" Her voice went higher. "Look how cute Ekstrom is. Doesn't she look mean? I love it. Hey, I wasn't done."

I'd closed the yearbook. I made my voice light, as if I were only speculating.

"What if Ekstrom knows something? She's lived here all her life. The girl we're looking for could even have been one of her classmates."

Ruth's gaze compacted, went clinical. "Interesting," she said, half to herself. "She did say on Monday she'd played the goddess game. So it had to have started before her time, right? Unless . . ."

Her eyes went to mine. For a moment neither of us spoke.

"You stay on her freshman year," she said. "I'll take '66."

This far back the yearbooks weren't indexed. I flipped through 1965 page by page, studying each face. By the end my eyes were burning, and Ekstrom hadn't shown up again.

Ruth had more luck with 1966. She pinned her finger to an open page, half frowning. "What the hell is a letter-writing club?"

I dragged my chair closer to look. A dozen girls, all white—as was most of PHS's population in the 1960s—looked awkwardly at the camera. Each brandished a pen in her right hand, as if to say, *I write letters, and I can prove it!* That was another thing about these old photos: people back then weren't used to being photographed five hundred times a day. It showed.

"Every one of these girls has brown hair," Ruth said. "*Six* of them have glasses. That is some old-school social sorting. Do you think all the cheerleaders are blonde?"

"Her hair's not brown."

Ruth leaned in. "Hm. You're right. It's hard to tell with it pulled back."

The letter-writing club's solitary blonde was curvy and very cute. She held her pen up rakishly. Her smiling face contrasted badly with Ekstrom's peevish one. Ekstrom stood beside the blonde in a skirt and sweater over a collared white oxford, holding the pen like she might use it to stab whoever was making her pose.

"That is one pissed-off fifteen-year-old," Ruth said.

"Who do you think they wrote letters to?"

"Jackie Kennedy," she said with certainty.

We moved on to 1967 together. "Here we go." Ruth rubbed her hands together. "Ekstrom's glasses era has begun."

The lenses only served to sharpen her eyes. She looked good in her junior year photo. Not smiling, but there was a surety to her that was previously lacking. Like she was becoming the person she would be. The letter-writing club was, tragically, missing from the yearbook's pages, but Ekstrom showed up as one of just two girls in a stiff group photo captioned *Honoring Scholastic Excellence*. We pored through the rest of the extracurricular photos, but she wasn't there. Not an athlete, our Miss Ekstrom.

At the very end of the book was a spread of candid shots. Students strummed guitars, sat in circles on the grass, made faces at the camera. It was the best part of the yearbook by far, the section in which they most seemed like actual *people*. Like us.

"Oh," Ruth breathed. She pointed at a photo on the right-hand page.

Miss Ekstrom, sixteenish, sat on a library table. Her legs were crossed at the ankles, her left hand rested on the tabletop, and she was turned to face the girl sitting next to her. The other girl's posture mirrored hers: crossed ankles, propped hand. The corner of her lip was caught lightly in her teeth, unmistakably flirty. They smiled at each other like they had a secret.

Ruth read the caption aloud. "'Bosom friends Rita Ekstrom and Patricia Dean on the hunt for a good book.' Bosom friends!" She literally cackled. "Now that is an unintentionally hilarious euphemism. What do you think *good book* is a euphemism for?"

She was right. There was a crackle in the air between them, Miss Ekstrom and this girl Patricia Dean. It was so lovely and apparent it made me smile. Until I remembered they were stuck inside small-town 1967.

"I've always wondered," Ruth said, "whether Ekstrom has someone, a girlfriend or a wife. Or a husband, I guess, though I was pretty sure not. She could, you know. She could be married with two grown kids and a pack of grandkids and we wouldn't even know it. She's so private."

I'd assumed Ruth knew more about Ekstrom's personal life than I did, because I knew basically nothing. Before I could say so she made a little sound of surprise.

"Wait! Patricia Dean is the hot blonde from letter-writing club! Literally Ekstrom scooped the hottest girl from the stupidest club." She clasped her hands over her heart. "I can't tell you how happy this makes me. Let's look at their senior year."

I went to the shelf, but 1968 wasn't where it should be. I tipped my head and scanned the years. A few were misshelved, and I moved them into place. By then Ruth was looking with me, but both of us came up cold.

"I'll ask the librarian," she said. "You can use my absence to eat that Mallomars you've been eyeing."

Joke was on her, I hated Mallomars. I ate the Kit Kat.

I was swigging water when Ruth came back looking sharp as a fishhook.

"Well," she said. "Want to hear something interesting?"

I slumped over until my forehead touched the table. "God, no. I'm sick of interesting. I want to be bored."

"Get over yourself, sit up and listen. Apparently there is no yearbook for 1968."

I lifted my head to find her watching me expectantly. "Really? Why?"

"Librarian doesn't know."

"Weird," I said slowly, and narrowed my eyes. "I can actually hear your brain going *click click click*."

"Well, I can hear yours, too," she said distractedly. "Look, you keep going on this, the memorial thing. I want to do some other research. I'll call you later, okay? We'll compare notes."

When she'd gone I reshelved the yearbooks. I knew somehow we were done with them, we'd found what we were looking for: whatever it was, it happened in 1968.

I could've gone to Ekstrom right then and asked her what she knew. But I kept running through the conversation we'd had on Monday after lit magazine.

She hadn't believed me when I told her Becca ran away. I walked away all self-righteous, figuring she was just another adult who assumed she knew something I didn't.

Now I had to ask myself. What if she *did*?

THREE MONTHS AGO

THEY DROVE TO THE HIGHWAY oasis twenty minutes outside town.

What did people see, looking at them? One picking cinnamon sugar bits off an Auntie Anne's pretzel, the other gripping a cup of black coffee. A girl and her grandma, Becca supposed. The thought made her chest ache.

"There," said the older woman, not bothering to be quiet. "Her."

Becca looked. A woman, fiftyish, pecking at her phone with an index finger. She had a frosty long bob and the clenched expression of a chronic manager-demander. It was easy to picture her in a shaky cell phone video, assaulting a minimum-wage employee.

"What'd she do?" Becca asked.

Her companion gestured dismissively. "It doesn't matter. The palette is so limited. It's only on TV that monsters are elegant or clever. In life they're just ugly."

Becca considered that. Over the past few months, her darkest views of humanity had been confirmed. People like the woman who killed her mother, then abandoned her body on the road weren't an anomaly, despite what her father told her all the way up to the day he died. Evil was banal, and it was *everywhere*.

That was why they were here, eating bad sweets and crap coffee at a rest stop perched like a concrete spider over the highway. So Becca could see what it was like to identify the bad ones, mixed into the crowd like arsenic in sugar.

"Do you ever . . . can you ever *not* see it? Or, do you ever get used to it?"

The older woman considered that. Then she answered a different question.

"People have so many things in their lives. Family, friends, community, hobbies, work. The little idiot boxes they carry in their pockets, to which they tithe away half their minds. I have *two* things in my life. One, of course, is this. The other is my work, the one thing that is only mine. I love my work, and I need the money to live. What I can't have is *people*. Friends ask questions, and family . . ."

She'd been fidgeting with a packet of Sweet'N Low. Now she tore it in half, its contents spilling out in a chemical puff. "What if I had a child and I looked into its face and—" Again she broke off. "I chose this life. But—I chose it *instead*. You understand that, don't you?"

It was a rhetorical question. She didn't even look at Becca for confirmation, only nodded toward a man who'd just walked in, a grade-school boy trailing in his wake. "Him," she said carelessly.

The man had a gentle paunch and a scrubby beard through which you could see patches of rosacea. Despite the cold he wore a thin denim jacket. The boy wore a puffer coat.

"Poor kid," Becca whispered. The boy was probably ten

or so, not much younger than she was when she lost her mother. Seeing him reminded her why this mattered.

"Poor *man*," the woman corrected her. "I was referring to the child."

Becca looked back at the boy. Overgrown hair licking his collar, shabby sneakers on his feet, trudging after the man with his eyes on a tablet. He must've felt her looking, because he glanced briefly back.

Then he looked away and moved on. And Becca stayed in place, cold to her marrow. Not because she'd seen something in him—some hideous potential, glowing in his pupils like twin flames—but because she'd seen nothing at all. He just looked like a kid.

One day soon she would look at him and see the taint of all he was capable of. She wouldn't be able to help it. And then she'd have to decide: Was he the one worth taking?

It wasn't the first time she had the thought. But it was the first time it came over her so powerfully, sucking her down.

What if I don't *want* to decide? What if I can't bear to see?

That night she stayed over at Nora's. It was year ten of an annual ritual: on the first cold Saturday of October, Mr. Powell lit the season's inaugural fire in the old gas fireplace, then left Becca and Nora to listen to the *Nightmare Before Christmas* soundtrack and eat burned marshmallows.

The ritual had a cozy continuity that both comforted Becca and inflicted a cognitive dissonance so severe it was almost vertigo: in the decade since it started, her entire life had blown down. But Nora's remained as sturdy as a museum diorama.

Becca acted weird all night, she knew she did. In response Nora was stiff and offended. But for the first time since midsummer Becca wasn't *trying* to push her best friend away.

Before today she thought she'd fully understood the deal she was on the verge of entering, as permanent and binding as a fairy's bargain. It was so noble in theory, so black and white. Until you're sitting at a rest stop full of tired people just trying to get to the next place, to get home. And even with your own human eyes the sight of them fills you with despair.

I have two *things in my life*, her tutor had said. *What I can't have is* people.

It was late now. Nora was sleeping. Becca watched the dying fire and let her mind run to the places it always went when she felt this irradiating loneliness. The memories were pools of warm streetlight in the dark.

She thought of the day she wrapped that horrible boy's hair around her fist, and cut it free.

Then the Kingdom game ran through her in a rush, all those golden hours spent making magic in the woods.

Next the goddesses they made appeared to her, one by one as they always did, each bright-burning girl.

And before them, the goddess game. Played just once, never forgotten. Nora's faith in her that day, so brilliant and complete, was a beacon in the dark years that followed. The game had compacted in her memory like a star.

Sitting in the drowsy light of the almost-dead fire, Becca was seized with the frantic need to feel that again: Nora's faith and love and perfect understanding. If she could remember how it felt to be anchored to her life and her person, maybe she wouldn't have to see this through. She could tell Nora everything, find another way forward.

"Wake up," she whispered. Watching Nora's eyelids flicker, then clench.

"Let's play the goddess game."

CHAPTER THIRTY—TWO

"NORA? COME IN HERE, PLEASE."

My mom called out as soon as I walked into the house. By the sound of her voice I guessed she knew what I'd recently confirmed: the story of the #PalmettoVanishings was spreading like the Black Death.

When I walked into the kitchen she turned her computer to show me a CNN article. *Disappearance of four in Illinois town confounds local authorities.* "I assume you saw this?"

Gripping the doorframe on either side, I let myself slump. "Not that specific one. But yeah." I leaned a little farther, relishing the burn in my shoulders. When my mom didn't reply, I lifted my head.

She was looking at me with an odd expression on her face. A look of distant but distinct alarm.

"Mom? What's wrong?" I let go of the doorframe and took two steps, arms rising to embrace her.

She flinched back against her chair. I stopped short, flicking a glance over my shoulder. When I turned back her eyes were glassy, alert. She'd flinched away from *me*.

"Mom," I said quietly.

She gave her head a little shake. "Come here," she said.

I felt a burn begin in my chest. An itch. I pointed behind me, toward the stairs. "I have homework."

"No." Her eyes ran over my face like she was searching for something. "Come here, and tell me what's going on."

"Like. How do you mean?"

"Don't," she said through gritted teeth. "Something's *wrong*." The words came one at a time, like she was dragging them out of the dark. "It's not just Becca, it's you. Talk to me. What *is* it?"

My chest pulsed with a sudden sharp pain. A burst of ball lightning above my heart. At the same time a thought burrowed wormlike through my brain.

Say nothing.

"Nora." My mom gripped the table with both hands. "Answer me."

I wavered, eyes filling with tears. She saw them and softened.

"Honey, come sit with me. Let me see you."

Another slippery thought. *Don't let her.* I twitched, clapping my hands together hard. To make sure I could feel them, to center myself. But my mom jumped, blinking, and I saw that I'd scared her. That the gesture was odd, and made her even more worried about me.

I had to get out of the kitchen. I had to do it before I fell apart. If my mom saw me break, she would never leave me to break alone. So I spoke from the thin angry place that just barely concealed my fear.

"You're being ridiculous."

"Ex*cuse* me?"

"And *really* insensitive. God, Mom, of course something's wrong with me. My best friend is missing. I'm allowed to act weird right now."

Her face was stricken. "That's not fair. That's not what I'm saying and you know it."

"I'm going upstairs. Please, just leave me alone."

She laughed angrily. "I'm your mother, it doesn't work like that. *Hey.* Don't you walk away when I'm talking to you."

I rounded on her. "Goddammit, Mom, just *leave it*."

Shock wiped her face clean. Before she could recover, I rushed from the room.

Upstairs, behind a locked door, I came apart.

I fell on my bed and shoved my face into a pillow and made a horrible sound I didn't know I was capable of. A scraping of confusion and guilt and sadness.

What was it my mother sensed when she flinched away from me?

Something was rising in me like a pitch-colored sun. A horrible comprehension that was too vast, too frightening. I cringed from it, taking refuge in excuses: I was being paranoid. I was overtired. I was sad and scared and *going through a lot*.

But.

I was writing notes to myself in my sleep. I was experiencing extreme dissociation, having thoughts that weren't my own.

I made myself uncurl and stand. On socked feet I crept toward the mirror.

A dark-haired girl stood there, posture tense. I looked her over, then walked right up close, until all I could see was my face.

It felt like looking at a stranger through a sheet of glass. Like that split second when you catch yourself in a mirror you didn't know was there, momentary displacement giving way to recognition. Except the recognition *never came*.

My phone went off in my back pocket, making me startle back from the mirror. Ruth. I hesitated, then picked up.

"Hey."

"Hello. You sound very unhappy to hear from me."

"No, I'm just." I visored a hand over my eyes. "Sorry. I'm . . ."

"You okay? I can call back."

I sat on my bed, pushing my bubbling panic aside. "I'm good," I said firmly. "What's up?"

"I found something," she said grimly. "A couple of somethings. 1968, year of the missing yearbook? I think I figured out why they didn't have one."

That had seemed so crucial a few hours ago. Now it took me a second to remember what she was talking about. "Oh. That was fast."

I heard a terse *tap tap* and knew she was dinging a pen-point against her teeth. "I told you a PHS teacher went missing back in the day? I was mixed up, she wasn't a teacher. She was the principal, a woman named Helen Rusk. She went missing April 4, 1968. As far as I can figure, she was never found."

I frowned. "And you think that explains the yearbook?"

"Well . . . there's another thing." She made a reluctant sound. "You know that blonde girl? Ekstrom's girl?"

I caught my breath. "Oh, no."

"Yeah." Her voice was subdued. "I made a run through old *Palmetto Review* obituary pages, just in case, and she came up. Patricia Dean. She died in January 1968."

"Shit. Did the obit say how?"

"Just funeral details and a list of surviving family. She had a *lot* of siblings. Nora." Ruth sounded uncharacteristically hesitant. "You don't think Patricia Dean is *the* dead girl?"

"Don't call her that," I said automatically.

"You're right. Sorry."

"But, I do. Think it's her. Patty Dean."

"Patty," she repeated. Then, "Yeah. I think so, too. Journalistic instinct, I guess. Plus . . . if she *is* the girl, and died at school, then the principal disappeared a few months later? You can see why they'd take a pass on the yearbook. Though Principal Rusk did *not* sound like a beloved local figure."

"Yeah? Why not?"

"The *Review* ran a longer piece about her one year after she disappeared. Like an obituary, but there was no body, so not quite. And *man*, was she a piece of work."

Ruth cleared her throat and read in a plummy BBC cadence. "'Though she chose family life over pursuing her dream of entering the sisterhood, Miss Rusk brought the principles of obedience, purity, and rejection of earthly vanity to bear in her leadership of the PHS student body. While most in the community supported her five-year tenure, it was not unmarked by controversy.'"

My throat thickened. "The *sister*hood? What kind of controversy?"

Ruth *tsk*ed. "All the shit you'd expect from an aspiring nun born in 1915. Girls sent home for wearing lipstick, showing their knees. Curriculum weirdness. There was a walkout in '64 after she tried to instate a mandatory purity pledge."

"Gross. So, what? Kidnapped by satanic teens?"

"Satanic panic was the eighties. Kidnapped by hippies? Or by one of her many enemies. Just the fact that she was a female principal, back in the sixties, you know she had to be full-metal bitch."

"But she got the nice obituary. What about Patricia Dean? What did *she* get?"

"Funeral announcement. St. Mary's."

"That's unbelievable," I said hotly. "It should've been big news. In a town where nothing ever happens, a girl dies, at *school*, and that's all they print?"

"It's a suburban weekly, Nor, not the *Globe*. They let little kids send in movie reviews. They have that annual column written by the editor's dog."

But I was remembering what Becca told James, about the death in school being a shady one. "Where'd you find all this stuff, just online?"

"In a mysterious diary. Hidden behind a loose brick. At the library, woman."

"Do you think there's any link between them? Helen Rusk and Patricia Dean?"

Ruth sounded hassled, put upon. Her favorite head-space. "Besides the school and the timing, doesn't seem to be. The timing's not even *that* close. And yet. Maybe some-one killed Dean and went for the principal next. Maybe the principal killed Dean and went on the run. Or Dean really did die of an overdose, and the principal peaced out to San Francisco. Summer of Love."

"Sure," I said, throat dry. "Nuns are all about free love."

"Hah," she said obediently. "Anyway, I'm gonna keep digging on this."

"Or we could just ask Miss Ekstrom."

I was testing her, wanting to see whether she was as reluctant to go to Ekstrom as I was. And there was an odd note in her voice when she said, "We *could*."

"Then why'd you say it like that?"

"Oh." Ruth laughed, but the sound was flat. "She's private. Like I said. *You* know."

"And . . ." I prodded.

"And . . . okay, this is kind of weird. And probably not related to anything. But I had this encounter, I guess. With Ekstrom, back in freshman year, that always made me wonder." She sighed. "I was in the city with my parents, seeing a play."

"Aww."

"It was very aww. I b*elieve* my mom made me wear an Easter dress and tights. We got dinner after, and on the walk to the car I saw Miss Ekstrom. She was dressed . . . it was funny, neither of us looked like ourselves. I was dressed like a communion child, and she looked like she was on her way to some boomer rock show. She's not young, but she's got that long hair, and she had, like, a Stones shirt on and these boots. She looked kinda cool, like if Janis Joplin got old. And of course I was obsessed with her, little freshman me, and I'm all *Miss Ekstrom! It's me, Ruth!*

"But when she saw me, her whole body *jumped*. Her face—she looked almost panicked. Like I'd caught her stealing a car."

"Was she with anyone? Was she drunk?"

"Right, you wouldn't want to be caught wasted by your student's parents, or even on a first date or something. But no and no. And it was bigger than that. I mean, a bigger reaction. It was *very* awkward. She halfway recovered and said hi, we said hi back, and my parents were like, *Let's go, Ruth.* And that was that."

"Did she act weird to you at school?"

"Not at all. It was like it never happened. But I always

wondered. What was she so worried about? Does she have some fascinating secret life? Or is she just incredibly secretive about her normal life?" She waited. "Nor. You there?"

"Can I tell you something?" I said abruptly.

I thought Ruth would lean into it, all *oooh*. But she just said, "Yes."

I listened to the quiet coming through the phone. Imagining her on the other side of the call, wondering what she was looking at right now. "The disappearances. What would you say if I told you Becca is the reason for all of it?"

Her voice was careful. "The reason like, she caused something? Or like she *did* something?"

"Did."

"I would say . . ." Ruth fell silent. It was a whirring, sharp-toothed silence. "Based on what we know. Timing, location, lack of leads or evidence pointing at *any*thing, unless the police are playing it seriously close. I would probably say that's not plausible."

"It wasn't a blood sugar thing in the library." I said it fast. "Something's going on with me. Something connected with Becca, with *all* of this, and I can't . . . I'm feeling like, sometimes it's like I'm not even me. Like my thoughts aren't *mine*. When I look in the mirror, it's like there's something *else*, something . . ." The pain in my chest returned as I spoke. I broke off, wincing.

"Nora," she said. The word almost sounded like a warning.

"But." My voice cracked. "I'm probably just tired."

"No, that's not . . . I think you need some company. Sloane's here but she's watching *SpongeBob*, she won't even notice if I leave. Let me come over. Or do you want to meet somewhere?"

"No. I'm good. Just tired, like I said. I'll see you tomorrow, okay?"

I hung up before she could reply. I was angry at myself, not her. Ruth was a fact-based person, her brain wasn't built for my quarter-baked rantings.

I tossed my phone aside and went back to the mirror. The pain in my chest was where the bruising had been, that quartet of dark spots I'd seen in the shower. In one brisk motion I stripped off my shirt.

The light was heavy, midwinter gray. It made the bruises on my chest look startlingly prominent. They should've been fading to yellow but instead they were darkening. I counted them. One, two, three, four.

Five. There was a fifth I hadn't noticed in the shower, slightly above and over from the rest.

With a dreamlike sense of foreboding, I raised my right hand and placed it, cross your heart style, on my chest. Each fingertip fit perfectly over a bruise. As if someone had pressed a hand cruelly to my chest, leaving its mark.

CHAPTER THIRTY—THREE

THAT NIGHT I PUT PEN and paper next to my bed.

I lay awake for a long time. I kept sliding toward sleep, then climbing back out of it, all my sharp insistent thoughts serving as handholds. But my mind couldn't fight it forever. Finally I blinked too long, and dreamed.

I stood in a place of brightness and heat. A place where sand and hard sun conspired to turn the world into a kiln. Ahead of me was a knot of people wearing light-colored clothes and hiking boots. Beyond them, hazy structures rose from the furrowed sand.

They were a tour group. Talking to each other, drinking from reusable bottles, holding phones out to capture themselves against the daunting landscape. They seemed like one organism to my dazzled eyes, a multicolored many-limbed thing moving over the sand.

One of the group turned her face to address the girl beside her. A woman with a buttery ponytail, midtwenties. She looked familiar in a generic way. She could've been any one of a hundred people I'd seen shilling products on my phone.

Except for the hovering shadow in her face. A darkness

I was learning to dread. She turned forward again, dismissing the person she'd been speaking to. As she moved over the sand, framing the world in her outstretched phone screen, I moved with her.

I was stalking her. As I'd stalked Logan Kilkenny. Logan disappeared; I bet this woman did, too. Because these weren't dreams. They were *memories*. But whose?

Now we stood inside the thick shade of the structures I'd seen from afar. Ruins of some kind, crawling with tourists. The woman I was following seemed irritated with her friend, and pointedly took a different path. Alone.

I followed. The passage we walked through was shady and cool, though I was close enough now to see the sweat on her neck.

Not just cool. *Cold.*

I was cold. The feeling didn't belong to the sweltering dream, I was waking up. I fell through a brief purgatory, not yet in the world but no longer dreaming. Then I came all the way awake with a horrible *splat*.

I was outside. It was night. I was on all fours in icy grass. My eyes were streaming and my bare hands were raw to the wrists.

I was more scared than I'd been the night before, waking up in my kitchen. But I was quicker, too. As soon as I was conscious I was placing myself. Trees all around me, a pearly pocket of cloud riding between them, concealing the moon. In the woods, but *where*? Panic hovered like a black bag over my head.

I saw the path first, to the side of me. Then the little break in the trees, beyond which was a grassy bowl of clearing. *Our* clearing, Becca's and mine. That was where

I'd been walking, I was sure of it. I stood on numb legs and stumbled forward, down the slick grass.

Just ahead of me was our tree, with its spreading arms and friendly, protective hollow. When I saw it I almost laughed out loud. I knew now why I was here. How had I not thought to check our tree? We'd been hiding things inside it since we were eight years old.

The wind picked up and the circle of trees moved hotly, all in a simmer. Our tree was backlit, its hollow matte black. Heart spiking, I stuck my hand into the dark.

Nothing. I swept it left to right, then put both arms into the trunk and felt around, disturbing grit and dead bugs and who knew what else. But the hollow was empty. I was wrong.

I slumped against the trunk, eyes filling, feeling the grain of the bark press into my cheek and palms. Behind me some nocturnal creature made a machinelike clicking. I wasn't as cold as I should be, and distantly I knew that was dangerous.

It was easier, out here, to let go of my denial. I sighed against the rough skin of the old tree and thought, There is something haunting me.

More than haunting. It bruised my skin, it slipped its thoughts into mine. It made me feel like a stranger to myself, and to my own mother. It whispered in Becca's voice. But it was *not Becca*.

Whatever it was, it slept when I slept. I knew that because it dreamed with me, filling my sleep with memories that weren't mine. And while we slept, this parasite and I, my hand wrote a message echoing the one Becca left behind. My body took me to this clearing, our most sacred place. Where we'd hid our treasures and made our altars and punished our enemies.

I summoned up the feeling I'd had in the kitchen last night, waking with a pen in my hand. Becca felt so close, as if she'd just been there.

What if, somehow, she *had* been? What if she was trying to reach me, and could do it only when I was sleeping?

And if, I thought with desperation, I could believe in any of this. If *any* of it could be true. Then it could also be true that I would see her again, that she might still be restored to me.

I held on to this foolish hope, because the alternative was unthinkable. It got me out of the woods.

CHAPTER THIRTY—FOUR

IF I DREAMED AGAIN IN the final hours of the night, I couldn't recall it. I woke around seven, trembling. The trembling turned to shudders, my body seizing like a fist around my ribs. As if the reality of what I'd decided in the woods had just hit me, and I was rejecting it like a bad transplant.

Maybe I was wrong. Lying in my bed in the dark of morning, no longer insulated by the dreamlike atmosphere of the woods, it struck me that I *had* to be.

I wanted to lock my door, ride this out without anyone bothering me. But when I stood, dizzily, the dark came up to meet me.

"Nora. *Nora.* What's going on in there?"

I sucked in a breath. I was standing in front of my mirror, fully dressed, lipstick in hand. A burgundy shade I'd dug from my drawer, too dark. Only my top lip was painted.

The doorknob jiggled. "Nora!" My mom's voice through the door edged on frantic. She must have been calling to me for a while.

I steadied myself long enough to yell, "I'm fine!"

She muttered something I couldn't make out. Then she said, "Good."

I thought I might throw up, and looked around for something I could use as a barf bag. But it passed. The sickness was in my head.

I wiped the lipstick off, threw both tissue and tube into the garbage can. I looked down at my clothes and pushed myself to remember picking them out. Putting them on. Buttoning my shirt, my jeans, hooking my bra, *anything*.

I couldn't. I'd lost time again, but this wasn't just a few chipped off seconds. When I checked my phone it was 7:16. About ten minutes were missing from my memory. As I stared at my screen, considering that, I got a text from Ruth.

Good. Don't let the bastards grind you down

I frowned at it, trying to think what she was referring to. I opened our thread to check for anything I'd missed.

She'd texted me first at 7:10, in the middle of my lost stretch of time.

How are you? You're coming to school today right?

With a feeling like a punch to the gut, I saw that I'd replied. From the fog of a blackout, at 7:12: *Feeling fine. I'll be there.*

I threw the phone away from me and looked around the room like I might see an intruder. But if there was one, it wore my skin.

I started cursing. One word in a whispered staccato as I tried to figure out what the hell I was supposed to do. I couldn't just sit through another day of school. Being alone in the house with my mother was even less of an option. I paced in my room until I saw through the window that my dad had left for work. Then I hurried downstairs. My mom's car keys were on the kitchen counter with a note. *Family meeting tonight at 7. Have a good day xo*

Family meeting, sure. I crumpled the note and bolted a triple batch of instant oatmeal, its top clotted with brown sugar. As I ate, my mind quested in every direction. What could I do, where could I go? *God*, my world was small. I could barely think past the northern rim of the city. Running away wasn't an option, anyway. My problem would run with me.

But I had to go *some*where. I pulled on my coat. What did I need right now, I asked myself as I walked to the car. An exorcism? Should I *pray*? The only church I'd ever been to held nondenominational services in the second-run movie theater, right before the Sunday matinee. Half the time was given over to God-themed comedy sketches and singalongs. I didn't think Pastor Andy was up for what I was dealing with.

I drove. I could buy a Ouija board. I could walk the labyrinth at the Unitarian Church. I could visit the Eyeless Angel, or a psychic in the city. I was on my way to the highway when I got a text from Amanda, sent to me and Ruth and an unsaved number I was betting belonged to Chris.

There are news vans at the back entrance, go through the front

Immediately my temples started to pound. I coasted for another half a block, then rerouted.

It was all related. I couldn't run from what was happening to me, and I couldn't run from the rest of it, either. Becca, the vanishings. I had to believe it could all be untangled, and I had to be in Palmetto to do it.

They must've closed the PHS lot's back entrance, because

the line of cars waiting to turn in at the front hit the corner and kept going. When I finally reached the lot its perimeter was dotted with faculty members looking disgruntled in zipped-up coats. Some were directing traffic, others hurried students along, not letting anyone linger.

I parked and joined the flow of people heading inside. Everyone was buzzing, looking at each other with astonished faces. Palmetto was trending, the world was at the gates. They must've felt like we were at the center of the universe. Ruth was right, I thought bitterly, this *was* the most exciting thing half these people would ever experience.

It all got worse once I was inside. The air was thick—with gossip, with tension, with humidity rising off a hundred winter-damp coats. I was one of the drama's minor protagonists, and today I could feel it. I walked a gauntlet of whispers and curious eyes, my skin singing with exposure.

Sharra's classroom was empty. The whiteboard was blank, no redrawn betting pool. I slid into my seat with relief. As the room filled around me, I pulled out my phone and avoided eye contact. I sent Amanda a thanks for the warning, then pulled up my thread with my sister. The last text I sent her—*I forgot my key when are you home*—was from over a month ago.

Cat would be in the locker room now, getting dressed after dive practice. She probably knew everything, but I messaged her anyway. *Hear about the news vans? Hope you're good x*

In my peripheral vision I tracked the entrance of Kiefer and Opal Shaun. Neither approached me, though Opal was blatantly staring. Mrs. Sharra arrived and class began without incident. I was just settling into her droning recitation of whatever lesson she'd been tasked with troweling into our brains when someone to the left of me said, "Oh, my god."

I turned, half expecting to see them scowling at me. But the girl who'd spoken was looking at her phone.

The people on either side leaned in to see. One put a hand to her mouth.

Sharra stopped talking as all around the room people pulled out their phones. My own lit up just as I was reaching for it. My sister, texting back with a link to a *Tribune* article. *Have you seen this??*

No. No. No. The word pulsed through me with every beat of my heart. It took a few seconds to take in anything around the bright scream in my mind that assured me a body had been found, a girl's body, with long auburn hair and a brilliant artist's eye and a hand that wore her dead parents' wedding rings and—

I gave a strangled sob that everyone around me was too rapt to notice. A cry of relief, because the article wasn't about her. It was about Kurt Huffman.

It was the prologue to a horror story we'd heard too many times before. But it had always been set elsewhere. Now it was here, drawn up so close the whole room was humming with it.

The article detailed what they found in Kurt's bedroom, under his bed. The chat room discussions pulled from his computer, the damning google searches. And in a notebook found in his backpack, a list of names. Each corresponding to a student at our school.

There are just so many bad people.

The intercom spat static and somebody yelped. There was a long gap. A hum of dead air. Then the principal's voice.

"PHS community, this is Principal Goshen. It has been a challenging week for our PHS family, and I want to address the—"

More dead air.

He began again. "All classes, please make your way to the gymnasium for a school-wide address. Please leave all coats and bags behind. No coats or bags will be permitted in the halls or in the gym at this time. Please proceed calmly and with respect."

The intercom switched off. There was silence.

We looked at Sharra. Her head stayed down for a few long beats. Then she shook it. "You heard him."

Kiefer made a sound of disbelief. "What's Goshen trying to do, herd us up?"

Judging by the ripple that went through the room, he wasn't the only one thinking it. Sharra looked pinched. "What do you want me to say, Kiefer? We're doing our best. I trust our security officers to keep us safe. Please leave your things and get in line."

The hall was full of people and unnaturally quiet. Just the stamp of feet and the hiss of low voices, mostly kids on their phones. "This is bullshit," someone called into the hush. "Send us home!"

I agreed. The air already felt thick as a milkshake. I wouldn't be able to breathe in the gym, in the crowd. I found myself looking for Madison Velez, and hoping fiercely I wouldn't find her. That she'd gotten the awful news about Kurt in time to stay home.

Then I thought, Was she on his list?

Someone behind me said, "Hey."

I paid them no mind, still thinking about Madison.

Then they were right behind me, touching my shoulder. "Hey. Eleanor."

I turned. A younger girl, feet planted wide, skin mealy around her freckles. I couldn't tell by her expression what she wanted from me.

"Hey," she said again. Her tone was conversational but her mouth was trembling. "So, uh, my brother, Evan? Evan Sewell? His name is on Kurt's list. And I guess what I wanted to ask you is—does Rebecca Cross have a list?"

I stared at her. It always took me a second to make the connection, *Rebecca* to *Becca*. The boy standing next to her grabbed the back of her sweatshirt, yanking it a little. "Jesus, Kate," he muttered. "Rebecca Cross is probably *on* his list."

"She isn't. None of the missing people are. I just talked to my mom, she *saw* it. So." She took a step closer. "Did Rebecca have her own list? Or did they make Kurt's list together?"

I was breathing in shallow bursts. Everything felt pleasantly unreal. When I opened my mouth I wasn't sure what I was going to say, but I knew it would come from the molten mysterious *thing* in me. The voice in my head, the ghost in my throat. I knew the words would burn and I would regret them later. Not now, though.

Then James was beside me. Not touching me but standing so close I could've tipped my head onto his shoulder. His hands were in his pockets and he was slouching but it was a burlesque of ease. His whole body hummed with tension.

"Fuck off," he told the girl civilly, eyebrows up. Then he did touch me, a gentle palm on my arm. "Come on."

I started to follow him. As soon as I turned the girl spoke again in a shaking voice.

"I bet they're dead now. Both of them. I bet they hated themselves more than they hated anyone on that list."

The thing in my chest went off like a firework. It wanted to drag me under but I wouldn't let it. Instead I moved *with* it, stepping forward to grip the girl's head with both hands, so my fingers met behind her skull.

I laced them. She was too startled to free herself. I put my mouth to her ear and whispered.

"You ingrate, she had her *own* list. Kurt was on that list. Do you understand me?"

The girl tried to pull back but I wouldn't let her. "Wait. Are you saying—"

"I'm saying you should be *grateful*." Louder now, my voice buzzing like a wasp's nest and stinging my throat. "All of you. You should be thanking me on your knees."

She blinked at me, eyes rabbity. "You?"

We stood in a circle of bodies. I could feel them breathing in a mass, hear their whispers. They seemed to me as undifferentiated as cornstalks. The girl wobbled, like she really would drop to the floor in gratitude. In a cut-crystal whisper one of the nobodies said, "Oh, my god. Is she *going* to?"

Then a teacher broke through the ranks. Miss Ekstrom, her face marked with feathering lipstick and a manic tension. She looked from me to the girl I was still gripping with both hands, then to the circle of watchers.

"All of you to the gym, right now," she said in a deadly tone. "You, and you, and you—everyone with a phone out, I know who you are and I will not forget. If *any* video gets posted, if I have an *inkling* it's being sent around, I'm not asking questions. Each and every one of you will be expelled. Don't test me."

The circle broke up, everyone rejoining the slow press of people making their way to the gym. Ekstrom watched for a minute, jaw locked, before switching her gaze to me.

I felt like I'd just woken up. For a horrifying moment I was sure I'd peed my pants. But it was sweat, soaking through my clothes like a broken fever. A sheet of flickering lights washed over my vision.

Ekstrom looked like she'd just woken up, too. "Nora," she said.

James was beside me, trying to keep me on my feet. I stumbled, catching myself on a locker. A wave of interest went through the crowd, peeling Ekstrom's attention away. She clapped her hands together like an animal trainer. "Gym, people! *Right* now."

I looked up at James pleadingly. "Get me out of here."

He did. We moved quickly, against our classmates, ignoring Ekstrom calling my name and the shouts of the teachers monitoring the crowd. Finally we broke free, stepping back into the cold.

CHAPTER THIRTY-FIVE

I FELL INTO JAMES' CAR with a feeling of homecoming. He leaned across me to rummage in the glove box, coming up with a granola bar he unwrapped and put into my hand.

"Eat this."

I took it down in two and a half bites. There were napkins in his glove box, too, and I grabbed the whole wad, mopping it over my face and neck. I watched the frosted landscape run past and thought about Miss Ekstrom. The way she'd looked at me today and the way she looked at Patricia Dean almost sixty years ago. *Do you know where Becca is?* she'd asked on Monday. *People are saying some outlandish things.*

Maybe she wasn't asking about Becca because she wanted to know. Maybe she was asking because she wanted to know what *I* knew.

When James spoke, I startled.

"Becca already knew about Kurt Huffman." It wasn't a question. "Like you told me yesterday. And Tate and Chloe, too. And she did something about it."

I cleared my throat. "Yes."

"That's what you meant just now. When you told that

girl she should be grateful." He paused. "'You should be thanking me on your knees.' Me. Is what you said."

Three cars passed us going in the other direction before I replied. "Yes."

Traffic was thin. I counted five more cars. Black, black, red, black, white, the colors of a card deck.

"What we saw in that photo." His driving shifted erratically as he spoke, bursts of speed and his foot all jumpy on the brake. "*What* did we see in that photo?"

It was bracing to see someone else doing badly. It allowed me to pull myself together and say, "Let's stop. Let's turn in somewhere."

"I have to get you home."

"I'm not going home."

He glanced at me. "You don't want to—"

"*No*. I'm not . . ." I laughed, and the sound was slightly hysterical. "I'm not myself."

James turned right at the strip mall with the comics shop, driving aimlessly now.

"Something's happening to me." I said it quietly, like there was something nearby that I didn't want to wake. "Something's *happened*. I'm being . . ."

Possessed. That was the word, wasn't it? But I couldn't say it. It belonged to midnight movies about killer dolls and pod people. The sun was high and we were driving past a Sally Beauty.

"Haunted," I finished softly. "I know you don't want to hear it, but . . ."

"No, I do." He gripped the wheel. "I was panicking yesterday, okay? It's a lot. I mean . . . honestly, I'm not *un*-panicked. But. I'm with you. Okay?"

I'm with you. The words scraped over my skin like a match on flint. "Okay."

"Good," he said with finality. "Tell me where we're going."

Sunlight dazzled over the packed snow, the salted roads. It smeared itself across the prismatic freeze bordering the windshield and lit the planes of his face. He looked like a still point in the speeding world.

I closed my eyes against a surge of longing, but there was no relief to be found inside my head. "We're going to Becca's house."

CHAPTER THIRTY—SIX

JAMES PARKED A BLOCK AWAY. I was counting on Miranda being at work, but it didn't hurt to be cautious. I checked the garage—only Becca's car inside it—and rang the doorbell a few times in case. Then we went to the backyard.

It was ringed around with high old trees that cast the grass and the pool deck and the square of concrete patio in a perpetual twilight that kept the pool water cool in all but the hottest weeks of summer. James and I were coatless, everything but our phones still in the classrooms we'd left behind. His arm jostled mine as we crossed the lawn, a brushing of warmth in the cold.

Together we walked up to the pool deck. "Here," I said. "This is where it started, Saturday night."

I'd rushed to Becca's house. I'd fallen asleep right here, and woke up changed.

I walked him through it. Getting Becca's text, running to her. Standing at the end of her driveway feeling time and the world go slippery. Was it nerves that made me hesitate there? Or a premonition? Would everything have played out differently if I'd just kept running?

Regret burned in my throat as I told him the rest. The coffee cup and the phone, the ashes on the deck and the odor of burning in the air. The sheer uncanniness of my spending the night out there without consequence. *You could've frozen to death*, Miranda had said, and she was right.

"What do you think she was burning?" James asked. "Photos?"

It seemed likely. I started to nod, then stopped, looking at the pool. In the morning light its water was the dusty green of a tumbled mineral chunk, surface pocked with debris. And I remembered.

"There's something in the pool."

James tensed, like he expected an alligator to breach its brackish surface.

"No, I mean—I saw something on the bottom of the pool, the morning she disappeared. I thought it might be a dead animal, but . . ." I stopped, unable to explain my certainty. "It's not."

He scanned the deck. Flush against the base of one chair was a skimming net on a long pole, the top few inches of its handle plastered to the wood with ice and snow. James bashed at it with the toe of his shoe until the net came free. Holding it like a fisherman, he leaned over the pool's murky surface. "Where did you see it?"

I took the net from him, using it to part the skin of frozen leaves. As I pushed it through the water, the water pushed back, gelatinous with cold. The net was too flimsy, I could feel it bending against the bottom of the pool. I pulled it out and flipped it over, trying again with the handle end.

This time it scraped stoutly against the pool's bottom. I stirred until I felt the interruption of some unseen thing. Firm, not organic. Not an animal.

With the point of the handle I dragged the thing against the pool's wall. But I couldn't drag it up. "I think . . ." I tried again, felt it slide upward a bit, then fall away. "I think I have to get it."

"*Get* it?" James had his sweatshirt sleeves pulled over his hands. "The water's shaved ice. What if it's just a big rock?"

"It's not a rock."

"I'll get it," he said grimly. "I've done the polar plunge at Coney Island."

A smile caught me by surprise, like a sneeze. "You've done the—never mind. Later. I'm getting it. I can get dry stuff from the house after, I know Becca's garage code."

I took my boots off, my socks. I stripped off my flannel shirt and the thermal henley I wore beneath it, clothes I didn't remember putting on. In a tank top and bare feet and jeans that scraped my naked ankles I crouched by the side of the pool. Wet denim was going to be terrible, but I didn't have the guts to peel down to my underwear in the morning sun.

It would be quick, anyway. Once I was in, the water would hit at my sternum. I'd brace myself on the side and pick the thing up with my feet. "Gross," I muttered, looking at the water.

"Wait, *let* me," James said urgently, but I was already in.

There was a bare shred of a second when my exposed arms and bare feet felt fiery and all my clothed parts oddly tepid. Then my clothes soaked through and the heat became cold and I went under.

I didn't mean to. But as soon as I breached the surface the thing inside me made itself known, shriveling in my belly like a lock of burning hair. Feeling nauseous, eyes squeezed tight, I used my hand on the side to push myself to the bottom. There I fumbled around until I found the mystery thing.

It was smooth and scratchy, and I knew at once what it was. I *knew*, and the awfulness of it shocked me into opening my eyes. Water pressed green fingers into their sockets and my body convulsed around a swallowed sob. I wrapped my hands around the thing I'd found, planted my feet, and pushed.

I came up gasping for air that wouldn't come. James was right there, arms catching me around the rib cage and dragging me out. He turned me onto my knees and whacked me twice on the back with the heel of his hand, then a third time. Wrist-warm water bubbled out of my mouth.

"Breathe. Don't try to talk." His hand was doing this infinitely comforting thing between my shoulder blades. I sucked in air and looked at the thing I'd dredged up from the water. I felt the moment when he saw what it was, and his hand on my back went still.

CHAPTER THIRTY-SEVEN

UNTIL BECCA WAS TEN SHE used her dad's old point-and-shoot. Her parents were supportive of her intense need to document the world through a camera lens, but they didn't really get it. Neither cared too much about art.

Then her talent began to emerge. Surprising at first, then thrilling. Undeniable.

When Becca turned ten her mom made strawberry shortcakes. Her dad turned the oven up perilously high and flash-baked homemade pizzas, scattered with basil we picked from the garden. A few kids rode their bikes up the block for a scavenger hunt that sent the crowd of us hurtling around the neighborhood.

When the cake was eaten and the other guests gone I gave Becca a wrapped stack of Chrestomanci books and a tiny synthetic opal on a chain. She opened the gifts by the light of the firepit and grinned, clasping the necklace under her hair. Then it was time for her parents' present.

I saw the way they leaned into each other as she lifted it into her lap. Her mom's face was so excited it almost looked scared, and her big charismatic dad was quiet for once. As Becca tore the paper away they reached out and gripped each other's hands.

Inside the wrapping was a camera. Daunting and beautiful, as inscrutable to me as a spaceship would've been.

Even then I knew it was expensive beyond their means. Meant for someone older. A professional. They gave their daughter a camera they couldn't afford, but the real gift was their faith in her. That she was a talent to be reckoned with.

For years I'd felt like the Crosses' second child, the fourth member of their little family. As Becca cradled her camera and looked at her parents across the firepit, all of them tremulous with an emotion too big to name, I remembered that I wasn't. Becca's family, boiled down to its true essentials, was a unit of three.

Now I gasped and shivered in the winter sun, hunched beside the drowned remains of that camera. Fire had warped and melted it like a piece of ugly art. I might as well have found my best friend's body.

James scooped me up like I wasn't wet or unwieldy. He carried me down the steps and over the lawn to the sliding back door, which, small miracle, was unlocked. His hair was against my mouth and it smelled like flowers and coffee and photo chemicals. The last of my delusions—that Becca might be close, might still be found—burst like a nail bomb.

I cried then for real. Finally. I cried like my best friend was dead, because I didn't know what was left to hope for. I cried because James was a lighthouse, and it scared me how much I needed the comfort he was giving me.

He tried a couple of doors before finding Becca's bathroom. My face was buried in his shirt but I could smell the room's familiar odor of wet towel and sandalwood matches. James set me gently down, my back against the wall, and turned on the water. I watched him stick a hand in the stream, then adjust the taps.

When the tub was three-quarters full he twisted off the water and with a complete absence of embarrassment said, "Do you need help getting in?"

Getting undressed, he meant. I stood and tried it but my fingers were too stiff to handle the buttons of my jeans. James kneeled in front of me and I watched him undo them with those purposeful artist's hands. He turned away as I kicked the jeans off and pulled my sodden tank top over my head.

I sank into the bath in my bra and underwear. James kept his back to me as I rattled the shower curtain closed. The hot water felt like a vast painful nothing, but my shivering subsided by degrees until I was still.

I lay against the tub's sloping ceramic side. James sat on the floor outside it, so we could see each other's faces in the gap. My sorrow felt like a glacier that would never fully melt, that would calve off shards of itself for the rest of my life. If she were really gone. How could she be anything but gone?

Becca told me once that she felt like an alien before she met me. Like the Doctor or Superman, the last of her kind. Was I the last one now? If she really was gone all our inside jokes and childhood shorthand were a dead language. One I spoke alone.

I started crying again, eyes closed, bathroom fan *whuzz*-ing above me. The water moved in tiny seismic ripples. I smelled the night-blooming scent of Becca's jasmine shampoo and wondered for a moment if I was dreaming. But it was James, holding the bottle. Asking me, "Can I wash the leaves out?"

I nodded. Then his hands were smoothing shampoo into my hair. I must have seemed so broken for him to feel he had to do this. But it was true that my limbs weighed a thousand pounds each, and the touch of his hands on my head was the kindest thing I'd ever felt.

I opened my eyes and his Erlking beauty hit me like a shot on an empty stomach. Breaking down had given me an uncomfortable clarity. All my self-deceptions were shucked away. For the first time I let myself think, really think, about kissing him. If he'd looked back at me my expression would've been as good as a confession. But he just slicked my hair carefully away from my face and murmured, "There," before standing to rinse his hands in the sink.

It was better that way. I knew it was better that way. Becca didn't deserve to have me push this grief away. James didn't deserve to be a distraction on the most fucked-up day of my life.

I sank into the bath until my sudsy hair floated around me. My heart hurt when I breathed. I pressed my hand to it, over the bruises. "That camera was her, James."

"I know," he whispered.

"And she destroyed it. She burned it like . . ."

Like an offering, I was going to say. But was that right?

The camera was her toolbox, her eye, her most powerful link to her parents. Had she burned it like a supplicant, looking for favor? Or like an acolyte, cutting her ties with the world?

I didn't want to get out of the tub. On the other side of this bath was the rest of my life. But I had things to do. I pressed pruning fingertips to my swollen eyelids and said, "I should get dressed."

TWO MONTHS AGO

AFTER THE FIGHT WITH NORA, Becca shook off her sorrow and rejected regret. It was better this way. When she stepped into her new life, there'd be no one to miss her. It wouldn't be much longer now until the goddess would come and ask her for a name. And she would say: *Benjamin Tate*.

But it was difficult, now, not to look closely at everyone she saw, thinking, What about you? And you? Are you a worthier target?

The whole world seemed haunted by hidden wickedness.

Her awareness of Chloe Park began like an itch. They were in the same math class, Chloe advanced enough to have tested into Algebra II and Becca behind enough to be re-taking it.

She knew a few things about Chloe, in the way you know a few things about everyone you go to school with, whether you talk to them or not. Chloe transferred in from Woodgate, she'd skipped a grade, she talked to no one and seemed not to want to.

But Chloe wasn't shy. She was *watchful*. A sponge that soaked up everything. Not the math stuff, which she seemed to have a handle on. She was absorbing something else. Becca went cold when she finally put her finger on it, what made it so her skin crawled when she looked at the quiet girl in third period.

Chloe was an actor. She watched people, took in the ways they were, and acted them back. Gestures, patterns of speech. Mannerisms tried on and then adopted or discarded, like spasms of machine learning.

Who was Chloe *under* that?

Security wasn't tight around Woodgate High School's pickup lot. No one noticed Becca loitering around the buses at the end of the day. She only had to approach a few people with her sob story—*My little sister has this new friend, Chloe Park, and I don't trust her. Do you know her? Are my instincts right?*—before someone spilled.

The scariest thing about the story was that Chloe had worked alone. What she'd done wasn't peer pressure or groupthink or toxic clique shit. It was just *her*, collecting information and using it to terrorize. Until a family's legal action drove her from Woodgate to PHS, where she embedded anew.

Now Becca had two names.

CHAPTER THIRTY-EIGHT

WHEN JAMES WAS GONE I let the water run out. I dried myself with a towel I found under the sink and finger-combed my hair into damp waves. In the cabinet was one of Becca's pomegranate lip gloss tins. I smudged some on and wrapped the towel around myself before peeking into the hall.

James was elsewhere in the house. I slipped across and into Becca's room.

As I eased the door shut I was struck by the uncanny sense I wasn't in the right place. It *looked* right, but it felt all wrong. Becca's absence had reduced her room to a shuttered stage set.

The furniture was spare—a bed and a desk and a chair, a long mirror on the back of the door. All the room's weird energy came from its walls. They were decked with dried blooms and wildflower plaits, pretty seedpods strung into garlands. All this curated wildness, curling around Becca's photographs.

Above the desk a neighbor boy's face was caught inside the sizzling halo of a sparkler. It transformed him into a Renaissance saint, hanging against a backdrop of perfect dark. Beside her window was the woods in winter, sunlight and ice sharpening the creek into a fairy road. The crook of wall around her bed was lined with shots of me, of us, of her parents. I didn't want to look at any of them too closely. Not now.

I moved to the closet, hoping to find something I could wear. But the photo that hung beside its doors stopped me cold.

James, standing before a tapestry of misty trees. Lean and straight and slightly smiling, his gaze so focused I could feel heat gathering in my cheeks. Becca had tweaked the contrast until the whole backdrop was *fizzing* with light. He looked like a dreaming boy Venus, served up on a gravel path instead of a shell.

I'd almost let myself forget she knew him first. Could have kissed him, even. Her first kiss, and if it happened she never told me.

Her first kiss. Her *only* kiss. The thought hollowed me out as neatly as an ice cream scoop. That faint ugly flush of jealousy drained, leaving behind it the fervent hope that she *had* kissed James.

Because there was so much she hadn't done. She'd never been to London. Never gone to art school. Never walked through the Fotografiska or lain on the grass in the Tuileries or been on a fucking *plane*, even.

The world suddenly seemed so churlish, so randomly cruel. I flung the closet open with too much force and started jerking her clothes around on their hangers. Nothing was going to fit me right. I should just throw my own clothes in the dryer, but I couldn't bear the thought of waiting another hour in this abandoned house. I stopped on a long-sleeved corduroy dress, deep blue with an empire bodice. When did she ever wear this? She hadn't, I realized. *I* had, for a goddess photograph. Becca found it on a Kohl's clearance rack.

I shimmied in, bracing for the sound of popped stitches. It was tighter than it had been a few years ago and hit too high up the thigh but I managed to zip it. From a drawer I took a thick pair of knit black tights that just barely made it to my waist.

And I liked how I looked in her mirror, surrounded by the reflections of dried flowers and black-and-white photographs. Wet-haired and shadow-eyed, rendered unrecognizable by the unlikely dress. That girl felt like a stranger, and now she looked like one, too.

James was in the family room. Propped against the arm of the couch, flipping through an old *Chicago* magazine. When I walked in he looked up. His eyes saturated darker, I could feel his intake of breath. He was going to say something, his mouth already pursing into the word *You*.

I spoke first. "Could you get my boots off the deck?"

He nodded to where my things were already piled, flannel neatly folded and boots on the floor. "I got it all."

"Oh. Thank you."

I pulled it all on slowly, delaying the moment when I had to leave him. And I knew I did. Because no matter what I wanted or what James was willing to do, I was alone. The thing I carried held me apart. Whatever was coming, wherever it would take me, I had to go through it alone.

When my boots were laced I checked my phone. Its screen was a mess of texts and missed calls. My sister and both my parents and Ruth and Amanda and even Chris, showing uncharacteristic sentiment: *Bruh you ok*

I'd never asked my little sister to cover for me, we didn't

have that kind of relationship. But maybe I wanted to. And anyway, I needed her.

Can you please tell mom and dad I'm dealing with Becca stuff and I can't answer my phone for a while?

I thought, then sent another.

I wouldn't ask you if it wasn't incredibly important. I promise I'll be home as soon as I can.

She replied right away.

Mom is reading this over my shoulder. She says, you didn't promise you'd be safe.

I pressed my lips together. *I'm safe, I promise.*

Once a liar, always a liar.

I looked again at my last message from Ruth. *I have an idea. Come to Sloane's house.* It was followed by an address and the words *Bring alcohol.*

I knew what I *should* be doing: talking to Ekstrom, the only person who might have the information I needed. I was only delaying that inevitability. But right now I didn't care.

I looked at James. "You want to come meet my friends?"

CHAPTER THIRTY—NINE

THE SUN WAS BRIGHT, THE neighborhood silent. We were traveling on foot, because you shouldn't drink and drive. And I was determined to drink. I'd found a bottle of orange-flavored vodka in Becca's freezer and we were passing it back and forth, its acetate flavor less objectionable with every sip. It blurred my edges like golden steam. It made my hope rebound: the camera *wasn't* a body. And there were things going on with Becca that I didn't understand.

According to the texts I'd received, which told the tale in patchwork, the principal's hastily convened assembly had ended after twenty minutes in a walkout. A lawlessness swept the student body, a kind of jittery carnival fervor in response to grim circumstance. Anyone who'd managed to escape their parents' oversight was now posted up in some-one's empty house, doing things they weren't supposed to be doing at 11:30 in the morning. Somehow it wasn't even noon yet.

"The last time I got drunk," James told me, "I stole a six-pound zucchini."

I cough-laughed a fine mist of vodka. He was trying to

distract me, and I was letting him. "Is that a . . . big zucchini?"

"*Very* big. It was someone's pride and joy. I stole it from a community garden and felt terrible the next morning, but I couldn't return it. I'd already used some to make zucchini bread."

I pinched my nose, manually pushing back the burn of approaching tears. I needed a break from crying. "Lemme line this up. You got drunk."

"Blackout drunk. In the morning I was like, where did this zucchini bread come from?"

"Blackout drunk. You found your way into a garden."

"Broke in. Climbed the fence. There are pictures."

"Uh huh. You found and stole a massive zucchini."

"Size of a baby. I also ate a *lot* of strawberries."

"Of course. So you go home with your huge zucchini." Obviously I perceived the sexual connotations of what I'd just said, but life was feeling too short to get flustered. "But you *don't* go to bed or drink more or whatever. You go to the kitchen and get an apron on. And you bake a nice loaf of zucchini bread."

He was smiling now. Our eyes kept meeting and catching, like links of delicate chain. "I like to bake."

But did you ever kiss her? The tipsier I got, the harder it was not to ask him. I forced myself onto a different course. "So did you used to go to a fancy prep school or what?"

He tipped his head. "Prep school?"

"Yeah. Before . . ." Even drunkish, I couldn't make myself say *Reykjavík*. In my flat midwestern voice, it would sound like a word I'd invented.

"I went to this tiny progressive school in Astoria. Queens. There were only twelve of us in each year. Everyone was named, like, Zephyr or Sway. Or, I don't know, Susan, but spelled with twenty letters and an umlaut. It was this experimental thing where half of us attended for free and the other half were millionaires' kids paying double tuition." He gave me a stern look. "I was the first half. My mom lived grant to grant. But she was just famous enough—New York famous, not other-places famous—that they gave me one of the scholarship seats. The headmaster was a star fucker."

I raised a brow at him. "You have to know how glamorous that sounds. Comparatively speaking." I gestured toward the flat lawns and faded houses, the snowbanks all dirt-chewed and raggedy. The glitziest thing in sight was the frosty coating of salt on asphalt.

"Okay, but . . . what's the capital of Montana?"

"Helena," I said like an automaton.

"Nice," he said amiably. "I couldn't have told you that under torture. It's like, you know how kids in books go to magic school and learn how to levitate cars and stuff, but they can't do basic math? Or find Canada on a map? That was my school. Except we learned sound mixing, because one kid's dad was a famous producer. Or, like, Nordic gastronomy, because the headmaster was dating a Norwegian chef."

I nodded seriously. "Oh, yeah. It's like how Ellen Culpepper's parents own Pepper's Pizza downtown, and once a year they let the elementary school kids come make their own pan pizzas. So, you know. I totally get it."

I laughed pretty hard at my joke. Hysterical hard. Getting drunk right now was either a great idea, or the all-time worst.

James looked briefly consternated. Trying to determine,

I guess, if my laughter was about to tip into weeping. When it didn't, he grinned. Shy and goofy and gorgeous, complete with a dimple in his right cheek I hadn't even known about.

"That was funny, huh? I can tell because you're still laughing."

I flapped at my face, trying to breathe. If I laughed any harder I *would* cry, and God knew when I'd be able to stop. "To get back to the point," I said, dabbing my eyes, "at what kind of magic school do you *levitate cars*?"

"Jedi Academy," James said promptly, still smiling at me. The sun lit his eyes two shades of honey.

I smiled back helplessly.

We turned onto Sloane's block. Her house was two down, an eggshell Colonial with tidy black shutters. There were no cars on the driveway, but the garage was closed. I figured whoever was here had carpooled and parked inside it, which was smart. Neighbors around these parts weren't above peeking in windows if something looked suspicious.

As we climbed the front steps I could hear faint strains of music. When I glanced at James, his warmth and openness were gone. He looked the way he did at school, utterly removed. But now I could sense the discomfort beneath his opacity. It made my throat hurt: the realization that, rather than being above our bullshit like I'd always assumed, he was actually just *shy*.

"Hey." I turned to face him. Again our eyes did that thing, that softly shining catch and release. "Cheers," I said, and wrapped my hand around his where it held the bottle. I kept it there as I took a tiny sputtering sip.

He put his other hand on top, so mine was sandwiched warmly in the middle. The way he looked at me made my skin feel as fiery as the vodka. Still holding my gaze, he lifted the bottle to his mouth.

Sloane opened the door.

For a second James and I just stood there, like raccoons caught in a flashlight. "Hey!" I slipped my hand free. "Uh. Sloane, this is James. Do you . . . know James?"

"Hi." He thrust the bottle at her. "Here."

Sloane gave me a slow smile, eyes unreadable behind her shag of bangs. But all she said was, "Flavored. Swanky," before turning to lead us into the house.

It had the same layout as mine, but a cluttered artsy vibe. We followed her to the den, where Stevie Nicks was singing off a turntable and the staff of the PHS lit magazine was three sheets to the wind.

"Hi," Chris said extremely loudly and with an extra syllable. He lay flat on his back in front of the record player, wearing a Minor Threat shirt. "Why did you attack that girl at school today?"

"Nuh-uh," Amanda said sharply. She was leaning against the couch holding a half-eaten loaf of what looked like sourdough bread. A Smucker's jar of red wine roosted at a dangerous tilt on the shaggy carpet beside her. "Ignore him, Nor. Ignore, Nor. Nor Nor." She laughed.

"These people . . ." Ruth tucked herself into Sloane's side, drawing the moment out for effect. "Are drunk. Shit, Nora, you look great. You should wear more dresses. And *you*. James Saito. I'm too drunk to pretend I don't know your name even though we've never met."

"Oh." He cleared his throat. "That's okay. You're Ruth, right?"

I'd been too shy to look at him since we walked in. But his quiet voice made my throat thicken, and I let the back of my hand touch his in a tiny show of support. I sensed his half-second hesitation. Then he laced his fingers in mine.

Every square inch of my hand lit up with zipping strings of LEDs. They pulsed in time with my heart, they wove themselves into the rhythm of "Gold Dust Woman."

I tried to act normal. Could he feel, through my hand, that I wasn't being normal? I attempted to hold his hand with the exact optimal pressure that a chill person would, while also preventing my palm from sweating with the power of my mind.

Ruth was looking between James and I with a canary-eating smile. Chris lifted his head and did a wobbly double take. "Whaaat. Are you and Hot James—"

Amanda threw her bread loaf, catching him squarely in the chin. "Christopher!"

He took a bite off the loaf, then put it under his head like a pillow.

Through it all James held my hand firmly, bravely. "So what's everyone's names?"

There was a round of introductions that might have been awkward if we were all fully sober. Ruth made a show of pouring James the last of a cocktail she'd just invented. Sloane swept it away when she wasn't looking, shaking her head firmly and giving him wine.

I looked around the room at my friends, at James, feeling grief and gratitude. If Becca were here. If no one had gone missing. If whatever was happening to me wasn't happening. Wouldn't it be nice?

When we were all sitting or lying down Ruth said, "Ready to hear my idea?"

Sloane ruffled her hair and said, "Mine."

"But I refined it."

"You yelled *good idea*," Amanda said, "then announced you were naming your cocktail the Hatchet Granny."

"It's a great name for a cocktail! Look it up, it's ironic."

James was next to me on the couch, his posture easy. I thought—I hoped—he was glad I'd brought him. I felt tipsy but solid, like myself. "Tell me the idea," I said, before Ruth could spin too far off course.

"Right. Well, first of all, I didn't mean to shut you down on the phone yesterday." She shrugged. "I'm a woman of reason. But after this morning I'm thinking that isn't actually what you need. So. Sloane?"

Sloane nodded and drained her glass. Then she leaned forward, clearing her bangs from her face. Without them in the way, I could fully appreciate the odd stone green of her eyes. "Yeah, so. My dad's a therapist. And some of his practices are pretty spiritual, bordering on, uh . . ."

"Quackery," Ruth said, and burped.

Sloane ignored that. "Ruthie said you've been feeling disconnected from yourself."

It wasn't exactly what I'd said, but I nodded. It was exciting to hear Sloane talk at length, I didn't want to throw her off.

"I could walk you through one of my dad's guided meditations. It's meant specifically to suppress," she made a gesture around her head, "your ego. Your conscious thoughts, your rationality. Let you get closer to your id. See what's there."

"I'm not gonna . . . think I'm a chicken or something, am I?"

"It's not hypnosis. You won't lose consciousness, you'll just become conscious of different things. If it works."

James said, "It's an okay idea to do this when we're all drunk?"

"It is so long as you don't report us to the Illinois Medical Board." Ruth gave him a stagey wink.

They were all waiting on my response—Sloane, James, Ruth, Amanda. Chris was eating bread, loudly turning the pages of a Tom of Finland monograph.

I had the terrifying thought that this might be *exactly* what I needed. If I could push myself aside for a moment, maybe I'd catch a glimpse of what was hiding below.

Was I stupid to risk bringing it any closer? This hidden thing that had already proven its power over me? Could be. But sometimes I lied to myself, too.

"Let's try it," I said.

CHAPTER FORTY

SLOANE WENT UPSTAIRS TO READY her dad's home office. Ruth went with her. Amanda looked between James and me, pursed her lips, and said, "We're hungry. Come on, Chris."

"I'm good," he said. "I had some bread."

"For fuck's . . ." Amanda pinched the bridge of her nose. "You're hungry."

She pulled him to his feet and out of the room. Then James and I were alone.

Sloane had put a record on that I'd never heard. The music was low, with a driving line I felt in my stomach and my knees. James stood there watching me with this shy light in his face. And I had a flash of knowing, like a nod from my future self, that I would never forget right now.

Of course I would remember all of it, this was the biggest thing that had ever happened to me. But I meant *this* moment, facing James from a few feet away, my body soft and heavy like I'd swum against a current for miles and was just now reaching shore. He didn't open his arms, exactly, but he shifted in this way that meant the same thing. We stepped forward together and collided.

I put my cheek against the soft front of his shirt and he pressed a hand to my back, steadying me. His shirt smelled of pool water and outside air. And like him, underneath. I breathed it in. Fully drunk now, swaying unsteadily at the crux of two paths.

I could wrap my arms around his waist and hold him there. I knew with a crisp certainty what would happen if I did. His other arm would come around me. In the dusty light, on a day outside time. And when this song was through, I'd tip my face up to find his waiting.

It would be the first step toward a place with just him and me inside it. Where Becca had nothing to do with what happened next. And I wanted it. The vodka in my system, the electric nearness of him, the swelling in my chest of a ferocious, almost desperate joy unlike anything I'd ever felt—all that made me *want it*. That wanting made my eyes prick with fresh tears. Of sorrow and of guilt, that I dared to feel happy. Of relief that, for a moment, I could.

Then I felt a scribble of pain, fleeting and electrical, right where my heart pressed against his rib cage.

With it came a wave of instant nausea. I *wasn't* in full control of myself, and this wasn't close to over. If I'd really lost Becca, it never would be.

I stepped back and felt his hand slide away. He'd been lifting the other like he was going to brush the hair from my face. It was still wet from when he washed it. When I moved away he gripped the back of his own neck instead, giving me a tight half smile.

Then he muttered, "Fuck it," and stepped forward to take my hands.

"Becca and me," he said urgently. "We're friends. *Just* friends. In case that's what—in case you need to know. It's never been more than that between us, not ever. We don't *want* it to be."

There was a rasp in his voice and I felt it in every bend of my body. It slid like velvet over the sharp places in my head and cut the last tether on my careful heart. He was shy and unsure of what I'd say and he was doing this anyway, awaiting my response with such gentle intensity it made my blood rush up. It was so brave I thought I might stop breathing.

And I knew I didn't have to tell him anything. I'd gone transparent. The velvet in my head, the ache of my yearning heart, he could see it. His eyes lightened, went sweet with hope. But I gave my head a negative jerk.

"It's not . . . I *want* it to be the right time," I half whispered. "I'm sorry, I wish . . ."

He was nodding. "Yeah. No, I know. God, *I'm* sorry. And drunk. And sorry."

"You don't have to be. At all. I just—"

The floor outside the room creaked, and we both turned. Sloane was there, looking chagrined, caught in the act of attempting a hasty retreat. She gave a little wave.

"Hey," I said. "You ready for me?"

"If you are."

I nodded. Before I followed her I looked at James.

He smiled, and made it easy on me. "Good luck."

The room Sloane led me to was tidy and spare, with blue walls and thin white curtains that cushioned the light. There was a pale blue sofa against one wall and two matching armchairs. It felt like a room in a cottage at the edge of the sea. It was just us in here, despite Ruth's protests that she could be very, very quiet.

"Should I lie down? I'll lie down." But I didn't. I sat awkwardly on the edge of the sofa. Sloane turned on a white noise machine and sat on one of the chairs.

"Okay," she said. "Before we start, do you want to tell me what's going on?"

I crossed my legs, uncrossed them. "Should I? Will it work better if I do?"

"No. It's a pretty nonspecific meditation. But I'm more okay than Ruth is with things that are hard to explain. And talking helps, in general."

She made a face like she knew that was funny, coming from her. It relaxed me some, and I lay back. The couch was the super-plush kind. I could feel it taking on the imprint of my body, like I was lying in heavy blue snow. Around the ceiling was a border of pretty plasterwork.

"I think . . . I don't want to talk." I blew out in a slow stream, settling a little deeper into the upholstery. "How do we start?"

"You close your eyes, and you listen."

I oriented myself. A window past my feet and another behind Sloane, sitting with her hands resting lightly on her knees. She looked like a person who would wait until I was ready, even if it took a thousand years.

I closed my eyes. "I'm ready."

"Good. Okay."

She breathed in, and I said, "Wait."

My eyes were still closed. I felt like a spotlight was on me, burning white. "If you get the sense that Becca is close. Is with me in any way. Please don't do or say anything to make her go."

She just barely paused. "Okay. I promise."

She started to speak, water-clear phrases designed to put me at ease, then be forgotten. I was worried I'd find it silly, and it wouldn't work. But my hyperalert state eased quickly to calm, then to nothing at all. Images passed over my eyelids like scudding clouds. Stars through a car window, snow falling from a black sky. Moonlight on marble, shattered glass on tile.

Sloane's voice faded out. I was told I wouldn't lose consciousness, but I had no sense of time passing, of anything happening within or beyond my body. When I opened my eyes, things had changed.

"Ruth. *Ruth.* Come here, please."

Sloane spoke from somewhere behind me. She didn't sound upset or panicked. She sounded like someone talking inside a dream.

The walls were still blue, the light cottony. I was in the grip of a benevolent kind of sleep paralysis: I couldn't move. I didn't *want* to.

The door banged open behind me.

"Sweetheart. What is it?" Ruth's voice, more tender than I'd ever heard it.

"Look at her chest," Sloane said.

The sound of approaching feet, then James spoke in a bass growl. "What *is* that? What did you do to her?"

He was here, he hadn't gone. But I couldn't turn to see him. The unnatural calm of Sloane's meditation was dropping away from me grain by grain.

"She didn't do anything," Ruth snapped. Her face moved into view like a frightened moon. "Nora? Does your—does anything hurt? Can you talk to me?"

I couldn't. I couldn't talk or move or even swallow. My body yawned around me like a vacant house. All I could do was look straight up into Ruth's face.

And it happened again. One of those disorienting flashes of *sight*.

It wasn't the dooming shadow-stamp I saw in Logan Kilkenny and the others I'd dreamed about. It began as it did with Kiefer in class: a sense of mist and motion, moving over her features like a storm on a weather map.

But it was different this time. Stronger, disorienting, unfolding into a moving, living vision that made the blue room and her worried face shiver away. In their place I saw

Ruth, elsewhere, kissing someone in a car. More than kissing. Their bodies met over the console, her hands twined hard in the other girl's bleached hair. There was frost on the windows, it must have happened recently. I could only watch it play out like a movie, then flicker away.

When it was over I found my body was coming back to me. I could move and blink and open my mouth to speak without thinking at all. "You're cheating on Sloane?"

Ruth's face changed. All the worry and color drained out, leaving her empty. And I was reminded suddenly of how scary she'd seemed before I knew her.

Sloane said, "You told her?"

"No," Ruth said woodenly. "And I'm not cheating. I *cheated*. Once. Sloane knows, and only Sloane knows. So how do *you* know?"

"*Jesus*, this isn't important right now!" James pushed past her to take my hand, moving into my line of sight. "Nora. Can you sit up?"

It happened again, so quickly. James was above me, then misting away.

I saw him in a high-ceilinged room. He was younger, face softer and tear-stained. Good light from tall windows fell over a poured concrete floor and brick walls and a pile of painted canvases. A dozen, at least. James cried as he shook the contents of a Seagram's bottle onto the paintings, and struck a match.

As it fell through the air I screamed. The vision broke.

"All of you, get *away* from me!"

I tried to stand but ended up on the floor. I could sense them moving in, and put out a hand. "Don't touch me. *Don't.* I don't want to see your faces."

"That's fine, don't look at me, just let me help you." James sounded pleading. "Something happened to your chest."

I looked down. Then I yanked the neckline of my dress away to really see it. The five little bruises had darkened. They'd *spread*, flowing together into the blue-black print of a lightly splayed hand. As if I'd dipped my own right hand in paint and pressed it to my heart.

TWO WEEKS AGO

KURT HUFFMAN WAS AN ACCIDENT.

Becca looked over his shoulder in class. He was hiding his phone behind a stack of books as he scrolled through one of those unreadable forums, text in blazing white on a black backdrop. Becca watched as he typed something very ugly about someone slightly famous. A female someone, obviously.

She clocked his username, then looked past him at the board.

That night, she went to the eye-burning forum and looked him up.

It was with a dull sense of inevitability that she found the posts. The bragging, the planning, the specifics. The forum wasn't big on moderation. Every one of his threads devolved into a comments battle among people who thought *You shouldn't joke about these things, man, fuck*, and people who thought *He isn't joking, get your head out of your ass, can anyone trace this guy's IP?*

Some people celebrated him, of course. Whether they thought it was a game or they really were monsters, Becca couldn't know. Neither would surprise her. It felt like nothing could surprise her anymore.

After gorging herself on Kurt's poison she felt sick all over. She took a shower and vomited down the drain.

This wasn't Mr. Tate and his predatorial creeping, or Chloe and her insidious, unpunished cruelty. Kurt had a deadline: with a child's sense of irony and the subtlety of a battleship he chose February 14. Just over a month away.

If Becca had any doubts left, she let go of them now. Even if she did nothing else, so long as she could stop Kurt Huffman it would all be worth it.

The plan had been to wait until the end of February, when Becca would turn eighteen. It was easier to disappear when you were eighteen. But this changed things. She felt electrified, halfway to divine already. It was time to stop dragging her heels. She had to *jump*.

When, the next day, she saw Nora and Kurt together—not *together*, but in the same stretch of hall, breathing the same air, her eye framing them ruthlessly into a double portrait—she lost all sense of caution.

Nora didn't even look up when Becca stopped by her locker. She only stiffened. It hurt Becca more than she thought it would to see her estranged best friend's face so guarded. This, too, hardened her resolve: it was time to go.

"You see that kid?" Becca said, ignoring the pain. "I need you to stay the fuck away from that kid."

CHAPTER FORTY-ONE

THE HEAD RUSH OF FEAR that I felt, looking at that inky handprint on my chest, burned the last of my torpor away. I leapt to my feet and sprinted from the room.

Amanda stood at the bottom of the stairs. "Everything okay up there? Thought I heard yelling."

"Sorry!" I said, winging her in the shoulder as I flew by, then out the door.

Everything was so sunny and still it seemed artificial. The sun was straight overhead, no shadows anywhere.

I didn't run for fun. Or for exercise, or at all, unless a gym teacher was yelling at me from somewhere nearby. But for the third time in under a week I found myself racing through Palmetto on foot.

School wasn't much more than a mile away. I went in through the front, expecting some kind of amped-up security presence. But I made it all the way inside before I saw any sign of life: one of the usual officers, sitting behind a dinged-up plastic screen.

I doubled over panting, avoiding his face. "I left my medicine in class," I said. "I need to go get it, I missed a dose and I have to take it *right now*."

"Is there a parent I can call to confirm this?" His hand hovered over the phone. "I'm not supposed to let anyone in today."

"*Please*." My tears came in a gush that must have startled him. Very soon it would start to seem suspicious, the way I refused to look at him. "If I'm too late taking it the medicine won't work!"

He dropped his hand. "*What* medication is this?"

"John, she's good. I'll escort her to her classroom."

Ekstrom's voice was brisk and bright. She approached me from the right, growing in my peripheral vision until she was right there, touching my arm. I'd come here hoping to find her, but that touch made my stomach turn.

"Hi, Nora," she said. "Let's get you to your medicine."

Neither of us spoke on the walk to her classroom. I kept my eyes ahead as she unlocked the door and switched on the lights. Its familiar odor of books and bergamot was cloying today. I sat on a desk. I'd pulled the dress's neckline as high as it would go but half the handprint remained visible. I could feel Ekstrom seeing it.

She took the big glass candy bowl from her desk and plunked it beside me. "Here. I bet you've had a sweet tooth lately."

My hand was halfway to the bowl when I really heard her, and stopped.

"I bet you've got a lot of questions, too."

"What," I whispered.

Her voice was steady, hypnotic. "To start, I can tell you it won't always feel like this. Your appetite will steady. Your thoughts and body will be your own. She's just getting used to you."

My brain popped like metal in a microwave. *She?*

"And you will get used to her. Soon you won't even know she's there. Until she's . . ." A tiny catch in her throat. "Ready."

It was hard, feeling this angry and not being able to look her in the face. "Until *who* is ready for *what*?"

A pause. "It wasn't supposed to go like this," Ekstrom said, quieter.

I snapped my head up. "*What* wasn't supposed to . . ."

Then I stopped. Because I'd looked into her face.

I didn't see a shadow in it, or a mist. I wasn't strafed by a cinematic vision of the worst thing she'd ever done. What I saw was so much harder to bear.

My teacher's face was a warped tunnel of *wrong*. Like the opening of a pit that ran clean through the world. It sucked me in and held me there and showed me the horrors it hid.

I saw Logan Kilkenny, his features distorted with terror. I saw the pretty blonde tourist, screaming, and the wiry man from the bar, his face wet with tears.

Mostly, though, I saw strangers. An old woman at a gas station under a nowhere sky. A businessman in a suit from another era. A teenage girl, younger than me, just outside the ring of torchlight on a tropical beach. I knew they were dead and I knew that she'd done it and the knowledge was dragging me under.

And then I saw someone I'd only ever seen in a photograph. But I knew him instantly: the man from the film roll Becca left behind. The person she'd spied on and photographed in the woods, facing off against a diminutive hooded figure I now knew was Ekstrom.

She had killed that man. Becca saw it happen, captured it on film.

What did you do to her? I tried to scream the words. But the horror overtook me, and I was gone.

CHAPTER FORTY—TWO

THE WORST PART WAS, I knew I'd been awake for a while when I found myself sitting up with a mug of coffee in my hand. It was grimy with sugar, half-drunk.

The worst part was I was sitting somewhere *different*, a table in a kitchen I didn't recognize, next to a window overlooking a yard that unrolled itself to a thick line of trees. Ekstrom couldn't have carried me here, which meant I must have walked.

No. The *worst* part was Ekstrom was sitting across from me, watching like she'd been waiting for the moment when I was the one behind my eyes. The darkness in her face was no longer visible to me. She looked careworn but alert.

She didn't talk right away, just cut a fat wedge off a half-eaten coffee cake and plopped it on the plate in front of me. I licked my teeth, wondering if I was the one who half ate it.

Her kitchen was pretty. Hanging copper pans, blue enamel kettle, herb pots, and exposed brick. I felt scared and angry and lots of other things, too, and the feelings were clear but very far from me, as if seen through a flipped telescope.

"I'm not a monster," she said into the silence.

I thought of one response after another. Finally I said, "Okay."

She nodded. Rhythmically she smoothed her right hand over the tabletop, both of us watching the motion. On its ring finger she wore a gold band. It had a chip of green stone that looked like peridot.

The hand stopped moving and she held it up. "Promise ring. I was sixteen when she gave it to me. I wore it on my index finger then. It was easier for us if nobody guessed."

Outside the light was fading, the trees' shadows lengthening over the grass. I wondered how long I had been here already. "What does that have to do with Becca?"

"Please. May I tell it in order?"

She was going to explain herself, probably in an effort to be absolved. "Fine."

"Thank you," she said, low. "I want to start with the day it happened. The last time I saw my Patty."

CHAPTER FORTY-THREE

THE PRINCIPAL WAS A BITCH, and she had it in for Patricia Dean.

You almost couldn't blame her. Patty Dean smoldered with mischief like a lit punk stick.

She was every single thing Principal Helen Rusk stood against. Her dirty mouth, her knowing eyes. Her generous body, round and ripe as a globe grape, that made even a T-shirt and jeans look more suggestive than lingerie.

It was predicted by many that she would be the death of her parents. But Patty was the last of eight, and by the time she came along they were half-dead already. She glowed and cursed and cracked jokes no churchgoing girl should. It was impossible to believe she came from those faded, unhappy people.

No one would blame them later for what happened to their youngest daughter. At least not out loud. At least not when they were in the room. But before all that, she was more alive than anyone. Rita Ekstrom marveled daily that Patty belonged to her.

*   *   *

Patty had a cold. She couldn't smell a thing. "Watch this," she said at lunch, eating her Salisbury steak in five fast bites. "Tastes like nothing. Silver lining, I guess. Hard to kiss, though, when you can't breathe through your nose."

Their friends laughed. Patty kissed lots of boys, and never the same one twice. It was smart, Rita knew, a necessary smoke screen. But even the reference to it made her fists go tight. Patty sensed it and waited for Rita to look at her. When she did, Patty winked. Quickly, practically a blink, reminding Rita who it was she really wanted to be kissing. Then she looked demurely downward, cool as an Alpine maiden.

Except she'd never make it up there in the pure driven snow. Not with that mouth, the way it looked and kissed and the things that came out of it. Not with that hair, those breasts, those hips and her waist nipping in softly above them, making two miracle curves where Rita's hands fit so perfectly you'd think they were factory-made for each other. A two-piece set.

"Oh, I almost forgot," Patty said primly. "I've got a physics test tomorrow, and I'm lost. Study date tonight, Ri?"

"I could do four o'clock," Rita replied. She'd loved Patty half her life, and still the girl made her heart go mad. "Come to mine?"

It was Thursday. Rita's mom went to Bible study on Thursdays.

"Make it six." Patty rolled her eyes. "I've got detention with Sister Bitch."

Rita felt a twitch of anxiety. "Again?"

Principal Rusk, aka Sister Bitch, creeped Rita out: her dry twig shape, her whispery voice and fundamentalist's eyes. Two years later Rita would watch news footage of

Charles Manson being brought to the courthouse in hand-cuffs, unrepentant, and taste stomach acid. Thinking, *Those are Helen Rusk's eyes.*

"What'd you do this time, Pattycakes?" Jeannie asked in a ready tone. She was a mousy Philip K. Dick obsessive who Rita had long suspected was in love with Patty. *Jealous girl*, Patty teased her when she shared her suspicions. *I have the most jealous girl.*

Rita *was* jealous. And uptight and funny and sharp as a tack. All the boys who wanted Patty blamed Rita for their bad luck. The dreaded prune of a best friend, scowling at them over folded arms. The boys weren't exactly right, and they weren't exactly wrong.

Now Patty said, "Oh, who the hell knows. Another drummed-up charge passed along by one of her spooks."

She meant for everyone to laugh with her, and they did. Only Rita could hear her frustration. Principal Rusk would've punished Patty for breathing wrong if she had nothing else to pick on. But Patty, stump-stubborn, *always* gave her something to pick on.

"Anyway." Patty stood up, a little too slowly. The basketball players at the next table were watching her, hungry as hounds. Jeannie, too. But it was Rita she was doing it for.

"Keep your noses clean, ladies, lest the good sister have you writing lines with me tonight. 'Thou shalt not have any fun.'" Patty picked up her tray. "See you at six, Ri?"

"Six," Rita agreed.

Patty didn't turn yet. She didn't turn. Maybe Rita remembered this part wrong, the endless stretch of seconds when Patty hovered there and Rita could have stopped her from going. *Stand up*, she says to the memory. *Run.*

It happened to her everywhere, anywhere. Swimming in

the municipal pool or standing in front of a classroom or smiling at a baby at the grocery store. The world receded and a voice said, *This is the last time you see her.*

And there was Patty again, standing up from the cafeteria chair. Beautiful buxom Patricia Dean. The dream girl, the only girl. Maybe there would've been others. If they'd lost each other in the usual way, surely there would, but not after it ended *this* way.

Not to mention what came then. After the end.

On the screen in Rita Ekstrom's mind Patty was picking up her tray. She was knocking her chair back into place with one plush hip. She was turning, walking out the door. She was gone.

CHAPTER FORTY—FOUR

SIX O'CLOCK CAME AND WENT. Seven, eight, nine. At quarter to ten Rita's mother came in from Bible study smelling of gin and gossip.

"Growing girls need their sleep," she said, weaving slightly.

"And grown women need to put something in their stomachs before they hit the bottle," Rita snapped back. She wouldn't have, only she was so scared. It began as a popcorn kernel in her stomach and grew into a horrible certainty: something had happened to Patty.

Her mom stood there a moment, mouth folded like a frog's. "Do not forsake your mother's teaching," she said, before wobbling haughtily down the hall.

When she was gone Rita allowed her imaginings to encompass the worst things she could think of, so she could be prepared: Sister Bitch kept Patty in prayer until midnight, kneeling on scattered sand. Mr. Dean finally roused himself enough to slap her across the mouth and demand she keep her sinful self at home, the way he'd done with his three elder daughters. Patty's sisters had always hated her for how easy she had it.

Then the very worst thing: Patty in a hospital bed, eyes closed, surrounded by a nebulous assortment of tubes and machines. But surely Mrs. Dean would call her if Patty were really hurt? Patty's mom liked Rita okay. Back when Mr. Dean worked second shift she and the girls would listen to Johnny Mathis records and bake butterscotch cookies on Friday nights. But that was a long time ago now.

Rita fell asleep waiting for Patty's call.

Patty didn't meet her at the water fountain like she always did. They had third period together, and Patty wasn't there either. Jeannie and Doreen and the boy Patty had been stringing along for a few weeks, whose name Rita couldn't produce to save her life, all of them asked her where Patty was.

Rita told them she was home with her cold. She wasn't sure why. There was a garishness to the light, a sickening quickness to the day's ordinary bustle. The pressure in her head intensified.

After third period she went straight for the doors. A hall monitor called after her and she yelled back, "I'm sick!" before bursting into daylight.

The walk to Patty's house was less than a mile and she'd made it a thousand times. She was on the front step and her hand was knocking on the door. Patty would open it. She would be in her nightgown, under the weather, laughing at Rita the worrywart.

It was Mrs. Dean who opened the door, her face like a watercolor that had run in the rain. She'd only ever touched Rita in careful passing—a tap on the shoulder, an accidental brush in the kitchen when she handed her a whisk. But now she said, "Oh, *Rita*," stepping halfway over the threshold before she collapsed. They held each other up, both of them weeping before Rita even heard the story.

It was the last time they would grieve together. By the time Patricia Dean's body was buried, eight days later, Rita hated Mr. and Mrs. Dean with an intensity that bordered on madness.

The only person she hated more was Principal Helen Rusk.

CHAPTER FORTY-FIVE

CARDIAC INCIDENT. THAT WAS WHAT Patty's dad said when he found her and Mrs. Dean embracing in the doorway. The words were ridiculous in his mouth, he sounded like a dog who'd been taught to read aloud. Rita didn't say that. He was a small and hateful old man, but he had lost Patty, too.

Cardiac incident. Rita's mother repeated it in low tones, mouth pressed close to the phone. Palmetto's phone tree was crackling, lit up like a burning bush.

Cardiac incident. Rita moved Patty's ring from her right index to her widow's finger, where her mother wore her own wedding ring. She spun it round and round. Remembering Patty's strong seventeen-year-old heart beating fast beneath her hands and mouth, then slowing to a drowsy drumming under her ear.

Patty, always the brightest point in any room. In the cafeteria, on Thursday. *I've got detention with Sister Bitch.*

Rita got out of bed.

Principal Rusk wouldn't see her. Would not. When she persisted, Rusk delegated the task of managing Rita to her most enthusiastic enforcer.

"I'm very sorry, dear," Miss Coates said in tones of impatient affront. She was a steel-haired spinster of the old school who taught home economics. It was half an hour past final bell and she and Rita were sitting outside Principal Rusk's office. Rusk might or might not have been inside it.

Miss Coates patted the back of Rita's hand, her fingers as dry and light as rattan pieces. "Loss is always difficult. Principal Rusk and I both think it's a thing best discussed with one's pastor." She smiled, doing something with her eyes that Rita recognized was a horrid attempt at *twinkling*. "And it wouldn't hurt to let your boyfriend take you out for an ice cream soda, would it?"

Rita yanked her hand away. Keeping her eyes on the old woman's she leaned slowly back. She crossed her arms and planted her legs wide, the way the boys who smoked on the low wall behind school did when girls walked by.

"I don't have a boyfriend, Miss Coates. Never have."

"I see." The woman's dim old eyes sharpened, her cloak of vague daffiness dropping away. "Girlhood friendships can run rather hot. Especially with a girl like Patricia Dean. Some young ladies live to subvert. It's a sad thing when a girl gets exactly what she's been asking for. But where drugs are involved, tragedy inevitably follows."

"Drugs?" Rita said faintly. "What drugs?"

"Now, I'm not an English teacher," Miss Coates said, voice cloying with false modesty. "But when they say a thing like *cardiac incident*, I believe that's what a clever person would call a euphemism."

Everything Coates said just barely reached Rita over the howling in her head. "Patty didn't do drugs."

"Oh?" Coates' eyes gleamed. "A sinner always wants another bite of the apple."

How could Rita have thought her just a lemming? Coates was Principal Rusk's malevolent equal. It had been a miscalculation to posture so arrogantly. "What kind of drugs?" she made herself ask.

Miss Coates made a moue of pretend sympathy. "It doesn't do you any good to dwell. Let this be a wake-up call instead. I'll be praying for you, Miss Ekstrom. Your mother doesn't need another grave to cry on."

Rita would spend years dreaming up blistering replies to this last twist of cruelty. But in the moment, she had no words.

Rita strode up to the front desk of the Palmetto Police Station and put two fingers on the bell, but didn't ring it. "Mary. Hi. Who was the responding officer on the Patricia Dean call?"

Mary Paulsen looked blankly up from her magazine. When she saw Rita, her eyes widened, then filled with tears. "Oh, my goodness, *Rita*. I'm so sorry. Oh, honey, it's just too horrible. I know you and Patty were like sisters."

Rita searched Mary's face for signs of double meaning or contempt. Seeing none, she said, "Thank you. It is. Could you please tell me who responded to the call about Patty? I'd like to talk to them."

Mary's father was deputy chief of the Palmetto police. She'd been working the front desk since she was fourteen. Before she graduated last spring, her classmates were always trying and failing to get information out of her—whose brother was in the drunk tank, whose mother pulled a gun on their dad. She was too nice to spread stories, and too scared of her dad to risk it.

Her head turned toward the door to the rest of the station, and Rita knew she was thinking of him. But when Mary looked back she wore an odd expression. "Why do you want to—"

The door swung open and an officer stepped out. Not Deputy Chief Paulsen, to both girls' relief. This man looked like an off-duty Santa Claus. Rita didn't know his name, but she'd seen him waving from atop the police float in the Fourth of July parade.

"You got a customer, Mary?" He smiled at them both.

"I want to speak with the responding officer on the Patricia Dean call." Rita said it as crisply as she could.

The man—his badge read OFFICER KAMINSKI—sighed and said, "Mary, honey, did you put in the dinner order?" He waited for her nod, then directed Rita toward a pair of folding chairs.

Once they were sitting, his belly settling comfortably over his belt, Kaminski gave her another good-cop smile. "Miss Dean was a friend of yours?"

"Yes."

"It's a terrible thing. Just terrible."

Grief was pressing in. Rita was almost at the end of what she could manage. "Were you the one? Did you see her?"

He patted her knee. His meaty hand was the polar opposite of Miss Coates' bundle of twigs. "It's an ugly thing to think on. The best thing you can do now is to help that girl's poor mother. She took it hard. Mamas always do."

It cost Rita all she had not to break into pieces right there. Everything, even the officer in front of her, seemed insubstantial. "It's just—I don't understand. Patricia was seventeen, she was healthy, she was . . ." *Mine. Alive.*

"It's not for us to understand, is it? That's God's way."

His eyes went misty, the way sentimental people's did when they were enjoying their own sentiment. His hand was still on her knee. Rita wanted to rip his throat out with her teeth.

"Patty wasn't a drug user," she said. "How exactly did she die, and how *exactly* did Helen Rusk explain the sudden passing of a seventeen-year-old student in her care inside an empty school?"

Rita heard Mary's intake of breath. Officer Kaminski retracted his hand. He was listening now. Now he actually saw the girl in front of him. Rita watched him marshal himself before responding.

"Listen to me, hon. I'm doing you a favor, talking to you. And I'm going to do you another by pretending I didn't hear that just now." He started and gave up on several sentences, then shook his head. "Patricia Dean's parents don't want any fuss. Do you understand me? They want to bury their little girl and grieve in peace."

Rita went cold all over. Even her scalp prickled with ice. Because she did understand. Patty's parents didn't care how their daughter had died. She was headstrong and difficult and now she was gone. They might even believe what Miss Coates said out loud, and what the neighbors were surely whispering: that she'd been asking for it.

Rita sat still as stone as the man gave her one last pat, one last sympathetic grimace. Still looking at her he raised his voice and said, "Mary, did you ask for double cheese on my burger?"

A pause. "And medium rare," Mary replied.

"Good," he murmured. "Good." Then he sniffed hard and stood.

"You take care of yourself, now. I promise you, it won't

feel this hard forever." He looked askance at her tricky features, her limp bob, the unflattering drape of her sweater and dungarees. "A pretty girl like you should just focus on being happy."

Mary Paulsen made an odd noise. When he and Rita looked, she was bent over her magazine.

Kaminski gave Rita a final nod. "Another pot of coffee," he told Mary, and disappeared through the door.

For a minute neither girl spoke. Then Mary said, "Now you know I don't like to tell tales out of school." She talked like that, like it was still 1950 and women's lib didn't exist yet, but once you met her dad you forgave her for it. "But the things that man does to our plumbing? I'm tempted to call a priest."

That startled a laugh out of Rita. It tasted bitter, though.

"Come here," Mary said.

Rita did. The other girl stood, leaning over folded arms on the counter, and spoke in a rush. "The responding officer was a man named Jake Bunce. He won't talk to you, believe me. But he is a talker. He's up here flirting with me the minute my daddy's out of the station. I think what he likes about me is I'm a captive audience. He wouldn't get too far with a girl who could walk away."

Their heads nearly touched over the counter. Mary kept going, low and fast. "He got the call Thursday and he came in Friday morning looking like hell. When I told him so he said, 'You'd look like hell, too, if you were me.' By then my daddy had told me about poor Patty. But I could see there was more to it, and I knew he wanted to talk. So I got him a cup of coffee. And he kinda slumped, like this, and he said . . ."

"Tell me."

Mary looked Rita in the eye. "Principal Rusk made the call. She was waiting outside the school when Officer Bunce got there, looking cool as a cucumber. She told him she found Patty with some kind of substance in her hand, some kind of drug she didn't recognize. She told him the first thing she did was flush it. And he asked her, 'The *first* thing? Before checking to see if the girl was breathing?' I don't know what she said to that. But when he went in there he found Patty just like she said. On her back, on the bathroom floor.

"Bunce never saw an overdose before. Not unless you count liquor. He didn't know what to do. But he looked her over anyway, because he figured he should." Mary's voice was just above a whisper now. "Her skin was . . . well. It was blue. And there were marks around her mouth. Raw and red, just made. He thought maybe she'd scratched at her skin when she—when she was at the end. But something made him touch her there and her skin was sticky. I mean, *tacky*, like there was something on it. He stood up quick and he looked in the trash can. It was empty but he couldn't shake the feeling. He told me, 'Mary. I think Helen Rusk taped that girl's mouth shut.'"

I knew it.

The words weren't a thought but a feeling, flooding Rita's entire body. She should've been horrified, furious. And she *was*. But five minutes ago she'd been at the end of her strength, and now she had purpose. It burned everything else away and left her with a feeling akin to serenity.

Behind Mary, the door opened again. A different uniformed man stepped out. Without skipping a beat or looking away from Rita, Mary said, "A casserole. In a tinfoil pan, mind. That way Mrs. Dean won't have to worry about returning your glassware. Do you know whether the wake will be held at home?"

"Mary?" the man said. "When's dinner coming?"

He was somewhere in his twenties, but his skin already had the grayish cast of bad living. Rita wondered if he was Officer Bunce. She hadn't gotten to ask Mary who else he'd told about his suspicions. Whether the whole station knew they were participating in a cover-up in the name of respecting the craven wishes of Patty's parents.

"Thank you," she said, holding Mary's gaze. "I'll do tuna, I think. *Thank you*."

CHAPTER FORTY — SIX

RITA HAD NEVER BEEN AT the receiving end of one of Principal Rusk's lectures, but Patty had described them. Sister Bitch, raw-boned with self-denial, looming over her like a marionette, rapturous and ranting. *Jezebel* this, *Christian womanhood* that. Patty even did an imitation, to the delight of their friends. Of course she did, she didn't have a self-preserving bone in her body. She could never just keep her mouth *shut*.

So Rusk shut it for her. And Patty had a cold. *Hard to kiss, when you can't breathe through your nose.*

Simple as that.

Rita didn't remember driving home from the station. She didn't remember taking all her clothes off and lying on her bed and screaming until her own ears rang. But here she was, naked but for her promise ring, her mother's face close to hers and terrified. Rita was burning hot and wished she had more to take off, would gladly have peeled her skin away.

"Please, Rita," her mother sobbed. "Shh, my baby, *please*."

Her mother's shushing reached a primal place in Rita, and she stopped. Her mother startled at the sudden quiet.

Through it Rita reached out to pet the older woman's soft brown hair. "I'm sorry, Mama. I'm done."

She wouldn't cry for Patty again until she'd earned it.

Rita returned to school one week after Patty died for want of air. Her friends hugged her and rigidly she hugged them back. They whispered that Principal Rusk hadn't said one word about Patty's death. No anodyne speech, no assembly. The funeral was tomorrow, and still nothing.

In sixth period, the sudden fuzz of the intercom. Rita snapped to attention, skin stinging. Everyone else fell silent, sure they knew what was coming. Principal Rusk's voice sounded even reedier through the speaker.

"This is Principal Helen Rusk speaking, with a reminder to all students that there is not and will never be a Beatles Fan Club here at Palmetto High School. Requests for such a club have been repeatedly denied. This includes unofficial meetings on *or* off PHS grounds. Meetings of *any* sort that *praise* or up*raise* offensive examples of secular culture are punishable by detention or even suspension."

As she spoke her breathy voice gained power. You could hear her spitting.

"Thank you, students and staff, for your cooperation," she finished. "Have a blessed day."

The intercom went silent.

Rita's jaw was tight. Her mouth tasted like a penny. She clocked the glances of her classmates in her peripheral vision. Sympathetic, mostly. All of them knew she and Patty were a pair, and most would be at the funeral tomorrow. Wouldn't they be shocked when Rita didn't show? She'd die before she played along with Mr. and Mrs. Dean's lies. She'd die *gladly*.

At the chalkboard Mr. Underhill had a look on his face like he'd swallowed a cockroach. He was thirty or so, with hair that fell just past his ears. While he wasn't permitted to add or remove books from the syllabus, he did read the class poetry every Friday. Allen Ginsberg, Anne Sexton, Gwendolyn Brooks. There was no way Rusk knew about that.

Finally he shook his head disgustedly and said, "Anyone currently under the pernicious influence of Ringo Starr, please blink twice." The class laughed nervously. "Anybody? Nobody? All right, then. Let's continue."

He looked angry for the rest of class. But Rita wasn't mad. She still didn't know how exactly she was going to destroy Principal Rusk. But she'd just figured out how to get through to her in the meantime. How to let her know a reckoning was nigh.

CHAPTER FORTY—SEVEN

RITA WENT TO THE HARDWARE store. Not the one downtown, where Mr. Gish sat half-comatose listening to sports radio, but would follow her movements and make note of everything she purchased. Instead she drove all the way to Skokie and stopped at a gas station for directions to the nearest Ace. What she bought fit neatly into her shoulder bag.

That night, for the first time since losing Patty, Rita slept deep and long, and opened her eyes at eight a.m. on the dot. It was Saturday morning, the day of Patty's funeral. Rita's mother, clad in the same best black she'd worn to bury her husband six years ago, pleaded with her again to come to the church. *To say goodbye to Patty*, she said, as if that would reach her daughter. As if Rita *wanted* to let Patty go.

When her mother was gone Rita took the bag she'd packed from its hidden place. She saw no one on the walk to school, and hoped no one saw her. In her pocket was a key Patty stole sophomore year, on a dare, and never used. With it she opened the side door to Palmetto High School.

Principal Rusk was a murderer, and not one person

but Rita was willing to do a damned thing about it. She could've gone to the church right now and screamed the truth from the dais, and it would only make them *tsk* and whisper about Elin Ekstrom's problem child. She'd lived here all her life, she knew how these people worked. They'd make polite small talk as someone's father dragged her down the aisle.

Rita couldn't tell them anything. So she would speak straight to Principal Rusk. Like some witch hunter of yore, Rusk targeted and punished Patty in the name of God. In response, in Patty's image and in her name, Rita would create a shadow devotion. Something fierce and pagan and *true*. A way of telling Rusk, *I see you. I* know. *And this is far from over.*

Rita hummed as she walked to the bathroom, then sang as she worked. "Lady Jane," "I'm So Glad," "Girl from the North Country," Patty's favorite songs. She lined up a trio of bloodred candles, arranging around them a fresh tube of Patty's signature lipstick, her favorite candy, and a Beatles 7-inch.

When her little shrine was set, she kneeled.

Rita didn't pray often. She didn't mean to pray now. She believed in God—the God her parents raised her on, not the false and hateful deity that existed in the vicious hearts of people like Helen Rusk—but she didn't intend to bring Him into this room. She wanted only to speak to Patty.

Rita told her she was loved. That she would never be forgotten. That Rita wouldn't rest until Rusk had paid for what she'd done. By the end it was close enough to prayer to be indistinguishable from it.

For the past week she kept succumbing to the notion that she could feel Patty with her. A disturbance at the edge of her sight, a warmth she kept reaching for but couldn't touch. It only made it hurt worse when she remembered it wasn't real.

But as she spoke to Patty, as she very nearly prayed, Rita became aware of a presence in the room. It was behind her. Neither mystical nor nebulous, just *there*. Its attention was so focused she felt it like a hand pressing hard between her shoulder blades.

There was an alien tang to the presence. An intrusive sense of something *other*, watching her from elsewhere. She registered this in a wordless way, beneath the skin.

Then her mind caught up. And she thought, Patty.

Rita didn't turn. She hardly dared to breathe. Patty was *here*. Drawn in by Rita's devotion.

Or maybe it was her rage that made Patty come near. Her absolute commitment to vengeance.

With shaking hands she ripped a match free and lit it. As she touched the flame to the first candle's wick, she heard her name.

Did she? It was whispered at the exact pitch of the radiator's hiss. Perhaps she only *wished* she did.

Rita moved on to the second candle. As its wick caught, her nose filled with the ghostly odor of synthetic citrus. Patty's lemon perfume. She was so startled she let the matchstick burn down to her fingers, and dropped it with a gasp. Ripping out another match, she scraped it frantically over the striker.

When it caught she stretched her arm slowly toward the third candle. It lit with a pop.

Nothing happened. Then she felt the faintest brush of air over her left cheek. Rita waited, trembling. And then: the press of a kiss. Unmistakable.

Rita closed her eyes and saw the trio of flames dancing in purple and black. Patty's mouth pressed gently against each lid.

She stayed like that as long as she dared. Memories curled behind her eyes, her whole body radiant with Patty's blessing. Then she rose and took out her spray paint. She'd planned to write something damning on the wall, though she wasn't sure what. As she stood with her feet planted in the place where Patty's body had lain, Rita felt the cool touch of words that came from outside her. Writing them relieved, briefly, the hammering in her head.

THE GODDESS OF RECKONINGS IS NIGH

She painted her message again on Principal Rusk's office door. In the parking lot she took out the spray paint can one more time, shook it, and wrote the message in tall red letters on icy asphalt.

It was risky in the open but Rita knew no one would catch her. Not with Patty's ghost beside her, riding the air. She was so *light* now. If she fell, she would fall upward, grip Patty's hand, and rise.

CHAPTER FORTY—EIGHT

ON MONDAY THE BATHROOM WALL where Rita had left her message was glossy-bright with fresh paint. The door of Rusk's office, formerly naked wood, was painted a soft blue.

Principal Rusk should've had someone pour paint over the words in the parking lot and been done with it. Instead a custodial worker in heavy gloves scrubbed at it as the lot filled. Curious students filed past him, smelling turpentine and casting curious glances at the words fading beneath his elbow grease. *THE GODDESS OF RECKONINGS IS NIGH.* They saw these words, the bathroom wall, the painted door. And they wondered.

All day Rita waited to be called to the principal's office. She wanted to face her enemy, see the truth in her anemic features. The call never came, but her skin prickled with her classmates' attention. They were putting it together: graffiti in the parking lot, fresh paint in the school. Rita's conspicuous absence from a funeral where she should have been in the front row.

Could studious, sarcastic Rita Ekstrom be behind this strange defacement? It was decided among them that she could. Her position as chief bereaved gave her a glamorous cast among her schoolmates. She was set apart from them now, Patty's death the axe blow that cleaved her from the rest of humanity.

But why did she paint *those* words? And what would she do next?

No one got to see the first shrine, swept up and trashed before school resumed. Rita made more. She got lucky, laying her shrines without ever getting caught. Patty was the seashell whisper in her ear that guided her to the places where, for just long enough, no one passed by.

She grew bolder. Alongside EPs and lipsticks she left empty gin bottles she dug out from where her mother hid them in the trash, and sexy magazine pictures of Twiggy and Mick Jagger and Penelope Tree. Anything to make Principal Rusk's skin crawl, to force her to retaliate.

Her classmates didn't know what to make of it. Some laughed, others were confused, a confusion that could shift quicksilver to destruction. The shrines never lasted long. Plenty of people ignored Rita and her bizarre project entirely.

But there were others who seemed to understand what she was doing. As if they, too, could sense Patty's nearness, her reluctance to be gone.

Since the moment Rita kneeled in the empty school and drew Patty in, anchoring her with love and promises, Patty walked beside her. Ephemeral yet undeniable. Keeping pace but never drawing too close. She was a shadow moving over the floor beyond Rita's closed bedroom door. A presence in the corner of the room, watching over her as she slept.

Of course Rita asked herself, Am I unwell? Griefsick,

lovesick, losing my mind? If so it was a benevolent madness. She'd take it over the cold alternative of absolute sanity. She kept up her lonely devotion, hoping it would keep Patty close. Hoping Rusk would break, and the unknown endgame of her revenge would make itself clear to her. What else could she do?

Two weeks after the funeral, sitting in mathematics, Rita slid her notebook aside to find words carved into the wood of her desktop.

The Goddess of Reckonings Knows Your Sins

She traced them with a trembling finger. Had *she* carved them? She couldn't recall doing it. But it was true that when she laid a shrine, she went into a kind of gentle trance, as if Patty were helping to guide her hand. She couldn't be sure she hadn't.

The next day, when Rita got to school, a crowd was gathered outside the front doors. She couldn't see what they were looking at until she was nearly there. A message, written in foot-high letters on the school's exterior wall: *THE GODDESS COMETH.*

It wasn't just the words that drew the crowd. It was the fact that they very much appeared to have been written in blood.

Rita's classmates parted for her as she moved right up to the wall. Close as she could get, until she smelled the iron, saw the unmistakable rusty catch of blood on pale brick. It lit her up. Patty's spirit shone on her like a second sun.

The cult of Patricia Dean, goddess of reckonings, had grown.

Why did the goddess craze spread so feverishly, so fast? Rita would ask herself this later.

The school was probably ripe for rebellion, teeming with the powder keg tensions of a student body just barely held at bay by a cruel and rigid principal. And it was the early days of 1968, the very air flammable with dangerous transformations.

Or maybe her classmates were responding to the terrifying neatness with which popular, vivacious Patty Dean had gone under and disappeared, her parents and the police and the school all conspiring to pretend she'd never been there at all.

But the goddess Rita made of Patty's spirit and memory had her own power from the start. A candle flame flicking to life between Rita's fingers. Passing hand to hand until it grew into a bonfire. Like any deity, the goddess began as an agreed-upon reality. And like any good story told when the lights were on, her power grew when no one was watching. In the dark.

The shrines took root everywhere, the work of dozens of unseen hands. In the crook of a stairwell or the cold shade of a doorway, words scrawled above them in marker or chalk. *The Goddess of Reckonings Is Watching You.*

The claustrophobic air of PHS opened up, shimmering with an unchained recklessness. Hanging on the air, Patty preened. Ever present, ever unreachable, the tart breath of havoc that stirred the room.

Her influence grew from a breath to a rebellious wind, sweeping caution away. Girls wore their skirts shorter, threaded hoops through their ears. They painted their mouths corpse-white or bright as blood and let their bangs skim their eyes like Grace Slick's. There was a glass-sharp edge to every argument, a chaotic sense of good-bad possibilities blooming. Everyone seemed to be dumping her boyfriend.

And Principal Rusk was nowhere to be seen. Though a permeating presence, Rusk didn't leave her office much. Mostly she was a voice on the intercom, a somber shape turning the corner just ahead. A black-garbed spider making her twice-yearly address to the student body, pale hands and face standing out like things left too long in the dark. Now she closed herself away entirely. A king teetering at the edge of overthrow.

Then a very ugly rumor started to spread.

Rita never said a word to anyone. It must've come from someone at the station. A policeman's wife, carrying a marital confession to her coffee klatch. Soon it was everywhere, spoken of in thrilled, horrified whispers: the suspicious marks around Patty's mouth, the unprovable claim of drugs flushed down the toilet. The indisputable fact that just one person had been in the school when Patricia Dean died so suddenly: Principal Helen Rusk.

Patty had been wild, they told each other, but she was still a daughter of their town. A churchgoer all her life. Suburban girls made mistakes, but they didn't know where to get *drugs*.

The burghers of Palmetto smelled blood. One by one, across grocery store run-ins and Tupperware parties and pre-dinner phone calls, people discovered they'd never really trusted Principal Rusk. Her piety was suspect, her reign approaching its death throes.

But no one accused her of the worst out loud. They barely allowed themselves to think it. Helen Rusk would be voted out of the job in some emergency session, shuffled off to the next school, the next monstrosity. And that would be that.

Rita's revenge plot had whipped up into a fad and a fever, half the school engaged in a rebellion in Patty's name. And part of what she'd set out to do had been achieved: everyone knew, or at least suspected, that Rusk had killed Patty. But not one of them, *not one*, cared to do shit about it.

Her anger became abhorrence, a soul-sickness that bordered on delirium. What could she do, alone, to punish a woman who refused to show her face?

In the shower Rita tipped her face up and stepped into the spray, letting shampoo run in suds over her closed eyelids. *I'm sorry*, she said in her head. *I'm sorry, Patty. I tried.*

She felt the odd muffled sensation that meant Patty was near, her presence pushing everything that wasn't her just a little bit farther away. Then, from just in front of her, a whisper.

Open your eyes.

Rita's eyes snapped open and right there, between the water and the wall, was a smoky shape.

She screamed. Soap ran into her eyes and burned them and by the time she could see clearly the shape was gone. Patty. Was gone.

In bed that night, at the very edge of sleep, Patty came to her again.

Open your eyes.

Rita did, and found herself sitting at a café table on a quaint European street. It was, right down to the pretty cane chairs and green awning, her vision of what her and Patty's life was supposed to be after graduation. Two American girls in Paris, living the expat writer's life.

Patty sat across from her. Rita had looked at and loved

that face since she was eight years old, but in the weeks since Patty's death the details had gone fuzzy. One day they would be washed clean away.

"What are you waiting for?" Patty asked softly. Rita heard the words not with her ears but inside her head. The feeling was a deep itch she could never reach. "You know what you have to do."

Patty was always good at that: making things simple. Rita overcomplicated everything. Running around playing mind games with a concealed opponent, making a mess of what could've been easy from the start.

Now the end came to her so clearly. She breathed out in a rush and reached for Patty's hands. Then woke in the dark, reaching for no one.

CHAPTER FORTY-NINE

RITA WAS GOING TO KILL Helen Rusk.

The clarity of it took her breath away. It was late March now, winter losing its teeth, but Rita didn't want spring without Patty. That the world had the *audacity* to wake back up when Patty never would made her want to kill Helen Rusk twice.

But she'd only get to do it the once. She didn't make some big plan. Didn't spend days thinking on how to get it right, how to cover her tracks. What she did was, she bashed the doorknob off the principal's office with a brick. It only took her two good hits.

It was just past five p.m. and the school was empty. The door was cheap particleboard, so thin she probably could've kicked through it as a backup plan. It swung inward to reveal Helen Rusk.

Patty's murderer didn't look like the monster Rita carried in her head. Rusk was fiftysomething, her body a study in deprivation. Crafted of bird bones, the face nearly fleshless.

Rita figured Rusk would hear the smash of the brick and go straight for her telephone, but that wasn't what had happened. She was on her feet, to the left of the desk, facing Rita. Both her hands were wrapped around a wooden baseball bat.

That's why you don't make a plan. Plans go awry, you waste time trying to adjust. Rita had no plan, so it was easy: she sized up the situation in half a breath and rushed Sister Bitch.

Rusk reacted fast. Her bat caught Rita in the belly, a little abortive half swing. Any higher and harder and Rita would've been curled on the ground around a set of cracked ribs. As it was, she let pain feed momentum and kept coming, the two of them falling to the carpet with Rita on top.

The brick and the bat crunched between them. Both made sounds of pain. Rita would have bruises later, and two jammed fingers and scrapes in places that made no sense. But that was later. Right now Rusk was beneath her, lashing like a tomcat caught in the black bag of her dress. Like a cat, she spat.

Her saliva hit Rita's left cheekbone with an acid splash. Did this woman misunderstand the situation? Did she not see who was on top, pinning her arms to the floor, her own hands still wrapped around a muddy brick? Rita lifted the brick and smashed it down on Rusk's shoulder.

The woman screamed. Until then their encounter had been wordless. But when Rita lifted the brick a second time Rusk shrieked, "I didn't!"

Rita paused. She couldn't care less what Rusk had to say in her own defense, but she did have questions. Had she drugged Patty first? Tied her hands before taping her mouth? How had it really happened, in the end?

"Didn't *what*?"

"She had a fit." Helen Rusk did not sound cowed. "The

girl did everything but dare me to muzzle her. She *laughed* at me until I restrained her and covered her filthy mouth. Then she had a fit. The Devil was in her, I didn't dare go near." Even lying on her back, panting through her teeth with pain, Rusk could've been pounding a country pulpit. "The Devil *is* a drug. The worst one there is."

Rita hadn't cried since the evening she talked to good Mary Paulsen. She'd be *damned* if she would cry in front of Helen Rusk. But her eyes blurred. Her voice came out very quiet.

"What'd she do, sass you some? Patty never could hush. That wasn't a fit, that was *panic*. She couldn't breathe and you watched her die struggling, because you'd rather believe in the devil on earth than lift a finger to undo your sin. *Your* sin, you murderer."

Rusk blinked. She seemed like she might speak, so Rita came down hard, pressing a sweatered forearm over the woman's mouth. "'I didn't know,'" she said in a dull, imitative tone. "'I just wanted to shut her up. I wasn't trying to kill her.'" Then, in her own voice, "I don't care. And I am going to kill you."

The world hitched like a creature catching its breath. Rita's skin hurt. She blinked and she was in bed with the flu, aching all over, her dad dancing an elephant over the blankets. She blinked again and saw a little girl with yellow braids and a face as beautiful as a wildflower. The girl grew up, and together they learned what love could be.

When was she? The world was wobbling now. It was ridiculous and random, a broken thing glued back together by a child. Rita had let herself think without thinking that killing Rusk would bring Patty back: a life for a life. She knew now that it wouldn't. Perhaps she would go to Patty.

Whatever Rita did next, she didn't want to do it with a brick. She threw it and the bat aside, far enough that Rusk couldn't reach them even if she did get an arm free. But Rusk sensed weakness in the move, and sent the fingers on her uninjured side questing in that direction.

Rita punched her in the face. Rusk made a horrible whining sound and Rita shook her aching hand like she'd seen men do in the movies. *Was* this a movie? The air rang with iron and ammonia, Rusk's bones shifted beneath her, and she knew it wasn't. The knowledge made her want to cry. She snaked a hand around to free the knife she'd taped to the middle of her back.

When Rusk saw the knife she started screaming. She brought her pelvis up so fast Rita listed to the side, freeing the principal's left arm. Immediately Rusk used it to clock her along the temple, a blow so glancing and pathetic Rita thought about laughing. Instead she took the tape she'd just ripped off her back and pressed it to the woman's mouth, where it wouldn't stay.

"Stop it," she said, as Helen Rusk went on screaming. "*Shut up!*"

She looked for the place she could cut or crush to make the noise stop and the only answer was the obvious one, the thin skin and rolling tendons of Helen Rusk's neck.

What would she be on the other side of this? Rita felt the touch of her mother's hand, soft with dishwater. She heard the rumble of her dead father's voice. She saw Patty laughing, Patty with lowered lids, Patty in the cafeteria that final day, turning away with a secret smile. Rita hefted the knife. Sweating, aching, her vision pulsing in time with her heart.

Then she folded, clutching it to her chest and crying out, "I can't!"

And Patty, who had been with her all the time, spoke to her as clearly as she had in the dream.

I can.

Rita's right hand, the one that held the knife, turned gold. Not Midas gold. Gold like a lion in the sun.

Rusk stopped screaming. Both of them stared as Rita turned her fist from side to side. They held their breath, watching the light flex and glister and become fingers wrapping themselves around hers.

And, oh. Rita hoped and she imagined but she didn't really believe she would feel this again. The hand that held hers was hot yellow light but it was *Patty's hand*, the exact press and texture.

Helen Rusk was babbling now. "My Lord, keep me, my God, hold me," on and on, and whether she was repenting or seeking His protection was unclear.

I can help you, Patty whispered. *Rita, my love, you can rest. If you'll just let me in*. Let me in.

Somehow Rita knew what to do. She raised her right hand, still caught in Patty's golden grip, and pressed it to her heart. She took her final breath alone in her body.

Then she welcomed Patty in.

Between that breath and the next was a slice of a moment, razor-thin, when it became too late to change her mind. In that instant the presence she called *Patty* felt like shrapnel, sharp-edged and unlike anything she'd ever known. The feeling took her back to the day she prayed to Patty in the PHS bathroom, and felt something watching her.

Something patient and intelligent, drawn in by the drifting perfume of vengeful fury and desperate prayer. A presence that Rita, in her grief, decided was Patty.

Then the thought was gone, as if she'd never had it. Banished with force from her head.

Through their layered hands, pressing hard to her heart, Patty melted impossibly into Rita's body. She was of her. *Inhabiting* her. They were one.

Rita felt drenched in hard sun. Overfull with it, scalp to toes, limned on the inside with liquid gold. Patty looked through her eyes and wound through her mind and flexed the fingers of her right hand, peeling it away from her chest. Rita saw the skin beneath it was marked with a perfect blue-black handprint. It showed the place where Patty, the goddess of reckonings, had opened Rita's body like a door.

At some point Helen Rusk stopped praying. When Rita looked at her now, there was something wrong with her face. A shadow was in it. It looked like a bad thing rising up through clear water.

Patty's voice was barbed velvet, soft and catching, a relentless lovely pain. *Ready, Rita?*

The sense of fullness expanded until it was overwhelming. There was no *space* for her, she was pressed against the boundary of her own skin. Until finally it broke open and released her. She fell rainlike through a long, plain dark, and when it was done she found herself lying on her back beneath a willow tree.

Rita lay still as the world returned to her in pieces: willow branches reaching down to graze her jeans. Cold air scented with mulch and snowmelt. A cedar waxwing singing, its voice like a sweet unoiled hinge. And pain, digging its fingernails into her inch by inch as she came out of the dark.

Standing up hurt, standing was *terrible*. The ground

listed and Rita went down, hand catching on the thing that nestled at the base of the tree, pushed into the dirt like it had always been there. A brick.

She looked but she found no knife. She checked her hands and saw roughed-up skin washed clean. There was a Band-Aid on her right palm. When she brought it to her nose she caught the tang of Mercurochrome and the industrial odor of powdered cleaner. Someone had washed her, patched her up. Cut a stretch of time from her head.

Rita wanted to scream. But her throat was already so raw with it.

CHAPTER FIFTY

MISS EKSTROM'S KITCHEN DIDN'T SEEM cozy anymore. It felt like an outpost on the moon. As she told the story her voice flattened and her face emptied out. By the end both were utterly without affect.

"But . . ." I shook my head, coming up from the deep water of her tale. "What happened? What did you do?"

"The goddess promised a reckoning. It came."

"And no one . . ."

"What? Arrested me?" She sniffed. "After Rusk disappeared, the fever broke. All anyone wanted to do was forget. Not just Rusk, but Patty, because they knew what had happened to her and they just stood by. But enough of them remembered. The ones who were a part of it, they remembered. They told their little sisters, and later their daughters. Even if they thought of it all as a prank or a mass delusion. Even if their tellings turned the goddess into a horror story, a granter of wishes, a *game*—all of it kept her memory alive. She stitched herself into the skin of this place. Patty will *never* be gone. I'll never forget the first time I heard the little girls chanting as they skipped rope."

Her voice lilted over the words, and there was triumph in it. "'Goddess, goddess, count to five.'"

In the morning, who's alive? The hair rose on my arms. The rhyme, the dangerous trust game in all its iterations: all were an homage to how far Ekstrom went to make sure the girl she loved wouldn't be forgotten.

And the dreams I'd been having that were memories— they were Ekstrom's memories. Every school break, every long weekend, she traveled far from home. Now I knew why.

"All these years," I said dully. "All these years you've been . . . taking people, for the goddess. Your whole *life*?"

"It's been a worthy life."

The kitchen was nearly dark now. What light there was settled uneasily over her face. I remembered the damning things I'd seen in it that eclipsed the human in her completely.

"But what do you do to them? What did *they* do, to make you think they deserved it?"

"Do you think they deserve my remorse?" she asked. "Since I was seventeen I've existed in a world of monsters. They are *everywhere*. With the goddess I saw the things they've done, the things they'd do. And I got to choose. It was a *privilege* to choose. Together we scoured dozens of monsters from the Earth. Saved uncountable lives."

She put her elbows on the table and leaned in, eyes raking my face with an envious assessment that made my stomach twist. "Do you think you'll choose differently? Will you walk through a crowd and see ten kinds of evil, a dozen time bombs, and do nothing? The hardest part will be knowing you can't do *enough*. And learning how to take proper care. Avoid returning to the same places, don't create patterns. Never let the goddess get too hungry."

My head felt like a cathedral, oversized and echoing with the beat of my own blood. "Hungry."

"For the wicked."

I stared at her. "Logan Kilkenny. Chloe Park. Tate, Kurt, that, that man in the bar, whoever he was. *All* of them."

"There've been lots of men. In lots of bars. All of them deserved what they got. Are you such a child that you can't understand that?"

"Chloe Park was a child," I said softly.

"She was an aberration. They all were." A desperate expression flickered over her face. "You do understand how important this is? If I weren't too old to keep it up . . . but, the hunger. The travel, and the act of it, *taking* them. Even just carrying it, the weight of what needs to be done. It's all so . . . *tiring*. Patty." Her voice broke. "She needs someone who isn't so tired."

"She needs . . ." I put a hand to my mouth. "*Oh*. My god. Becca. You were *recruiting* her."

It killed me to think how *ready* Becca would've been for it. She'd been preparing for this kind of power since we were ten. It must've felt like fate to her. Like she'd been chosen by a sister creature to our own goddess of revenge.

A quieter part of me understood that it could've been more than a mission for her. Working for the goddess, becoming what Ekstrom had become—maybe it was an escape hatch.

Ekstrom was shaking her head. "Recruit," she said dismissively. "Becca saw me. Last summer in the woods, she saw the goddess take someone. I waited to see what she'd do, if she'd tell. But the goddess knew Becca was meant to replace me. And sure enough, she came. Becca found *me*."

"No," I said hollowly. "You isolated a girl without a family and tried to pass her a *parasite*. This thing in me? It isn't Patty. It isn't human, and it never was."

Miss Ekstrom looked down at her fisted hands. "She doesn't understand yet," she murmured, "but she will." It took me a second to get that she was talking *about* me, not to me. "I promise, I'll teach her, too." Then she did address me. "I will help you understand why this is a burden worth carrying. I'm sorry it happened this way. But even if it wasn't going to be you, everything happened as it was meant to. The goddess doesn't make mistakes."

"Really? Because this looks like a mistake to me." I yanked the neck of my dress down to display the bruise-colored handprint.

Ekstrom ticked her tongue disgustedly. "I expected more of you, Nora." For the first time since I opened my eyes here, she actually sounded like my teacher. "Do you have *no* respect for what you carry? Even now, knowing what you do about Kurt Huffman, knowing all of it started with Becca's choice—none?"

I glared at her. "If all of this was her choice. If the goddess never makes mistakes. Then *where is Becca*?"

My voice thickened and shook. I watched sympathy spark in her face and instantly die, like the flick of a failing lighter. "She's gone."

"Gone," I repeated. "Gone *where*? Did your goddess—" *Eat her up*, I was going to say, but I couldn't bear to be so glib.

"I don't think so," she half whispered. "I don't know. I am sorry."

I stood. I didn't know everything, but I'd heard enough. I pitied Ekstrom more than I hated her. She was a death cult of one, the goddess's real first victim.

But in a twisted way, she inspired me. She never ever gave up on Patricia Dean, even when she should have. And I wasn't ready to give up on Becca.

Ekstrom and I were more alike than I wanted to admit. She followed Patty beyond the line of death and was ensnared by something there. I was ready to do the same; I was, like teenage Rita, the *only* one who would.

Becca was mine and I was hers and I didn't have the space to consider whether that was good or bad. It just *was*. We'd nourished and stunted each other in turn. Grown toward and around each other, fed on love and loss, resentment and dependence.

And death was already in me. Hijacking my sight, ticking like a clock toward some unconscionable hunger. So what did I have to lose?

"You can't go yet." Ekstrom's voice was edged with something frantic. "I know this isn't what you wanted, but there's more you need to hear. The goddess will ask so *much* of you."

I looked at her one last time. Haggard in the near-dark, stooped beneath the weight of all she had carried.

"I'm sorry," I said, and meant it. "I'm off to play the goddess game."

I slid the back door open and let myself into the night.

CHAPTER FIFTY—ONE

I'D THOUGHT THE NOTE I wrote to myself was a question: *play g gm rembr.* We played the goddess game, remember? But now I wondered: What if it was a promise? Play the goddess game, and you will remember.

I knew now that as I lay in Becca's yard last Saturday night, Ekstrom's goddess had found its way into my skin. But I wanted to know *how.* If I did, I might understand what happened to Becca.

Night had fallen as I sat at Ekstrom's table, listening to her confession. A few flakes gusted down from the black. *Diamond dust.* I had no sense of time anymore, it could've been eight or midnight or two in the morning. I sprinted over her lawn and into the woods.

It was one of those icy-clear nights when you can make out the bones of the world. Naked branches and furrowed earth and a sky so empty you could guess at the curve of the Milky Way. I pounded down the path, sliding on slush and patches of black ice, stepping in puddles that broke with a crushed-glass sound and flooded my boots with meltwater. Everything else was snow-globe silent.

I reached our clearing and Becca was all around me.

Setting up her tripod, pulling candy from our hollow tree, unrolling a Kingdom map. Mouth Icee-blue, Band-Aids on her knees and chains of wildflowers wilting in her hair. I walked through the ring of imagined girls and at the clearing's center I stopped, slipped my flannel off my shoulders, and spun it into a rope. I tied the rope over my eyes.

The quiet was so different than it was in summer. There were no leaves to soften the wind's lonesome sound, no sun to warm it. Inside me the thing Miss Ekstrom called *goddess* was very still. I had so many questions but only one mattered now: whether Becca was with me somehow. Not entirely gone.

I would play the goddess game. If I was right and she was close I would walk through the trees unscathed. I'd play the game, and remember.

First, I reached for her. My best friend's magnificent mind and daunting talent and flashing silliness. Her sun freckles and gimlet eye and that wild October hair, apples and firelight and butterscotch candy. It took me so long to *listen*, but I was listening now. I gripped the thought of her like a heat-bright wire, and when I trusted my hold, I began.

On the way here I'd slipped and stumbled. Now I walked smoothly through the trees. Beneath my boots was grass and ice, earth and snow. Steadily I went, and I knew I traced perfectly the path I'd walked seven summers ago. I stopped, put my hand out, and felt the rough trunk of the maple. Gripping the branch just above me, I swung myself into its arms.

I climbed. The blindfold tipped the nervous sound of my breathing back into my ears. Bark scraped my bare legs. When I'd climbed high enough I felt for that thick branch and found it, then crawled across it belly down. I was heavier than I was at ten. My rib cage pressed hard around the branch, threatening to separate. I let my body fall.

CHAPTER FIFTY—TWO

AS SOON AS I HIT the water I could feel the squatter in me spread, numbing me out. I thought of the way I lay all night in Becca's frozen yard and didn't even get frostbite. It was *protecting* me, then and now. Protecting its vessel. I lay still beneath icy water and didn't feel it at all.

And a steely new purpose presented itself: if I stayed long enough in the killing cold, I might *force* this parasite to go.

Get out, I thought.

My chest tightened around stale air. My heart thudded slow and deep like the pulse of a hibernating animal.

Get out.

I could drown. If this didn't work, or maybe even if it did, I would drown. I didn't have it in me to feel sorry or afraid or to watch my life run before my eyes in a melancholy reel. What thoughts I had came in hollow flashes, timed to the beating of my heart.

Get out, I said. *Get out get out get—*

No.

It spoke in Becca's voice. I couldn't feel my body at all, but my fury at that seemed physical.

Don't. I know you're not her. Who are you?

Her voice again, ordinary and a little impatient. *I'm your best friend, Nor.*

No. Who are you?

Its speech changed completely, became scratchy and sweet and the faintest bit mocking. *I'm Patty Dean.*

No. You're not. Who are you?

Now it was a voice made up of many voices, corded and rolling, vibrating in my back teeth. *I am the Goddess of Reckonings.*

There is no goddess. She doesn't exist.

A long silence. Then out of it slid a voice that was sticky and heavy and slow. Not the thing in the dark, but the dark itself.

She did, it said. *I was her. I am always what you believe me to be.*

I believe you are nothing.

Nothing? Its voice was neither angry nor impatient nor amused. *I have been goddess and monster. An eater of sins in the service of man, and the devil who takes the unshriven. Prayed to and guarded against in turn, though my appetite for wickedness is always as it has been. But I have never been Nothing.*

I took that in. The small corner of it I could fathom. *What do you want? Why are you here?*

If you were banished, hungry, to the endless dark. And you found an open door back to the bright world, and a way to feed again on the food you like best. Wouldn't you walk through it?

I'm sure I would. But that door is gone, and this one I'm closing to you. If I could've moved at all, I would have lifted my hand to the print on my chest. *Get out.*

No.

Then I'll starve you out. It'll take longer but you'll go in the end.

You won't, and I won't. I could feel the thinning of its perfect patience. It was doing its best to keep me alive, but my body would need air soon. *I'll feed myself.*

No. I expressed it with all the force I had. *Get out, I don't want you,* get out. *You think I'll give up but I won't. If I can't starve you out, I will die to* force *you out, and you'll go back to the dark. I will* never *let you feed on anyone.*

Stupid girl, it said. *You already did.*

Inside me crouched a creature that called itself *goddess.* Cupped carefully in its hands was a slice of last Saturday night that it had been hiding from me. Not much, just an hour or so.

It opened its hands and let the hour out.

LAST SATURDAY NIGHT

NORA

HER TEXT CAME JUST BEFORE midnight.

I love you

Only that. I read it and my eyes went wide in the dark. I replied in an anxious flurry.

Hi

I love you too

Okay I just tried to call. Lmk youre ok

Becca??

I'm coming over

I had to go on foot. In January, at night. As I walked my mood flipped from fear to fury and back again. The text was weird, but on the other hand it was classic Becca: dropping a line in the water. Waiting to see if I'd bite.

I went through the woods and they felt unfriendly, the night around them deep as an underwater trench. I was craving the slap of instant relief that would come when I saw Becca's face through her bedroom window, screwed into an expression of *what are you doing here?*

I walked faster. Down her block, to the edge of her driveway. The air smelled of snow but none had fallen yet. Everything—me and the weather and the world—felt perched at a tipping point, on the verge of some change.

I hurried up the driveway, along the side of the house. Through the back gate.

And into a nightmare.

BECCA

BECCA KNEW GOODBYES WEREN'T AN option. After tonight she would simply slip out of her life as she'd known it and into a new one. She had a plane ticket, a burner phone, a short-term studio rental in a town she'd never heard of, twenty minutes outside a city she had. Miss Ekstrom had arranged all of it. Becca would have to find work when she got there, the money the older woman gave her wouldn't last long.

Ekstrom had impressed upon her repeatedly that she couldn't tell anyone anything. She implied the transfer might not work if she did, owing to the capriciousness of the goddess. But Becca doubted that. She knew Ekstrom and the goddess needed her as much as she needed what they were offering: not just a life of unassailable purpose, but a change so transformative it would rip her clear of her history, and cauterize the exit wound.

The transfer would begin at midnight, which was either crucial or completely arbitrary and she couldn't decide which. She would wear white, like a vestal virgin or a human sacrifice: Ritual 101. She suspected Ekstrom was making this up as she went along.

But Becca had always respected a sense of theater. And everything was arbitrary until you gave it purpose. Once, she took her own tragedy and formed it into a goddess of revenge, burning irreplaceable photos of her lost mother to petition the supernatural. Tonight she would commit her final link to this life to the flames: a summer-camp photo of herself and Nora in a hand-painted wooden frame, and the beautiful camera her parents gave her, which had served as her translator for the past eight years.

At six o'clock Becca took a shot of Miranda's embarrassing orange vodka to settle herself. By seven, she'd had three. Then she switched to coffee, because otherwise she might actually fall asleep. When Miranda walked in on her making a French press at eight in the evening, Becca considered saying something pithy and mysterious, so Miranda would think of it after she was gone and wonder. She settled for mumbling, "I'll be out of your way in a sec."

Her stepmother wasn't really so terrible. She was just profoundly unlucky.

By eleven Miranda was, as usual, fast asleep with her earplugs in and her sleep mask on and her TV set to play old episodes of *Friends* all night long, episodes she would neither see nor hear but that would populate the room with companionable motion. On top of all that she took a nightly pill from the bottle of generic Ambien Becca skimmed only rarely. Miranda wouldn't be bothering anyone.

At 11:30 Ekstrom texted, *I am on my way*, which was funny because she used contractions just fine in real life, why couldn't she manage them in a text?

At 11:35 Becca felt so sick and shaken she had to remind herself she wouldn't be dead tomorrow, just different, and far away. Her life would still be recognizable. She would still read books and watch movies and take photos and drink tea. Not Earl Grey, though. Ekstrom had turned her off it for life.

At 11:40 she walked outside with her phone, her camera, and a cup of coffee dosed liberally with more vodka. Beneath her coat, as instructed, she wore a plain white dress. In her pocket were three names written in pen on a Post-it. Ekstrom had asked for one, but this was her rodeo now, wasn't it? Besides, she and the goddess would never come back to Palmetto. Might as well leave with a bang, three sinners vanished.

Four. She would be wrapped up in the story, too. She hoped she'd left Nora enough to understand there were deeper mysteries afoot, to get that she wasn't *really* gone. Enough that she might even forgive Becca one distant day, when she showed up to surprise Nora in some coffee shop or lecture hall. By then she'd have tattoos and a pink pixie cut, let's say. And spilled blood, invisible but indelible, all over her.

Maybe she wouldn't surprise Nora after all. But the dream—the lie—made it easier to sit still and wait. The stars through her camera lens were the color of dry ice, fizzing in space like little chemical reactions. She snapped a photo she'd never develop and chanted a snatch of the old rhyme.

> *Goddess, goddess, count to three*
> *If I'm good, will you pick me?*

For weeks she'd been telling herself she was giving up nothing she hadn't already lost. But now everything she was leaving behind shone with a painful brightness. The slipstream feel of the woods between seasons, the little house where she had lived very happily for many years of her life. The hopeful quiet of the PHS darkroom, the unexpected entrance of James into her life, an honest-to-god new friend who understood her, or at least listened with enough care to decipher.

From the start, she'd paired him with Nora in her head. Becca didn't want her best friend to be alone. She wondered what would come of her pushing them to meet, and longed fiercely to see it.

She let the wave of wanting wash over her. When it had receded enough for her to breathe properly, it was 11:48 and she had another text from Ekstrom.

I am coming around to meet you now.

Becca dropped her head and blew out hard, like a person in a Nike commercial. She deleted all her messages from Ekstrom and removed them from her Recently Deleted folder. Then, quickly and without thought, she texted Nora.

She found she couldn't not say goodbye. She hadn't planned ahead, hadn't figured out some perfect combination of words, just dashed off the truest thing and hit send.

I love you

Then Ekstrom was opening the creaky gate. Becca dropped her phone and nudged it under a pool chair and waited for the next part to begin.

NORA

IT WAS 12:14, NOT HALF an hour after Becca texted me. I stood in her open back gate, unable to make sense of what I was seeing.

Up on the pool deck Becca stood barefoot in a stark white dress, spotlit by the moon. Arms out, right palm forward, feet planted. Her hair was pulled back, showing her expressionless face.

Facing her, right palm out to mirror hers, stood a person who didn't belong here. In this yard, in this picture. Someone who was part of *my* life, who, as far as I knew, Becca had never even spoken to. Miss Ekstrom. She, too, was dressed in white, she, too, stood on vulnerable bare feet. They could've been dancers in some experimental play.

Between them was a flickering orange fire. An awful smell rolled from it, burning plastic and ozone, the electrical odor of a rip in the world.

Did I scream when I saw them? I wasn't sure. If I did they didn't hear me. Didn't sense me, didn't seem to exist inside the same world as me. Becca's dress was made of some flyaway fabric and it rippled around her legs. Ekstrom's clothes, too, moved in a wind I couldn't feel. Her face shone with tears, lit orange by the fire below.

I didn't run to them. I *couldn't*. I moved steadily forward, hugging myself, bent against the treacherous desire to get away from whatever was happening here. What was *happening* here?

I was close—just a few steps from the deck, looking up at their faces—when it really began.

What it looked like was fog, rolling off Ekstrom like smoke off the sea.

No. It was a sheet of black chainmail, lifting away from her chest. A glimmering swarm, shushing free of her rib cage.

Dark rain. Black ink. A chittering data cloud of unpossibility, a phenomenon that did not, *should* not exist.

Whatever I was looking at, my eyes weren't made to see it. My brain couldn't bear to comprehend it. All the possibilities collapsed into this: a furling dark ribbon of compressed gray smoke, issuing from my teacher's chest like blood from a kill shot.

Her head lolled on its stem as the smoke unwound itself. She looked so frail, but she didn't fall. Something was keeping her on her feet. The same thing that held Becca so utterly still.

The smokething broke free of Ekstrom's chest with a meaty snap. It hung between them, undulating like a banner on the breeze. I blinked and for half a breath I *saw* it: an intelligent vastness with a woman's face and a gunmetal gleam, the edges of it sizzling to steam on the air.

An explosion of pain behind my eyes made me close them. As I did, I thought, It can't stay here. The thing that came out of Ekstrom had been comfortable where it was. It wouldn't last out here in the open.

Oh.

I surged across the last few yards of grass. I was hoisting myself onto the deck when the thing compressed itself, winding like searching fingers around Becca's outstretched hand. With an inexorable sweep she brought the hand in and pressed it to her chest.

Her head snapped back. Her limbs stiffened and bowed, taffylike. *Horrible.* Her hair stood out in a crackling halo and the sound that came from her mouth was not human. It wasn't a sound of agony or terror. It was deeper and worse: a sigh of satisfaction.

She fell to her knees with a bruising crack. Ekstrom fell farther, until she lay prone, squeezing and releasing her fists as she gasped for breath. The sight of it froze me, drained the strength out of me. I could no longer lift myself onto the deck. Instead I walked lead-legged to the steps and climbed them.

I felt I was moving through a dream. Ekstrom lay on her side, limply struggling. Just past her the fire had gone out. I could see now what was burning: Becca's camera. What used to be her camera. I noted it and went on. Becca lifted her head just as I crouched beside her, our faces a foot apart.

The alien reach of that gaze hit me like lightning and ice. It wasn't Becca looking at me.

Its eyes were Becca's, the odd flat blue of grass before the sun comes up. Its solemn face was hers, framed by wisps of Pre-Raphaelite hair. It was Becca's face and hair and body. Something else was using them.

We were kneeling so close I could've cupped its borrowed cheek. The idea of touching it—of it touching me—filled me with revulsion. But it didn't *have* to touch me. I was flayed to my core by its regard.

It smiled. The smile was heavy-lidded, *benevolent*, unlike any expression Becca had ever made. It unstuck me. I thumped onto my tailbone and slid backward. I smeared the ashes, I knocked the ruined camera into the pool. The creature that wore my best friend like a captured skin said,

"Stop."

I stopped. The word was an order, with the gravitational pull of a planet. The voice that spoke it sounded tinny and far away, as if the thing were still figuring out how to use Becca's voice box.

Behind me, Ekstrom cursed. "No. No, no. Not her, Patty, *not her.*"

The thing rose to standing, watching me impassively through Becca's eyes.

"I'm sorry," it said tenderly.

I shuddered, and couldn't speak.

"I'm sorry," it said again, stepping forward. Its voice thickened. It made my ears ring, my palms tingle. Then it hissed, "Sinner."

I shook my head, thoughts replaced by white noise.

It took another step. "Inconstant."

Another and it loomed above me. "*Liar.*"

"Not her." Ekstrom wobbled on her feet. "Your right hand already chose. This girl is *ordinary*, she's not worth taking, Becca wouldn't want you to . . ."

None of what she was saying made any sense. Even if it had, my mind was frozen dirt, terror given way to dissociation. Then something happened that broke me out of my trance.

Sluggishly Becca's hand rose to her chest. She raked it hard, opening the skin in four bright lines. Her mouth shaped itself tremblingly around one syllable, then another.

"Nor," it said, "uh."

Ekstrom spoke sharply. "Don't fight it. Becca, *don't*, you'll only make it—"

Becca's body tilted sideways at an impossible angle, her feet shuffle-stepping closer to the pool. "*Shut*," said my best friend's voice, struggling upward.

The hand that scratched her climbed falteringly to her throat, but there was no strength left in it. Her other hand plucked it off and threw it back with enough strength that her shoulder popped, body losing its balance and falling to the boards.

Whatever manner of possession I was witnessing—because that was what this was, and I had to rewrite my sense of reality to make it fit—Becca was fighting it. I saw it in the quiver of her lip and the jerk of her head. Then, as if she'd marshaled all her strength to get it out, her own voice spoke in a rush.

"Not Nora," she said, and tipped her body sideways into the pool.

There was no splash. She slid beneath its grimy surface and was gone.

I shouted, scrambling to the water's edge. It wasn't deep, but it was dark and murky and dangerously cold. I swung my legs around, getting ready to jump in after her. But Ekstrom grabbed me under the armpits and yanked me back. "The goddess will win," she said breathlessly. "She'll keep Becca alive."

"The *what*?" I said shrilly.

Impatiently she said, "Look."

Becca burst into sight at the center of the pool. Her body was arched, fighting the frigid water, but she wasn't fighting her way up. She was trying to stay *down*. Her hair had tumbled from its knot and it looked so much like drowning I tried again to wrench myself from Ekstrom's grip. But she'd caught me in a hold that made even small movements send pain twanging through my shoulders. Why did she know how to do that?

Then I felt a burst of ferocious triumph, because Ekstrom was wrong. The dark—the thing she called *goddess*—wasn't winning. It was leaving Becca, streaming from her chest in a pixelated double helix flashing chrome and black.

Ekstrom's grip tightened.

"Let me go," I said, "*please,* she's gonna drown, she's—"

I cut out. Because with an almost audible crack the thing flattened into a sheet like poured tar and folded around Becca's body. In an instant she was out of sight.

Before I could scream the thing that held my best friend reverse jackknifed out of the water with acrobatic suddenness. The goddess hung shimmering on the air, vast and starry and *not possible*, like a window onto a land of nightmare.

Just before she went for me.

I braced for attack but the goddess only took my hand. And her touch wasn't cold or sick or terrible. It was warm and it filled my head with light. She felt—god help me—she felt like *Becca*.

Where is she? I said. *What did you do to her?* I knew the goddess would hear me even if I didn't speak.

I'm here. It was Becca's voice. *Nora, let me in.*

"Let you—in?" Now I spoke aloud, through tears. Beside me Ekstrom was wide-eyed and silent.

Please, Nora. Her voice ratcheted up. It warped like an audio error. But it was *her* still. Becca. Wasn't it?

I'll die if you don't. I'm dying. This is the only way. Please, *Nora.*

Ghostly fingers bent around my hand, soft and made of light. A thousand summer twilights slid through me, swimming with fireflies lit up that very color. I raised my right hand, trembling.

"I love you," I said. I put my hand to my heart.

The goddess went through breast and bone. She opened my chest like a door.

And when she was inside, she tucked me somewhere safe and small, because I wasn't needed.

What came next was soundtracked by the oceanic workings of my body. Sonar clicks and the warm red rush of my blood, my breath a tide. Conscious thoughts slipped past me like neon fish, unreachable.

I was sunk fathoms deep inside my own body as the goddess used me. I could look if I wanted to, and see: Chloe Park slipping on broken glass in a modern kitchen, vinegar and steel to the very end. Mr. Tate in the front seat of a family car, sighing with a sound that was chillingly like relief. Kurt in the cemetery, weeping like his heart was breaking. The goddess took them all.

We sped from place to place via rushing black corridors, not of this earth nor made for the passage of humans. But she kept me safe inside them, as I kept her safe in my world. When her feast was through and the goddess eased me from my hiding place, I spoke to her.

You're not Becca. Where is she? I can't feel her anywhere.

The goddess didn't answer.

What have you done? What have you made me do? I can't live with this. I can't live knowing I've done this.

And the goddess said,

Okay.

Benevolent goddess. She took me back to the start, dropping my body at the end of Becca's drive. Like a seamstress she scissored away everything I'd witnessed in Becca's yard, and the massacre that came after. She stitched the raw edge of my first arrival, not long after midnight, to whatever time it was now, around half past one in the morning. Then she curled away inside me to digest what she'd taken.

I blinked back to full consciousness, a little dizzy, at the bottom of Becca's snow-dusted driveway, watching her unlit house.

Time felt slippery, the night endless. I'd been standing

there a while, but not too long. I'd come running right after receiving her unsettling text.

I shook it off and headed up the drive.

Near the end the memories started flickering. I was in them, in the creek, back and forth as the goddess lost her perfect grip. I think she was using most of herself just to keep me alive.

I couldn't feel my mouth, my lungs. But I could feel how she'd used Becca's voice to trick me, and what it was to cower like a mollusk as she turned my body into a murder weapon. *I* could use my body as a weapon, too. With muscle memory and the very end of my strength I sucked in a breath of black water. It was frigid and filthy, a benediction that scoured me from the inside out.

Get. Out.

I didn't think she would. I could sense a banked fury in her that I'd taken it so far. I wondered what would happen to her if she were inside my body when I died.

Then the goddess-creature spoke to me one last time, a coarse and furious word in the language of another world. She burst from my struggling body like a maddened bat and was gone. Banished, I hoped, to an unreachable place. Back to the endless dark.

I heard Becca's voice in my ear, very clear.

Nora, she whispered. *I'm sorry, Nora.*

I wanted to reply but I was just so cold. My jaw locked tight and my lungs were dead flowers and I thought *Don't go away, not again, don't leave me, Becca, don't—*

Then I was alone, drowning.

Except I wasn't, because someone was holding me. They were dragging me from the water, onto the frosted bank. Laying their body on mine to warm it, to press the water from my chest, to put their mouth near my ear and say it again, cracked and crying. *I would* never *let you die*.

Becca. Then flashlights and voices, up in the trees. Light wobbling over us, a person crying out.

I fell out of consciousness uncertain whether they and Becca were hallucinations. Real, or the wish of a dying mind.

CHAPTER FIFTY–THREE

NOT LONG AFTER I RAN from Sloane's house—leaving my friends in a panic, chugging water, googling *how to get sober fast*—my mom called me. My phone was where I left it, by Sloane's record player. Ruth made the executive decision to take the call and tell her everything, right down to the handprint on my chest.

Together they searched for me. By nightfall my parents went to the police, who were unusually prepared to take them seriously, given recent events and bad press and the fact that I was the best friend of one of the missing four.

The search party found Becca and me on their second sweep of the woods. It was Cat who saw us first, tromping along the path with my dad and James and a trio of Maglites.

I was released from the ER less than thirty-six hours after I arrived, having been treated for hypothermia, various lacerations, and three frostbitten toes.

Becca was transferred after four days to a long-term care facility. When James carried her from the woods, her body was that of a person who'd been bedbound longer than she'd been gone. Her muscles showed signs of atrophy, she had bedsores over her hips. The fact that she dragged my dead weight out of the water in her condition was as unlikely and adrenaline-driven as a mom lifting a car off a baby.

Worse was the scarring in her lungs that no one could explain in a previously healthy seventeen-year-old. That kind of scarring was irreversible, they said. Except it was reversing itself, bit by bit.

There were stranger things, too. Even less explainable. Marks of an unfathomable imprisonment that would stay with her for the rest of her life.

CHAPTER FIFTY—FOUR

WHERE DID SHE GO?
Becca was asked that question a hundred times in the week after we left the woods. By police officers and hospital staff, legal counsel and an enterprising journalist who made it all the way to her room by wearing scrubs and wheeling around an IV stand he must've bought online.

She told them all the same thing: *I don't remember.*

No one was allowed to visit her at first. I'd been treated and discharged and spent a full twenty-four hours at home—napping and watching old movies in my parents' bed, avoiding my phone for a million reasons—before we got the news that Becca was cleared for visitors.

I walked into her hospital room to find her sitting up, looking out the window with a Canon held to her eye. I'd had my dad buy it with the last of my summer-job cash and drop it off the day before, with instructions to leave it by her bed.

That was how I saw her first: behind a camera. Turning, smiling, snapping a picture of me as she'd done so many times.

When she lowered it, she looked uncertain. I felt shy,

too. Turning the camera in her hands, she said, "I can't always tell if I'm awake. When I look through this, I'm sure."

Her voice—*her voice*, not in my head but in the world—was small and hoarse, unspeakably dear. I crossed the room and did what they'd told me not to: climbed carefully into her bed, the two of us just barely fitting side by side.

Her breath smelled like green Jell-O. She was wearing a Bikini Kill sweatshirt Miranda must've brought her from home. We could've been nine again, sewn up in one sleeping bag, if it weren't for the hovering half-moon of machines.

"I'll tell you everything," she whispered. "But not yet."

We fell into a routine. I visited her every day except Monday: lit mag meeting day. We were advisor-less, but Ruth had finagled emergency access to the magazine inbox. There had been, of late, a major influx of submissions, everybody translating the shit PHS had gone through—was still going through—into art. Or, as Chris would say, "art."

Monday was James' day to visit. He brought her last week's photos and fresh film, took her finished rolls away for developing. She was doing a lot of portraits these days.

I didn't know what they talked about, how much she told him. But her story came to me in pieces. Around long bouts of blackout sleep, physical therapy sessions and blood draws, meetings with specialists and curious medical students and the lawyer hired by Miranda on her behalf, Becca told me what I'd missed, starting with what she saw in the woods. Finding Ekstrom's address and confronting her there. Being drawn into the teacher's lonesome war.

Former teacher. Miss Ekstrom had very recently retired.

In return, I told Becca what it was to remember what

I'd done. To have the images living in me, to know it both was and wasn't *me* who had done those things. She listened like a penitent, guilt-stricken. But I knew what had happened could either draw us even closer or kill us completely. And I couldn't lose her again. She was, literally, the only person in the world who could understand what I'd been through.

Becca turned eighteen a month after her return. They planned to discharge her a few days later. She could walk on her own again, she only needed oxygen at night. Her lungs continued their miraculous repair.

She would go home to the house she'd grown up in, that Miranda would end up selling not a year later. By summer Becca would have an apartment of her own, and her GED. She would never spend another day at PHS.

I couldn't blame her: Becca was the capital-G Girl Who Came Back. There would be podcasts and book deal offers and "where is she now" follow-up pieces down the road. Even a prestige miniseries that would run for two seasons, somehow skirting the black hole at its center: the fact that the only people who knew where Becca came back from, and why the others never would, refused to speak a word of it.

On her birthday we sat in her hospital room, eating strawberry shortcakes. Becca finished hers, took a photo of me where I sat on the windowsill, and said, "I want to tell you where I went."

She laughed at the look on my face. She'd gained back the weight she'd lost in her days away. Her skin wasn't disturbingly plasticky anymore, her ribs didn't pull when she breathed. But there were changes in her that weren't so transient. Some more unsettling than others.

"Okay," I said.

"Okay," she mimicked me, smiling. But she was nervous.

"I remember all of it," she said. "Ekstrom and the pool and . . . I remember the goddess screaming. In my head."

We were still calling her—it—the goddess. We always would. "What was she screaming?"

"One word, again and again. Not a word I knew. Or a language. Then I saw the stars and I felt so cold and I heard *you*, your voice, and then . . ."

She lifted a hand, touched the mark on her chest. Hers looked like a blue chilblain, undefined. Mine was sharp-edged, its handprint shape undeniable. It had faded but would never fully disappear.

"There was this pop," she said. "Like a brain injury pop, I thought I was dead. I was in the dark for a while, and when I opened my eyes I was in a house."

I blinked. "A house."

"Not a real house. I think . . . I think that wherever I was, whatever I was seeing, I wasn't *built* for it. When I was with the goddess, or *inside* the goddess, I was somewhere no human should ever be or see. I think my brain was protecting me. And the way it did that was, it made me believe I was walking through a house. There were no stairs or hallways or in-between places, just an endless series of rooms. Some were ornate and beautiful, some just looked normal, like motel rooms or rooms in a regular house. Some I swear I recognized from movies or photographs.

"Every room had two doors, the one I came in by and the one I walked through when I left. And none of the rooms had windows. Not one. I'd been walking through this house for what felt like ages when suddenly the lights went out. I was in absolute dark.

"The first time this happened I sat down where I was and waited until the lights came back on. Then I started walking again. But the second time, I was standing inside an old-fashioned bedroom, sort of bare, like a maid's room from another century. I knew where the bed had been, when I could see it, and tried to feel my way toward it. But it wasn't there. I walked and walked, way past where the room should've ended. That was when I really got it, that what I was seeing wasn't what was *there*.

"I walked until I found a door. I banged right up against it, and felt the doorknob. But I didn't open it. I didn't feel much of anything in this house, emotionally speaking, but this door scared me. It was warm, first of all. Almost hot. And at first it seemed like it was some kind of synthetic material—very smooth—but as I stood there with my hand on it, it started to feel almost alive. Like skin, right over the bone.

"The lights went on again, and that door was gone. I spent another—day, I guess, not that I really knew—just wandering. The longer I stayed in a room, the more I looked around, the more detail there seemed to be. Shelves filled up with books and walls with, like, sconces or complicated wallpaper, and if I opened a drawer there were always little things inside it, coins and keys and dice and beads, junk drawer stuff. But I swear I could almost see it *becoming*, before my eyes.

"Maybe a wall would give the impression of being empty, but if I looked there was a painting there. And it was a painting of some trees at dusk, but what I took to be trees were people, and each had the most detailed face, and I thought they stood on grass but it was actually green water, and deep in it you could see a seabed covered in treasure, and on and on until I almost got pulled in, another level deep, into a painting or a book that wrote itself as I read it, or a card deck I took from a drawer and shuffled. And I knew if that happened, it would be over for me. I wouldn't know my own name for much longer.

"After another long time of all that, the lights went out for a third time. I was ready. I started moving through the dark right away. It took time to find the door, and when I did, I didn't wait. I threw it open and stepped through."

"And?"

She dipped her chin, almost ruefully. All along her part was a half inch of silver-white. Her hair, since she'd returned, was growing out colorless. One day it would look like the mane of a toy-store unicorn.

"And I was you," she said. "I walked through the door, and when I opened my eyes—your eyes—I was in your bed. Because the goddess was in *you*, and I was—tucked away somewhere by the goddess. When it was dark, I think that was when you and the goddess were sleeping.

"I keep thinking . . . remember when Mary Poppins pulls that whole big lamp out of her little bag? I think I was that lamp, tucked away nowhere. In a place that could've exploded my mind into snow. But I shaped it into a house with a hidden door inside it, that I could find only when the lights went out and everything I kept inventing was out of my way.

"I thought fast. I didn't have time to waste. I couldn't find a pen in your room, so I went downstairs. I had to go so carefully to keep from waking you up. I didn't have perfect control of the vehicle."

"My *body*, you mean." It was harder than I expected, hearing her narrate this from the other side. I felt myself perched on the edge of hysteria.

"Yep," she said remorselessly. "And I left you that cagey note, because every letter of it was hell to write and I kept thinking you'd wake up."

"I got it, though." I took a breath. "Play the goddess game, and remember."

She squinted at me. "I was trying to get you to—this doesn't sound good, after everything. But I knew if you endangered yourself somehow, the goddess would react. Would *leave*, hopefully, like with me and the pool. And that's exactly what happened. Eventually."

A nurse came in then. One of the younger ones, pristine white sneakers and a pair of pink cheetah scrubs. She took Becca's vitals, then approached her with a tongue depressor extended.

"Lemme get a look at that throat," she said brightly.

Becca gave her a narrow smile. "You want to see the teeth." She tipped back and opened her mouth wide. *Wide*.

It had taken them almost a week to discover she was growing a pair of new teeth, tucked right alongside her last upper molars in a place teeth never grew. She said they didn't hurt, and showed me when I asked. They were thinner than incisors, a milky blue-white.

The nurse took a cursory peek and hustled out.

When we were alone again, I said, "That night, when I woke up next to the clearing. If you weren't trying to make me play the game, why was I there?"

"I was trying to get to Ekstrom's. My plan was to break in and hide somewhere. And then when you woke up in her tub or closet or someplace, she'd have to tell you everything."

"Yeah, *that* wouldn't have been terrifying for me. Waking up inside a strange bathtub."

She just looked at me. Absorbed and a little distant, a smear of strawberry on her lip. Sometimes I felt like she was holding two conversations, one with me and one with herself. Sometimes she seemed to lose the thread of the one she was having with me. After a while I gently said, "What was it like at the end? When the goddess let you go?"

"She didn't *let* me go, you yanked me out of her hands. I went from the house to the water, and I had—a minute, maybe two, before I could really feel my body. How beat up and miserable it was. I was in the middle of giving you fake TV chest compressions when it all hit me. The cold and the *everything*."

For a second she looked exhausted. "In all my dreams since then I'm in the house again. I don't really know what to do about that."

We were quiet for a long time. Then she said, "Nora."

"Becca."

"Did you like what I left for you?"

I laughed a little, swiping tears away. "Oh, yeah. Gotta love a knife. Gotta love film so supernaturally fucked up it lights a Walmart on fire." Then I caught her expression. "Oh, my god." I covered my reddening face. "You mean James."

For just a moment her smile was what it used to be, all made of light. "I'm a *matchmaker*," she said. "I am a certified maker of matches. One *hundred* percent success rate. Now you talk for a while, I want to catch my breath."

I left the hospital and drove downtown, heart drumming. Arches of pink and red lights still blinked over the main road, though Valentine's Day had come and gone. Palm

Towers had a row of visitor parking spots, and that was where James was waiting for me.

I had the same feeling every time I saw him. A sense of disbelief that he was for *me*. Even now—watching the way his posture changed when he saw me, seeing the sweet anticipation in his face—I had to make myself believe it.

With Becca I could embrace how altered I was by what I'd been through. With James I could almost forget. Sometimes going from one to the other caused whiplash.

I got out of the car and walked toward him slowly. Sometimes this was my favorite part, where nothing had happened yet but it was about to. Then I reached him, and it was even better. He gave me that slow-simmer smile that I'd never seen him give anyone else. "You ready?"

I laughed, because we were both pretending this was no big deal. Just me, coming to his apartment for the first time, to eat dinner with and made by the fiercely protective grandmother who thought the sun rose and set on him, and had her reservations about me: the new girlfriend with the fantastically weird baggage. Of course my parents had known and loved James since the night of the search party, a frankly unfair advantage.

"I'm ready. I think."

"She'll like you," he said firmly, then his brow furrowed. "Your hands."

They were unmittened, raw. I curled my fingers in, embarrassed by their redness. With the same unhurried economy with which he did everything, James took my hands in his and unfolded them. He brought them to his mouth and breathed slow and warm into my cupped palms.

"Better?" He dropped the word between them.

I looked at the crown of his hair and said, "Yes."

It came over me sometimes, this hopeful feeling. If all the hard things in my life—the guilt, the nightmares, my fears for myself and my radically changed Becca—were structures in a looming city, it was moments like this that felt like seeing, at the end of a narrow road, the shine of the open sea. Shifting under the sun, sending up sparks of pure light. I would get there. And for now, I could at least catch glimpses of it. Smell the salt.

Together we stepped into the space where our breath met in white smoke on the air. He ghosted his hands over my arms and up, unloosing my hair from the collar of my coat. I hadn't noticed it was tucked in there, but once he'd freed it I was struck with a sense of lightness so powerful it felt like levitation. I was smiling when he cradled my face in his hands and kissed me.

ACKNOWLEDGMENTS

Thank you, Sarah Barley, for being an editor, cheerleader, and friend. We've gone to some very strange places together, and I'm grateful. Many, many thanks to my wise and unflappable agent, Faye Bender.

Thank you for everything, Team Flatiron! Sarah (again), Bob Miller, Megan Lynch, Malati Chavali, Cat Kenney, Erin Kibby, Sydney Jeon, Nancy Trypuc, Marlena Bittner, Erin Gordon, Kelly Gatesman, Louis Grilli, Jennifer Gonzalez, Jennifer Edwards, Holly Ruck, Sofrina Hinton, Emily Walters, Melanie Sanders, and Cassie Gitkin. And thanks once again to dream team, Keith Hayes and Jim Tierney, for a cover that practically glows with sinister intentions.

Thank you to Alexa Wejko for your crucial early read, Kamilla Benko for saving my life with one eleventh-hour phone call, and Tara Sonin and Sarah Jane Abbott for writing dates that helped break walls when I was stuck.

Thank you to my fellow staffers on Libertyville High School's *Slant of Light* magazine (and our short-lived yet deathless shadow publication, *Tilted Darkness*) and *SoL* advisors Karen LeMaistre and Meredith Tarczynski. I had so much fun inventing a lit mag staff for this book (none of you are Chris).

Thank you to my very favorite bookworm, Miles. Reading to you and with you remains the best thing about life on Earth. Thank you to Michael, for making me laugh for seventeen years and counting. Just four more years! . . . on repeat. Thank you to my parents, Diane and Steve Albert. I love you dearly and am grateful for the safety and security you gave me that allowed me to be a shy and book-devoted kid for as long as I needed. (It was a Good Long While.)

And thanks to you, if you're reading this. The support of every reader, bookseller, librarian, teacher, parent of a kid who finds their way to these books: I'd need at least as many words as I've already written to fully express my gratitude, so I'll just say, one last time, thank you.

ABOUT THE AUTHOR

Melissa Albert is the *New York Times* and indie bestselling author of the Hazel Wood series (*The Hazel Wood*, *The Night Country*, *Tales from the Hinterland*) and *Our Crooked Hearts* and a former bookseller and YA lit blogger. Her work has been translated into more than twenty languages and included in the *New York Times* list of Notable Children's Books. She lives in Brooklyn with her family.